Polonaise

Polonaise

JANE AIKEN HODGE

Hodder & Stoughton

LONDON SYDNEY AUCKLAND TORONTO

British Library Cataloguing in Publication Data

Hodge, Jane Aiken
    Polonaise.
    I. Title
    823'.914[F]   PS3558.0342

    ISBN 0-340-40673-9

To the Reader

The more I enjoy a historical novel, the more maddened I always am by not being sure where fact ends and fiction begins. So in the hopes that you will enjoy this one, may I tell you my own policy on this? All the historical facts are as accurate as I can make them. Events took place when and where I say they did. I hope. When it comes to historical figures, I have allowed myself a little more latitude. They too only appear where and when they actually did, and much of what they say is direct quotation from historical record, but inevitably some is not. What I do hope is that all their speech and behaviour is compatible with their characters as I have read them.

J.A.H.

EASTERN EUROPE

NORTH SEA

Dantzig

R Elbe

Berlin

R Weser

R Oder

Poznan

London

Walcheren

R Rhine

Weimar

Dresden

Breslau

Erfurt

Olmütz

Valmy

Bartenstein

Brunn

Austerlitz

St Cloud

Ratisbon

Paris

R Seine

Wagram

R March

Schönbrunn

Vienna

Mödling

0   100   200
Miles

1

'How dare you! Let me go!' The angry voice carried clearly across Cracow's Palace Square and Glynde Rendel turned quickly at the sound of English spoken, and saw a scuffle taking place outside the cathedral.

He hurried across the square that Poland's Austrian occupiers had turned into a parade ground. 'What's going on here?' His German was fluent and the Austrian soldiers recognised authority in his tone and stopped manhandling their prisoner, whose round hat had fallen off in the struggle, revealing closely curling black hair over a wide brow and the dark, sparkling eyes of a Polish aristocrat.

As if to confirm this, he was speaking again, furiously, in Polish – recognisable but not intelligible to Rendel.

'Thought so.' The larger of his captors tightened his grip. 'A bloody Pole!' The German word he used was stronger. 'No need to trouble yourself, sir.' His tone to Glynde was civil enough. 'It's just one of the natives come to spy, on the pretext of visiting this damned cathedral of theirs.' He used a couple of adjectives Glynde had heard only on the field of battle.

'What's he saying?' The young man turned eagerly to speak to Glynde in his slightly nasal English. 'You're British? Speak German? Ask them what in tarnation they mean by grabbing me. All I want to do is look at the cathedral. Why in Tophet shouldn't I? I even have an ancestor there. As if they'd care!'

'You're American of course!' It explained both the odd twang of the young man's speech and something faintly outlandish about his straight trousers and short greatcoat. Glynde turned away to greet a minor officer who had sauntered over to see what was the matter. 'Sir.' He knew just the tone for this level of authority. 'There seems to be some misunderstanding here. This gentleman is an American visitor; he merely wishes to see the cathedral. As a tourist, you understand. He speaks no German.'

'He speaks damned good Polish,' said the soldier who was holding the young man's right arm. But his grip slackened slightly; he was beginning to look unsure of himself.

'There's no law against that is there?' Glynde addressed the officer.

'Not yet.' The officer turned to his men. 'What was he doing?'

'Skulking about like a damned Jew of a spying Pole. We told him to halt and he took not a blind bit of notice.'

'He didn't understand you,' said Glynde. He smiled at the furious young man and spoke to him again in English. 'They say you took no notice when they challenged you. I take it you didn't understand?'

'Not a word. Confound it, here in Cracow hasn't a man the right to be addressed in Polish?'

'Not by the Austrian garrison. You can't have been here long.' He turned back to the officer. 'My name is Glynde Rendel. I've been visiting my cousin, Lord Falmer, in Vienna. I dined with the Governor here last night; met your commanding officer. Either of them will speak for me, and I have no doubt, if your men will just let him go, this gentleman will show you his papers.' Another smile for the scowling young American. 'Glynde Rendel, sir, very much at your service. And you're . . .?'

'Warrington. Jan Warrington. From Savannah, Georgia. If these dolts will just let me go, I'll show the officer my papers. I've a letter from Mr. President Jefferson, if that means anything to him. He's a connection of my father's.'

Swiftly translated, this information was enough to get him his freedom and a grudging apology from the officer. 'Tell him to learn some German if he means to spend any time here in Austria,' he told Glynde, who thought it best not to translate this, or at least, not at once.

'I will act as his interpreter for the time being,' he said instead. And, in English: 'The officer has apologised. The incident is closed, except that I have volunteered to act as your interpreter, here in Cracow. It could save you further trouble.'

'Keeping away from these Austrian bastards will be more to the point.' He smiled for the first time, the dark face transformed: 'Forgive me! Damned ungracious. I rather think I'd have ended up in one of their filthy prisons if it hadn't been for you. It's this temper of mine! But to be here, at home, in Poland, for the first time in my life, and find our own language useless! Of course, I should have tried them in French.' And, with an odd little smile for Glynde he turned back to the officer and made him a civil enough speech in that language, ending with: 'And now, if we might continue my interrupted visit to the cathedral? I take it there is no objection to foreign tourists visiting it?'

'Not the least in the world.' The officer's French was only workmanlike. 'It's the Poles make the trouble. They will bring in messy little bunches of flowers, bits of ribbon, God knows what, and lay them on the tombs.'

'Quite so.' Glynde Rendel took his new companion firmly by the arm and led him away before he exploded.

'Messy little bunches of flowers.' Jan Warrington's voice was loud but he was back into English with no risk of being understood. 'The Poles make the trouble! And who makes trouble for the Poles, pray?'

'Everyone. But if we are going to go into that, don't you think we should save it until dinner and begin by paying our visit to the cathedral, which I wish to see quite as much as you do. Did you say you had an ancestor buried there?'

'Yes. My mother was a descendant of the Polish King, Jan Sobieski, who saved Vienna from the Turks. I'm named after him.' They moved together through huge doors into the cooler, incense-scented twilight of the great church. Like every other building Glynde had visited so far in Austrian Poland, it showed signs of neglect. He saw tarnished gilding and holy pictures darkened by time as they walked silently down the aisle, to pause at last by the shining tomb of St. Stanislas, Bishop of Cracow and patron saint of Poland.

'I'm surprised the Austrians haven't seized the silver,' he said, low-voiced.

'Not even they would dare! The Catholic Church is a powerful mother. The only protector Poland has.' When they came at last to the huge marble sarcophagus of King Jan Sobieski, his namesake reached into the pocket of his greatcoat and produced a little box. 'It was my mother's.' Opening the box,

11

he took out a silver brooch in the shape of an eagle. 'She always wore it. When she was dying, I promised her . . .' He laid the shining emblem gently down among the bunches of flowers that already lay on the tomb.

'The Polish eagle?' Glynde looked at the flowers. 'The Poles don't forget, do they?'

'They never will, not so long as there is one still living.'

'You feel so strongly, even though you have never been here before?' They were moving back now towards the great doors.

'Yes.' It was an absolute statement. 'I sure was lucky to meet you,' he went on as they climbed the wide stairs to the old royal apartments with their unpolished parquet and ragged tapestries.

'It's depressing, I'm afraid.' Glynde was amused to find himself almost apologising to his companion. 'But I imagine the decline here started long before the partitions of Poland, when the Kings moved their capital to Warsaw. Here's the audience chamber. The King's subjects keeping their eye on him!'

The carved ceiling of the huge room was divided into squares, and from each one a carved head looked down, amazingly individual and lifelike. 'Listening.' Jan gazed upwards. 'I wonder what it felt like to dispense justice under so many eyes and ears.'

'Characteristic plight of the Kings of Poland,' said Glynde drily. 'Always aware of the threat from their nobility.'

'You know a remarkable deal about Poland.' Something distracted him. 'Ah, there she is, the one my mother talked about. See! The woman in the gag. I wonder what my cousin thinks of her.'

'You've relatives still in Poland?'

'I'm grateful to you for calling it Poland! It's not many do since the final partition in 1795. Seven years ago! I was only a boy, but I remember that day. I think it's when my mother began to die. Yes, I've some kin here still, though one whole branch of the family died in the massacre of Praga in '94. You know about that, too?'

'Yes. I'm sorry.' What was there to say? 'How did your mother get to America?'

'Her father was a friend of the hero Pulaski, fought with

him at the time of the Confederation of Bar, went into exile with him. Was killed with him, too, in the American attack on British-held Savannah in '79. No hard feelings, I hope!'

'Not the least in the world! That war between our countries was a bit of idiocy. But what chance of reasoned argument between a mad King, an obstinate minister, and, excuse me, a bunch of hot-headed colonists? I just hope to God it never happens again.'

'You think it might?'

'Not if this peace holds in Europe. If we should find ourselves fighting Bonaparte again, and I am very much afraid that we may, there is no knowing what may be the end of it.'

'You really think the peace they made at Amiens won't hold?'

'It will be a miracle if it does.' Glynde turned to look at his companion as they picked their way over huge cobbles on the steep slope down from Cracow's Wawel Hill where the palace and cathedral stood. 'You can't want war to break out again.'

'As a Pole, I must. Napoleon betrayed us at the peace conference. After all Dombrowski's Polish Legion had done for him, all the blood they had poured out fighting his wars, he let the partition stand! Another war, another peace; it's our only hope.'

'I'd be careful how you say such things here in Austrian-occupied territory. Even in English.' They had left the Wawel now and plunged into the narrow, crowded streets of Cracow itself. 'I was warned in Vienna that there are spies everywhere.'

'Thanks!' Bitterly. 'Of course their spies would speak English even if their soldiers don't! I begin to think that the sooner I get to my cousin's, the better.'

'I'm sure you're right. In the meantime, come and dine with me at my hotel. I've a private room, such as it is. At least we can speak freely there.'

'Thank you.' The young American turned and held out a friendly hand. 'And thanks again for what you did back there. I could have been in real trouble.'

'I'm afraid you could.'

Glynde had rooms in a hotel on Cracow's main square, overlooking the handsome old Cloth-makers Hall. Instructing his servant to order them a neat dinner as soon as possible, he poured a glass of wine for them both, and raised his own. 'To our lucky meeting.'

'Lucky for me, and no mistake. But tell me, what brings you to this God-forsaken country?'

'I'd have said God was Poland's only hope right now. You're not a Catholic?'

'No. I was brought up as one, of course, but father's a Unitarian. It seemed to suit me better, somehow. It's the only argument I have with my sister. She stuck; I didn't.'

'Is she as passionate a Pole as you, then?'

'Not quite. She was younger, when mother died. She doesn't remember so clearly. Mind you, she speaks Polish as well as I do, maybe better. And German! Pity she couldn't come too.'

'I'm surprised your father let you.' But then, he thought, fathers . . .

Jan laughed. 'It took some persuading! When I finished at Harvard College, he wanted me to stay home and learn to manage the plantation. A life sentence!'

'A pleasant one. I'm a younger son, myself; no estate to manage.'

'But not exactly starving,' said Jan with transatlantic frankness. 'Those damned Austrians were your servants on sight. Do you think they would treat me as well if you were to lend me that caped greatcoat of yours?' He had begun by dismissing his new acquaintance as a typical English fop, the kind of young aristocrat who was obeyed simply because he assumed he would be. Now he began to revise his opinion, aware of a hint of steel under the charming manner, a firm twist to the engaging smile.

Glynde laughed. 'It would hardly fit you!' Slender, though strong himself, he had approved his companion's broad shoulders. 'I think that if I provide the language for the pair of us, you're the one who will keep the footpads at bay. That is, if you are going to agree to let me join you in exploring Cracow, as I hope you will.'

'Frankly, I hadn't reckoned to spend much time here. I had to see the cathedral, but the rest of the place gives me the glooms. All these relics of former splendours! Have you seen the university? It'd break your heart! And the poverty everywhere, the beggars . . . the way they cringe . . . I hate it!'

14

'I know. But you can't blame it all on the Austrians. It goes further back than that, if you ask me.' He had been about to mention the evils of serfdom, remembered just in time that his new friend came from one of the slave-owning states of America, and held his peace as his man reappeared to usher in a pair of inn servants.

'It's a kind of stew, sir.' The man's tone was apologetic. 'The best they can do, they say.'

'*Bigos*,' said the young American with relish. 'My mother used to make it. You might as well eat the food of the country while you're here, Mr. Rendel.'

'Spare me the "Mister".' He was refilling their glasses. 'And tell me where you are heading when you leave Cracow. I'm not hell-bent on staying here either; I mean to spend more time in Warsaw, so if by any chance you were going that way, maybe we could at least start off together, and I'll teach you some useful German phrases as we go.'

'Thanks! Yes, I'm going north too, to my cousin's at Rendomierz.' He coloured. 'I'd like it very much if you would join me that far. And of course you must meet my cousin. I'm sure . . . that is, I don't quite know . . .'

'I'm a fool!' Glynde interrupted him. 'When you said cousin, I thought of a man. Well, one does. But, of course, it must be the Princess Sobieska. You're here for the wedding! And she'll have enough on her hands without entertaining a stray Englishman she's never heard of. But I would most certainly like to meet her. They say she's a great beauty, and a great lady. And Rendomierz itself one of the most famous Polish palaces. What do they call it? The Polish Urbino?'

'Drawing rather a long bow,' said Jan. 'But, yes, when we got news of my cousin's marriage last fall, it was the feather that turned the balance. My father knew mother would have wanted me to come. Says he hopes a year or so here will cure me of my Polish mania, and from what I have seen so far, I think he's likely right. But, what I don't know is whether the marriage may not already have taken place; it was a while before I could get a ship, see. Father insisted I travel on one of his.'

'I can set your mind at rest there.' Rendel made a mental note that Jan Warrington was clearly the son of an affluent father. 'The marriage contract seems to have presented various problems. Well, it most certainly is a dynastic alliance; the heiress of the Sobieskis with a man who claims the blood of the Jagiellos, that old, great, royal family.'

'You do know your Polish history.'

'I've tried.' Deprecatingly. 'It's partly why I've rather made a set at you. A real live Pole. Well, Polish American. I've an eye to the diplomatic service, you see. A man must do something. I've money for my tailor – as you've remarked – left me by my mother, but that's no reason for sitting idle. I'd meant to join the army, but a damned inconvenient wound I got at Valmy put paid to that idea.'

'You were at Valmy?'

'Yes. I'm not so good a son as you. I didn't wait for my father's consent. I'd have waited for ever! He meant me for the church. He doesn't change his mind, my father.' He ran an angry hand through fashionably cut fair hair. Even now, ten years later, the memory of that scene enraged him. 'So – I ran away, got myself taken on with the Duke of Brunswick's staff. And a sad, mismanaged business that campaign was, I can tell you. The Duke's a soldier; no diplomat.'

'And you were wounded? You must have been a mere boy.'

'Old enough to know what a fool I'd been as I lay there in the mud, with the rain pouring down. Not my cause, not my army . . . And nearly the end of me. Damn fool boy. Your glass is empty. It's a long time since I thought about Valmy. Ten years ago! And how I've wasted them. Well, let's not go into that. This fricassée is good. What did you call it?'

'*Bigos*. My mother used to make it when she could get the cabbage and enough bits of meat and sausage. We always loved it, Anna and I.' He turned and spoke in rapid Polish to the inn servant who had remained in attendance, and got a flashing smile and a flood of speech in response. 'I told him you liked it. They don't often get praise from foreigners, he says. Complaints mostly, because it's not what they're used to.'

'He said it at some length!' Glynde was wishing he had made himself learn Polish as well as Russian before he came on this odd venture. But there had not been much time for preparations. His friend Canning, the Tory politician, had

16

approached him about this secret mission the moment the peace was signed at Amiens, and Europe open to travellers again.

'It's mostly like this. They're so pleased to find I'm a fellow countryman. Tell me terrible tales of the occupation. I think it helps them to be listened to.'

'I'm sure it does. What now?' The man had bent forward to speak again to Warrington, then left the room.

'He's gone to order us their special dessert. Told your man there was nothing in the house, but of course he was lying. It's a kind of pancake. I hope you'll like it.'

'I'll eat it anyway,' he promised. 'You Poles certainly hang together.'

'Odd you should say that. It's just what my father doesn't think. He says we need a foreign enemy to stop us fighting amongst ourselves.'

'I'd like to meet your father. He studied Polish history too?'

'What is there to study? No, but he was a friend of Pulaski; did his best to help him over his various problems with George Washington and the government. He was a hothead, too. Pulaski, not my father. Father said, in a way, he was lucky to be killed gallantly at Savannah. *Enfant terrible* one day; dead hero the next. You know how it is.'

'What did your mother say to that?'

'Father never said it when she was alive. She'd not have borne it. Pulaski and Sobieski were her heroes. It was after she died, when I started to grow up, that father began really talking to me about Poland. When he saw how mad keen I was to come here.' He looked round the shabby room. 'I still feel I owe it to my mother. She was only ten when they went into exile in '72. She owed Poland a life, she said.'

'Your life?'

He emptied his glass. 'I hope not.'

2

In the snug English vicarage on the banks of the Arun, the discussion had been raging for three days, ever since the letter had come. Now Mr. Peverel banged a hand on the dining table, rattling glasses and china. 'I say that, since she wishes it, the girl should go. It's a damned flattering invitation, and a damned surprising one, as you must admit, Mrs. Peverel. That the Princess should have remembered our Jenny, these eight years since they met at Petworth, and remembering her, want to see her again –' His impartial gaze, summing up and dismissing his twenty-two-year-old unmarried daughter, finished the sentence for him. His wife made to speak, but he raised a formidable hand to stop her. 'Times are bad, as you know, and this peace won't change things overnight. Taxes up; tithes down. If it wasn't for the farm, I'd have to give up the carriage, and then where would you be, ma'am? No more jauntings to Petworth then. A mouth to feed has to be a consideration these days, not to mention the laces and ribbons, the fans and furbelows for the Chichester Assembly. And all of it wasted.' He fixed his daughter with an angry eye. 'Young Forester that you turned down in your first season's a Rural Dean now. Told you there was good stuff in him, remember? To think I was fool enough to listen to your pleadings! He has influence with the Bishop, they say. Didn't take him long to marry that friend of yours, what's her name? Maria Kemp, pretty little puss. I remember her.'

'I met her in Petworth the other day.' His daughter spoke at last. 'You'd not know her now, father. Four children in four years; and a husband who never listens. She looks an old woman.'

'Never listens? How do you know he never listens? Been tittle-tattling with her, hey?'

'He didn't listen when he was courting me. Just talked. Men

'don't change, father.' She met her mother's horrified eye and blushed crimson.

'That settles it!' Another thump on the table. 'I'll not be preached at in my own house. By a chit with only one offer to her name! And no wonder. Bella was a beauty; Araminta had style; what have you got, hey, Jenny?'

'Jenny has very good sense,' said her mother. 'It's selfish of me not to want her to go, and I know it. I had so hoped . . .' It was her turn to blush and to suppress a surreptitious tear at the thought of those hopes for her youngest daughter's company through the years as some modification to life with her husband. 'But if you really wish it, Jenny love? You're sure? It's such a long way to go . . . Everything so different . . . And on so short an acquaintance. You'll be entirely dependent on the Princess, remember. Suppose you should not suit?'

'I'll see to it that I do,' said Jenny. 'It will be an adventure, mama. Such an adventure! To go all the way to Poland . . . I've only ever been to London once.'

'And a sad waste of money that was,' said her father. 'But how to get you there; that's the question. No one goes to Poland any more, now it's not a sovereign state. No Ambassador, no diplomats. Tell you what, I'll put on my hat and ride over to Petworth House. See if Lord Egremont has any suggestions to make. It was there that you met the Princess and her mother after all. Sad about the young Prince. I remember him. Shaping up for a proper young blade, he was. These duels are not at all the thing . . . And with a Russian too. Awkward for everyone. You'll need to turn your mind a bit to politics if you're going, Jenny. Or at least remember to still that tongue of yours and keep quiet when you don't understand. For God's sake, what's the matter now?' He spoke to his wife, for his daughter had risen, mute and scarlet-faced and hurried from the room.

'I thought so,' said Mrs. Peverel with a kind of gloomy satisfaction. 'I should have had more sense than to let her run tame with those two young foreigners. But at the time it seemed such a chance to get her a little social polish. And so young as they were; and surrounded by that train of tutors and governesses . . . She profited by it, too. Look at the languages she speaks. She's kept at them most faithfully, ever since that summer they were all here. I wonder if she really hoped . . .'

'You don't seriously mean to suggest that she set her heart on young Prince Sobieski? Is grieving for him now? I always knew our daughter was a fool, but not such a fool as that, surely? I'll never let another of those damn fool novels of yours into the house!'

'A bit late in the day for that? I said before that Jenny has great good sense, and I stand to it. If she lost her heart a little to the Prince, I can't entirely blame her. He was one of the most charming boys I ever met. In a careless kind of way.' She thought about it. 'I think it could just be possible that he said something, casually, and our Jenny took it more seriously than it was meant.'

'Well, if the little fool's been wearing the willow for him all this time, at least it's over now he's dead. You think that's why she turned down Dick Forester?'

'The Prince set a high standard.' Mrs. Peverel wisely refrained from mentioning various other young men from whom she had seen her daughter gently edge away almost before they knew themselves that they were approaching her. 'I know our Jenny's not a beauty, Mr. Peverel, but I sometimes think that if you didn't tell her of her plainness quite so often, she might make more of herself. She has a kind of something, you know . . .'

'I'm glad to hear it,' he interrupted her. 'Because I begin to lose faith in that sense you speak of. Dare I let her go, if she's already made such a fool of herself? Tell me that, Mrs. Peverel.'

'You have already said she may,' replied his wife. Since his favourite phrase was that his word was his bond, this was unanswerable, and, expecting no reply, she went on, 'I wish I could remember the Princess Isobel better, but what with her brother and that powerful mother of hers she didn't stand out very much.'

'She was set to be a raving beauty,' said Mr. Peverel, surprising her. 'I remember those eyes of hers, dark, set deep . . . She was a young thing, of course, what – eleven, twelve? Very much in her mother's shadow, but I'd lay you any odds she's a stunner now. Pity to think she's to throw herself away on an old roué twice her age. I wonder if that means the

Sobieski estate's entailed away from her? By what I've heard, Polish ladies can often inherit in their own right, like the Russians, but it might not be so in this case. God knows her fiancé Prince Ovinski's rich enough; owns half Lithuania, I believe.' He gave a firm tug to the bell-rope. 'I'll have my horse sent round and ride to Petworth right away. Egremont will advise me what to do for the best, but if we can get her there, I think there should be a good enough future for Jenny in such a household. Palace, rather. Odd to think of the chit living in a palace.'

'Yes.' Her mother swallowed a lump of tears.

Peverel returned late, full of port and good news. 'Took me a while to get his Lordship alone,' he confided to his wife, who had already retired to bed. 'Full house as usual: artists, children, dogs – fellow called Turner I never could abide. Open house, mind you. I always enjoy going there.' He dropped his clothes on the floor and reached for his nightshirt. 'Egremont says she's a lucky young woman.'

'Jenny?'

'Who else? Now her mother and brother are dead, Princess Isobel is absolute mistress of the estate at Rendomierz and God knows what else. And won't lose possession when she marries. I always knew those Poles were a set of barbarians. Wife setting herself up independent of her husband! No wonder she's had a bit of trouble finding one.'

'Has she?'

'Must be rising twenty. They can't have been exactly flocking forward, can they?'

'Maybe she's hard to please,' said his wife sleepily.

He snorted with laughter. 'Can afford to be, God knows. One other thing.' He put the candle on the table at his side of the bed and climbed in. 'You'll have to say a word or two to Jenny about the husband, Ovinski.'

'Oh?' She shifted a little away as his heavy bulk settled into the bed.

'An old rake, as I thought. Nearer sixty than fifty and a sick man, Egremont says. Never married before; wants an heir in his old age; dynastic arrangement; you know the kind of thing.'

'I don't like it! Mark –' How seldom she called him by his

21

given name. 'Let's not let her go.' She reached out a hand to him.

'Nonsense. Gave my word, didn't I?' He blew out the candle. 'My word's my bond. Always was, always will be. No need to fret yourself about the chit. Plain as a pikestaff; probably why the Princess wants her. Lots of prettier girls in Rendomierz.' Enflamed by the idea of them, he rolled over and caught her in the hot, familiar grip.

'It's all settled,' he announced at the breakfast table, to which the two women had come heavy-eyed from lack of sleep. 'You're in luck, miss. Egremont knows of a very good sort of merchant, a Mr. Richards, who is taking the chance of the peace to get his family out to Petersburg by the land route. Wife can't face the Baltic. So they are going by sea as far as Hamburg, and then overland by Berlin and Warsaw. Egremont had heard from the Princess too,' he explained belatedly. 'Wasn't a bit surprised to see me. She'd written to him, old friend of her mother's, asking his help in a host of commissions for the wedding. It's going to be quite an affair. She mentioned you, Jenny.' His surprise was obvious. 'She really wants you, seems like. You'd better bustle about, girl. The Richards leave in two weeks. Can't waste a moment if they are to get to Petersburg before winter sets in; Mrs. Richards don't stand the cold any better than she does the sea. Going to have a hard time in Petersburg, I fancy. Egremont's written Richards telling him you'll join them in town Monday week.'

'So soon!' exclaimed Mrs. Peverel. 'It can't be done!'

'Has to be. You can have the horses tomorrow; go into Chichester; buy what you must. Little as possible. You should be there well before the cold sets in. Didn't the Princess say something about that?'

'Yes.' Jenny had the amazing letter almost by heart. 'She gets her wadded clothes for the winter from Vienna, she says. It will be her pleasure to outfit me. Imagine Isobel so rich, so sure of what she wants! Do you remember, mama, what a little bit of a thing she was when they were at Petworth? She couldn't keep up with Casimir and me; we used to run ahead and hide from her in the pleasure gardens and she'd come calling after us: "Wait for me! Wait for me!" It's good of her to remember me so kindly. I wonder what she is like now.'

'A great beauty, they say,' her father told her, 'but of course so rich as she is, she might well be called that. Well, I'm glad she promises to rig you out for the winter, Jenny, because the expense of your journey is going to be quite bad enough, without spending a mint of money on clothes for it.'

'You shall have my fur pelisse,' said Mrs. Peverel, making the supreme sacrifice.

'Oh, mama!' Jenny recognised it as such. But a messenger, bearing gifts from Petworth House, made the sacrifice unnecessary.

'It's from Mrs. Wyndham!' Jenny stroked the smooth fur of the pelisse. 'How good of her!'

'Lady Egremont, you should say.' Her father corrected her. 'The word is that they've hardly spoken since he married her two years ago. Pity, after all those years together, and all those children.' And then, aware of a fulminating look from his wife, 'Come now, ma'am, if the chit is going on her travels she must learn to call a spade a spade; a mistress a mistress. You'll mind your behaviour, girl, in this Polish palace you're going to, and remember you're my daughter, an English clergyman's daughter.'

'Yes, papa.'

'This Prince Ovinski, now, that the Princess is marrying. Egremont told me a thing or two about him. You'll take care not to be alone with him in any dark Polish grottoes. An old goat! Caught the Empress Catherine's fancy back in the seventies, after the first partition. Took over from Stanislas Augustus for all I know.'

'Stanislas Augustus? You don't mean the last King of Poland?' Now he really had shocked her.

'You didn't know that was how he got the Polish throne? One of Catherine's cast-offs. Just remember that when they tell you what a great romantic figure he was. Probably a cousin of Princess Isobel's, come to that. They do all seem to be related. So don't go blabbing about any of this to her. Or to anyone else!'

'No, papa. Is he really so old? Prince Ovinski?'

'Sixty if he's a day. But rich as Croesus and belongs to one of the first families of Poland. I expect the Princess knows what she's doing. But I can see how she may feel the need of some other companionship than that of her husband. I just hope she doesn't find you a bore. Which she most certainly will if you make great shocked eyes at her like that!' He retired to his study to choose himself a sermon from Blair's invaluable five volumes.

Left alone, mother and daughter sat for a moment in silence, Jenny still lovingly stroking the fur. 'May I really accept it, mama?'

'Oh, yes, I think you should, my dear, and write a pretty thank you.'

Applied to by their mother, her two married sisters also searched their wardrobes for outmoded garments that might be of use to their sister in launching herself into the world, and since Jenny was adept with her needle and had a good eye for what suited her, she had soon assembled what seemed to her a more than adequate trunkful of clothes. It was merely a matter of removing frills from Araminta's dresses, and blonde from Bella's, and letting them out a little at the seams to allow for the sturdy build that Prince Casimir had once called classic proportions . . .

That was no way to be thinking. Casimir was dead. Dead in a duel against one of the Russians he had talked of with such hatred. And Isobel was about to marry an old man of sixty who had been the Russian Empress Catherine's lover. It made no sense. No sense at all. Isobel had adored her brother. It was when she recognised that Jenny adored him too that she had dropped that curious prickly reserve of hers, and made friends. And now she was marrying a Russian. No, not a Russian. A Russian-loving Pole. Surely worse? More despicable? They had played a game that summer the Sobieskis stayed at Petworth House. One of them would be the King of Poland. Jenny had found his name hard to pronounce then, Stanislas Augustus; she knew it well enough now. The one who played him − often Isobel, because it was the smallest part − would stand in the little Greek temple in the pleasure gardens and look down towards the London road, now in their game the Vistula, shading her eyes, watching the Russian soldiers massacre the innocent citizens of Praga. The less popular of the children staying at Petworth House played the Russians and all the rest were Poles. 'Where are my gallant Poles? Where is Kosciusko?' Isobel was supposed to cry, and then all the rest of the children would fall upon the 'Russians' and drive them out of the gardens, sometimes right down into the fields beside the London road. Casimir had thought of the game, and it was he who finally put an end to it by losing his temper and nearly strangling a visiting English boy. Later that day, deep in disgrace, he had caught Jenny for a moment on the nursery stairs. 'My mother says we must leave tomorrow, but I shall come back. You'll wait for me?'

Had she really been waiting? Not knowingly, she thought, unpicking the stitches of some blonde trimming. And she smiled to herself, remembering Dick Forester's proposal, his absolute certainty that she was his for the asking and angry amazement when she refused him. A dangerously good listener, she had been more careful after that, choosing just the moment for a small question or quiet comment hinting a flaw in the male argument. It had worked like a charm. Too well? But now: Isobel certainly wanted her. With her mother and brother both dead, she wrote, she had no close relatives left, since one whole family of cousins had died in the massacre at Praga. No wonder Casimir had struck the Russian officer who made a joke about that day. 'You're the nearest I have to a sister,' Isobel had written. 'Come to me and we will mourn him together.' Of course she was going.

Travelling to London by the night mail, with some discomfort and considerable saving, she reached Mr. Richards' brother's house in Holborn very early, since the mail coach got to London at six in the morning, and found only Mr. Richards himself up to greet her. He was younger than she had expected: a stocky, fresh-faced man, maybe in his thirties, and looking anxious.

'Miss Peverel? Delighted! Can't tell you how glad. You must let me –' He took over the business of paying the boy who had brought her trunk from the General Post Office, and she could only be grateful. She had never travelled alone before and had fretted over the problem of tipping the boy. 'No, no.' Richards refused her timid offer of repayment. 'More than delighted.

Company for Maria. She's not quite the thing this morning; you'll cheer her up, I'm sure of it. A seasoned traveller like you; all the way from Petworth by yourself! Now: breakfast. Kidneys, perhaps a chop, a little bacon? Maria's having her chocolate in bed; not at her strongest first thing, poor girl. We start in half an hour.' An anxious glance at his watch. 'Easy stages: Ipswich tonight; Yarmouth tomorrow; packet leaves tomorrow night; mustn't miss that.' He watched with satisfaction as Jenny dealt with her loaded plate. 'Pleasure to see you eat, Miss Peverel. Keep your strength up! Poor Maria! Homesick, of course. Never left her mother before; sad business yesterday; feel better once we're on our way. Of course she will.'

'I'm sure of it.' But when Maria Richards appeared Jenny felt less so. Tall, fair and sylph-like, Mrs. Richards should have had an English cream and roses complexion and been very nearly a beauty, but this morning her skin was blotched and her eyes shadowed from sleeplessness and tears. She acknowledged her husband's introduction of Jenny with something between a sob and a greeting and sat down as far away as she could from the breakfast table where Jenny was still eating kidneys.

'How you can! The very thought of food makes me feel queasy. My dear mama will be just the same this morning, I know. Missing me. We've never been parted before,' she confided. 'George says – Where is George?'

'He said he was going to see to the packing of the carriage. What a kind man your husband is.' Anything to distract her from these damp thoughts of her mother.

'Oh, yes! The best man in the world!' A blush restored the beauty of her skin and a little, tremulous smile gave life to her face. 'He's so good to me! He's a Bristol merchant. Came to the Bath Assembly on a visit; saw me; got himself introduced.' Her colour was high now, her eyes sparkled. 'He says he nearly bankrupted himself courting me, so wasn't it kind of him – when he saw what it would mean to me to leave mama – he sold his house in Bristol and bought one in Laura Place. Just a step from mama's apartments. George said mama would be best living her own life. Well, of course, there's no separating mama from pug, and George thinks dogs are for outdoors.

26

Mama's not over fond of children either.' Now the betraying skin flushed crimson.

'You have children?' It was a question she had been wanting to ask.

'No. N . . . not yet. Mama says two years is nothing. Just as well, she says, for a young thing like me; just a child myself, but I sometimes wonder if George isn't beginning . . .' She stopped. 'How I am chattering on. You've told me nothing of yourself. You're a friend of Lord Egremont! And going to visit a princess! It's like a fairy tale.' Her dubious glance took in Jenny's altered riding habit and whole unromantic person.

Jenny laughed. 'If it's a fairy tale, I'm most certainly not the heroine. But then, I've always thought being a heroine would be remarkably uncomfortable. Just think! If I really was one, I most likely would not have got here at all. The mail coach would have been held up by footpads last night, and I'd have been spirited away, out of the kingdom most likely. Or, if I got here safely, you and your husband would be villains, taking me off to durance vile in a moated castle somewhere on the continent.'

'Oh, no!' Shocked. 'I told you, George is the kindest of men.'

'Bless you! I was only funning. You'd make a much better heroine than me anyway, so beautiful as you are.'

'You really think so?' She jumped up and crossed the room to study herself in the big glass over the chimney-piece. 'George does, of course.'

'What does George do?' Returning to announce that all was ready, her husband was surprised and delighted to find her in so much better spirits and thanked Jenny with a speaking glance.

But the long day's drive took its toll. As soon as they got out of London, George Richards elected to ride beside the carriage, pointing out that this would mean more room for what he called 'the girls', and give them a chance to get better acquainted.

'Sacrificing yourself?' asked Jenny drily.

'Well . . .' He looked at her for a moment, puzzled, then roared with laughter. 'You're a cool one. No, you're quite right. I much prefer to ride. I'm glad you're with us, Miss Peverel.'

Settling back in the carriage, Jenny found her companion eyeing her cautiously, as one might a strange foreign creature, possibly dangerous. 'Do you speak to all gentlemen so?' she asked. 'Is that perhaps the way they talk at Petworth House?'

'Bless you, no. I've hardly been there since I was a child. Don't go thinking I'm anything but a poor clergyman's daughter.' But she saw this would not do. Her companion was actually hovering on the verge of jealousy and that was no way to start a long journey together. 'Forgive me if you think I spoke somewhat freely to Mr. Richards,' she said, meaning it. 'It's a bad habit of mine. My mother says I'll never get a husband if I don't cure myself of it.'

'Your mother? How could I forget? You've just parted from your mother, too. And your father and brother.'

'No,' Jenny told her. 'My brother Giles was killed on the *Bellerophon* at Aboukir Bay.' She almost kept her voice steady.

'Oh, I am so sorry.' Maria reached out a hand and caught hers. 'So very sorry.'

They were quiet for a long time after that, but Jenny was anxiously aware that her companion was not bearing the journey well. Neither of them had come this way before, and she was fascinated by these new views of flat, agricultural England, each village marked by its dominant church. She could not interest her companion in any of this. 'Forgive me,' said Maria. 'I don't find myself quite the thing. I'll try to sleep a little.' She had eaten hardly any lunch, and when she only picked at her supper in the bustling Ipswich inn, Jenny began to share Mr. Richards' anxiety. The crossing to Hamburg was a long one, she knew, and her midshipman brother had told her often enough what the North Sea could be like.

'We must try to get her to eat some breakfast,' she told George Richards, saying goodnight.

But there was no question of breakfast in bed in this crowded post house and Maria gave the loaded tables a sickly glance, then hurried from the room, pursued by her anxious husband. Jenny, quietly finishing an ample meal, was coming to a conclusion. She might be the youngest of her family, but she was also its only available female and had spent a good deal of time in nursing duty at the houses of her older sisters.

Having finished her breakfast she found the Richards standing in the doorway of the inn, considering a fine June morning. 'I think I should join you in the carriage today,' said George. 'My poor Maria is not in the best of spirits.'

'Always so considerate,' said Maria. 'Dear George.'

Jenny gave her a thoughtful look. 'I wish I could ride,' she said. 'Then, perhaps you could manage to sleep a little in the carriage. Those inn bedrooms are so noisy, are they not?' She had slept like a log herself, but it seemed a safe enough assumption.

'You're right, of course,' said George, disguising his pleasure. 'Thoughtless of me to suggest joining you on what, I am afraid, is going to be a hot day. You'll be much better on your own, and I know Miss Peverel will take the best of care of you, Maria.'

'Thank you.' She was blushing again, Jenny noticed, and wondered just what it meant this time.

Once established in the privacy of the carriage, she began a series of casual-seeming questions about Maria's state of health, and soon established, not much to her surprise, that she was pregnant and did not know it. Sparing an angry thought or two for a mother who could have left her child so ignorant, she went a stage further and discovered that the poor girl was wretched because she felt too ill and tired to . . . Another flaming blush finished the sentence.

Jenny had got hold of her hand in the course of this slow and hesitant conversation, and now patted it soothingly. 'You poor lamb.' She felt immensely old and experienced. 'It had really not struck either of you that you might be increasing?'

'In – Oh!' Maria's hand clasped hers convulsively. 'You can't mean it! Mama never said . . . But how would you know?'

'It sounds very much like it to me, and I'm something of an expert. My mother always sends me to my sisters as soon as there is the least sign – and I have five bouncing nephews and nieces now. In fact,' she could not help a smile at this new thought, 'I rather wonder what they will say when they realise I won't be there for the next time.' And having thus established her authority, she managed a few even closer questions which brought her companion to tears of embarrassment, but established the facts of the case beyond a doubt. 'So now we have to think what is best for you to do.' Her heart had sunk as she recognised the implications of the discovery. 'Will you wish to go home to your mama? Will your husband be able to abandon his trip to take you?'

'Oh, no!' Horrified. 'I know what it means to him. Do we have to tell him? He might make me go back to mama, and she would be in such a taking. She doesn't much like people to be ill, you see.'

'But you're not ill,' said Jenny robustly. 'My sisters do feel a bit queasy, like you, for the first few weeks, but after that they go about their affairs just as usual – well, they have to, so busy as they are.'

'You mean in public?' asked Maria, shocked. 'In Bath, ladies stay at home . . . Mama says it's not decent . . .' She turned suddenly and looked full at Jenny. 'Please, help me to persuade George that I may come with him. I'd so much rather be with him than with mama. And with you, too. You'll look after me, won't you?'

'If it's what you want.' She could not help feeling that the girl had made a wise decision. To be cooped up in Bath with a mother who obviously disliked and disapproved of the whole business might easily be disastrous. 'But you must most certainly talk to your husband.'

'Oh, but please, Jenny, you'll do that. I couldn't! I may call you Jenny?'

'Of course you may, but, dear Maria, surely you should be the one to tell your husband?'

'I can't.' And then, on a totally different note. 'I wish you would call me Mary. It's the name my father gave me, for his mother. I like it so much better, and so does George, really. He only calls me Maria to please mama. You will tell him for me, won't you, Jenny?'

But a cracked splinter-bar, losing them a precious hour in repairs, so delayed their arrival in Yarmouth that there was no possibility of a quiet word with George Richards before they found themselves breathlessly on board the Hamburg packet. Jenny, exchanging one speaking glance with Maria – Mary – could not decide whether she was relieved or appalled.

3

'Do you think that's Sandomierz at last?' Glynde reined in his tired horse and pointed ahead to the silhouette of gothic towers against a clear evening sky.

'It must be,' said Jan. 'And only a day's ride to Rendomierz from there, praise be! Mother used to talk of doing it by boat down the Vistula, but the state of rack and ruin everything is in in this wretched country, I don't suppose there's a boat fit to travel in. It breaks my heart to see the farms so neglected.'

'Well, it's an occupied country,' said Glynde. 'Though how much difference that makes to the peasants, I don't know.'

'Serfs,' said Jan.

'Exactly.' Glynde changed the subject. 'Do you think we can look forward to a few basic comforts tonight? Some edible food, and a bed without bugs? I'm tired of sleeping in the carriage.'

But when they rode across the Vistula and up the dark tunnel through the town's thick, red-brick walls, they found it in an even more advanced state of decayed splendour than Cracow. Carvings on the old houses round the market square and its town hall were crumbling away and many stood empty, with gaping, glassless windows.

'It must have been a great centre of trade once.' Glynde was looking sadly at what had been a stately Renaissance town hall. 'Wealthy merchants all round this square, with money enough to build their town hall and market centre. And now, is there even an inn?'

There was, on the lower side of the square that sloped slightly downhill, so that one had the feeling that in the end the whole place might slip gently down into the Vistula below. Any idea of luxury they might have entertained was dissipated when they entered under the once elegant portico of the shabby building. They were greeted with the usual subservient zeal by the unkempt landlord, but Jan's eager questions were met only with shakes of the head.

'I shall know the Polish words for "no" and "impossible" before we part, that's one thing certain,' said Glynde, when Jan had conveyed the gist of the landlord's refusals to him. 'But we can hardly sleep in the carriage here in the town square, do you think? Not with all these beggars about.' Their arrival always drew swarms of these.

'He's promised clean straw.' Jan had given up apologising.

'But will we get it? Have you noticed with what overwhelming courtesy they fail to produce anything one asks for? I've never been so civilly neglected in my life.'

Jan laughed. 'It's a comfort you find it comic too. The landlord promises us a delicious dinner.'

'And I'll believe that when I taste it.'

It certainly took long enough in the preparing, and Jan had just made an impatient visit to the back of the house to ask how much longer they must wait, when they were surprised by the arrival of the first travellers they had met since leaving Cracow.

'Good day to you.' The two men who came in from the dusk outside seemed to know the house, shouting casually for the landlord by name: 'Isaac, some vodka now, quick, we're famished. And for the gentlemen, too. You speak Polish?' the taller of the two men went on.

'I do.' Jan returned the greeting. 'But my friend speaks only German, English or French.'

'Then let us by all means speak French,' he turned to Rendel and greeted him civilly. 'Since we seem to be doomed to spend a deuced uncomfortable evening together. I hope old Isaac has dealt well by you?'

'He's promised us fresh straw,' said Glynde.

'And a *ragoût*, whatever he means by that,' said Jan. 'In which we hope you gentlemen will join us.'

'With pleasure.' He strode through the room and out towards the kitchen, shouting again for Isaac and vodka.

'Knows his way round,' said Glynde in English to Jan.

'You're regular visitors then?' Jan asked the younger man.

'We've been here before. And you?'

'Our first visit. You live in Cracow, perhaps?' Jan was

32

having difficulty in placing these strangers, but then, a stranger himself, this was hardly surprising. They were both armed, both wore a kind of compromise between the old Polish costume of long coat and high soft boots and the modern trousers that had spread from revolutionary France. Neither had his head shaved in the old Polish style which Jan found so shocking, but each sported a villainous growth of whiskers.

'No.' The older man returned from the kitchen, driving Isaac before him with vodka and glasses. 'We're from north of here. Rendomierz way. Your health!'

'And yours.' Glynde sat down on a backless chair the landlord had produced. 'Then you can tell us if we will get to Rendomierz tomorrow?'

'You're going there?' The younger man leaned forward so eagerly that he almost fell off his three-legged stool.

'For the great wedding, I suppose.' The grey-haired stranger seemed to have taken charge of the proceedings and refilled their glasses. 'Here's to the bride! May she bear nothing but sons.'

'It's true then that the wedding has not yet taken place?' asked Jan.

'No. Prince Ovinski's not come yet,' said the younger man. 'Trouble getting the Tsar's permission to marry her, they say. Bloody Russians. To hell with the lot of them. The Princess would do better to marry a right-thinking Pole, if you ask me.'

'Which no one did,' said his companion repressively. 'You perhaps know the Princess, gentlemen? Her family were great travellers when her mother was alive.'

'No, we have never had the pleasure.' Glynde thought that Jan had left the answer to him, and rather sympathised with his reluctance to claim kinship with the Princess Sobieska. There was something he did not like about these two strangers; hard to say what. They were tossing down the vodka, too, and he was glad when the landlord produced the promised *ragoût*, which proved to be a surprisingly delicious stew of mixed game, cabbage and beans.

'No thanks.' He refused more vodka, applying himself to the sharp small beer and was glad to see that Jan did likewise. 'I'm a little inclined to sleep in the carriage after all.' He seized a chance to say it quickly in English to Jan while the other two men were arguing about the likely date of the wedding.

'Tiresome to be robbed.' Jan had had the same idea. 'And an early start in the morning? I don't altogether fancy their company on the road.'

But to their surprise and relief, when they had mopped up the last sops of gravy with coarse wholemeal bread, the older man rose. 'The gates will be locked in half an hour. We'd best be on our way.'

'You're riding tonight?' Glynde asked.

'There's a moon. And the road to Rendomierz is good; the Princess sees to that. You'll see the difference in the morning. We'll get halfway tonight, sleep at a cousin's of mine, be at Rendomierz at noon. I've commissions for the Princess. Shall I tell her who she has the pleasure of expecting? Or perhaps she knows you are coming?'

'I'm a cousin of hers,' said Jan. 'From America.'

'A cousin! Her aunt's child. But, sir, why did you not say so?' He wrung Jan's hand. 'I should have seen the likeness! What a happy day; a cousin from the other side of the world to grace her wedding.'

'Now perhaps the bridegroom will turn up,' said his surly companion.

'A thousand pardons,' the other man interrupted him, 'that we did not introduce ourselves before, but you know how it is these days, travelling the roads. One does not altogether know . . .' And he proceeded to name himself and his companion in two of those unfathomable groups of Polish consonants that always defeated Glynde, who was amused to see them make just as heavy weather of his own name. But the time when the town gates were locked drew near, the flurry of congratulation and compliment was soon over, and the two men paid their shot and left.

'Well, thank the Lord for that,' said Glynde.

'Agreed! I'm sorry I unleashed that flood of compliment on us, but it suddenly struck me it might make sense after all to say I was the Princess Isobel's cousin. Just in case they had any little idea about ambushing us tomorrow and leaving us dead in a bog.'

'I noticed you didn't mention that she doesn't know you're coming,' said Glynde. 'Frankly, I'm grateful to you. I shall

34

sleep sounder tonight and travel more peacefully tomorrow for knowing we are expected.'

'If they tell the Princess. I didn't much like them, did you?'

'No. Are they what are called the *schlachta*, do you suppose? The petty nobles who have no land, only their so-called nobility, and no way of earning their living, because a noble can't take to trade?'

'I imagine so. Hangers-on of my cousin, I would think. Mother used to say that any great house had swarms of such men, useful only when it was a question of swinging the vote in the diet, or impressing a neighbour. Will my cousin look down on me, do you suppose, because my father is in trade?'

'I shall think the less of her if she does.' But Glynde wondered what his own father would have said if he had suggested becoming a merchant when his wound closed the army against him. Sometimes he found himself thinking it might have been a more honourable calling than the diplomatic service, but his father would most certainly not have agreed with him, and his elder brother would have been enraged. A Rendel of Ringmer in trade. Unthinkable. 'I imagine things are quite different in your United States of America,' he said now. 'I'm for my bed. I wonder if there is clean straw.'

There was, and a chipped jug full of cold water. 'The lords should have told me they were kin to the Princess Sobieska.' The landlord was more obsequious than ever. 'If I have failed in any way, they must forgive my ignorance.'

'I like him still less when he fawns on one like that,' said Jan impatiently as they made their minimal preparations for sleep.

'Yes. Intolerable. As if he expected us to kick him.'

'Perhaps people do,' said Jan sleepily.

No armed robber disturbed their sleep, and the landlord amazed them by producing coffee for their breakfast. What with this, a fine morning, and the better road that the strangers had promised, they started out for their day's ride in good heart. And the country was more interesting here as the hard dirt-road ran sometimes along the Vistula, sometimes at the other side of the broad valley it had made by constantly changing its course. The land was better cultivated, too, and the villages began to look more prosperous, with here and there a paned window visible in one of the larger houses, and a pale, clean look to the one-storeyed peasant huts.

'The women scrub them down each spring,' Jan explained. 'My mother told me about it. To get rid of the lichens and grubs that otherwise destroy the wood. It must be a terrible job.'

'Women's work? They do seem to bear the burdens, don't they? The oriental influence, I suppose. Like those outlandish shaven heads. I cannot get used to them.'

'No more can I,' admitted Jan, 'though one has to see that they have advantages from the point of view of cleanliness. I'm ashamed to arrive at my cousin's so very far from presentable.' Travelling even lighter than Glynde, he had been reduced to borrowing a clean cravat from him that morning but was still unhappily aware that his attempts at shaving in the exiguous supply of dirty water had not been totally successful. 'I wish I was fair like you,' he said now. 'I feel shabby all over. Mother always made their trips to Cracow or Vienna sound like parties of pleasure . . . picnics almost.'

'I imagine it was different then. Mind you, even now, with a sufficient retinue it would be another case altogether. I was warned that travellers in these parts were judged by their servants and the lace on their coats, but who wants to be cumbered with a lot of grumbling retainers?' All the same, he liked the prospect of meeting the Princess Sobieska in his present travel-stained condition even less than his companion did. And when they got their first view of Rendomierz that afternoon even he, who had grown up in one of England's smaller stately homes, felt daunted. 'It really is a palace!' They paused by common consent to gaze at the cluster of buildings set back in a fold of the foothills that separated the Vistula from its tributary, the Renn. Westering sun caught the glass of windows in the gothic tower and central block and sparkled on what must be an immense orangery.

'Or a village! I had no idea . . .' Jan put up an anxious hand to the borrowed cravat, then withdrew it hurriedly, aware that it was bound to be dirty. He met Glynde's eyes ruefully. 'Frankly,' he said, 'just now, I wish I'd taken father's advice and stayed home. This is no place for me. A cousin who owns all that! She'll be proud as the devil, of course.

Making a dynastic marriage –' He looked wildly round him and Glynde actually wondered whether, on his own, he might not simply have turned and fled.

But it was too late. Glynde's sharp eyes had caught sight of a group of horsemen galloping towards them from the direction of the palace. A cloud of dust at first, they were soon distinguishable as wild, Cossack figures, lances and sabres gleaming in the sun. 'I hope that means we are expected,' he said drily to Jan. 'I think we wait for them here, don't you?'

'Lord, I'm glad I ran into you,' said Jan. 'I suppose it is a reception committee.' He did not quite make it a question.

'Oh, I imagine so.' And as his hand almost unconsciously reached towards the pistol he carried, a shouted order halted the oncoming mob in its tracks, horses foaming to a halt, their riders suddenly motionless and silent. One man rode slowly forward, sabre raised in salute, shaven head gleaming in the sunshine. 'Welcome, the Princess's cousin!' The greeting, in admirable French, was spoken equally to the two of them, but his eyes were fixed on Jan.

'*Zenkue*,' Jan chose the Polish word for thank you and went on in that language, introducing himself and Glynde, then switched to French to explain that Glynde did not understand Polish.

'Then we will speak French, though it makes me happy and will delight the Princess that your Lordship has taken the trouble to learn our language. She bids you both welcome to her home, and looks forward to meeting you when you have recovered from your journey. I am her chamberlain, Leon Wysocki, entirely at your service.' They were riding forward now, at a reasonable pace, the Cossack escort skirmishing round them. 'This is where we leave the road.' He shouted an order to one of their outriders. 'I have told him to guide your coachman to the stables,' he explained. 'We will ride through the park; it is the shorter way to the guest-houses. The park was planned by an Englishman, a pupil of your William Kent.'

'He certainly knew what he was doing.' Glynde looked across the close-cropped grass to its groups of ornamental trees; beech, and live-oak and towering pine.

'It must take an army to keep it like this,' said Jan.

'The Princess has an army of serfs, and more acres than she

can count.' He pointed. 'The kitchen gardens are behind that wall, and the maze over there, but I am going to take you by way of the ornamental waters. The Princess's father designed them himself. They were his pride.'

'I should think so,' said Glynde as they paused for a moment beside the ornamental pool at the end of a long yew walk lined with statues. 'I've seen the ornamental water at Chatsworth and it is nothing to this.'

'So other gentlemen have said.' Wysocki was pleased. 'It used to be a great sport with the Princess and her brother, God rest his soul, to take guests to see the statues in the yew walk and then drench them from the secret outlets. There's a stone you press,' he explained to Jan, who was looking puzzled, 'and water spurts out of their mouths.' He led the way across an ornamental bridge and round the corner of the yew walk. 'Rendomierz,' he said.

From here, the house looked still more enormous, the symmetry of its pale yellow and white front relieved by the orangery glittering to one side and the church with its gothic tower on the other. The huge front door under its classic pediment stood hospitably open to late afternoon sunshine, but their guide turned his horse down a neatly gravelled side-path that led towards the orangery. 'The Princess has given you one of the guest-houses,' he explained. 'You will not mind sharing it? She thought you would be more comfortable there than in the main palace, where we are all at sixes and sevens because of the wedding. Each of the family used to have their own house,' he went on, as they rounded the corner of the orangery and saw what looked like a village street running up the centre of a small valley, a stream sparkling beside it, houses on either side. 'The Princess had this one made ready for you.' He stopped outside the first house. 'It's the most convenient for the Turkish bath, which her father built at this end of the orangery. And here is Jadwiga to welcome you.' A smiling servant in tight-fitting velvet waistcoat over voluminous striped skirts stood curtseying at the open door. 'Ask for anything you need. She will send a boy to conduct you to the Turkish baths, and I will come – shall we say in two hours? – to take you to the palace, where the Princess hopes you will sup with her.'

A boy had appeared from nowhere to take their horses; their guide bowed and left them; the smiling servant stood back to let them enter the house.

'Not exactly a cottage.' Glynde looked at the luxurious living-room. 'And we didn't need to worry about our appearance after all.'

'No, thank God. Mother never said . . . I had no idea.' He crossed the room to where Jadwiga was standing at the far door. 'Dining-room through there, kitchen beyond . . .'

'And bedrooms on each side.' Though he had immensely taken to his new companion, Rendel was nevertheless delighted at the prospect of a room to himself again. There was so much writing to be done.

'You will take some vodka, lords, while you wait for your baggage?' asked Jadwiga, in Polish. 'Or anything clsc?'

'She's offering us vodka,' Jan translated. 'Or anything else.'

'I wonder how all-inclusive that is,' said Glynde thoughtfully. 'She's a striking creature, isn't she? It's the first time I've seen the Polish national dress worn with style, as it should be. But no vodka for me, or anything else. I cannot begin to tell you how I look forward to that Turkish bath.'

Two hours later they were ready, glowing with cleanliness, scrubbed and pummelled and soothed by the willing staff of the Turkish bath, and dressed in the formal best each had saved for this occasion. They made a comic enough contrast, Glynde thought, he in full court-dress of knee-breeches and silk stockings, Jan in another of his loose-fitting coats over straight trousers, but these of the finest alpaca. 'Father said I should get a rig-out like that,' he looked a little anxiously at Rendel's costume. 'I said he was crazy. I'm an American. This is how I dress.'

'And very comfortable it looks. Frankly, I envy you.'

'Thanks. But what will she say?'

'Nothing,' said Glynde. 'Whatever else she is, your cousin is a great lady.'

Which did not do very much to calm his young companion's nerves, but luckily the chamberlain appeared at this point, cast an approving glance over Glynde's costume and a puzzled one over Jan's, and said, 'You are ready, lords? Then come with me.'

They entered the palace by a back way that was only marginally less stately than the front one and passed through ranks of liveried, bowing footmen to a grand stairway that swept up through the centre of the building. Dusk had fallen while they were in the bath, and every third footman held a flaming torch, while candelabra on the walls had their myriad candles reflected over and over again in the huge looking-glasses that adorned the stair. 'I feel like Tom Thumb,' muttered Jan. 'I wish I'd stayed home.'

4

'But why didn't she tell me?' asked George Richards, distracted. 'I'd never have brought her. You must see, Miss Peverel, that I would never have brought her.'

'I suppose not,' said Jenny, 'but whether that would have been a good thing is more than I can tell. I haven't met her mother, but I did wonder . . .'

'A terrible creature,' said George Richards. 'A blood-sucker. I'd thought to get Mary clean away to Bristol, but not a bit of it. Can't leave dear mama. Or rather, dear mama won't be left. So I bought a house in Bath – only thing to do, hoped for the best. Drew the line at her living with us. Better living on her own, I said; her own life, all that. But in and out all day; Mary quoting her to me till I thought I'd choke on it. Planned this trip as a last recourse. And now, look what's happened. If only she had told me!'

'But she didn't know. And really, Mr. Richards, from everything you say, I think it may be all for the best, if we can just get her safely through this first difficult time. My sisters were always poorly at first; merry as grigs the rest of the way. By what Mary says – if I may call her Mary – I would think she is probably almost over the worst of it. If we take great care of her for the next few weeks . . .'

'How can we? If only you had told me at Yarmouth,' he said again. But they both knew it had been quite impossible during the chaos of embarkation the night before. Now, Mary was prostrate in the tiny cabin and Jenny had asked George Richards to take her up on deck for a breath of air after the noisy, crowded ship's breakfast. It was a fine morning with the ship running easily under what she thought Giles would have called a following wind. She found she liked the live feeling of the deck under her feet; felt herself automatically yielding to its movement.

Impossible not to feel exhilarated by the fresh, keen air, the cheerful bustle around her. She pushed back the hood that warmly framed her face and smiled at him. 'That inn was no place for her. It would have meant going back to Bath, I think. Which would have been bad for her too. She says young ladies in Bath stay at home with their feet up when they are in her situation.'

'Ridiculous! If I could just get her to Petersburg! Safe enough in Holy Russia from ma-in-law – and from Bonaparte. It's a handsome city. Their customs are strange, of course, take a bit of getting used to, but there's a British colony centred round the Factory, and this new Tsar of theirs is quite a fellow, they say. I've not been there since that madman Paul was killed last year. I'd never have considered settling there while he was alive. Do you know, Miss Peverel, if his carriage met yours in the street, you had to stop and get out and stand bareheaded while he passed? In the snow, even, with the temperature well below freezing. Women, too, and children.'

'And if you didn't?'

'Siberia the least of it. Well – a foreigner might just have been ordered to leave, but I wouldn't have banked on it. He was army mad, you know. It's a fortunate thing for us all that he died, or he might have come to blows with Bony in the end, though he seemed to think well enough of him. Well: two tyrants! His son Alexander's a liberal, a man of peace. He'll do great things for Russia and I mean to be there to see them. Profit by them. It's bound to mean more trade. Do I shock you, Miss Peverel? It's hardly the kind of talk you can be used to.'

'I like it,' she said. 'It reminds me of when my brother Giles used to talk of life in the navy. It's real, somehow. Different.'

'I'm sorry about your brother. Mary told me last night. She didn't seem to be able to settle. She's . . . worried about herself, I think. Frightened, maybe?' He was half ashamed to admit it. 'I'm from a family of ten. Mother never had time to fret. Too busy keeping us out of trouble, I reckon. I wish she'd lived so I could give her a bit of comfort in her old age. I'm selfmade, Miss Peverel, proud of it. I've been wanting to tell you, so you know where you stand. Mary never would tell, poor girl. She's ashamed of it. I'm not, but I understand how she feels. Course, we did have to pretend a bit for her ma. She'd never have swallowed me whole, not as I really am. Wasn't it a lucky thing for me that when I started making my mint I had the wits to get me a speech master?' His voice changed, rose a note or two, took on an accent she had never heard. 'Born and reared in Liverpool, miss, if you call it rearing. Begging in the streets; fighting for crusts; holding horses for halfpence. Mary's ma would never have stood for me, talking like that, would she now?' He reverted to the King's English. 'And even you might think twice about being seen with me, Miss Peverel.'

'I wish you would call me Jenny.' It was the most complete answer she could think of.

'Thank you, Jenny.' He took it as such. 'Well, there we are. Yarmouth's behind us. Hamburg won't do. How long do you reckon we are going to have to cosset the lass?'

'Not long. Another few weeks at most. What are the country inns like in Prussia?'

'Terrible. But I planned to start by way of Lüneburg – that's in Hanover, practically British,' he explained. 'It don't make much difference to their inns, but there's one in Lüneburg I've found snug enough. I aim to do a bit of business there on the way. It's one of the Hanseatic League Cities, you know, quite a centre of trade.'

'I didn't know,' she admitted. 'To tell truth I'd not thought of Hanover as being exactly British. Even if our King does reign there, too.'

'You're right,' he said. 'It ain't. But I reckon we could stay there a few days, and let Mary rest, if it won't make you too late for that wedding of yours.'

'Oh, never mind about that.' She smiled at him. 'It will save me worrying about what to wear. And, of course, Mary must come first. My invitation to Rendomierz is a very general one. Princess Sobieska seems to feel she will want company after she is married.'

'As well she may. This Prince Ovinski she's marrying don't sound at all the thing to me. We merchants have our sources, bound to have. Oh, his credit's good enough; no trouble there; but as to his character . . . And an old man, too. No, I reckon that Princess knew what she was doing when she sent for you.

I only wish . . . Miss Peverel, you wouldn't think again and come to Petersburg with us instead?'

It was, for a moment, enormously tempting. Then she shook her head. 'It's most kind of you, but my father –'

'Wouldn't much like your running off with a self-made cit and his wife. And quite right too,' he added handsomely. 'But I wish you could, just the same. Mary will miss you badly. And so will I.'

'The Princess will receive you in the small salon.' Leon Wysocki led the two young men through a series of brilliantly lighted rooms hung with tapestries Glynde longed to stop and study, catching a glimpse of a unicorn here, a flower-studded landscape there. He could hear music now, a piano played quietly as background to a buzz of talk; Mozart, he thought, or old Haydn.

The small salon would have been a large reception room anywhere else. As they paused in the doorway the pianist played a final chord and was rewarded with a brief hush and a small flutter of applause. Then the conversation started again, on a rather louder note, as Wysocki led them forward through a group of men talking Polish, who drew aside with curious glances to let them pass. Beyond them, six women were sitting bent over their work, talking quietly. Three of them wore widow's black and could be dismissed at once, but Glynde, eagerly scanning the other three, felt a pang of disappointment. Could one of these very ordinary young ladies really be the almost royal beauty of whom he had heard so much?

Apparently not. With a brief greeting, Wysocki led them on to where the pianist was looking up eagerly at a tall young woman, dressed in plain white, who had her back to the room as she leaned against the piano to leaf through a pile of music. Glynde had dismissed her as the pianist's page-turner until he drew near enough to see the look of hopeless adoration on the man's face. And at the same moment, he saw them coming and said something.

She turned, smiled, held out both hands in welcome. 'My cousin!' She had singled out Jan unerringly, and Glynde, watching, thought it no wonder. There was an obvious likeness between them. Both had dark curling hair, wide brows and sparkling black eyes, but where these made Jan merely good-looking they gave the Princess an absolute beauty.

She was turning to him. He must not gape like a boy at his first party. 'And welcome to you too, Mr. Rendel. It is a long time since we have had the pleasure of entertaining an Englishman here at Rendomierz. You will have to bear with me if I speak your language with a little difficulty. I have not had much practice of late years.'

'But you speak like one of us.'

She smiled at him, making him her absolute slave. 'Believe me, I was not – you say hunting for a compliment?'

He returned the smile with good measure. 'Fishing, as a matter of fact.'

'Thank you! I remember now, my governess used to say it to Casimir and me. "Never fish for compliments, children." She was English, of course. My brother and I made it our private language.' The expressive face clouded. 'She died last year, my dear Miss Pratt. It spared her a great sadness. She loved me, but she adored Casimir. Well, we all did. You look a little like him,' she told Jan. 'I am so very glad to see you, cousin. You will both stay for the wedding, of course. You come on a happy day. We have just heard that my affianced is on his way from Petersburg. He should be here within a week or so. He does not like to travel fast, which is perhaps as well, since the ceremony is to be performed as soon as he gets here and there are naturally a million things to do first. I am afraid you find us all at sevens and sixes –' A challenging glance suggested to Glynde that she knew she had got this phrase wrong.

'The ceremony will take place here?' he asked.

'But of course. In our church, with our people present.' She turned to Jan who was gazing at her, as spellbound as Glynde. 'Are you a Catholic, cousin? You are my nearest male relative, you know, even if your name is Warrington.' She made heavy weather of it, on purpose, Glynde thought.

'No, I am so sorry, I am afraid . . . My father . . .' Glynde thought, amused, that for two pins Jan would have abjured his father's religion there and then. 'My sister still is,' he went on, as if that might help.

'But she is not here. I wish she were. I am sadly lacking in female relatives to talk to.' Her meditative gaze rested for a moment on the little group of women still rather ostentatiously busy with their handiwork. 'That is why I am so grateful to Monsieur Poiret for his music.' She smiled down at the pianist, translated the last sentence into French, and introduced him: 'Monsieur Poiret and his parents escaped from France in '89,' she said, still in French. 'They saw the storm coming before most did.'

'And found a most blessed asylum.' Poiret's look of adoration was so blatant as to be painful. 'May I play the sonata you picked out, Highness?'

'Would you like it?' she asked the two men in English.

They exchanged glances, Glynde's suggesting that as her cousin, Jan should speak first.

'Well, as a matter of fact –' Jan was actually blushing '– mother was a great one for music; used to sing to us when we were little. Anna loved it, but, me, I'm afraid . . .'

'It means nothing to you? And you, Mr. Glynde?'

'Highness, I like it so well, and thought so highly of Monsieur Poiret's playing, what I heard of it, that I would much rather have a real chance of listening to him some other time.'

It got him a pleased look from Poiret, and one of the Princess's ravishing smiles. 'You put me quite to shame, Mr. Rendel. Let me introduce you to my friends.'

Presented to six ladies in a row, Glynde sorted them out as best he might. One of them might be a young cousin of the Princess, since she had the dark hair and sparkling deep-set eyes that Jan shared with her, but combined with a squat build and sallow complexion that denied her any hope of good looks. The Princess introduced her simply as 'My beloved Marta,' and passed on to present him to Madame Poiret, the pianist's mother, who plunged at once into so doleful and extended a tale of lost glories in France that he was relieved when the Princess came back to claim his arm to lead her in to supper. 'I treat Jan quite with disrespect, as a member of the family,' she explained, smiling at him. 'You will bring Madame Poiret, Jan. And you will not mind my calling you by your given name.'

'I will not mind anything you do,' said Jan, and Glynde,

46

taking the Princess's arm to lead her back through the long
range of rooms, thought how used she must be to this instant
adoration.

Over a meal that would have seemed luxurious in any
palace from Vienna to London, the Princess questioned Glynde
eagerly about the international situation. 'We are so cut off
here, in what should be Poland,' she explained, 'that we are
quite savage for news of the world outside.' But her questions,
close, intelligent and showing her surprisingly well informed,
kept him at full stretch. Secretly and thoroughly briefed by his
friend Canning before he left on his unofficial and unorthodox
mission, he must be careful not to reveal more knowledge than
might be possessed by an ordinary tourist.

'This new Whig government of yours,' she was asking now.
'You think it will last?'

'If the peace does. And for that I think I must refer you to
Bonaparte.'

'If we only knew what was in his mind!' She gestured to one
of the liveried servants to refill their champagne glasses.

'I doubt it's peace.'

'Ah.' Again that distracting smile. 'So you are a Tory, one
of Mr. Pitt's men. I thought so. And being in opposition has
left you free to travel. Well, we are the gainers, but I wonder
how long you will find you can stay away. I think we are just
holding our breath, myself, waiting for the next act. And, when
it comes, what hope for us Poles, Mr. Rendel? If your Mr. Pitt
has the negotiating of the next peace, will he do something for
us, do you think? You British talk very handsomely of liberty,
but when it comes to practice at the conference table . . . Oh,
I know England is a long way off. What do you care what
happens here in central Europe? I met your poet Mr. Campbell
at Ratisbon two years ago. I'm afraid I told him it was all
very well to rhyme about *The Pleasures of Hope*, and freedom
screaming when Kosciusko fell, but that we Poles need more
than fine phrases.'

'What did he say to that?'

'He had no answer, poor man. I thought it served him right
when he had to run from the French army a few days later.'

'And you, Highness? Did you run from the French?'

'No, why? I invited their commanding officer to dinner. A

47

charming man; we have corresponded ever since. You must see, Mr. Rendel, that the one advantage of being a nation without statehood is that there is nothing to stop you being friends with everyone.'

'Even your occupiers, Highness?'

'*Touché!*' She raised her glass and drank to him. 'But, yes, in fact. I have cousins and good friends in Vienna and go there from time to time – to shop, mainly. And, as I expect you know, my future husband is a close friend of the Emperor Alexander and of his right-hand man, another Pole, Adam Czartoryski. We are not a simple problem, we Poles.'

'You most certainly are not. Tell me about Prince Czartoryski. Do you know him well? I long to meet him. Will he be coming to your wedding, perhaps?'

'We're related, of course. You will have noticed, I expect, that we are mostly cousins here. No, I'm afraid the Emperor cannot spare him for the wedding. You will have to go to Russia if you wish to meet him.'

'I intend to.'

'I imagined so. In fact, though you are too polite to say so, you are merely passing through Poland on your way there. Nobody comes here now we don't exist any more. Why should they?'

'For the pleasure of meeting you, Highness.'

'Compliments, Mr. Rendel? I thought better of you.' And she turned to Jan, leaving him enraged at his own obviousness. But on the other hand, thinking about it afterwards, he decided it had gone well enough. If he lingered a while at Rendomierz, she would think it a natural tribute to her. And so it would be. For once, duty and inclination ran side by side. No doubt about it, Rendomierz, and the society wedding to take place here, was the ideal scene to study the chances of a national Polish uprising actually taking place if the moment should come – part of the purpose of his secret mission.

Two nights later, something roused Glynde from his first sleep. They had retired early, the Princess having pleaded fatigue after a long day spent riding with her guests to show them the model village she was building south of the palace. He had fallen asleep at once, now waked, as always, into complete consciousness. Absolute silence, but some sound must have waked him. A night bird probably, or the dying scream of a small animal out there in the park. But something made him open his eyes. A faint glow of light in the far corner of the room. Fire? He smelled nothing. And now, surely the sound that had wakened him, a loud creak as the light focused itself into a narrow band where a piece of the floor was slowly rising. An oubliette? An attack? Incredible, but his hand had already found the pistol automatically tucked under his pillow. He lay still, finger on trigger, as the section of floor lifted completely back. A hand, holding a lantern. A woman's hand?

She emerged slowly, quietly, and Glynde lay still as death, watching. He knew her almost at once. Marta. The Princess's beloved Marta, her visibly adoring shadow through the days he had spent at the palace. It was entirely fantastic, something out of the thousand and one nights, and he lay still, finger now slack on the trigger, waiting to see what would happen next.

'Mr. Rendel?' Her English was heavily accented, but adequate enough. 'Mr. Rendel!' Just a little louder.

He would play this comedy her way. He turned over heavily in the bed, pretended to wake, let the pistol drop back under the pillow. 'Yes? What is it?' He sat up straight. 'Miss Marta! What is it? What's happened?' Instinctively, he kept his voice low.

'Hush!' She put a warning finger on her lips. 'We must not wake Mr. Warrington.'

'No? But — I don't understand.' And he had never said a truer word, he thought, watching her embarrassment, as she stood there, confronting a strange man in his bed. Could this, possibly, be part of the Princess's idea of hospitality? It was a thought to disgust, to enrage.

'The Princess sent me.' She put down the lantern on a small table. 'She asks you to come to her. She needs your help, badly. Here.' She handed him a folded note. It was short and to the point. 'Please come to me. You will understand, by the drastic means I use to send for you, how badly I need you.'

'She wants me to come now?'

'Please.'

'You're a good friend.' He needed time to think.

'I love her. She would not ask if it was not urgent. Please –' she said again.

'Very well. If you will be so good as to look the other way while I put some clothes on, I will be with you directly.'

'Thank you.' She moved away, to look out into uncurtained darkness while he climbed hurriedly into the riding-clothes he had worn that day.

'There.' He shrugged himself into Mr. Scott's well-fitted coat. 'I'm at your service, Miss Marta.' And then, on an afterthought. 'Should I, perhaps, lock the door?'

'Please.' She watched him push down the bar that held the latch immovable. 'Now –' She was eager to be off.

'Close it behind me?' He was following her down a solid enough flight of stairs from the trapdoor.

'No need, since the door is locked. It will be easier, coming back.'

'Yes.' The trapdoor had squeaked, as if it had not been used for years. They had reached the bottom of the short flight of stairs, which opened on to an arched tunnel. Musty with long disuse, it stretched darkly before them, the lantern only illuminating the first few yards. The ground was damp as the tunnel sloped gently downwards. It must be following the line of the lane that ran between the houses. Over the years, water would have seeped down from the stream that lay somewhere to their left. Marta turned and put a finger to her lips, but it had not occurred to him to speak; he had far too much to think about. The going was level now; they must be under the palace, to which this secret way must lead.

Marta paused at an open arch where a winding stair twisted up to their right. 'Not a word now, and be careful how you go.' She held the lantern low to illuminate the worn treads of narrow stone steps. The hem of her skirts was soaking, he saw, and reached out to take the lantern gently from her. She would need both hands for this steep climb.

She nodded her thanks, picked up her skirts with one hand and clung to the rope that served as hand-rail with the other. This was a much longer and steeper climb than at the cottage and he remembered the imposing height of the palace's grand stairway.

The top now, and a crack of light ahead. She turned, finger

again to her lips and motioned to him to stay where he was, then pushed open the door where the light showed. It led into what must be the back of a huge closet and she moved forward and out of sight through a whisper of stirred silk and satin.

'All's well.' She was back again, speaking normally now. 'Come, Mr. Rendel.'

The Princess's dressing-room? Blue velvet curtains; he was facing a Chippendale dressing-table flanked with ormolu-framed looking-glasses. Doors to right and left gave on to lighted rooms. He followed Marta through the door to the left, found himself in a luxurious boudoir also hung with blue velvet, but had eyes only for the Princess who stood there awaiting him, dressed in a plain white gown like the one she had worn when he first met her.

'Mr. Rendel. I am more grateful than I can say.' She held out her hand and he badly wanted to kiss it, but pressed it firmly instead and was angry with himself at what the touch did to him.

'I am at your service, Highness. But . . .'

'Deserve an explanation. Marta, will you keep watch in the anteroom. I gave strict orders, but just in case . . .'

'She should change her slippers,' said Glynde.

'What? Oh,' looking down. 'Thank you, Mr. Rendel. Take a pair of mine, Marta dear.' And, as she left them, 'It's a long time since the tunnel was used. Since my father died . . .'

'He built it?'

'The branch that runs to the Renn was part of the old fortress he replaced with this palace. I'm afraid he must have seen its possibilities at once. He had it made good and built the extension up to the guest village. I'm afraid you can guess what he used it for, Mr. Rendel.' And then, for the first time, he saw her blush, a slow crimson flood that drained as slowly away and left her white and drawn. She moved over to an inlaid side table. 'Let me pour you a glass of vodka, Mr. Rendel, after your damp journey.'

'Thank you.' It was the last thing he wanted, but he thought she needed it. 'You must tell me how I can serve you.' Could she possibly have learned of his secret mission? The question had been hammering at him as they talked.

'Yes.' She handed him the brimming glass and sat down in

a heavy straight-backed chair. 'This is even more difficult than I expected.' Her eyes met his. Appealing for help? Extraordinary from this great lady he had watched directing a palaceful of courtiers.

'I am yours to command. Just tell me . . . Short of murder, that is . . .' The days he had spent with her had taught him how passionate a Pole she was. Could she want him to use his diplomatic entrée to assassinate one of the enemies of Poland? In this fantastic situation, it seemed entirely possible.

But, surprisingly, she was laughing. 'Oh, no, not murder, Mr. Rendel. Quite the contrary.' And again that miraculously becoming blush. 'But, first, your promise that even if you refuse my request, you will never speak of it to a soul.'

'You have it.'

'Thank you.' Gravely. 'Then, forgive me if I tell you something about myself. It will help you understand . . .'

'I shall be honoured, Highness.' But his eyes moved involuntarily to the gilt and marble clock on the chimney-piece.

'It's early,' she said. 'There's time. Do I need to tell you how much I care about my country, Mr. Rendel?'

'No. Everything you do and say shows it.'

'Thank you. Believe me, if it would serve Poland, I would gladly die. As my brother died, defending it.'

Now, for the first time, he was sorry for her. To delude herself that her brother's absurd duel had done anything for Poland . . . 'You know how sorry I am,' was all he could find to say.

'Thank you.' A regal inclination. She had herself in hand again. 'His death leaves me the last of our line, the last of the Sobieskis.'

'Yes?'

'And, as you know, I am marrying a man of equally ancient line. A Jagiello.'

'Yes.'

'You know about my future husband?'

'Know?' This was difficult ground.

'Of course you do.' She stood up, almost violently, reached for the decanter, refilled their glasses. 'I've not met him for years, but he's an old man, Mr. Rendel, an old roué, his health

52

wrecked by the life he has led. My brother's was the smaller sacrifice.'

'Then why?' And why in the world was she telling him this? He had never felt himself so entirely out of his depth and dared no more than these scant monosyllables.

'You really don't see? What easy lives you must have in England! And yet you strike me as having thought a great deal about Poland. Has it not struck you that what we so gravely lack is a leader? Freedom did die when Kosciusko fell.'

'But you can't possibly imagine that the Prince Ovinski . . . forgive me, Princess, but even married to you . . . And so committed as he is to the Emperor Alexander.'

'No, no.' She had tossed off her vodka, like a man, in one draught. 'But his son, Mr. Rendel. Our son. Sobieski and Jagiello; the heir of our two great houses. And – brought up to it by me. Might he not prove the leader behind whom the Poles would cast off faction and unite, once and for all, to throw out the invaders?'

'But –' How could he say it? The whole conversation was fantastic, unreal. 'But, Princess . . . an old man, you said it yourself . . .'

'Yes.' She stood up, one hand tense on the arm of her chair, looking half away, as if she could not face him with what she was going to say. 'I'm not a fool. I thought of that too, Mr. Rendel. You met two of my men in Sandomierz?'

'Yes?' He was most absolutely in the dark.

'I have had my emissaries out as far away as Cracow and Warsaw, talking to travellers, weighing them up for me. With no idea, of course, what my purpose was.' She turned now and faced him, head up. 'From their reports, I have had to decide if they had found someone fit to father my child. The future King of Poland.'

'Dear God!' He had risen when she did, now moved almost blindly over to the decanter to refill their glasses. 'You cannot possibly be serious.'

'Would I have sent for you like this, secretly, if I was not?' Her hand trembled as she took her glass from him. 'I do not take after my father, Mr. Rendel. The tunnel has not been used since he died. Monsieur Poiret is the nearest I have come to a male friend. While he lived, my brother was enough. I

53

dread my marriage, Mr. Rendel. Have dreaded this still more. But, for Poland, it must be done. Now, perhaps, by the lucky chance of your coming, it need not be quite so bad.' She was blushing now, uncontrollably, and so he thought, amazed, was he. 'It's a great deal to ask,' she said now, as he stood silent, dumbstruck, gazing at her.

'Highness, it's impossible!' But he was ashamed to feel a change in the way he looked at her, at this Princess suddenly become mere woman. 'You can't mean it?'

'You say that here, at this time of night, my reputation gone already if you choose? Oh – I know you won't. I trust you absolutely, Mr. Rendel, or you'd not be here. As to its being impossible, you, a diplomat, must know better than that.' Her request made, she seemed more at ease, her tone almost teasing. 'You know perfectly well that this kind of reality lies behind much of politics. A woman sacrificed, for dynastic reasons, one way or another. It's no more than that.' And then, colouring more than ever. 'Forgive me, when I said sacrifice, I didn't mean . . .' She stopped, speechless.

'Don't marry him!' Explosively. 'There must be some other way.'

'Don't think I haven't searched for one. I had hoped that perhaps Adam Czartoryski . . . but he's even more tarred with the Russian brush than Ovinski, and besides, there's talk of an engagement with the Princess of Courland.'

Not to mention his affair with the Empress of Russia. But he did not say this aloud, just sat there, gazing at her, struck speechless by a confused mixture of respect, sympathy and rising desire.

'Of course, if you can't face it . . . It's a great deal to ask.' She had misinterpreted his silence, and no wonder.

'Highness, you're not a fool. You must know . . . I'm just a man.' Just a schoolboy, he felt, embarking on that first flurry of petticoats. He stood, reached for the decanter, poured for them both, raised his glass: 'To the King of Poland.'

'Thank you!' She drank it, looked up at him, a question. 'Marta is safe?'

'Entirely. She's my half sister, you must have seen?'

'Oh, God.' He took her glass, put it, with his, on the table, stood for a moment looking down at her. 'You have not exactly had it easy,' he said, his hand reaching out, almost without his volition, to touch the place where pearl-coloured shoulder emerged from white dress.

'Oh, easy! For someone like me, what is easy?' She looked up at him. 'Is this how it begins?'

'This is how it begins, Highness.' He was entirely mad. He bent, gathered her into his arms, amazed at the light strength of her, and carried her through the dressing-room to her bedroom beyond. And, much later, rational for a moment despite the fused ecstasy he had never felt before, knew that she had spoken the truth. It was the first time for her. He thought he wished it had been for him too.

5

'I shall never be able to thank you enough.' George Richards wrung Jenny's hand once more. 'Remember, if you ever need help; if you don't find life with the Princess to your liking; there will always be a warm welcome and a home for you with us in Petersburg.'

'Yes, do change your mind and come with us.' Did Mary's tone lack conviction? 'I don't know how I will go on without you.'

'You'll do very well now,' said Jenny bracingly. 'George will look after you.' And recognised another mistake. She should have called him Mr. Richards.

'I don't much like letting you go alone,' he said. They had originally planned either to take her down to Rendomierz or wait with her in Warsaw until she could hear from the Princess. 'But we have lost so much time already.' He looked at his wife with a hint of reproach. It had taken a great deal of tactful persuasion from Jenny, and in the end, a strong word or two from him to get Mary up from the comfortable goose-feather bed after her near miscarriage at Lüneburg.

'And the sooner Mary is settled in her own house the better. You have the child to think about now, remember.' She was sure that Mary's jealous tantrums were the worst possible thing for the unborn child.

'All thanks to you! It seems a poor return to let you go jauntering off on your own, but the girl seems reliable enough.' He had been relieved to find a young Polish woman, who wanted to visit her brother in Sandomierz but lacked funds for the journey and would gladly keep Jenny company.

'Yes.' Jenny managed to keep the doubt out of her voice. She could not like the girl, Olga, but George had said, once too often, 'Jenny doesn't fuss.' It was high time they parted.

They did so early next morning, George and Mary leaving by the bridge of boats that led to the Praga Suburb and the long road to Moscow and Petersburg, while Jenny and Olga started south, past the old royal park and the Lazienki Palace. The carriage George Richards had hired for them smelled a little, but was comfortable enough and he had loaded them with money and provisions for the journey, and made sure they had the papers necessary for passing from the Prussian zone of Poland, in which Warsaw stood, to the Austrian region to the south. 'The Austrians have divided their territory into a series of circles,' he had told Jenny. 'Each with its own captain, who will pass you on to the next one. They'll give you authorisations for horses, too, when you need them. I'm sure it will all go smoothly enough.'

She had done her best to reassure him, aware of how guilty he felt; now breathed a sigh of relief at finding herself safely through the first hurdle, the frontier between Prussian- and Austrian-held Poland, with nothing worse than an overtly leering glance for Olga from the soldier in charge.

'This is something like,' said Olga in her guttural German as she leaned forward in the seat facing Jenny for a last view of the town. 'This is the life! Fancy me, a fine lady, riding through the countryside in my carriage. And did you see the look that man gave me!'

Jenny could not share her enthusiasm. 'I wish you would teach me some Polish phrases,' she said.

'You'll never learn! It's quite different from any other language. Besides, you'll never need it, an aristo like you.'

'An aristocrat? Me?' She could hardly help laughing, and yet there was something in the girl's tone she did not much like. 'What in the world gave you that idea? I've not got a penny of my own in the world; never had; never shall. I was travelling as companion to Mrs. Richards, and really don't know what position I am to fill at the Princess Sobieska's.' This was too good a chance to be missed. 'That's why I don't like your trying to wait on me,' she went on. 'I'm not used to it, and I'm sure you're better born than I am.' George had told her that Olga's father was one of Poland's penniless minor noblemen.

'Oh, I'm noble enough.' With a toss of the head. 'But nobility boils no broth, here in Poland. Why should it? The French revolutionaries had the right of it. Liberty, Equality,

Fraternity! When we get our freedom, you'll see what a splendid new state we will build. No more Kings to spend the nation's wealth on books and palaces. An elected President, who will live like the rest of us and do the nation's will. Once we've got rid of the vultures who batten on the land, we'll have the money to do great things. They're the ones who keep us down; they care nothing for Poland, only for their own wealth and ease. Look at this Princess you're going to toad-eat. Marrying a dirty Russian-lover! A landlord who never comes near his estates. I warn you, Englishwoman, enjoy your life of luxury at Rendomierz while you can. When the day of reckoning comes, you may wish you had stayed in England.'

'You can't be serious.' Jenny felt a sudden stir of alarm, not so much at what her companion was saying, but that she should feel safe to say it.

Olga smiled. 'Who would believe you, Englishwoman, if you were to report that I had talked such nonsense to you? I would simply claim that you were a hysterical foreigner – had misunderstood my German. Anyway, you should be on our side if you are really the poor dependent that you say. We could do with an informant at Rendomierz, someone to be our eyes and ears there.'

'We? There really is a group of you?' Now Jenny felt real fear.

'Tell me you'll help us, and I'll answer that.'

'You must see I'd need to know more before I could make any such promise. I'm a stranger here in Poland, I know so little about your country.'

'I'm glad that at least you call it "Poland" and "our country". You English are supposed to be friends of liberty, though I never could see it myself. Your crazy old King sounds worse than Stanislas Augustus. That's one good thing the Russians did for us, taking him away, letting him die in exile.'

'They imprisoned Kosciusko too.'

'You know that! But he's free now!' She paused, looked hard at Jenny, then changed the subject.

After that, conversation was desultory, uninteresting, like the flat landscape through which they endlessly drove. From time to time, Olga would rouse herself to comment on a particularly ruinous village, or a place where the dark fringe of forest closed threateningly in towards the road. 'Why should we till the soil, when the foreigner takes the fruits of it?' she asked once. 'Free the land; free the people, and then you will see something!'

George Richards had suggested they spend their first night at a little town on the Vistula, where there was said to be a very good inn. But their progress was slower than he had reckoned. This road was even worse than the one by which they had reached Warsaw, and their twelve-year-old postboy had no idea of pressing his four small horses as they lumbered along through heavy sand. Dusk was beginning to emphasise the threatening darkness of the forest, very near to the road here, when Josef, their guard, brought his horse up to the carriage window, and looked in to say something in Polish, making Jenny wish more than ever that George Richards had managed to find a man who spoke a language she understood.

'What is it?' she asked.

'He says we'll never get to the inn before dark. The horses are flagging already; he thinks they must have been overworked yesterday. Of course, being women, we got the worst. Luckily for us, he has a cousin, a nobleman, whose house is a mile or so east of the road. We will be most honoured guests there, and it will be interesting for you to see how a Polish nobleman lives.'

'It's very kind of him.' Doubtfully. 'But are you sure . . .'

Apparently sensing her doubt, the guard leaned in again to speak urgently to Olga.

'I thought so,' she said. 'He says that boy's not fit to be driving his grandmother's old goat, let alone a team of horses. If we go on in the dark he's bound to overturn us. A wheel off, or a broken splinter-bar would be the least of it. Madness. I'm not prepared to risk it. I've told him we'll be glad to spend the night with his cousin.'

Nothing for it but to agree with as good a grace as possible, but Jenny's heart sank as the carriage turned ponderously off the main road on to what looked little more than a forest track. Her point gained, Olga now laid herself out to be pleasant. 'You'll see the true Poland now,' she said. 'The old hospitable land where any guest is welcome.'

'How far is it from the road?'

'Oh, nothing, Josef says. A Polish mile or two.' But Jenny had already learned about Polish miles and sat in increasing, if silent, anxiety as darkness and forest closed around them.

At last she saw lights ahead; Josef paused to speak to someone holding a torch and then led the way into a wide forest clearing. The long, low house had lights in all its windows and Jenny was surprised and relieved to see several carriages outside and a couple of boys walking pairs of horses to and fro. 'Josef's cousin must be entertaining,' she said. 'I hope he won't mind . . .'

'He will be delighted to welcome us,' said Olga with an overemphasis that was doubtless due to her faulty German.

Another boy had run up to open the carriage door and Olga alighted first, spoke to him quickly in Polish and turned to help Jenny down. The boy was talking now, pointing not to the main doorway of the building but to a path that led down the side, past the range of lighted windows.

'This way,' said Olga. 'The boy will bring our baggage. The women's quarters are down here, he says.'

An odd phrase, surely? Jenny smiled dismissively at the boy who tried to take the little valise that held her money, clinging to it a little more tightly as she followed Olga along the side of the house, aware of sounds of merry-making from within. Now she was not so sure that she was glad to find their involuntary host entertaining. What kind of party was it? 'Women's quarters'? It was only men's voices she was hearing, the voices of men free of female constraints. Now someone was singing, a song she had heard before, but always surreptitiously, a phrase now and then, quickly suppressed. As she listened, more voices joined in, exulting, triumphant.

'What is it?' she asked Olga, who was listening, too, eagerly.

'Dombrowski's March,' the girl told her. 'The march of the heroes of Poland. They sang it when they won the battle of Lodi for Bonaparte; it is our national song now.'

'What is this place, Olga?' Jenny stopped in the doorway. 'Why have you brought me here?'

'Because it is my duty,' said Olga. 'You should be proud, Englishwoman, to have this chance to help Poland in her fight for freedom.'

'How do you mean, help?'

'You'll see. Or rather, you will be told. Now, come; no more questions.' She put a firm arm through Jenny's and drew her into a big kitchen where two women were busy at an immense stove while others worked, sleeves rolled up to the elbows, at a long table that ran down the centre of the room. One of these left her work to come forward and speak rapidly to Olga.

'We are in good time.' Olga turned to Jenny. 'I thought we must be when I heard them singing. The meeting has not yet begun. There is all the ritual to be gone through before they are ready to see you.'

'What in the world do you mean?' Jenny felt her command of German slipping away. 'What is this place?'

'It was once a hunting lodge belonging to Stanislas Augustus. When he died it was forgotten. It's our headquarters now.' Proudly. 'These ladies keep it ready for our meetings. It's an easy ride from Warsaw. A hunting trip – any excuse. No questions to be asked or answered. Don't fret yourself, you will be sent for when they are ready for you. They will explain what they need of you, pani.'

'They? Who?' *Pani* meant lady, she had learned.

'The freedom fighters. The Free –' She stopped, as the woman who had greeted them made a warning gesture. 'You'll see,' she said again.

Jenny looked about her. Josef, who was supposed to protect her, had vanished, undoubtedly part of the plot. What naïve fools she and George Richards had been. Was she glad or sorry that she had refused the little pistol he had offered her in a moment of extra anxiety? Well, he had been right to be anxious, but what use would one little pistol be now, among this group of Amazons? She must rely on her wits. And, as she thought this, the talk and laughter in the next room stopped suddenly.

'Soon now,' Olga said. 'You must do exactly what They tell you, or we'll both suffer for it.'

'You're frightened!'

'So should you be. These are powerful men. Their arm stretches as far as Paris or Petersburg; make Them your enemy and there is nowhere for you to hide.'

'Who are They?'

'It's not for me to tell you.' She turned as the door to the next room opened and a hooded figure appeared.

'Be silent, and follow me,' he told Jenny in French. 'If you value your life, you will speak only to answer questions. It is a rare honour for a woman to appear before the Brotherhood.'

'It is not one for which I asked,' said Jenny.

'Princess!' Once again, she lay in his arms, smiling up at him, and the nights when Marta had not come for him were black holes in his memory. 'Princess!' Why was it that he still could not bring himself to call her Isobel?

'Yes?' She raised a lazy hand to trace the line of his mouth. 'So serious, Mr. Rendel?' They had made love, frantically at first, tearing each other's clothes off the moment Marta left them alone. He had never known anything like this, like her . . . In the daytime, she was the Princess Sobieska still, treating him just as she did Jan, as a valued guest and friend, but at night . . . He was consumed by her. 'Marry me!' He got it out at last. 'I can't let you sacrifice yourself to this old man who comes so slowly to his wedding. To an idea, a chimera, an illusion about Poland! Marry me, come back to England with me, I'll make a life for you there, a good one, and for our children, I promise it. With you beside me, what could I not do, what not become?'

'First Minister? But I am a Princess of Poland.' The smile was tender now, the hand gentle. 'You do me great honour to ask me, and I thank you from my heart, but you must know that I cannot do it.'

'Cannot, or will not?'

'Metaphysics, Mr. Rendel? Perhaps a little of both.'

'Call me Glynde, for God's sake! Speak to me as your equal, Isobel, just this once.' Had he already ceased to hope?

'No, Mr. Rendel.' Her hand, busy among the short curls at the back of his neck, took the sting out of it. 'You are no fool; that's why you are here. You know as well as I do that that is the way to discovery. In some moment of relaxation, in public, I call you Glynde or you call me Isobel. And then . . .'

'Then you marry me, Isobel. Then our child –' Why was he so sure there would be a child? '– will be a freeborn Englishman.'

'The greatest creature on God's earth?' But the laughter in

her voice was loving. 'Dear Glynde, I could so very easily love you.' She stirred in his arms, her whole body an enticement, and he roused into flame with her, forgetting the future in the imperious now. Much later, aware that at any moment, Marta must come to take him away, he tried again. 'Marry me, beloved. Please? If you wish it, let me stay here and be your consort, help you rear our child for a great future, perhaps to be King of Poland.'

'With you for his father?' It was unanswerable, and the light kiss that went with the words did little to lessen their sting. 'But I do thank you for offering. I shall never forget you. Nor that, once in my life, I have been happy. You will always be somewhere warm about my heart. I shall not be able to tell my son of his father, but I promise he will be a son for you to be proud of.'

'Don't speak as if this was goodbye!' He pulled her closer, kissing her angrily, trying to possess her whole. 'There are still tomorrows before this reluctant wooer of yours arrives to claim you.'

'Yes, there are still tomorrows, but today, Marta will be waiting for you. Goodnight, my dear love, sleep well, and dream of me.'

'Goodnight, Isobel.' This was a quiet kiss, and something about it frightened him. 'You'll send tomorrow?'

'If I can.'

Following their hooded guide into the main room of the hunting lodge, Jenny saw that it had been turned into a meeting hall by the construction of a small platform opposite the main door. Three hooded figures sat there in heavy, armed chairs facing the equally anonymous crowd, close-packed on wooden benches. Entering from the kitchen, she and Olga found themselves standing just in front of the dais, intensely aware of secret eyes on their backs.

The silence was absolute. Jenny had never been so angry in her life. Standing here, unmasked, before all these hooded figures, she might have been naked in front of them. Meant to frighten, it merely enraged her. She felt the men behind her summing up her small figure, dismissing her as unattractive, negligible, and the more she felt it, the angrier she got. Awareness of Olga's terror merely increased her rage. What promises, what threats had made Olga bring her here?

The silence drew out. At last, the man in the central chair rose slowly to this feet, anonymous like the rest, except for the small, ceremonial leather apron tied round his loose robe. Jenny took a deep, furious breath. She knew something about the mysterious order of Freemasons. Her father had been invited to join them by a fellow clergyman who promised great things, promotion in the church, maybe even a political post, a state pension. He had told her about it once, when her mother was ill and they were dining alone. 'I might be a Bishop now.' He had drunk deep, missing his wife's attentive ear. 'If I'd joined them. But they don't believe in God! They speak of the "Great Architect of the Universe".' Was he regretting his decision? 'And if you tell anyone I told you that, it may cost me more than my vicarage. I don't know. My life, perhaps.' He had refilled his glass and gone on to tell her about the initiation meeting to which he had innocently gone, so that she recognised this one. 'And they're revolutionaries, too, like those madmen in France. Talked about liberty and fraternity and all that trash. How could I join them?'

That had been years ago, but Mr. Peverel had never got promotion in the church. Remembering this now, Jenny stood very still and stared at the man in the ridiculous hood and apron. Ridiculous. That was the way to think.

He spoke at last. 'You are Jennifer Peverel, an English-woman, on your way to servitude with the Princess Sobieska.' It was not a question. Was she supposed to be too frightened to reply?

'Janet Peverel, as a matter of fact.' Speaking French, like him, she made her voice cool, steady. 'Yes, I am on my way to visit the Princess. Nobody mentioned servitude. And may I ask by what right you have had me brought here?'

'I ask the questions, woman. You are here because we think we can use you. If we find you an unhandy tool, it will be the worse for you.'

'Then you had better tell me what you want of me.' Jenny had not thought she could do the aristocratic English lady's voice so well. 'Nothing you have said or done so far much inclines me to help you; but the fact remains that if, as I assume, you are conspiring in this curious way for the freedom of Poland, then you most certainly have my sympathy. What I can do for you, I will.'

'Insolence!' A voice from behind her somewhere. And at the same moment hands snatched the valise from her. She had expected this, but it made her angrier still. 'I did not take you for thieves,' she told them. 'If you really want me to act as your agent at Rendomierz, you will have to leave me funds to get there.'

'The woman talks sense.' This was the man on the right of the first speaker. 'She has promised to help us, and if she is to do so she must get to Rendomierz in the ordinary way, as if none of this had happened. She has spoken up for herself boldly, Brothers; I think we owe her an explanation. But, first, Grand Master, should you not administer the oath?'

'As to a man?'

'If we honour her by asking her to help us, I think we must treat her like one of ourselves. But not the other woman. Has she not served her purpose? I propose that she be rewarded and dismissed, and that the rest of the Brotherhood adjourn to their supper while we go into private session and explain to our guest what it is we ask of her. The night is going on, and those of us who need to be back in Warsaw by morning must not linger.'

There was a murmur of agreement from the crowd, doubtless aware, as Jenny was, of savoury smells from the kitchen. 'May I speak?' She pitched her voice above the buzz of the crowd.

'Yes?' Impatiently, from the first speaker.

'My companion – Olga. You speak of dismissing her. I hope you will not do so until you have told me more. It seems to me that I shall need her both to add respectability to my arrival at Rendomierz and as a messenger between you and me. She told me a tale of a brother at Sandomierz. It may even by true. Surely this could be useful?'

'Very well.' He raised his voice once more to address the crowd who were beginning to dissolve into murmuring groups. 'Brother Katowice, you will look after the woman, Olga. Brother Lublin, you will count the Englishwoman's money and hold yourself responsible for it. Brother Poznan, you will preside over the supper tables and make sure that all the

Brothers leave here in good time and good order. We will retire and confer further with the Englishwoman, and you will all of you remember that from this day forward, she is our known friend to be helped in all things, whether small or great, until such time as we, your Brothers and your Masters, tell you otherwise.' He raised an imperious hand for silence, got it, absolute, and spoke for the first time in Polish, what sounded like a long catechism, to which the crowd replied in sonorous ritual. Beside her, Jenny was aware of Olga, silent, rigid with terror at what she was hearing, and was glad she had spoken up for her. It would be useful, later, to find out just what was being said.

'Come.' The speaker reached down a hand to help Jenny up on to the dais. 'We will leave them to their supper. Your servant will be cared for in the kitchen. It was well thought of, that.'

Resisting the temptation to say that it had seemed obvious enough to her, Jenny accepted his arm, muscular under the folds of black cloth, and let him lead her through a door at the back of the dais to a small room beyond, where refreshments were laid out on a round table. A door to the right must lead to the kitchens and another one, facing them, presumably straight out into the forest, for secret exits and entrances.

'This is our conference chamber.' He seated her on his right. 'You would probably prefer wine to vodka?'

'Yes please, and I wish you would do me the courtesy of removing your hoods.'

Angry exclamations, and 'Impossible,' said the leader. 'If you value your life, Miss Peverel, you will not even think of attempting to identify us. You would merely compel us to have you killed, which, believe me, we do not at all wish to do.'

'You had much best stop playing the society host and administer the oath, Brother,' said the man who had not previously spoken. He sounded older than the other two, Jenny thought, and a man of authority, so that she was surprised he did not act as leader.

'Well advised, Brother Vilno. We are glad to have you with us at last.' He turned to Jenny. 'You will repeat after me, and from your heart, Miss Peverel. It will seem a strong oath to you, but as you take it, remember the strong griefs Poland suffers, and be glad of this chance to help her.'

It was a strong oath indeed, and Jenny, repeating it after him, wishing unspeakable horrors on herself and her heirs to the fifth generation if she should betray her Brothers, comforted herself with the thought that it was framed so entirely in male terms as almost automatically to let her out. Odd that this did not occur to the three men who leaned eagerly forward to hear her follow the leader's fluent French with her own. But they were so taken up with the honour they were doing her in letting her swear their oath at all, that it might well not occur to them how it would strike her. The very fact that it was all in French left her feeling just slightly detached. As much as her life was worth to let them see this. At the end, her mentor broke into Polish. 'You will not understand this,' he warned, 'but you will repeat it after me.'

She hesitated, then did so, word by word, as best she could. 'What did it mean?' she asked afterwards, as he refilled the wine glass that she seemed to have emptied while she took the horrible oath. He hesitated, shared a glance with the other two, then: 'It means, "If I betray you, Poland, may all my hopes be ashes." And you have sworn it.'

'Yes.' Without understanding. But a cold chill ran down her spine. 'Now,' she reached out, took a piece of black bread, ate it hungrily. 'Tell me why you want me to spy on the Princess Sobieska.'

'We don't,' he said, surprising her. 'The Princess is a great lady, and a great Polish patriot. You are fortunate to be going to live with her. But there is an Englishman staying with her at Rendomierz, a Mr. Glynde Rendel. You have heard of him? You know him, perhaps?'

'I know of the family, of course. Their main estate, Ringmer, is not very far from where I live in England. They are one of the great, quiet English families. I cannot believe that one of them –'

'We are not asking for your views, Miss Peverel.' This was the third man, who had spoken so little. 'We are telling you of our suspicions of this man. We want to know what he is doing in Poland, now, when there is so little to bring a man like him to this country. Our English friends have told us of him; he is an associate of Pitt and Canning, a member of the war party, in fact, and out of office like them. He was in Vienna for a while before he moved on to Cracow and Rendomierz but our friends there could find nothing out of the way in his behaviour. His contacts seemed entirely social; he did not meet the British Ambassador except at balls and parties. If he is some kind of emissary, he is a very secret one indeed. We had expected him to go on to Russia, but instead he picked up a young American at Cracow and the two of them have settled down at Rendomierz to await the wedding there.'

'Is that so strange?' she asked.

'Not for the American, who is a cousin of the Princess, but Rendel is something else again. He fought at Valmy, a friend of the oppressors. It may be one of them he is representing now, Austria, or even Prussia or Russia, not England at all. It may even be that he is part of a plot against the Princess Sobieska. As a known patriot, she is a very possible target for our enemies. You will make friends with this Mr. Rendel – it will be easy for you, his countrywoman – and find out for us where his real sympathies lie.'

'I'll do my best. I have no doubt I shall find he is just an ordinary young Englishman making the Grand Tour now the peace allows it.'

'Not so young as all that,' put in the third man. 'He fought at Valmy, remember. And there is more to it. A very strange question hangs over him. His parents were in Paris before he was born. His mother was a great beauty.'

'We will not trouble Miss Peverel with that,' interrupted the one they called Grand Master. 'It is enough for her to know that we have cause to suspect him. You will watch him closely, Miss Peverel, get his confidence, find out what makes him stay so long at Rendomierz.'

'The wedding, surely? Or is it already over?'

'I ask the questions here.' Angrily. 'You have your instructions. The woman, Olga, will get your reports to us. Let them be full, and frequent. No need for you to know how she sends them. What you do not know, you cannot betray, even by accident.' He refilled her wine glass. 'Be warned. Our arm is long. If you have any idea of going to Rendomierz and telling either Rendel or the Princess about this meeting, give it up,

68

now. You will not be our only informant there. And it is not only you who would suffer if we learned you had betrayed us. Our friends in England could easily reach a country vicarage. You would not wish to know yourself responsible for your parents' death.'

'You wouldn't!'

'Where the future of Poland is at stake, we would do anything. Risking our own lives, why should we care about those of others? I tell you, now, once and once only. If we so much as suspect that you are betraying us at Rendomierz, your mother will die. You will live on, to mourn her and serve us. And if you fail us again, it will be your father's turn. Now, do you understand us? And the oath you have sworn?'

'Yes.' Wine spilled from her glass, making a blood-red patch on the table. 'I understand.'

6

Night after night, Glynde prowled his room, waiting for the summons that did not come. The trapdoor was securely bolted on the underside, or he might have ventured, uninvited, down into that dark and secret corridor. In the daytime, there was never a chance to be alone with the Princess, since Jan was always at his side, while she was surrounded by an ever-increasing throng of wedding guests.

Daily messengers arrived now from the bridegroom, each one bringing a more impressive gift: one perfect pearl, a thoroughbred Arab mare, a set of sables . . . Prince Ovinski was not far behind. Brass and silver in the ornate little baroque church had been polished and polished again; peasants from miles around were camping in the pleasure gardens, waiting to see their Princess married. She moved always surrounded by a loving crowd. Watching her, Glynde felt his right hand raking through his hair, that old nervous gesture his Aunt Maud had worked so hard to cure. And at night, sleep would not come, or if it did, brought passionate, frustrating dreams.

Jan was restless, too. 'I hate to stay and watch it,' he said, as the two of them returned from an intentionally exhausting ride in the forest. 'To see her throw herself away like this. What do you say? Shall we cut and run for Warsaw?'

It was enormously tempting. But suppose she were planning to send for him just once more? On her last night of freedom perhaps? Besides: 'How could we? It would be the most appalling affront. And specially from you, her cousin.'

'You're right, of course. And, who knows, when she sees the man, she may change her mind. And if she did, would need all our support.'

'Yours perhaps, as a member of the family,' said Glynde bitterly. But how could he even think of leaving, his commission for Canning so totally unfulfilled? Fathoms deep in love with the Princess, he had put off, every night until the next one, the questions he should have been asking her. He was paying for it now. Talk among the wedding guests who thronged the salons was curiously superficial; no information to be gathered there. Family news was enthusiastically exchanged, down to the last marriage of the remotest cousin. When the ladies rose and left the gentlemen after dinner, hunting stories, not politics, were the rule, with an occasional reference to a campaign of long ago, but even this was obviously dangerous ground.

'Is it us they don't trust, or each other?' he asked Jan now, reining in his horse at the bottom of the pleasure gardens, before they reached the noisy bustle of the stables.

'A bit of both, don't you think?' Jan knew what he meant. 'When you come right down to it, after all, it's a police state, isn't it? Even here, under all the luxury, you feel it. And there are Austrians here for the wedding, don't forget. Not to mention Russians and even a Prussian or two. It's amazing how the family web is woven across Europe. Don't you find it so? Or is it the same in England?'

'Not quite to such an extent. We have political differences within families, of course. I'm a Tory, for instance, my older brother is a Whig, we're as unlike as chalk and cheese, but we're not at daggers drawn about it. And we can talk politics when we do meet. If we want to. But then, we aren't a police state.'

'We're lucky,' said Jan. 'I didn't realise . . . Sometimes I think I'll be glad to get home.'

'You'll go when the wedding's over?'

'I'm not sure.' Slowly. 'I've thought about it a great deal. I don't suppose I'll ever come to Europe again. My father's a young man still, but he plans for me to begin to take some of the load of business off his hands when I get back. And once I've started . . . I had my first letter from him the other day. He suggests I go on to Russia before I leave; seems to think that with this new Tsar Alexander there may be a chance of business openings for us there.'

Entering the stable yard by a side gate they found it in an even greater commotion than usual. A cortège of carriages and waggons was filing in from the front of the house, while

71

an escort of Cossacks shouted angrily for attention. They exchanged glances. 'He's come,' said Glynde.

'Yes.' Jan seemed to square his shoulders. 'Too late to cut and run. I rather wish I had, now, don't you?'

'Oh, thank goodness!' A woman's head appeared at the window of what they had thought an empty coach, and a shabby one at that. 'You speak English! Would you be so good as to interpret for me? My Polish maid has been in strong hysterics all morning, and nobody seems to understand my German. Or they pretend not to! Well, of course, with the Prince's arrival.' Bright eyes under an unbecoming bonnet surveyed the usually immaculate stable yard, which was now littered with filthy straw and horse droppings as the newcomers vied for the attention of harassed grooms. 'I hate to seem missish, but this is hardly the place for a lady to alight.'

'You came in the Prince's train?' Glynde was trying vainly to place her.

'Much against my will. He overtook us and swallowed us whole. Are you acquainted with the Prince Ovinski?'

'I have not had that pleasure.'

'He gets his own way. Oh, Olga,' she turned to her companion, and to German, 'do stop that crying. We're here now; it's all over; the Cossacks didn't rape you; all we have to do is find some way of getting to the house without absolutely filthying ourselves, and I am sure these gentlemen will take care of that. I'm so glad to meet two Englishmen!' She smiled at them impartially, the plain face transformed. 'I'm Jenny Peverel, come to stay with the Princess.'

'Delighted to make your acquaintance, Miss Peverel.' Glynde smiled back at her. 'Glynde Rendel, at your service. My friend here, Jan Warrington, is American.' But Jan had moved forward to speak rapid Polish to the coachman. Returning, he greeted her apologetically. 'I'm afraid the man says it will be some time before he can get you back through this mêlée to the house door. I cannot imagine how he came to be so stupid.'

'I can,' said Jenny Peverel. 'The Prince's orders. He would not want to make his state arrival with two draggle-tailed females in tow.' She said it entirely without malice and Glynde found himself thinking the Princess was going to be lucky in

72

her companion. 'There it is then,' she went on, confirming his good opinion. 'If you would be so good as to tell the man to do the best he can for us, we'll just resign ourselves to the wait.' She turned and explained the situation to her snivelling companion. 'But don't let us keep you two gentlemen. I've a very interesting book to read. *Clarissa Harlowe*, it will last me out nicely.'

'It most certainly will, all seven volumes,' Glynde smiled with her. 'But we can't abandon you to your fate here.' A Cossack, sidling his horse nearer to peer in at the far window of the coach, helped to make his point for him. 'Ah.' He saw the groom who looked after their horses. 'Tell him to stable them for us, Jan?' And then: 'If you ladies would allow us to carry you in?'

'Sir Walter Raleigh himself.' Drily. 'But I'm afraid we're not exactly a couple of sylphs.'

'We're stronger than we look.' He opened the carriage door and gathered her up, a compact bundle inside the broadcloth riding habit, firm, and resilient and smelling curiously like his mother. She was laughing, listening to Jan expostulating with Olga in Polish. As she leaned forward in his arms to add her persuasions to his, her bonnet fell off into the filthy straw, revealing a tumble of unruly curls. 'Oh, what a relief,' she said, 'I cannot begin to tell you how I have come to hate that bonnet! Olga, do stop screeching and let the gentlemen pick you up. We really cannot stay in this shambles for ever. We're causing a bit of a stir!'

They were indeed the centre of amused attention by now, the Cossacks crowding round, on horseback and on foot, with what were obviously fairly ribald comments.

Glynde said something short, sharp and unintelligible. The comments ceased; a lane opened. 'Well, you are a dark horse,' said Jenny as he strode towards the house, carrying her as if she weighed nothing. 'Russian! And the kind of Russian they understand.'

'Yes,' he said, 'the Russian of the camp and the knout.'

'I don't think I'd better ask you what they were saying.'

He laughed shortly. 'I most certainly won't tell you, but I'm afraid you're probably guessing quite right.' Odd to find himself liking her so much and yet to be so fiercely aware of

73

how totally she was not the Princess. After the long starvation, the desperate nights of waiting, it was maddening, almost horrible to hold this strange woman in his arms.

Get it over with. He lengthened his stride, tightening his grip on her as he pushed through a crowd of grooms.

'Gently!' She spoke as she might have to a jibbing horse. 'You're hurting me a little, Mr. Rendel.'

'I am so sorry!' Had the Princess ever made him blush? He certainly was now. 'Here is *terra firma* for you at last.' And then, apologising, 'Dry land, I mean.'

'Solid ground, perhaps? I'm not entirely without education, Mr. Rendel, even if I have been compelled to seek my fortune miles from home, here in Poland.'

'A female Quixote?' He smiled for the first time and her heart gave a little jump. 'Well now, we must think what's best for you to do. Shall we hand you over to one of the Princess's retainers, or would you wish to greet her at once? She is doubtless still in the main salon, with Prince Ovinski.'

'Then let's go there.' She ran a hand through shaggy curls. 'I never shirk my fences, Mr. Rendel.'

But when they reached the main entrance hall, they found that the Princess had chosen to meet this honoured guest almost at her front door. She was standing at the foot of the grand stairway, dressed in her favourite plain white, looking up at the tall man who held her hand in both of his. Entering from the rear of the hall, it was his face Glynde could see, and it surprised him. This was not at all the old fop he had expected. Keen eyes under heavy, greying brows had left the Princess for the moment to focus on the little stir their entry had caused.

'So!' He released the Princess's hand with what struck Glynde as an odiously proprietorial pressure. 'Here are my lost sheep, and in good hands.' By what magnetism did he make the crowd of his retainers and hers melt away so that a clear passage opened for the four of them? He had said nothing, done nothing, but the way was clear and Glynde, aware of Ovinski's careless elegance as he led Jenny Peverel forward, was angrily conscious of his own dusty riding breeches, his cravat undoubtedly dishevelled from carrying her. This was not at all how he had intended to meet the Princess's future husband.

'A thousand apologies, Miss Peverel,' the Prince held out a friendly hand to Jenny. 'A most unfortunate misunderstanding. But let me make you known to our hostess. This is Miss Peverel, my dear, whose company has so much brightened the last days of my journey.' His French was impeccable, and the courtesy title he gave his future wife equally so, Glynde thought, respecting him, and angry at having to do so.

Jenny was smiling and curtseying, apparently quite unaware of tousled curls and crumpled skirts, but the Princess moved forward to prevent her. 'We are to be friends.' Much the taller, she leaned down to kiss her, formally, first on one cheek then on the other. 'I remember you so well! When Casimir would not wait for me, you used to make him. I was a poor little shrimp of a younger sister then,' she turned back to the Prince. 'Casimir was always impatient!' Were her eyes clouded with tears? Jenny's certainly were. 'I've made you cry, the last thing I wanted.' And, giving her time to recover, she turned to introduce Glynde and Jan to the Prince.

'Your two cavaliers. I must thank you, gentlemen, for keeping my bride company while I made my elderly way to her.' His keen glance moved from one of them to the other, friendly, dismissive. 'If I had known, would I have come faster?' He shared the question with them all, without expecting an answer. 'No. Age must have its privileges.' He had got the Princess's hand back, now bent to kiss it. 'You were that same little shrimp of a younger sister when we last met. I remember it well! You kicked me on the shins because you thought I was treating Casimir with insufficient respect. Of course, even then, I was old in your eyes. I have grown no younger, Princess, but I hope I have grown just a little wiser. Not much! When they told me you were beautiful, I am afraid I did not believe them. I had my picture, you see, of that little minx of a younger sister.'

'If you had known, you would have come faster?' It was almost a challenge, as she moved up on to the first step of the stairway, so as to be able to look him in the eyes.

'Oh, no,' he said. 'More slowly.'

75

Prince Ovinski's party had overtaken Jenny and Olga the second day after they had left the Brotherhood's hunting lodge, just when Jenny had begun to wonder whether the little of her own money they had left her would in fact be enough for the rest of their journey, overcharged as the two of them, women travelling alone, inevitably were. There had been some moments of pure terror when the Prince's cortège caught up with them, but after that she had travelled in great comfort as his companion, to allieviate, he said, his boredom. She had enjoyed it all, developing a taste for caviar and vodka and learning a great deal about European politics from the Prince. She had not been in the least surprised when on the last night of the journey he had toasted her in champagne and told her she must travel in her own coach the next day; but she had not reckoned on finding herself marooned in the stable yard at Rendomierz.

It had meant a dramatic introduction to Glynde Rendel. She felt his strong arms round her still. It had felt like being carried by an explosion, a charge of dynamite. He was not nearly so handsome as his tall companion, this man of mystery on whom she must report, but being touched by him had felt like being touched by lightning. She would send the Brotherhood the reports they demanded, but there would be nothing in them to harm Glynde Rendel. And that would be easy enough. Only minutes after that first overwhelming encounter, she had seen him with the Princess, seen that he saw no one, thought of nothing but her. No need to look farther for his reason for staying on at Rendomierz, though now the Prince had come he would probably soon leave. Which would end her usefulness to the Brotherhood, and begin her struggle to forget him.

7

The wedding took place next day in a blaze of candelabra and a cloud of incense. The bride was a hieratic figure: her plain white abandoned for cloth of silver, her hands full of white roses, her veil anchored by a diamond tiara. When the service was over at last and the couple turned to face the packed congregation it gave a sigh of pure awe, acknowledging a Queen, the future mother of Kings.

Glynde's hands gripped each other as he stood. There had actually been a moment when he had been tempted to rise from his place at the back of the church and interrupt the service. To forbid the banns. Could it have been the quiet presence of Jenny Peverel between him and Jan Warrington that had put this out of the question? Something matter-of-fact about her made such a melodramatic action impossible.

The celebrations seemed to go on for ever. Palace and gardens were open to the world; wine flowed from the fountains; peasants from miles around drank the couple's health, ate more food than they had seen for years, and fell asleep in the pleasure gardens. Very much the same kind of thing was going on in the palace, with servants always ready to remove the guests who succumbed to wine, food or emotion. And through it all moved the Prince and Princess, cool, composed, hand in hand, always ready with a friendly word, an instant recognition, an introduction if the guest was known to one of them only.

Musicians had come from all over the country and Monsieur Poiret had organised them, so that as one passed from room to room, the music of one group gave gradual way to that of the next. Late on that first day, the Prince and Princess led off a stately polonaise from the great salon. As their guests fell in, two by two behind them, Glynde saw Jenny Peverel standing in a corner of the room, white with fatigue, plainer than ever, and felt a quick qualm of conscience. In his own misery, he

77

had forgotten all about her, a stranger, just arrived, and the kind of person inevitably neglected by servants. He moved through the crowd to join her. 'A long day.'

'Yes.' Even the monosyllable cost her an effort.

'What have you had to eat?'

'I don't remember. Not much ... Everyone's been so busy ...'

'Come along.' He took her arm. 'There's a buffet in the music room. What would you like?'

'I could eat a horse,' she told him. 'But if there should chance to be vodka and caviar? Only –' she held back for a moment '– should we not be joining in this odd dance the Prince and Princess are leading?'

'The polonaise? Don't fret; it will go on for hours. It always does. The dullest dance in Europe. But the music is different tonight.' They had reached the music room, where Poiret himself was conducting a string quartet.

'Yes.' She was silent, listening, as he pulled up a gilt-backed chair for her. 'I know it! It's variations on something called Dombrowski's March. A kind of national song. How very bold, Mr. Rendel.'

'Making a point of a kind.' He tried to make it sound light; was not sure that he had succeeded. 'Sit there, Miss Peverel, rest, listen to this brave music, while I find you your vodka and caviar.'

Returning with a flunkey bearing a tray loaded with food and drink, he found that she had been joined by Jan Warrington, rather flushed of face and slow of speech, and was making him tell her about life at Rendomierz. Had he really meant to drink himself insensible? Instead he ended the evening demurely leading Jenny Peverel through the long, dull, graceful routine of the polonaise. 'It's as good a way as any of learning your way round the palace,' he told her, leaving her at last at the entrance to the private apartments where she was lodged. 'Goodnight, Miss Peverel, and thank you.'

'Thank *you*.' She smiled, and left him.

Back in the little house, he found Jan snoring like a pig in a chair in the main room, tried and failed to rouse him and left him to sleep it off where he was.

*   *   *

'It's a while since we came.' Olga had brought Jenny a pile of freshly laundered linen. 'They'll be expecting a report.'

'Then they'll have to wait for it,' Jenny told her. 'Absurd to expect me to make any sense of things here while the festivities are still raging. If anyone should approach you, tell them I've hardly had a chance to speak to Mr. Rendel.'

'They already have. And you spent the whole wedding evening with him.'

'Dancing the polonaise! Who told you?'

'I'm not to say. But to remind you of what they threatened.'

Jenny shivered and let Olga see that she did so. She was frightened, wanted the girl to think her terrified. 'Tell them they must give me time,' she said. 'Tell them Mr. Rendel is so deep in love with the Princess that I am having trouble getting him even to notice me. If you know we danced the polonaise together on her wedding night you doubtless also know just how little we talked.' Terrifying to think that the palace must be full of spies. 'It will be easier when more of the guests have left,' she went on. She had hoped and feared that Glynde Rendel himself would be one of the first to leave, but neither he nor Jan Warrington showed any sign of doing so, though both of them looked quite absolutely wretched, and tended to follow the Princess with their eyes when they thought no one was noticing.

She herself felt entirely useless, a most unusual and unhappy state of affairs. At home she had never had a moment to call her own; here time hung endless on her hands. The Princess must honestly have thought she would need her, and she had been most happily proved wrong. If the Prince had found his wife unexpectedly beautiful, she had obviously found him immensely good company. Always together, they talked as if they were catching up on a lifetime of separate experience, which was now to be shared. No wonder Glynde Rendel and Jan Warrington looked so miserable. But there was also no chance of speaking to the Princess without a strong risk of being overheard. She should be grateful for the unconscious warning conveyed by Olga's message. She must speak alone, or not at all. Any of the servants, any of the guests could be a spy for the Brotherhood, or even a member. Sometimes, listening to a group of men talking, she wondered if she recognised a voice, but what chance was there, granted the muffling hoods the group had worn?

And although she was both angry and frightened by the Brotherhood's threats, she did not at all wish to betray them to the Austrians. Even here, in the luxury of Rendomierz, there were constant reminders of the enslaved state of Poland. Remembering how freely political talk had flowed in Petworth House, where Whig and Tory threw facts and figures like debating points across the dinner table, she found the contrast here wretched indeed. She said so to Glynde Rendel one morning, when she had strolled out for a breath of autumn sunshine before breakfast, and met him on his way to the palace from the guest-houses. Had she hoped to do so? She was afraid she had, and not for the Brotherhood's sake.

'Yes, the talk's dull as ditch-water.' He smiled, and her heart jumped. 'But can you blame them? I was warned in Vienna that every third man in Warsaw is a spy and I suppose the same must be true here.'

'Every third man? Yes, that would figure: one Prussian, one Russian and one Austrian.' She was pleased with her note of cool interest.

He laughed. 'On the nail, Miss Peverel, but don't you think probably a Frenchman and an Englishman as well? Or at least, people in their pay. I hope you are a little careful in those long letters I see you writing to your family. I've been wanting a chance to say this. I should think letters from here are bound to be open to some kind of censorship.'

'Thank you! Yes, I do confine myself rather to generalities. It makes for sadly dull letters.' Here was a chance, if she could trust him, to tell Glynde Rendel that she was in fact supposed to be spying on him. But could she trust him? His devotion to the Princess was all too obvious, but what had that to do with his reasons for being in Rendomierz? The fact that he had stayed on after the marriage he had obviously found so painful did seem to suggest some hidden reason, though she found it hard to believe it as sinister as the Brotherhood had suggested. She took his proffered arm, angry as always at what his touch did to her.

'Homesick, Miss Peverel?' What had he sensed?

'A little.' She seized on it. 'Thinking of England certainly.'
It was true. She longed for the simple duties of her English
life. To be needed; to be useful. To be away from Glynde
Rendel? But here came Jan Warrington hurrying after them,
and the moment alone with Glynde Rendel had passed.

Glynde greeted Jan cheerfully but swore to himself. He was
convinced that Miss Peverel had something on her mind, and
had hoped much from his rare chance alone with her.

'I only asked if you were going on the hunt today?'

'Oh, I think so. And you?'

'The Princess has very kindly promised to lend me a horse.
I love riding . . . and to get into those great forests!' She meant
it, but the thought of plunging once more into those dark
woods was frightening, too.

The hunting party gathered in front of the palace soon after
breakfast, and Glynde, sparing an anxious glance for Jenny
Peverel, saw with relief that she sat her lively little cob firmly,
very much mistress of it and herself. The men were after bear,
and the ladies would follow at a discreet distance, joining them
at last for a picnic at a remote hunting lodge where a posse of
servants had been working for several days, making all ready
for them. A ride had been cleared into the forest, too, and
Glynde marvelled, as he often did, at the lavish use of serf
labour. If only one could find out what the serfs thought about
it all, but by all appearances they adored their Princess. Her
father had actually freed them, during the brief period of
progress and enlightenment before the Russians foreclosed on
King Stanislas Augustus, but so far as he could gather the
experiment had not worked very well. They were not trained
to cope with freedom, and he thought that what the Princess
was doing in the way of education and medical advice was
probably very much more to the point.

'Keep close to the others,' he told Jenny, when they reached
the place where the men were to follow a tracker into the deep
forest, while the ladies, and the Prince, took the cleared ride
to the meeting place. He watched for a moment as Jenny set
off down the ride, side by side with Marta, the Princess's half
sister. Her messenger. His hand worried at his hair as he
looked farther down the ride to where the Princess and her
husband were leading the way, their erect backs rising in

unison, the Princess leaning towards her husband to hear what he was saying.

It was only much later, when they had found their bear and loosed the hounds on it, that he remembered something that had faintly troubled him as he watched the ladies setting off. Something about the way Marta was looking at Jenny Peverel? Ridiculous. But, a trained watcher, he had seen Marta looking at Jenny before, as if she did not much like her. Suspecting perhaps a new friend for her half sister? Someone who might displace her?

The bear was killed messily, with two young men both claiming to have delivered the *coup de grâce*. 'Let's go.' Glynde sought out Jan Warrington. 'Let's join the ladies. I'm sick of this quarrelling.'

Why did he feel this passionate need to hurry? When he heard the screams, he was hardly even surprised. Without a word, he and Jan put spurs to their horses and galloped down the ride, pausing at last at a point where it crossed an old forest path. Dead silence now. Which way?

'You go that way.' Glynde pointed to the left. 'I'll go this.' He turned his horse into a little-used path and pushed it as fast as possible under the low-hanging trees. On impulse, he shouted, as loud as he could, 'I'm coming, Miss Peverel.' And, emerging into a little glade, found Marta trying to catch her horse.

'Miss Peverel!' She pointed into the forest. 'Something frightened the horses. They bolted.'

'That way?'

'Yes.'

Should he believe her? He thought so. 'Wait here. I'll be back.' Large trees here, and small scrub under them. He pushed forward in the direction Marta had indicated, and called again. 'Miss Peverel, can you hear me? Where are you?'

No answer. But the sound of a horse thrashing about somewhere ahead of him. She must have been thrown, too. Or worse? His own horse had instinctively turned towards the sound, and he let it have its head, calling again. And, at last, a faint answer. 'Here. This way. I'm here.'

He found her at last, sitting very still and small under a huge oak. She did not rise as he emerged from the trees, but sat there, motionless, looking at him, the scarlet weal across her face startling against its dead white.

'What happened?' He jumped to the ground beside her, and still she did not move.

'Something frightened the horses.' She was holding on to herself with an immense effort. Blood seeped from the wound on her face. 'They bolted.' It was exactly what Marta had said. Too exactly? 'Thank you for coming so quickly.'

'But your face?'

'A tree branch. And – I've twisted my ankle. I can't stand. I'm . . . so sorry!'

He did not believe a word of it, but picked her up gently, recognising once again that elusive scent that reminded him of his mother. Her breath came fast; her eyes were bright with tears she would not shed. 'This was worse than a fall.' He settled her sideways on his saddle. 'Tell me.'

'No! Mr. Rendel, I am most terribly sorry, but I believe I am going to faint.'

'Don't be afraid. I have you safe.' He held her tight as she drooped against him, sure she was faking it, but what could he do but admire her quick wit and high courage? And here came Marta, riding towards them.

'You found her! Thank God.' And then, seeing the drooping figure, the savagely marked face. 'Mary, Mother of God! What happened?'

'She says her horse bolted. A branch marked her face. She twisted her ankle. She has fainted.'

'No. I'm better now.' She stirred a little in his strongly encircling arms. 'Did you get thrown too, Marta? Are you hurt?' And that was all she said.

8

By the time Jenny was able to walk again, most of the wedding guests had left the palace. Days of lashing rain had been a warning of the morasses forest roads would soon become. The nights were getting colder, too, and armies of servants were at work preparing the palace for the rigours of winter. Venturing downstairs at last on the day the huge majolica stove was lighted in the main salon, Jenny found the Prince and Princess enthroned side by side on a wide, gilt-backed sofa, busy over an immense batch of mail from Warsaw.

Her first thought, as she curtseyed and acknowledged their enquiries, was that the Princess did not look well. The glow of health had faded from her clear skin and been replaced, she suspected, by a finely applied touch of rouge. She looked eagerly around, her heart sinking. Glynde and Jan must have left, and Olga had not thought to tell her. She would never see Glynde again. And a good thing too. It was extraordinary how it hurt.

'A chair for Miss Peverel,' said the Prince. 'You must not be standing yet, ma'am. Your ankle hurts you still, I can see. Did you not say there was a letter for Miss Peverel, my dear? News from home will be just the tonic she needs.'

'Oh, thank you!' It was the first that she had had, and she read it eagerly, half aware as she did so of the Prince and Princess discussing their own mail. It was extraordinary how completely the Prince was now established as master of the household, which, Glynde had told her, had once revolved so entirely round the Princess. If only she had arrived before the wedding, instead of in the Prince's train, she might have had a chance of achieving some kind of relationship with the Princess, making herself useful to her. But the Princess, who had greeted her as an old friend, had subsided into cool indifference after the wedding, totally absorbed in her new relationship. If only her mother's letter were a summons home.

But it was nothing of the kind. Between every loving line lay the clear message that whatever happened, her father did not want her back. He was not well, her mother wrote, and even thought of retiring.

'Here are your cavaliers back from their ride at last.' The Prince sounded amused. 'None the worse for your drenching, gentlemen?'

'Not the least in the world.' Jenny's hands clenched on the letter at the sound of Glynde's voice.

'That's good.' The Prince was at his most urbane. 'For I am afraid I have some news from Paris that you will not much like, Mr. Rendel. The French have reoccupied Switzerland, and show no sign of evacuating Holland, as they undertook to do under the terms of the Treaty of Amiens. I am sure you will feel, as I do, that this must mean a renewal of hostilities between your country and France. As your host, I dislike suggesting it, but as your friend, I think I must advise you to think about leaving us, sad though my wife and I will be to see you go. The First Consul is an unchancy man. I think you would be wise not to be anywhere his long arm can reach when war breaks out. Of course, we would do our best to protect you, my wife and I – I know I can speak for you, my dear – but these are unhappy times. You will forgive me, I know, for speaking so frankly.'

'Highness, I am most grateful. I would not dream of involving you and the Princess in any kind of unpleasantness. I will make my arrangements to leave in the morning.'

'And Mr. Warrington?' The Prince turned to Jan. 'I have news which must interest you, too, both as an American and as a man of business. The French seem to have concluded their arrangements to take over Louisiana from Spain. I wonder how even your peace-loving President Mr. Jefferson will relish the prospect of having Bonaparte's France for so near a neighbour. I hardly imagine that you renounced your allegiance to one European power in order to find yourselves dominated by another.'

'Dominated?' Jan's transatlantic drawl was more pronounced than ever. 'I doubt Mr. Jefferson will allow that to happen. Nor yet the British!' He stepped forward, took the Princess's hand. 'Highness, I shall never forget your hospi-

85

tality, but the time has come to thank you and leave you.'

She smiled up at him. 'You were to call me cousin, cousin. You'll go to Warsaw, the two of you? You must let me give you letters to my friends there. And could I persuade you to stay one more day? My beloved Marta has decided she must quit me and yield to her vocation. She longs to be in her convent at Warsaw and has waited only for a suitable escort. You will take care of her for me, I know. And,' turning to Jenny, 'Jenny dear, you will take her place at my side?'

It was only when the whirl of preparations and the silent anguish of the parting were over, and the oddly assorted trio were on the road to Warsaw that Jenny had time to sort out the impressions of that scene and remember the shock of surprise on Marta's face. It had been the first she had heard of the plan too. Happily busy in taking her new place at the Princess's side, Jenny warned herself never to forget the surprising streak of ruthlessness in Isobel, who could dismiss even a half sister so suddenly. The Prince's doing, perhaps? She had never thought he quite liked Marta.

For herself, it was an immense relief. Marta had lured her into the Brotherhood's ambush that day of the hunt, and it was small comfort that Marta had been appalled at what had happened to her. It had been savage enough. She would remember until she died the quick brutal movements with which the hooded figure had slashed her face, twisted her ankle. 'That happened when the horse bolted,' he had told her. 'In future, you will report regularly.'

She had done so, and had stuck to her story about the bolting horse, grateful to the Prince for putting a brusque stop to his wife's questioning. 'Some salve for the wound would be more to the point. We do not want Miss Peverel marked for life.'

In fact, a natural healer, she had soon been able to face her reflection in the glass with no more than her normal stoicism, and in the end the only lasting reminder of the blow was a slight, ironic twist to her upper lip which she rather liked. But relief at Marta's going was small consolation in the wrench of Glynde's. She would probably never see him again. She made herself face it, and plunged heart and soul into the business of making herself invaluable to Isobel.

The first snow showers worked their magic on palace and park; preparations for Christmas were going on apace; Jenny was increasingly puzzled by the Princess's behaviour. All the symptoms she knew so well suggested that Isobel was pregnant, surely a matter for great rejoicing, but the most delicate of probings were met with a kind of regal blankness. Perhaps this was the way Polish ladies behaved, and there was nothing to do but go along with it, and take as much care of her as she could.

She then noticed that the Prince was doing so too, refusing, for instance, his wife's suggestion that they ride out through an early snowfall to show him her model village, and insisting that the Christmas festivities at Rendomierz be kept simple. It was not until well into the New Year that they made their announcement, and then it was precipitated by a messenger from the Tsar.

'He wants me back at Petersburg.' The Prince had joined his wife and Jenny where they sat sewing in a small south-facing salon, which caught every bit of the rare winter sun. 'Not immediately. He says he would not ask that of a newly married man, but before the spring, while the roads are still frozen and travelling possible. He flatters me by saying he needs my wise counsel. Of course, he expects that you will come with me, my dear. He says he longs to meet you.'

'Too kind,' said the Princess. 'In the ordinary way, naturally, I would like nothing better, but as it is, in my condition, a winter journey . . .'

'You would get the very best of medical attendance in Petersburg. The Tsar, I am sure, would offer his own doctor, Dr. Wylie.'

'I have the greatest confidence in my own Dr. Scott,' said the Princess. 'And in my dear Jenny, who I believe has had some experience . . . You do understand what we are saying, Jenny?'

'I cannot tell you how happy I am, Highness.'

'Miss Peverel could accompany us to Petersburg,' said the Prince. 'I know her for an intrepid traveller. And indeed it might be best for her to do so. The threat of war between France and England is my master's reason for summoning me.

She would be much safer in Russia than here. The First Consul's hand will never stretch that far.'

'Nor to here,' said the Princess. 'Besides, Jenny will always be entirely safe, as a member of my household. And the heir to Poland must be born on Polish soil.'

'The heir?' He took snuff. 'You are so very sure, my dear? Should you not, perhaps, be preparing yourself for a Jadwiga rather than a Jan? The one I am descended from played a great part in Polish history by her marriage to the Duke of Lithuania. I sometimes think union by marriage has its advantages over that by the sword.'

'Compliments, Michael?'

'If you wish to take it as one. But, coming back to small Jan, or small Jadwiga, as the case may be, you hold to it that you prefer Poland in chains to free Russia for its birthplace?'

'My child must be all Polish.'

'Our child.'

'Yes. And not Jan, Casimir.'

'Ah. For your brother. Why not? And the European spelling your mother favoured? Wise, I think. But Miss Peverel thinks we are counting our cattle before the market and I am superstitious enough to agree with her.' He turned to Jenny, who was moving to leave them. 'Don't go, Miss Peverel, you have a part to play in this decision. My wife, I know, counts more on you than on Dr. Scott. But are we right to let you stay? If war does break out, your chance of getting back to England is gone. This is your moment of choice, to go or to stay. To return to your family, or to throw in your lot with us, which I promise you will never regret.'

'You're very kind.'

'Don't go, Jenny, please.' Isobel took her hand. 'I need you.' Pregnancy had changed the Princess, softened her, Jenny thought, made her less remote.

'Thank you. I'd not thought to trouble you with my sad news, Highness. But my father is dead. My mother has had to leave our home and is sharing her time between my sisters. There is no place for me in England now. It makes me very happy that you want me here.'

'I am so very sorry,' said the Prince. 'And, selfishly, so glad. I mean to write and ask my master for leave to stay until the birth, but longer, I know, he will not allow. It will be the greatest comfort to me to know that you are here, Miss Peverel. I just hope, my dear, that your little Casimir does not keep you waiting too long.'

'Our little Casimir,' said the Princess.

Glynde and Jan had been settled in the Hôtel de Londres at Petersburg for some time. Neither of them had much wanted to delay in Warsaw, where there was an absolute dearth of hard news, but where they first encountered a disquieting rumour that Bonaparte was imprisoning any Englishmen caught in his territory by the outbreak of war. Jan's father had been urging for some time that he move to Petersburg and get down to business, and Glynde had been sent in the same direction by a long, irascible letter from Canning. Reading between the lines of their prearranged code, he could tell that things in England had not gone at all as Canning had hoped. The office of Foreign Secretary still eluded him, and nothing had improved his soured relations with his old friend Pitt. Glynde thought he needed a brilliant diplomatic achievement to re-establish himself. Perhaps because of this, Poland, that home of lost causes, had become less important in his thinking than Russia, and he urged Glynde to go there. England's chances of success in the new war against Bonaparte would be immensely improved if the Tsar Alexander could be persuaded to join in. But Alexander and the group of liberal-minded young men who surrounded him still seemed beglamoured by Bonaparte. 'Even the subjugation of the independent Swiss has not undeceived them.' Canning went on to thank Glynde for the information he had sent him from Poland, even though much of it had been negative. Now, he wanted him to move to Petersburg: 'Your friendship with the Prince Ovinski will be of the greatest use there.'

Friendship! If Canning only knew. He did not at all wish to be beholden to Ovinski for his introduction into Petersburg society. Luckily, he had letters from Simon Vorontzov, the Russian Ambassador in London, to his older brother Alexander, who had been Foreign Minister under the previous Tsar, and he and Jan found themselves welcome in his house as well as the British Ambassador's, where a restfully masculine atmosphere prevailed while Sir John Warren's wife was in England. And wherever they went, they heard the praises of the new young Tsar Alexander, and whispered descriptions of his dead father's mindless tyranny.

'They say Alexander is a great liberal.' Jan turned to Glynde as they walked along the quay by the River Neva admiring the throng of boats. 'Plans great things for Russia since his sudden accession to the throne. What a blessing . . .'

'Let's not talk about that.' Even in Alexander's freer Petersburg, discussion of his father's murder was dangerous. 'But I agree with you,' Glynde went on, 'I long to meet the Tsar.'

'Do you think Adam Czartoryski would arrange it for us? It does seem quite extraordinary that the Tsar should have a Polish Foreign Minister.' They had met Adam Czartoryski at Simon Vorontzov's house and he had claimed Jan as a kind of cousin after hearing of his relationship to the Princess, reminding them that his family home, Pulawy, was not far from Rendomierz.

'He's a brilliant man,' said Glynde. 'I just wish I knew whether he's more Pole or Russian these days. He was pure Pole when I met him years ago, as an exile in England.'

'And look at him now! I wonder how he and Ovinski get on.' He paused for a moment to look at the busy crowd crossing the bridge of boats. 'I wish there would be news of the Princess.'

Glynde was silent. She was never out of his thoughts.

Calling on Sir John Warren, they learned that Prince Ovinski had reached Petersburg the day before. 'He has come to announce the birth of his son,' Warren told them. 'It was a bold marriage that; two dynastic Polish families; I do rather wonder if the Tsar was not counting on their remaining childless when he gave permission for it. The Tsar Paul, of course,' he explained a little hurriedly. 'Permission was naturally given before his death. I think it surprised everyone. But then, he was a most unpredictable man.'

The two young men walked home rather silently. 'What is the form?' Jan asked as they reached the Hôtel de Londres.

'I think a note, don't you?'

They duly wrote the notes and delivered them at the Ovinski

Palace on the Fontanka Canal. Civil, non-committal replies told them that the Prince very much looked forward to meeting them, but made no positive suggestion.

'So that's that,' said Glynde, relieved.

'Yes.' Jan's laugh was forced. 'Blood may be thicker than water in Rendomierz, but not here, it seems.' He took an irritable turn to the window. 'Let's go out! I need to stretch my legs. What do you say? Shall we take a walk in the summer gardens?'

'What a noble view, now the sun's out for once.' They were returning along the quay by the Winter Palace and Glynde paused to look across the grey Neva at the spires and domes of the Peter Paul Fortress and the twin lighthouse towers in Vasily Island beyond it.

'Peter the Great certainly knew what he was doing. I've never seen New York, but Petersburg certainly has London or Paris quite beaten when it comes to design and coherence.'

'I thank you, gentlemen, on my ancestor's behalf.' The handsome, fair young man who had come up from behind was taller than either of them and stooped slightly, graciously to speak to them. Piercing blue eyes looked, for a moment, from one to the other. 'Mr. Rendel, I think, and Mr. Warrington? I have hoped for the chance of making your acquaintance.'

'Your Majesty!' Glynde had known him at once, but still found the situation more than he could handle.

'No, no!' His laugh was friendly, engaging. 'I have slipped the leash. I am strictly incognito!' He looked around him on the crowded quay. 'I pretend very hard not to recognise the secret police who follow me. They are no affair of mine.' But he had made a point of a kind, Glynde thought. 'I am happy to welcome you both to Holy Russia, and only sad that protocol has made it impossible for me to do so formally.' He had taken his place between them and they found themselves walking along the quay, one on each side, aware of the stares of the crowd. 'Now, Mr. Warrington, you must tell me about your United States of America, and how you manage to govern yourselves in a country almost as vast as mine.' And he proceeded to put Jan through a remarkably knowledgeable cross-examination about his country, then turned at last, smiling, to Glynde. 'Forgive me, Mr. Rendel, but I know more

about your great country. We must meet again. I count on it.'
And, as easily as he had come, he was gone.

'What an amazing man!' Their eyes met.

'Yes.'

Sir John Warren was more surprised than pleased to find their
names included with his in his invitation to the Tsar's Peterhof
Fête, early in August. Their carriage followed his on the
three-hour drive from Petersburg to the palace Peter the Great
had built on the Gulf of Finland as a setting-off point for his
new naval base at Kronstadt. Used by Tsar Paul it had fallen
into disuse since his murder and was only opened for this
annual fête.

Strolling on the terrace to admire the view of the sea and
the imperial yachts dressed overall, they came face to face with
Prince Ovinski, very elegant in full court-dress. 'We are to
congratulate you, Prince, on the birth of a son.' Glynde had
the phrase ready for such an occasion. 'I trust you left the
Princess well?'

'Both her and the child, thank you. And Miss Peverel.'

'She's not gone home?'

'No. When war was declared, she chose to throw in her lot
with ours. To my great satisfaction. What news do you have
from England, Mr. Rendel? Are your friends glad it's war
again?'

'Bonaparte must be stopped, Highness. This high-handed
imprisonment of innocent British travellers must enrage all
right-minded people.'

'You would certainly think so.' Ovinski shrugged. 'An un-
principled nobody. I will see you later, at the ball, gentlemen.'
He turned and walked slowly away past the waterfall with its
brilliant golden statues.

Much later, after an excellent dinner and a ride through the
pleasure gardens in luxurious carriages provided by their host,
they put on dominoes and masks for the ball and awaited its
opening in the crowded central chamber of the palace, a
handsome hall painted all over with female portraits. At last,
the Emperor and his brother, the Grand Duke Constantine,
passed through to the dancing-hall, followed by the Empress
and the Empress Mother, with the young Grand Duchesses

Catherine and Anna and the rest of the royal family, resplendent with jewels.

Following them into the ballroom itself, they found it already packed with people of all classes who were admitted to this part of the festivities. As a result, only the very senior members of the court were able to walk through the inevitable polonaise, but Glynde recognised Prince Ovinski among them, despite the mask. He was leading a very lissome young lady, whose whole bearing, as she let him guide her through the formal movement of the dance, showed adoration, the unqualified surrender of a young girl to an older man.

'It's intolerably hot in here,' Glynde turned to Jan. 'Let's get outside!'

They were soon followed by the Tsar himself, who moved on to the balcony outside the Portrait Hall to watch the illuminations, accompanied by those of his court who could crowd on to the balcony. Watching from the terrace below, Glynde thought the illuminations disappointing, over in less than a quarter of an hour and suffering from the fact that it was still not fully dark. But had he really been watching them? The picture of that elegant young female form, bent adoringly upwards towards the Prince, kept superimposing itself before his eyes. And what right in the world had he to object? He, who had cuckolded the Prince before he was even married, who was almost certainly the father of the young Prince Casimir?

He loathed himself. 'Let's go home,' he said suddenly to Jan. 'Let's not wait for supper!'

'Someone told me the bridges would be raised between here and the city,' Jan objected.

'Nonsense! Impossible! With this crowd on its way home!' It was beginning to get light again already as their coach pushed its slow way through the line of carriages and crowd of walkers that extended almost the whole way from the Peterhof to the city gates.

'How many people in all, do you think?' asked Jan as the carriage paused once again.

'God knows! Forty thousand? Fifty perhaps? A chance for the world and his wife to see their beloved Tsar.'

'Yes. Shall we call on the Prince?'

'I think we must.' And then, 'Damnation!' The bridge was indeed raised against them and they had to sit there waiting for a furious hour.

There was not much hard political news in Petersburg, but gossip was plentiful, and Glynde soon heard the stories about Prince Ovinski and the ladies, notably the beautiful young Princess Irene Landowska. He longed to go back to Rendomierz, to tell the Princess about it, make her come away with him. And he made himself face how she would receive such a suggestion. He could see the lift of those strongly marked eyebrows, so oddly like Jan's, the light laugh with which she would dismiss the idea, and him. He stayed in Petersburg and amused himself as best he could, which was not well.

9

'I still don't believe it,' Jan said again. 'It's murder, no more no less. To kidnap the Duc d'Enghien on neutral soil in Baden would be bad enough; but to arrange his judicial murder, without even a pretence of a trial . . . Even Bonaparte would surely not do that!'

'It seems he has,' said Glynde. 'Oh, some sort of a trial, but condemned and executed all in one day . . .! One of the oldest families of France wiped out. And all on some flimsy pretext of conspiracy. Bonaparte has finished himself. It will mean ostracism in all the courts of Europe. And Baden's the home of the Russian Empress. The Tsar will be outraged.'

Alexander was indeed shocked and furious. He put his court into mourning for the murdered Duke and recalled his Ambassador from Paris, but the rest of Europe had learned to fear the formidable First Consul. Reaction in England was violent, but elsewhere the protests were surprisingly muted. And Alexander's own protest had met with a disconcerting reply. Bonaparte's Foreign Minister, Talleyrand, pointed out that so far as he knew, no one had ever been punished for the murder of Alexander's own father, the Emperor Paul. And when Napoleon crowned himself Emperor, a couple of months later, in May 1804, with the Pope looking on, Europe once again stirred uneasily and did nothing.

'But I really believe it has opened my master's eyes at last to the true character of the upstart Bonaparte.' The Russian Foreign Minister, Adam Czartoryski, had found he could speak freely with Glynde and Jan, and made no secret of his own Polish sympathies. 'My hopes for an independent Kingdom of Poland are rising,' he went on. 'The Emperor begins to see the need for it as a buffer state between him and that madman in France.'

'You think the Tsar might really allow Poland its independence?' asked Glynde.

'With a King of his choosing? Yes.' Unspoken between the three of them was the chance that Czartoryski might be that chosen King.

'Czartoryski is related to the last Polish King, Stanislas Augustus, after all,' said Jan back at the Hôtel de Londres.

'For what that is worth. Stanislas Augustus was the Empress Catherine's appointment, remember, but not much good came of it in the end.'

'Poland had almost thirty years of quite remarkably humane rule under him.'

'The tyrant from whom your mother fled?'

'You've got me there! Whatever else you say about Polish history, you do have to admit it's complicated. But, surely, Glynde, anything would be better than its abject state today. To have even the shadow of independence! If only there were a real rallying point, but you know as well as I do that Adam Czartoryski is practically a Russian by now. He was only in his twenties when they brought him here as a hostage for his family's behaviour ten years ago. And look what a friend of the Tsar's he has become!'

'But he fought gallantly against the Russians in 1794.'

'A long time ago. If the Poles do remember, do you think they will forgive him for all his collaboration with the Russians since?'

'Collaboration's an ugly word. We know how he has stood his country's friend with the Tsar.' But Glynde was thinking of something else, of the little Prince Casimir Ovinski, now a year old, scion of two royal Polish houses, a planned rallying point. 'Have the Richards heard anything from Miss Peverel?' he asked now, surprising Jan.

'Not for a while. The posts are quicker between Petersburg and London, they say, than between here and Rendomierz.'

'And more reliable, I expect, since they doubtless send by British merchantmen. But there's not been one yet, has there, since the Neva thawed?'

'No. Richards thinks there should be one any day. I just hope it's not from the United States, with a letter from my papa demanding my instant return.'

'I should think he must be beginning to find you quite useful to him here.' Jan had made firm friends with George Richards, was spending a good deal of time with him and obviously enjoying this rather informal apprenticeship in the world of business.

'George says Mr. Addington's government is bound to fall,' Jan said now. 'He's a little anxious about what Mr. Pitt's war party may do to trade, when they get in.'

'He says "when" not "if"?' Glynde had developed a considerable respect for George Richards' judgment. If Pitt came back to power, so, surely would his own friend Canning, and his roving commission might turn into something more official – what he had always hoped for. If not, it was time he went home, stopped enraging himself by watching Prince Ovinski and his series of exquisite mistresses.

But when news finally came of the new British government formed in May, Canning's name was not listed among the members of Mr. Pitt's cabinet. 'Your friend's still out of favour, it appears,' said Jan. 'Richards seems to think it is all for the best. But he believes that Canning's friend Lord Granville Leveson Gower may replace Sir John Warren as Ambassador here. Do you know him too?'

'Yes, indeed. We were at school together.' Glynde laughed. 'He'll cut quite a swathe among the Petersburg ladies, I can tell you. If Lady Bessborough lets him come, that is.'

'Lady Bessborough? How does she come into it.'

'She's been his very good friend for years. But I hope he comes; I'm sure he could do more in a week to persuade the Tsar to ally himself with us than Sir John has done in all his years of grovelling flattery. He's a straight talker, and a very persuasive man, Granville.'

A letter from Canning later that summer, confirmed Granville Leveson Gower's appointment and asked Glynde to put himself at the new Ambassador's disposal. 'He counts on you rather than Warren to point his way in Petersburg society.'

'So you'll stay?' Jan was delighted. His father had decided that he should continue in Petersburg as his representative to explore the increasing possibilities of trade between the United States and Russia. 'Then how about moving out of this hotel? George Richards knows of a good little house to let on the English Quay. What do you think? I'm sick to death of hotel life.'

'We'd be robbed blind by our servants.'

'No more so than we are here. And you'd not be everlastingly worrying about my free tongue.'

Glynde laughed. 'Am I such a bore? I warn you, there will be a spy among our servants just as much there as here, but I agree with you. Some domestic life would be a pleasant change.'

The negotiations for the house took time, and they finally moved in just before it became necessary to put up the double windows and hermetically seal themselves in for the winter. Granville Leveson Gower reached Petersburg shortly afterwards and was soon very much at home in the snug little house on the English Quay, describing the palace in which he was staying until Sir John and Lady Warren left as an intolerable barracks of a place. He was also soon allowing himself the relief of telling them what he thought of Sir John himself. The previous Ambassador had not been pleased at being recalled, and relations between the two men were frigid throughout the necessary formalities of the handover.

'Three bows for an Ambassador, two for a Chargé d'Affaires,' Granville told Glynde and Jan. 'And one should take one's own yardstick, to get the depth just right, or risk precipitating a diplomatic incident! I begin to wonder if I was really cut out for the diplomatic service. I had to ride forty miles to her country palace the other day to pay my respects to the Empress Mother, and then translate my pretty speeches into diplomatic French, all in the third person. Now that I do really call work!'

'But you know you are enjoying it,' said Glynde.

'Now the Warrens are gone, yes, I begin to. She was the proudest woman it's been my misfortune to encounter for a long time.'

'And so little to be proud about,' said Glynde.

'Well, birth, I suppose. You are laughing, Mr. Warrington?'

'I was thinking how restful to be an American.'

'Where you make no distinction between classes? I might call on you and confidently expect to sit next to a black gentleman at table?'

'You have me there!' Jan threw out a hand. 'But we do not treat our slaves as badly as the Russians do their serfs!'

'And yet the serfs seem devoted to their masters. Is that true of the Polish peasants, too?'

'The Princess's certainly were.' Granville had learned that so far as Glynde and Jan were concerned, there was only one Polish Princess.

'I long to meet your Princess Ovinska,' he said now. 'I've seen her husband often enough, and his *belle amie* the Princess Landowska. I rather think that if I were the Princess Ovinska, I would come to Petersburg and present my son to the Tsar. What news do you have from Rendomierz?'

'None directly,' said Jan. 'But my friend Mrs. Richards corresponds with Miss Peverel, the Princess's companion.' A touch of defiance in his tone suggested that he had taken to heart the remarks about pride of birth and knew that a merchant's wife would not seem a very elegant acquaintance to his two companions. How strange it was to find himself associating on these easy terms with an Ambassador, who was also a lord. He was afraid his father would be delighted.

'A letter from Mrs. Richards in Petersburg?' Princess Isobel was playing with her stalwart little black-haired son in the garden, and looked up smiling as Jenny joined her.

'Yes. It's taken for ever to get here.' She bent to pick up the toy soldier Prince Casimir had dropped and hand it back to him.

'Well, at least it got here! What news from Petersburg?' She had had only a few brief letters from her husband in the two years since he had returned to Russia.

'George Richards and Jan Warrington seem to be thick as thieves. I am so pleased. Mr. Warrington is to stay another year at least at Petersburg, and so, she thinks, will Mr. Rendel. He's an old friend of the new British Ambassador. They went to school together.'

'Those very important English school-friendships. Then I have no doubt Mr. Rendel will stay.'

'Yes. He and Jan Warrington have taken a house together. On the English Quay, wherever that is.'

'On the River Neva, and very pleasant, I should think. What's the matter, Jenny? Something is troubling you?'

99

'Not precisely. It's something Mary Richards says. It almost reads like a message.'

'A message?'

'For you. Jan told her, she says, that the new Ambassador, this Lord Granville Leveson Gower . . . what a name!'

'I believe you pronounce it Lewson Gore,' said the Princess.

'Well, however you pronounce it, Mary says he was talking about you, and –' she blushed crimson '– about the Prince.'

'And also, no doubt, about the Princess Irene Landowska? Don't look so wretched, Jenny, I've friends in Petersburg too. What else did he say?'

'Well . . . He asked Mr. Warrington if he was in touch with us here, and went on to say that if he were you – forgive me, Princess – he thought he would take Prince Casimir to Petersburg and present him to the Tsar.'

'Did he so?' said the Princess thoughtfully. 'Now I wonder just what he intended by that? And whether it was good advice?'

Jenny wondered, too. She had had very similar instructions from the Brotherhood only the other day. They had left her in peace for a long while after Glynde and Jan had gone, then, at Christmas, she had had a message by way of Olga. 'They want to know all about the little Prince; how he goes on; what he is like.'

Her hand had gone automatically to the scar that still lifted the corner of her mouth. 'Prince Casimir? Do they so?' But in fact it confirmed what she had always thought about those sinister, hooded figures. Their methods might be savage, but their aim was one with which she could only sympathise: freedom for Poland. She was glad that she had never thought of trying to betray them, despite the brutal, unnecessary attack on her. And it was a pleasure to let them know what a bright, promising child Prince Casimir was. An expert aunt, she could report him as advanced in every stage of his development, a great hope for the future. She had done so, and had had, just the other day, further instructions through Olga. 'You are to urge the Princess to send for her husband, no matter what the pretext.'

Ever since the Brotherhood's messages had begun again, Jenny had felt she ought to tell the Princess the whole story.

Shameful to be afraid to. But now, she knew, the time had come. She waited until the Princess was changing for dinner. 'Princess.' She was in the big closet, selecting a white dress.

'Yes?' The Princess was at the glass, brushing her long hair.

'There's something I ought to tell you. Should have long ago.'

'Oh?' The Princess's eyes met Jenny's anxious ones in the glass. She stood up, finger on lips, moved forward, took Jenny's hand and led her through to the boudoir, all in silence. Then, 'Close the door, Jenny, would you? I'm tired; I feel the draught.'

'It's been a long day.' There was no draught, but Jenny moved obediently to close the door into the dressing-room, and saw the Princess move to the other door into the corridor, open, look out, and close it.

'No one,' she said. 'What is it, Jenny?'

It was most absolutely terrifying to have her own fears thus confirmed by the Princess's caution. 'You think that even here?' The Princess had seated herself on a chaise longue in the centre of the room and motioned her to join her.

'Everywhere.' Quietly. 'I am glad you are going to tell me at last, Jenny.'

'You knew?'

'I'm not always stupid. What happened to you, Jenny?'

'It was before I even got here.' She poured out the story of her first meeting with the Brotherhood and ended by telling of their new order, so oddly like Mary Richards' message.

'So!' The Princess thought about it for a moment. Then, 'You're a brave girl, Jenny. I'm glad you are here. And have told me. What do you think it means?'

Here was a question. What use beating about the bush? There had never been any secret about the dynastic reason for the Princess's marriage. 'Don't you think, maybe, that they want to make double sure? Time for you and the Prince to meet. Two little Princes better than one? Two hopes for the future? What's the matter?'

Princess Isobel was laughing, quietly, desperately. 'Do you think there is a branch of the Brotherhood in Petersburg too? That they are urging the Prince to come to Poland?'

'I expect so,' said Jenny. 'Don't you?'

'Yes. But he won't come. Not for their asking. So – not at all. I don't know him well, my husband, but I know him well enough for that. Besides, there is Princess Irene – and his other ladies.'

'And the Tsar,' said Jenny. 'Who values his advice, it seems.'

'His and Czartoryski's. Do you think I should take Casimir to St. Petersburg, Jenny?'

'I just don't know.' Jenny had noticed that the little Prince was never without a male attendant when he was out in the palace grounds.

'It's difficult, isn't it? On all kinds of counts. First and foremost,' she blushed, painfully, 'my husband has not suggested that I go. He has – other occupations. And then, as to Casimir. You know what my hopes are for him. I think he should grow up pure Pole, not half Russian like Czartoryski.'

'Well, yes, but one visit? Mary Richards writes in glowing terms of the Tsar. Suppose he were to see Casimir –' They were both convinced that to see their little Prince was to love him. 'Might not that affect his thinking about Poland's future?'

'I suppose it might. He'd make Casimir King, as the Empress Catherine did Stanislas Augustus? But Poland needs her own leader, not someone thrust upon her by even the most benevolent of foreigners. I don't think I'll go to Russia,' she decided. 'And I most certainly will not invite the Prince to come here. But tell the Brotherhood that I will bear in mind what they say.'

'I can't do that,' Jenny protested. 'I'm not supposed to have told you.'

'Of course. Stupid of me. I sometimes think I am hopelessly stupid, Jenny. Well, tell them you have done your best to persuade me! More than that you can hardly do. And – I know! – Ask them what their views are of my taking Casimir to Petersburg.'

'Clever,' said Jenny.

She put the question in carefully general terms in her next report to the Brotherhood and received an answer with disconcerting speed, confirming the Princess's instinct that their presence loomed very near indeed. 'They say he should stay here. Whatever that means.' Olga, acting as mouthpiece for the Brotherhood, did not necessarily understand the verbal messages she carried, and, as she could not read, was equally unaware of what Jenny said in the written reports she transmitted to them. It had been tacitly agreed between them that the less either of them knew about the other's activities, the better for both. But Jenny sometimes worried about Olga, who had grown proud in the comfort of Rendomierz and made no attempt to hide how much she disliked waiting on a foreigner. It was just as well that she was also deadly afraid of the Brotherhood.

The hot summer of 1804 drew into autumn, with the Prince still at Petersburg, the Princess at Rendomierz. Jenny had a rare letter from her oldest sister, describing invasion panic on the south coast of England and telling her how lucky she was to be living safe and in luxury in the centre of Europe where Bonaparte's long arm could not reach. 'Emperor Napoleon indeed!' Araminta concluded. 'That's what he wants to be called, but never by us!' Her husband was vicar of a seaside parish in Sussex, and she gave a vivid description of the preparations for swift evacuation if the enemy should land. 'Only our gallant navy and Lord Nelson stand between us and the monster. That little business of Lady Hamilton is quite forgot, and Nelson is all the cry now.' She went on to complain about the high cost of living. Taxes were up again, to pay for the war, tithes were hard to collect, and their sister Bella's husband had decided he could no longer afford to have Mrs. Peverel stay with them for the six months in the year that had been agreed upon when her husband died. 'So the burden falls entirely upon us, Jenny. What a mercy that you, at least, are settled in the lap of luxury. And so far from danger, too. With no one to care for but yourself. I cannot begin to tell you how I envy you. Remember us in your prayers.'

10

'It's signed at last.' Granville Leveson Gower had dropped in
as he so often did to the little house on the English Quay
between dining at home and starting on his evening round of
diplomatic engagements.

'The Anglo–Russian Treaty of Consort?' Glynde poured
wine for them all. 'Then let us drink to it. We British provide
the money, I take it, and Russia the troops?'

'That's it. If the Austrians and Prussians come in too, we
shall see some action.'

'Will they?'

'I wish I was sure of that. Oh well,' he rose. 'I must be
about my duties. Thank God, with this treaty signed at last,
I can begin to hope for my recall.'

'You wish to leave us?'

'As soon as I decently can. It's all very well for you two free
men; I am strangling in protocol. Feel for me! I am off now to
make my round of bows and scrapes.'

'Ending up, as usual, tête à tête with the Princess Galitzin?'

'The only place in Petersburg, except here, of course, where
I have found the kind of talk I am used to.'

'She's a great beauty, they say.'

'And a good friend.'

'I do wonder what Lady Bessborough thinks about it all,'
said Glynde, when Granville had left them.

'I shall never begin to understand you Europeans.' Jan had
been a silent listener. 'Behave like this in the United States
and you'd be run out of town on a rail. But here, so far as I can
see, Prince Ovinski spends his time with Princess Landowska,
while his wife lives at home with the little boy; the Emperor
is devoted to Princess Narishkin while Adam Czartoryski –'

'Is the Empress's devoted friend,' Glynde broke in. 'Which
goes far to explain why Adam has never made the kind of
dynastic marriage one would have expected. There's been talk

of a very rich Princess of Courland, but she's little more than a child, they say, and he's not interested.'

'Nothing but unhappy dynastic marriages,' said Jan, 'and scandalous liaisons as a result. I do feel we manage things better at home.'

'Your father has never urged you to marry a rich neighbour's daughter?'

'Oh, well, fathers!' Glynde could only agree with him. He would soon have been two years in Petersburg and his only word from his own father had been a message, sent by Granville Leveson Gower, urging him to stay.

As the days became longer and the weather more clement, with green showing here and there at last, everyone moved out of Petersburg to *dachas* in the surrounding countryside. The Tsar was mostly at his summer palace of Tsarske-Selo, though he came frequently to Petersburg to oversee the great mobilisation of the Russian army, which was going on apace now that Austria had joined Russia and England in their alliance against Napoleon. Taking after his father in this, Alexander was passionately interested in military matters, particularly in uniforms, and showed signs of meaning to lead his army himself.

'I do hope wiser counsel prevails.' Granville had invited Glynde and Jan to the country house he had taken on the banks of the Neva some way out of town, but they were all being eaten so horribly by mosquitoes that it seemed doubtful if they would repeat the visit. Besides, Granville's dear friend, Princess Galitzin, had taken a house so close to his that the ensuing outburst of gossip had been too much, even for her. 'Mind you,' Granville went on now, 'I do rather selfishly hope that the Tsar decides to go with the army when they move west. It will be a tremendous chance of seeing something more of Russia, and Poland, too, most likely.'

'You would go too?' asked Glynde.

'The whole court would. A most appalling nuisance for the army. But one can understand the Tsar's wanting to go. He does tend to imitate Napoleon, and the French government officials go with him on all his campaigns – inevitably, since he's about as absolute a monarch as even the Tsar himself. But he's also absolutely in control. Most unlike Alexander, who is as hamstrung by protocol as the rest of us. I can imagine him expecting his armies to wait for his permission, or the requisite number of bows given and acknowledged, before they can join battle.' He slapped irritably at a mosquito. 'I do sometimes wish that Peter the Great had not chosen to build his capital city in this wilderness!' And then, as if to explain his unusual ill-temper, 'I've been ordered to stay on here, much against my will.'

'Good news for us,' said Jan.

'Thank you. Which brings me to the real reason why I asked you to risk marsh fever with me here. I'm hoping to persuade you two gentlemen to come with me if I do go west with the Russian army. I am sure you would find it enormously interesting.'

'Why, yes,' said Glynde doubtfully. 'But you know we have no official position. We have not even been presented.'

'Ridiculous,' said Granville. 'Just like Sir John. That's to be taken care of. The Tsar himself was asked to have you presented. He says he can't go on for ever gossiping with you on the quay.'

'Very civil and agreeable he's been,' said Glynde. 'It's amazing how freely he walks about the city.'

'And a great headache for his ministers. There's no end to the tales one hears – in strictest confidence, of course – of the trouble they have making good after one of his quixotic gestures. He loves to grant people's wishes; promise them what they want. Someone else has to make it possible. Or explain to them that it's not. And now, he wants you two gentlemen to be made officially known to him.'

'All that kissing of hands and standing in line,' said Jan, surprising them. 'I'm sorry, Granville, but not I. You go, Glynde, if you've a mind to, but it's not my line at all.'

And from this stand he would not budge. 'No. I'm a free-born American. I like the Tsar; I enjoy talking to him when we meet on the quay. He asks very interesting questions. But treat him as if he were God walking on earth I cannot and I will not.' Urged once again by Glynde, he rounded on him. 'Look, friend, why do you think we Americans fought and beat you twenty-five years ago? It was for just this kind of freedom, and I'm not going back on it now.'

It might not be reasonable, but it was final, and, in the end, the impasse was broken by the intervention of the Tsar himself.

'We're to meet him and Czartoryski "by accident" in the summer gardens,' Granville told Glynde. 'Do you think you can manage that?'

'Oh, I should think so,' Glynde laughed. 'I begin to think you want our company quite badly on this western journey.'

'Frankly, I do. And for two reasons, closely connected. I like Adam Czartoryski immensely; he's a man it's a pleasure to work with, but he is also the servant of an autocrat of the most unpredictable kind. I've tried to learn Polish; it's no use; I need you as an interpreter, Jan. I need to know what the Poles really think, not have their views filtered through a Russian's incomprehensible mind. Even in all innocence, Adam could so easily mistranslate them.'

'Yes, I can see that. Though mind you, all the Polish aristocrats speak French, and a great many of them English as well.'

'But what about the serfs? They are the cannon fodder, after all. And the middle class, what there is of it. It is always the lower classes war hits hardest.'

'You speak as if war were certain.'

'Oh, I think it is. It's just a question of where and when it starts. It may be just as well that Jan has made an informal presentation to the Tsar the only way. There might not be time for anything else.'

'You leave so soon?'

'As soon as possible. The Tsar wishes to sound out feeling in what used to be Poland, both Austrian and Russian. And maybe even Prussian too. He's planning to go and stay with Adam's family at Pulawy, in the Austrian zone, and, entirely between ourselves, I rather think he means to make one of his "surprise" visits to Rendomierz while he is there. He's certainly brushing up his Polish. You can see why I need you and Jan. You will come, the two of you?'

'Oh, I think so.' Did he long, or dread to visit Rendomierz again? He was not sure, but he knew, given the chance, that he must go. He must see both Isobel and the child. His child?

Jan, too, agreed at once. George Richards would look after his business interests, he said, while he joined this irresistible expedition. 'It will be good to see Rendomierz again.' Besides, now that they had had their formally accidental introduction to the Tsar, they were being plagued with invitations. 'It's as if we had been invisible before! I don't know about you, but I'll be glad to get away. Are we going to this solemn "Te Deum" in the cathedral?'

'I think we should. The Tsar will expect it. And whatever one's beliefs, it should be an interesting spectacle.'

'All that incense! And nowhere to sit down.'

The Tsar left Petersburg the day after the service to join one of the two Russian armies already deployed in the west of the country. Led by the old General Kutusov who had been so surprisingly successful in Turkey, it was to join the Austrians against Napoleon in the south, while the other one, further north, was poised to invade Prussia if its King refused to cooperate.

'The trouble there is,' Granville had dropped in to see his friends on the night of the 'Te Deum', 'that the Tsar has one of his friendly passions for Queen Louise of Prussia. She's a great charmer, and Alexander has been her faithful servant since they first met; will do anything to avoid injuring her. Poor Adam's on tenterhooks! Every hope for the rebirth of Poland lies in the Russians invading the Polish lands the Prussians hold. He is sure that would mean a mass uprising of Polish serfs, who hate their Prussian masters much more bitterly than the other occupied Poles do their Austrian and Russian ones. A successful nationalist rising there might be a real beginning for a new Kingdom of Poland.'

'It's a strange position, Czartoryski's,' said Glynde. 'Foreign Minister to the Tsar, and yet hoping for Poland's freedom from Russia.'

'It certainly is. Risky, too. When he urged, at dinner the other night, that Alexander take Warsaw and Poznan from Prussia and reconstitute the Kingdom of Poland, Prince Peter Dolgoruky turned on him: "You speak like a Polish Prince, and I speak like a Russian Prince." The Tsar said nothing, but Adam turned white as a sheet. I think his position hangs on a hair. Anything could happen. It's absolutely maddening that I cannot come with you tomorrow, but I must wait for the courier from England. I'll catch you up in a day or so, I am sure; he is overdue already. But if anything should detain me, I count on you for every detail of what happens when the Tsar visits Pulawy.'

'And Rendomierz?' asked Glynde. 'Is the "surprise" visit still in the programme?'

'Oh, I think so. Ovinski goes with the Tsar, and I am sure he will urge him to visit Rendomierz as well as his own estates further north, near Vilno. Did you remember to ask Mrs. Richards to warn Jenny Peverel?' He turned to Jan with the question.

'Of course. Though I still think it hardly necessary since the Prince must have written to the Princess.'

'A message from Them.' Olga had cut across the pleasure gardens one fine September morning to join Jenny and Prince Casimir, who were feeding stale bread to the golden carp in the lily pond. The serf who always attended the little Prince when he was outside the palace was standing, arms folded, some little distance off, watching the scene with a benevolent eye.

'Yes? Careful, Casimir, don't throw yourself in too.' Jenny managed a casual note as she half turned to Olga, still keeping a firm hand on the little Prince's loose blouse.

'You're to tell the Princess. The Tsar is coming to Pulawy on his way to the war. He plans to surprise her with a visit.'

'The Tsar? Coming here?'

'Yes. He is to be made welcome, they say.'

'That's all?'

'Isn't that enough? The tyrant! Coming here. And to be made welcome!'

'Olga's cross? What's the matter?' The little Prince, who seemed not to like Olga, asked the question of Jenny.

'Nothing's the matter with *me*, Highness.' Olga made a deep, half-mocking curtsey to the little boy, and left them.

'I don't like it,' said Jenny, reporting the scene to the Princess that evening. 'I'm sure she knows something more, something that pleases her and would not please us.'

The Prince's messenger arrived a few days later, bringing the same news. 'It's all very well,' said the Princess, reading her husband's letter, 'but I don't quite see how we contrive to be surprised by the visit, and at the same time have the state apartments swept and garnished, and a crowd of guests here to greet the Tsar. All by accident!'

'Well,' said Jenny. 'They could be here to greet the Prince perhaps? You are surely allowed to be expecting him?'

'You're right. Stupid of me. It's . . . unsettling.'

The Prince arrived a week later and acted as if he had only been away for a few days, taking up life in the palace exactly where he had left off, behaving with his usual impeccable courtesy, and approving all the arrangements his wife had made for the Tsar's impromptu visit. If the fine September weather held, he was to find his hosts entertaining their friends with a display in the famous Rendomierz water gardens. Workmen were busy checking the elaborate mechanism of the fountains which had not been used since the wedding three years before.

'It must all go like clockwork.' The Prince and Princess had joined Jenny by the big fountain of the Three Graces, and he spoke to them both. 'Czartoryski and I want the Tsar to feel adored and welcomed here in Poland, to understand what an asset we Poles can be in the coming war against Napoleon. He may even have been moved to declare an independent kingdom of Poland at Pulawy, before he comes here, but if not, perhaps Rendomierz will have the honour to be the scene of the declaration.'

'And who is to be king of this independent kingdom?' Princess Isobel gave him a very straight look.

'Oh, the Tsar himself, for the moment. Czartoryski and I are agreed on that. It's the only way. I imagine Czartoryski thinks the arrangement will be permanent, but he's been away from Poland too long; he does not understand. The Tsar is a man of high ideals . . . and . . . persuadable. I think the sight of you and our little Prince may do what a thousand arguments could not. If not now, then later, after we have given him loyal support in the fighting.'

'I see.' But Jenny did not think the Princess quite liked what she saw. It was maddening that the arrival of the Prince had put an end to their close, daily communication She should have foreseen this, but had not quite realised how her relationship with Princess Isobel had changed during the Prince's absence. Now, badly wanting a chance to talk to her about Olga, she never managed to see her alone. The Prince and Princess's apartments adjoined each other; the communicating door had been unbolted when he arrived. In his absence, she had joined the Princess while her maid was brushing her hair and getting her ready for bed. It had been their chance to talk over the happenings of the day, free from the Princess's observant crowd of hangers-on. Now, Prince and Princess retired together. It was as if a stage curtain had fallen between her and them, and she could only wonder what went on behind it, and be angry with herself for doing so.

The great day dawned fine and bright; many of the guests had arrived the night before, but more kept driving up all morning, and by midday the gardens were crowded with people, many of whom Jenny had not met since the wedding three years before. In theory, they only knew that they were come to welcome the Prince back, but a feeling of tense expectation in the air made her wonder just how open a secret the surprise visit really was. Liveried servants were circulating among the crowd now, pouring vodka for the first toast of the day. Nobody had moved yet to help themselves from the lavish collation of cold meat and smoked fish set out on tables on the main lawn. Everyone seemed suspended, waiting . . .

'Jenny!' Prince Casimir tugged at her hand. 'I have to go!'

'Oh, no, Casimir!' A stir among the crowd, the far-off sound of carriages told her that the surprise guest was arriving at last.

'I'll take him!' Olga appeared at her elbow. 'I don't want to see that man!'

'Oh, thank you!' In her relief, because the Prince had made a point of her being there to join in the welcome of the Tsar, she let Olga take Casimir's hand and lead him away. Only afterwards, too late, did she remember how Olga had gone around, the last few days, looking as if she was enjoying some secret joke.

No time for that now. A procession of carriages swept round the last curve of the drive. The crowd was suspended, hushed as she moved swiftly to join the Prince and Princess near the flight of marble steps that led down from the carriage sweep to the first of the lawns.

Whips cracked, postilions shouted, the first carriage stopped at the top of the steps and a lithe young figure jumped down as the doors opened, sunlight gleaming on golden curls. 'My dear friend,' he paused for a moment at the top of the steps, smiling down at the Prince and Princess, 'I am come to beard you in your country den, and make the acquaintance of your Princess.' He was down the steps while they were still in full bow and curtsey. 'You never told me how beautiful she was!' He bent to raise the Princess and plant a fraternal kiss on her cheek. 'I am delighted to find you at home, ma'am, and among your friends – and mine, I hope.' This, louder, as he turned to greet the reverently silent crowd.

Is he going to make a speech? Jenny thought, appalled. How can he, here on Austrian soil? But the next carriage had drawn up behind the Tsar's, which she saw with amusement was merely an open calash, nothing like so impressive as the Prince's. The Tsar turned back. 'I have brought some old friends of yours to be my introduction, Princess.' He had her by the hand and led her back to the bottom of the steps, the Prince following with a close eye on his wife, Jenny thought. The first man who alighted was a handsome stranger, but – her heart gave a curious, uncomfortable jump – he was followed by Glynde Rendel and Jan Warrington. The Tsar was presenting all three of them. 'My good friend and minister, Prince Czartoryski; Mr. Rendel, Mr. Warrington, both of whom you know.'

'A delightful surprise, sire, as is this whole unexpected visit.' The Princess's colour was high. 'Would you care to take a walk in our park? We were about to show our guests the water gardens for which Rendomierz is famous in a modest way.'

'Famous indeed, and rightly so.' He made it a personal compliment. 'I long to see them.' And then, an afterthought, 'But where is the Prince, your son? I have heard fine things of him from his father, fortunate man, and looked forward to meeting him.'

'Jenny?' Princess Isobel turned to her with the question. And then, 'Sire, may I present my friend and companion, Miss Peverel.'

'An Englishwoman? One of my new allies!' He had a great gift, Jenny thought, for making one feel the only important person, for the moment. Answering his kind questions about her family in England, she was intensely aware of Glynde, talking to the Princess. And at the same time, at the back of her mind, was a growing anxiety about Prince Casimir. He and Olga should be back by now.

But the little group was moving off towards the water gardens, the Tsar graciously acknowledging the salutations of the crowd as he went, bending his handsome head this way and that, pausing from time to time to greet an acquaintance like an old friend. He had given his arm to the Princess; the Prince was talking to dark-haired, handsome Prince Adam Czartoryski; inevitably Glynde and Jan were on either side of Jenny.

'*You* really are a surprise,' she said.

Glynde laughed. 'I did think you seemed not entirely unprepared.'

'No, they've been working on the water display like madmen all week. It's not been used since the wedding; some of it not for longer than that. Dear God!'

'What is it?'

'I've remembered something! But it's not possible. She couldn't . . . They wouldn't . . .'

'Stop it!' Glynde's voice was sharp. 'Pull yourself together, Miss Peverel, and tell us what it is you fear.'

He had stopped, turned to face her with the question. 'No, we must keep up with them,' she said breathlessly, 'be ready to do something, God knows what. Do you remember the joke fountains?' she asked. 'The Princess's father's idea of humour; she never uses them. The statues in the long yew alley, between the Pool of the Graces and the ornamental water. Fountains come out of their mouths. The Prince used to have them switched on when a guest was halfway down the walk. Trapped by those thick hedges. Go on, or go back, he was soaked to the skin, a laughing-stock.'

'You can't think!'

'Imagine what it would do to this visit, to us all! The Tsar would look a fool. He'd never forgive that. And, there's worse. I think it may seem that Casimir did it. He might even have done so. He's into everything. And, I saw him there with Olga, my maid, one day last week.'

'Where is the water controlled from?'

'The grotto at the top of that hill.' She pointed. 'It's a long way.'

'I'll go,' said Jan. 'You do your best to detain the Tsar.'

'How?' Glynde and Jenny looked at each other. It is not easy to detain an absolute monarch. But the group ahead were pausing now to admire the Three Graces, who were pouring silver streams of water from their cornucopias on to a central female figure.

'I have always thought my father intended it for Poland,' the Princess was telling the Tsar as they caught up and mingled in the little group. Much too close together to chance any kind of warning.

'You are sure he did not intend it for his daughter?' asked the Tsar, smiling down at her as if she were the only woman in the world.

'Oh, no, sire, I was a squalling infant then, a bitter disappointment to him: a girl.'

'And now you are the mother of a Prince. But where is Prince Casimir?'

It was a chance, and Jenny took it. Colouring to the roots of her hair, intensely aware of the busybody she must seem, she took a step forward, made her deepest curtsey, and said, 'I am beginning to wonder if he has not run away to play in the grotto.'

Dead silence for a moment, while the Tsar looked through her as if she was most absolutely not there, then turned to the Princess again. 'I really sometimes believe that I suffer just a trifle from deafness. Shall we set forward down this handsome alley of yours? I have heard that the fountains at the bottom of it are the most beautiful of all.' He offered his arm once more to the Princess.

But as the two Princes loomed forward at Jenny, as if to erase her from the Tsar's sight, the quicker-witted Princess looked up at him appealingly. 'Sire, forgive a mother's anxiety for her only son. Casimir is not allowed in the grotto; it's not safe for a child. Will one of you gentlemen very kindly go and look?'

'Mr. Warrington has gone already,' said Glynde. 'It is but to wait a few moments and be sure all is well with the child.'

'Mr. Warrington is a very capable young man. You may rely on him, Princess. And now, we must not keep your guests waiting.' The Tsar had the Princess's arm once more and led her to the opening of the wide alley between dark yew hedges, at the far end of which they could see the crowd gathered to welcome him by the ornamental water. The Princess exchanged an anguished glance with Glynde, who shook his head just imperceptibly. There was no chance that Jan could have reached the grotto yet. But the Tsar was laughing at her a shade impatiently, teasing her for being an over-anxious mother, leading her forward. Small consolation that she would be soaked as well as him. Whichever way they turned, when the water hit them halfway down the alley, they would cut a publicly ridiculous figure, something he could never forgive.

'Prince!' Glynde spoke desperately to the two Princes at once. 'They must be stopped. There's just a chance that the water may be turned on.'

'Water?' asked Czartoryski.

'Mary, Mother of Heaven!' said Ovinski, remembering. But how do you stop an autocrat? Oddly, they all looked at Jenny.

'It's all right,' she said. 'I think the Princess understood. But we must go after them. Yes,' she went on as they all moved in a huddle down the alley after the two figures who were almost halfway. 'Look!'

The Princess was swaying on her feet. She looked up at the Tsar, said something, drooped towards him, was caught in his strong arms as she fell. For a long moment, the watchers were silently terrified that his basic obstinacy would make him carry her forward, the way they had been going, but all logic pushed him the other way. He turned and came back towards them, carrying her lightly, as if she weighed nothing, looking, Jenny thought, enormously pleased with himself.

'I am afraid it has all been too much for the Princess,' he said, as he approached them. And then, as Prince Ovinski stepped forward. 'No, Prince, I am younger and stronger than you. She is my hostess and my responsibility. Just show me where to take her. I am afraid your ornamental waters will have to wait for another day.'

After that, his visit was almost miraculously successful. He could not do too much for the hostess who had swooned so touchingly in his arms. He even postponed his return to Pulawy, telling Czartoryski that they could await a reply to the messenger he had sent to the Prussian court just as well at Rendomierz.

'It's another of his sudden passions,' said Glynde rather wryly to Jan, back in their little house in the guest village. Had he hoped or feared a chance to talk alone with the Princess? Either way, monopolised as she was by her royal guest, he was most certainly not going to get it.

'Yes.' Jan sounded anxious. 'All very well, so long as he never finds out how she fooled him. He wouldn't like that. And it was touch and go. Casimir's hand was on the lever, with Olga watching from the grotto window to give him the word, and that serf who goes with him everywhere, standing looking on and grinning all over his face. I pretended to see nothing, of course. Just picked up Casimir, told the girl his mother wanted him, carried him off.' He smiled. 'Not a cent's worth of fear in that child!' A total stranger, but he thought it a great game, rode me like a horse all the way to the palace.'

'That's a remarkable little boy,' said Glynde. 'And the image of his mother.' Had he been relieved or disappointed to see no trace of himself in the boy he was sure was his own?

'And with her brains, too. A small Polish eagle who will fly far.'

'Please God.'

11

Rendomierz had never been so festive. Day after day, the Tsar rode out with the men; night after night Prince and Princess entertained him with one 'impromptu' concert or dramatic entertainment after another.

'Monsieur Poiret says he is going to bed for six weeks when this is over.' Jenny had happened on Glynde and Jan knocking balls about in the vast billiard room on a day when a light, drizzling rain had kept the men at home.

'Poor man, I don't wonder. And after all the years of idleness, too.' Jan missed an easy shot. 'It's no use, Glynde, you could beat me with your eyes shut. Or half your mind, which is what you've been using today.'

Glynde laughed. 'Forgive me! I was wondering how long this charade would continue.' And if he would ever get a chance of a word alone with the Princess, who walked, always, between the Prince and their guest.

'Charade?' asked Jenny. 'What do you mean?'

He moved over to close the door. 'What does the Tsar mean, is the question. He's been here almost three weeks now, courteous, delightful, the perfect guest, listens to everyone, smiles at everything. Says nothing.'

'Or rather, says a great deal.' Jan was stacking the billiard cues. 'None of it to the purpose. If one could only get a word alone with the Princess. I would give a good deal to know what she thinks of it all. You must know, Jenny. Has she hopes for Poland?'

'Miss Peverel wouldn't tell us, even if she knew.' Glynde smiled at Jenny, and her heart lurched.

'But I don't know,' she said. 'I'm just as much outside of things as you two.'

'Except so far as little Casimir is concerned. You play a very important part there.' Glynde moved to reopen the door. 'And here he is to prove it!' They could all hear the child's voice now, calling imperatively for Jenny. 'He's wonderfully lucky to have you.'

'Why, thank you!' Blushing, afraid of tears, she was glad to be distracted by Casimir hurling himself at her and demanding a story.

'Back in the nursery.' She picked him up, spoke angrily to the serf who now appeared. 'You know the Prince is not allowed in the public rooms alone.'

'Forgive me, pani!' The girl looked terrified, as well she might. 'Don't tell? We're all topsyturvy above and belowstairs. It's the farewell dinner, you see, and so little notice.'

'Farewell?' Jan pounced on it. 'The Tsar is going?'

'Yes, in the morning. But not the master.' The girl rather looked as if this had been bad news for the household.

'We'd better get packing.' He turned and explained quickly to Glynde what the girl had said. 'So, no chance of that word with the Princess.'

'No. And not much joy for the Poles, who have built such hopes on this visit.'

'Unless he makes an announcement tonight?'

'Of a Kingdom of Poland? Don't delude yourself, Jan. If he'd been going to do it, he'd have done it when he came; got the good of it.'

'He might have been thinking it over,' said Jan, obstinately hopeful. 'And he's been closeted with Adam Czartoryski all afternoon. That has to be promising.'

'Has Prince Adam said anything?' The Princess asked her husband, who had joined her in full dress for the evening.

'There's been no chance. But he looks remarkably cheerful. I really do allow myself to hope . . . And much of it thanks to your influence with the Tsar. The dress is excellent . . . Will you wear the Ovinski diamonds tonight?'

'I had thought the Sobieski emeralds.' She stood by the cabinet, opening their morocco case.

'No, the diamonds.' It was courteous but deadly firm. 'You are to queen it tonight.' He moved over to shut the door into the dressing-room. 'And, apropos, I think we should be planning another Prince.'

'Another . . .?'

'Prince. And, this time, may I have the privilege of being the only possible father? I am glad,' he went on smoothly, before she could speak, 'that you have not tried to use that tunnel of yours this time.'

'The tunnel?' She looked up at him, aghast.

'You really did not know it was being watched? Satisfactory. And I'm glad that no disaster has had to befall either Mr. Rendel or Mr. Warrington, my two very good friends. That being so, and I cannot tell you what a relief it is to me, may I count, in future, on fathering my own heirs?'

'You knew?'

'Naturally, I knew. I may be an old man, but I am not absolutely a fool, still less without experience. And, luckily for you, for us all, I also had the wits to understand your motive. I'm just sad you had so little confidence in me. I may be old; I am not precisely in my dotage. I wish I thought you could prove to me that that charming child Casimir is my son.'

She looked up at him, the diamonds hanging from her nerveless hand. 'I am so very sorry. I had no idea . . .'

'That I knew. Just so. That is why I thought I had better tell you. Now that I have decided I can trust you in the future.'

'You've had me watched?' She was taking it in slowly.

'Not you, my dear, the tunnel.'

'And if someone . . .'

'He would have been killed. Let me do that for you.' He took the necklace from her shaking hand and fastened it round her neck. 'We must go down. The Tsar is not a man to keep waiting.'

'No. Yes.' She looked up at him. 'I'm sorry,' she said.

'I really believe you are. A misunderstanding . . . A pity. We will not discuss it again.' He looked around the luxurious apartment. 'We will pretend it did not happen.'

'And Casimir?'

'May be my son.'

She was white as her dress. 'If we should have another?'

'We will cross that bridge when we get to it. Come.'

Chandeliers glittered; champagne flowed; Monsieur Poiret's music echoed from room to room. The Tsar took the Princess's hand to lead her in the first polonaise. 'You are pale, Princess. I have been an exhausting guest?'

'Oh, no, sire. It has been the most immense pleasure.' Looking up at him, she thought it almost true. Impossible not to like this tall young man who bore the burden of empire so seriously. 'I shall pray for you, sire, if I may,' she said impulsively.

'In Polish? Dear lady –' He broke off. 'What is that tune?'

'It's a Polish marching song.' She recognised it with a pang of horror; hoped the Tsar would not.

'Played by Napoleon's Polish Legion?' He smiled down at her reassuringly, bending towards her. 'Paler than ever, Princess? No need. I may be Tsar of all the Russias, but I am no tyrant, as you must know by now. I only try to serve God, like everyone else. I wonder,' he paused for a moment, listening to the music as it rose to a dramatic climax. 'An omen, perhaps? I have an announcement to make, later; one that will give you pleasure. I am glad to make it here, in your hospitable house, where I have been so lovingly served. What's that?' A stir on the grand staircase; a mud-stained messenger was pushing his way through the crowd.

'Despatches for the Tsar! From Berlin.'

'No.' The Tsar spoke as Adam Czartoryski moved forward to intercept the man. 'A message from my sister, Queen Louise, at last. I will read it myself.' He did so, fast, once, then more slowly. Turned to the Princess. 'Dear lady, I must leave you! It is a cry for help from a dear friend. The monster, Napoleon, has violated Prussian territory. Now they must throw in their lot with ours. With them on our side, we will defeat the Godless tyrant once and for all. A new era will dawn for the world, a time of peace, of the worship of God, of goodwill among men.'

'And your announcement, sire,' asked the Princess, desperately daring. 'Will we hear it before you go?'

'Ah, dear lady, that must wait.'

'And so he goes.' The Prince had joined his wife much later, after the banquet had drawn to its dreary conclusion.

'I can't bear it,' she turned to him for comfort, forgetting their painful previous talk. 'He as good as said he was going to announce an independent Poland, and now, one message, and he's off –'

'To tilt at another windmill. It's a pity you're not his only

Dulcinea, my dear, but there it is. And now, we have business of our own to attend to. Send away your maid; I'll be your attendant tonight.'

'I wish Granville were here. He might have some idea of what's going on.' Glynde turned to Jan as they rode away from Rendomierz in the Tsar's train.

'The Princess looked pale this morning.'

'It must have been an exhausting visit for her.' Maddening beyond belief to have had to ride away without a single private word with her. He had caught Jenny that morning, asked her quickly: 'The Princess, how is she?'

'I wish I knew,' Jenny had said. 'She looks like death this morning.'

And so did Jenny, he thought, and found himself wondering what life must be like for her, so far from home: 'Miss Peverel –'

'Yes?'

'If ever you were unhappy here, wished to go home . . . If I could serve you in any way . . . We are old friends, are we not?'

When she smiled, he noticed the slight twist to her lip, found himself remembering that day in the forest. 'I like to think so, Mr. Rendel,' she said. 'And it's good of you to ask, but my life is here, with the Princess. And Casimir.'

'You'll look after her!'

'In so far as she will let me.' And with that he had to be satisfied.

The Tsar moved on from the Czartoryski palace at Pulawy to Natoline, the country home of another powerful Polish family, the Potockis, just outside Warsaw. Lavishly entertained, he was charming, agreeable, diplomatic as ever, and said nothing positive.

'He really is a genius at hiding his feelings,' said Glynde. 'Natural enough I suppose, after growing up between a mad father and tyrannical grandmother.'

'Czartoryski looks black as thunder,' said Jan. 'Whatever is happening, it's not good news for Poland.'

'What is?'

They reached Berlin to a hero's welcome for the Tsar from

his 'brother and sister' the King and Queen of Prussia, who had been thrust towards his side when Napoleon's General Bernadotte marched through their territory. The secretaries were soon at work drafting a treaty between Russia and Prussia, while all the world turned out to honour the friend who had so nearly been an enemy. While the diplomats argued and the armies gathered, the Tsar seemed happy to dance attendance on Prussia's beautiful Queen Louise. And when he did leave Berlin at last, early in November, he still did not go straight to his army, but paused to visit his sister Marie, wife of the Crown Prince of Saxe-Weimar. He stayed with her several days, enjoying the talk of Goethe and Wieland and the other men of letters who illuminated the Weimar court. It was there that news reached him of one of Napoleon's lightning movements.

'Ulm has capitulated? The French are in Vienna? Kutusov is retreating?' Glynde repeated the catalogue of disasters. 'Why didn't Kutusov stay to help the Austrians defend Vienna?'

'Maybe after Mack's shameful capitulation at Ulm he did not look on them as very reliable allies,' suggested Jan, who had brought the news.

'Fair enough,' Glynde groaned. 'The Austrians do seem to have let Napoleon fool them up hill and down dale. Both Mack at Ulm and the Austrian General at Vienna who let himself be persuaded not to destroy that vital bridge over the Danube. God knows why.'

'He's been sent in irons to Königsberg, for what that's worth.'

'*Pour encourager les autres?* I wonder if it will. Well, one good thing, we are off tomorrow, at last, to join Kutusov at his headquarters at Olmütz. I devoutly hope that Granville has heard the bad news, and contrives to meet us there, rather than heading for Vienna, as he wrote he intended, and certain captivity.'

'Or even death. Another "suicide" like Pichegru and that unfortunate Captain Wright.'

'Or barefaced murder, as with the Duc d'Enghien. But Granville has a great deal of sense. He'll never walk into the lion's mouth.'

They were both immensely relieved when Granville Leveson

Gower arrived at last at Russian army headquarters at Olmütz in mid-November, and were spellbound by his tale of adventures since he had left Petersburg early in October, expecting to meet them at Pulawy. He had got as far as Minsk, the capital of Lithuania, when he learned that the Tsar meant to meet the Emperor of Austria at Vienna and set out for there, only to learn when he reached Brunn, fifty miles from the city, that Napoleon had taken it.

'So it was across country to find you,' he told them. 'And very glad I am to have done so. I can tell you, the prospect of sleeping in a bed after all these nights in the carriage is a very pleasant one. But, tell me before anything else, is news of our naval victory at Trafalgar confirmed?'

'Yes. And of Lord Nelson's death, which almost overshadows the great victory he won,' Glynde told him. 'But you will find that both the sorrow and the joy are ours alone. They don't reckon much to sea battles here in the centre of Europe.'

'They have other things on their minds,' said Granville. 'The Prussians still seem to be standing shilly-shally on the side lines, and the Tsar is mad for a great battle to defeat Napoleon once and for all. The Russians are formidable soldiers; they've fought like demons every inch of the way in this retreat, but whether their Generals can match Napoleon is something else again. I know Kutusov wants to rest his forces first and wait for reinforcements from Poland, but the Tsar and the young aristocrats round him are getting impatient. They call Kutusov General Slowcoach and put all their hopes in the Austrian General Weyrother. I just hope good comes of it.'

'You don't sound sure?'

'Frankly, I'm not. Napoleon is at Brunn now, where I was just the other day. He moves like lightning, that man. I'm sending my heavy baggage away, and keeping a guard on my carriage and horses at all times. If I were you, gentlemen, I would do the same. Specially living as you do, here to the west of headquarters. You're wise, of course, not to be in Olmütz itself, granted the overcrowding and the risk of disease, but I rather wish you had chosen to place yourselves to the east of the town.'

'It was a question of beggars can't be choosers,' Glynde told him. 'All very well for you, who must be found lodgings close to the court.'

'You'd not think it very well if you saw them. We're all slumming it.' He rose. 'Never mind. Maybe I will be proved a false prophet and we will be dining in luxury in Vienna next week.'

Glynde and Jan were waked early next morning by the shrill of trumpets and the call to arms. All that day, December the first, they watched the allied troops marching west to meet the enemy, and chafed at having to remain where they were. After a restless night, they woke to a world charged with rumour. The Tsar was ill; he had fallen from his horse; he and the Emperor Francis still insisted on taking part in the battle. Soon they began to hear the thud of gunfire from the west.

It grew louder as the day wore on. 'It's nearer,' said Jan. 'We must be retreating. Should we pack and run, do you think?'

'Not yet.' But soon, towards evening, the first fugitives appeared, bloody, desperate, heading east on the four-hundred-mile flight that separated them from Mother Russia.

'The Tsar?' Glynde asked a bearded Cossack.

The man spat. 'He's running too. Just a man, like the rest of us. He should have kept off the battlefield. Him and that milksop Austrian Emperor. Austerlitz, they're calling it. Bloody muddle, I say. I'm going home!'

The two young men were very quiet as they loaded their few possessions into the small carriage that must be their safety. 'Pity the roads aren't frozen enough for sledges,' said Jan.

'Pity about the Tsar.'

'Of course he's just a man. What else? But unfortunate his soldiers should have found it out. Come on, time to start.'

With the roads half frozen and crowded with desperate fugitives, the going was intolerably slow. They had paused once again at the long, wretched queue for a bridge across a tributary of the March River, when Jan caught Glynde's arm. 'Isn't that James Wylie?'

'Good God, yes.' They knew the Tsar's Scottish doctor well enough to be sure that if he was here, desperately scanning faces as they passed, the Tsar himself could not be far away.

124

By unspoken consent they got their carriage pulled with difficulty to the side of the road. 'Here!' Glynde leaned out, shouted against the uproar, waved to catch the doctor's attention.

'Mr. Rendel! Thank God.' The doctor's Scottish accent was more pronounced than usual. 'Have you a drop of wine for my master? He's in a hovel; here by the roadside; ill!'

'Dear God! Get in, Dr. Wylie, show the coachman the way. Naturally, we've wine; whatever the Tsar needs. We're at his service.'

'Thank you, gentlemen.'

Fortunately the ground here was frozen enough, so that it was possible to take the carriage slowly across the fields to the little town of Czeitsch where the two Emperors had found refuge after the disasters of the day. By Wylie's direction, they drew up at last outside a peasant hut.

'Good God!' exclaimed Glynde. 'This is where your master lies?'

'On straw! Come in, gentlemen. Warm yourselves while I heat the wine and give my master an opiate. He is very far from well; must have some sleep.'

Since the main room of the hut had no chimney, it was full of smoke from the small fire that burned in the centre of the room. They could just make out the figure of the Tsar in the corner, the handsome face grimed with smoke, and they thought tears, the golden hair tarnished and in disarray. They could hear his teeth chatter on the silver cup in which Wylie proffered the warm wine and its soothing draught.

Next morning, Alexander was himself again, convinced that Austerlitz was merely a temporary setback, that he now had the measure of Napoleon. It was but to regroup and defeat him. But the Emperor Francis had other ideas and signed a separate peace with Napoleon the next day. Under its terms, all hostilities would cease, and the Russians would not be molested so long as they retired across the River Bug on to Russian territory.

As the long retreat began, the Tsar was still pinning his hopes on help from Prussia. He learned his mistake in mid-December when news reached him on the plains of Austrian Poland that the Prussians, too, had signed a separate peace with Napoleon, who had bribed them with the offer of British

Hanover. Alexander had been travelling up to then with his defeated army, doing his best to put new heart into the sullen troops; now he gave up. 'Everything I've tried to do has been a disaster.' He must get back to Petersburg. A triumphant Tsar might safely stay away from his capital. A defeated one faced the threat of deposition and death. A death like his father's. And the only place to fight this was the capital, Petersburg itself.

12

Jenny was relieved when Prince Ovinski left at the end of November. He had seemed his usual agreeable self throughout his stay, but something had been wrong just the same. Even Olga had noticed. 'They want to know what is the matter between the Prince and Princess.' She never mentioned the Brotherhood by name if she could help it.

'Then they will have to find out from someone else, because I have no idea.' Jenny had been tempted to insist that Olga be sent away after the episode of the water gardens; had decided, on thinking it over, that it was better to hang on to the devil one knew. The little Prince had a new bodyguard called Lech, a member of a family who had been devoted to the Sobieskis for generations. She did not think she need worry about him, but the Princess looked exhausted, hag-ridden. She had grown thin; her cheeks had lost their glow and her dark eyes their sparkle; even her hair, usually so crisp and curling, hung limp and lifeless in its stylish short cut round the pale face.

It was snowing hard the day the Prince left for his estates at Vinsk, near Vilno and the couple said their public farewell in the main hall. 'Take care of yourself and the child.' Ovinski bent to kiss his wife formally on the cheek. 'I will expect you at Vinsk before the thaw. And you too, Miss Peverel.' He had his usual friendly smile for Jenny. 'It will interest you to see how we go on in Russian Poland.'

'You do not mean to join the Tsar, sir?' It was a question she had longed to ask.

'On his triumphal march against Napoleon? I think not. My master knows me for a counsellor grown old in service; I am of more use in the court than the camp. Besides, my steward writes that it is time my serfs at Vinsk saw their master. You'll take good care of my wife, Miss Peverel.' He flicked a finger at his secretary, standing just behind him. 'Here.' He handed her the leather case. 'This is for you. For a faithful —' Had he been about to say servant? If so he changed his mind: 'Friend.'

'Oh, no!' It was a magnificent chain of rubies. Something he carried about with him for a possible mistress? 'Please, I would much rather not. No need . . .' For a bribe, she would have said, but thought better of it.

'You must indulge me, Miss Peverel.' It was final. She caught the Princess's anxious eye and was silent. And after all, despite the kind things the Prince had said before Casimir was born, it was the first actual payment she had received. Impossible to say that she would much rather have a small salary.

A few minutes later the great doors closed behind the last of the Prince's train, leaving the hall still ice-cold despite its great stove. The Princess was shivering. Jenny took her hand and felt the tremor run right through her. 'Come to your room, ma'am. You're worn out.'

'Yes.' She seemed to pull herself together. 'Yes, I am a little tired.' She looked round the circle of curious faces. 'I believe, perhaps, an early night. Madame Poiret, if you would preside at dinner in my place?'

'Send away the girl.' She had got as far as her boudoir; subsided on to the chaise longue. It was warm here, the stove red-hot in the corner, but Jenny found a light cashmere shawl and threw it over her. 'Thank you.' She pulled it close. 'I don't think I'll ever be warm again. These last weeks . . . Jenny, can I trust you?'

'You know you can! He tried to bribe me! I'm sorry I had to take it. What's the matter, Isobel?' Had she ever used the given name before?

'Jenny!' The cold hands clutched hers convulsively. 'I told him I was pregnant. The only way to make him stop. It was horrible, Jenny, horrible. An old man . . . trying . . . not for pleasure . . . not for lust even. Just for an heir. Night after night. Over and over again.' She was crying at last, the cold calm broken.

'But you're not pregnant?' Jenny went to the heart of the matter.

'No, thank God. If he'd stayed much longer, he must have known. I've had no peace, Jenny, no privacy . . .'

'You say, "Thank God,"' Jenny said. 'But Princess, why?'

'Call me Isobel. Please. I like it. I'm so alone . . . But you'll stand by me.'

'Of course I will. If only you will explain.' She tucked the shawl more snugly round the Princess, moved across the room to pour vodka for them both. 'We need this, I think.'

'Yes.' Her teeth chattered against the glass. 'You'll help me, Jenny? I'm going to say I've miscarried. Tonight. The cold; the shock of the Prince's going; all kinds of reasons. You'll help me make it convincing? By the time he hears – the messenger will be slow – he'll be at Vinsk. Busy. Please God, he won't come back. He must have hated it just as much as I did. And – he trusts you. If you tell him, he'll believe you.'

'But I don't understand. Princess –' She corrected herself. 'Isobel. A brother for Casimir. Or a sister. Why not?' But she was afraid she knew.

'Because then he would kill Casimir. Oh, he'd not do it himself. He never stains those white hands of his. But he would click his fingers, and Casimir would die. Do I need to say more, Jenny? Do you understand what I'm saying? What he thinks . . . what he suspects?'

'I'm afraid I do.' How could she ask: 'But, Princess, is it true?' How could she not wonder? Look back, those years of Casimir's life, and before, to her own arrival in the Prince's cortège. To that scene at the stables, where Glynde and Jan, very much at home, had rescued her from the filthy yard, the crowd of serfs. The Princess had been awaiting her affianced husband. Pregnant already? Glynde? Jan? Monsieur Poiret? Who else? And, more important by far than what she imagined, what did the Prince think? What might he do to the man he thought had cuckolded him? Had they all been on wafer-thin ice, all this time? 'Princess! Isobel!' But the Princess, her secret shared at last, had fallen deeply asleep.

She stayed in bed for several days, quite obviously ill, and her little court was in a buzz of sympathy for the miscarriage proclaimed by her doctor. Scott had grown old and lazy in her service, and gratefully accepted the hint Jenny threw him. 'Poor lady. What a bitter blow to her. No, of course I'll not trouble her with questions.' She thought it a great relief to him. 'Should we inform the Prince, do you think?'

'I wish you would, Doctor. Better from a man.'

'Yes. Yes, of course. Man to man. Naturally it is for me to do . . .' She knew he would find it extraordinarily difficult; would put it off from day to day. No fear of a messenger catching the Prince before he reached Vinsk and the problems that awaited him there.

There was another bull to be taken by the horns. Jenny sent for Olga on the pretext of needing clean linen for the Princess; made sure they were alone. 'You'll let the Brotherhood know about the Princess, Olga?'

'That she has miscarried? They'll hardly be interested in such women's work.'

'I'm not so sure.' She had thought a great deal about the attempt to implicate little Casimir in the practical joke on the Tsar; had never been able to understand the Brotherhood's motive. Was it possible that they too had their doubts about his legitimacy? Or was it that they wanted Poland to turn to France, not Russia for help? She knew herself for a moral coward because she had boggled at asking the Princess if there was any truth in her husband's suspicions. But how could she have? And the subject was now closed between them.

'What's going on downstairs, Jenny?' The Princess had waked looking much better, demanded coffee, and asked Jenny to share it.

'Everyone sympathises deeply with you, Princess, in your sad loss.' The maid who had brought the coffee was pouring it. 'I am charged with so many messages for you that I hardly know where to begin. Dr. Scott has undertaken to break the sad news to the Prince.' A quick exchange of glances told her that the Princess understood just how many glasses of vodka stood between the intention and the act.

'Any other news? Thank you, Gabriela, you may go.'

'Rumours only, but disquieting ones. You know how news travels among the serfs. They seem to think that there has been a battle somewhere in the west; that the Austrians and the Russians have been defeated. Of course, hating their Austrian occupiers as they do, they may be deluding themselves. I believe, though, there has been some trouble in Sandomierz; stones thrown at the Austrian troops; that kind of thing.'

'And reprisals, I suppose?'

'Savage ones. Which makes me think there may be some truth in the rumours.' She had asked Olga to try and find out if the Brotherhood knew anything.

'The Austrians are afraid?'

'I think so.'

'I must get up. Find me something dark, Jenny. I'm in mourning, remember. How odd that a woman isn't really expected to mourn her unborn child.'

'I expect the assumption is that it would have been a girl.' Jenny moved towards the big wardrobe in the next room. 'Not black, I think, granted the real state of the case. What's the matter?' A strangled exclamation from the Princess brought her hurrying back to her bedside.

'Not in there! Never in there! Jenny – What's that?' Someone was tapping at the door of the boudoir.

'Highness!' It was Leon Wysocki, her major-domo. 'There's a stranger at the gate, demands admission.'

'Demands?'

'Yes. Shabby and travel-stained, in a broken-down calash, and demands admission. Insists that he see you. Highness, there is something about the way he talks. I thought at least I had better let you know.'

'Thank you. What do you think, Jenny?'

'Oh, I always believe in saying "yes".'

'Very well.' She pulled her negligee more closely round her. 'Admit him, Leon. Let him cool his heels in one of the small parlours while I get ready to receive him.' And back to Jenny, 'The dark green, don't you think, Jenny?'

'The crimson suits you better. You need colour just now.'

'I need to look ill. I've just miscarried, remember. But very well, the crimson it is. Oh God, Jenny, how would I have managed without you?'

Half an hour later, refusing to bother with jewellery, or any other aids to beauty, she pronounced herself ready. 'Give me your arm, Jenny. I will receive this importunate traveller among my friends.'

She bore the loving questions of her little court with equanimity, but cut them short by announcing that they had a guest to receive. 'Fetch him, Leon.' She turned to Dr. Scott who was clucking round her like an incompetent hen. 'Have you written my sad news to the Prince?'

'Not yet, Highness. It must be delicately done . . .'

'Yes. There is no great hurry. Bad news travels fast enough . . .' She looked towards the little stir in the doorway where a tall figure had appeared, the collar of a shabby greatcoat pulled up around his face.

He swept off the hat that had been pulled down over his brows, revealing unkempt golden curls. 'Princess! I am come to claim asylum in your hospitable house!'

'Sire!' She went down into the deepest of curtseys, her court following her example.

'No, no!' He strode towards her, raised her gracefully. 'I am plain Pan Thaddeus while I travel through Poland, and must be treated as such. But what is this? You have been ill, Princess?'

'A little. Nothing to signify. But you, sire . . .' She corrected herself: 'Sir. You look exhausted. What can I get for you? Vodka? Schnapps? Wine?'

'A cup of tea, dear lady. Just a cup of your delicious tea and a warm bed for the night. I have been travelling night and day since the Corsican upstart outwitted us. You've not heard?' He was quickly aware of the stir of interest in the crowd around them.

'Nothing certain. Rumours only . . . The Austrians are not lavish with information.'

'Specially not now, when the news is all of their shame. My Russians fought like heroes, like demons, but the Austrian Generals were outfoxed by Napoleon. I never thought I would lead my armies for the first time into defeat.'

'You were on the field of battle? You risked your life?'

'Naturally, I did. It was my privilege . . . my duty. Send your people away, Princess. It would ease my heart to tell my sad story to a friend like you. I am only sorry not to have found the Prince here; I had hoped for his wise counsel as well as your loving sympathy.'

'Your Highness is too kind.'

'The kindness is all on your side, beautiful Princess, and I am going to ask for more from you. Never was monarch in sadder plight, in more need of comfort. But my desolate story is for you alone, and besides, your pale cheeks betray you. You would be better in the seclusion of your own rooms; indulge me as an old friend of your husband's, and let me join you there for the cup of tea I long for?'

A request? A command? The Princess exchanged a long, thoughtful look with Jenny and then gave the necessary orders.

'This is better! This is what I need!' He seated her on the chaise longue in her boudoir, motioned the servant to place the tea things beside her and moved a chair closer. 'Send the girl away. You will serve me with your own fair hands?'

'With pleasure.' Her hands were not quite steady on the urn. 'But you were to tell me what happened.'

'Defeat! Disaster! Both Austrians and Prussians have betrayed me. I stand alone against the Corsican tyrant.'

'The English?'

'Will give money, but never their blood. Isobel.' He had drained his tea at one draught, put down the cup and took her hand. 'I need comfort! I have never felt so alone. These last days; a nightmare! I, a fugitive! Driving through Austrian territory; wondering whether my "brother" the Emperor Francis will decide to hand me to the French tyrant. Suspecting friends and foes alike.'

'No need to suspect me, sire.' She used his title on purpose. 'We Poles do not betray our friends.'

'Your Poles fought gallantly at Austerlitz. On the wrong side.' He moved his chair nearer hers. 'I should have listened. To you and to Czartoryski. Would the tide of battle have flowed in another direction, do you think, Isobel, if I had fought it as King of Poland?'

'I am sure it would!' Was she? 'It is not too late, sire. Speak now! Announce it now, and see what will happen! The rumours of Austrian defeat have been rife for days; there has been trouble; disturbances savagely put down. Only place yourself at our head, you will have a new army of loyal Poles.'

'At the moment of defeat? I would rather it was on the tide of victory.' He reached out and took her hand.

'Sire, I sometimes think we Poles are at our best in time of defeat. It unites us, you see.' She tried to withdraw her hand; failed. 'You would gain yourself a whole nation of allies. Ones who will never fail you.'

'You say that? But what of your son? Of Prince Casimir's claim?'

'I would bring him up to be the first and most loyal of your Polish subjects.'

'Would you? I think I would need a guarantee of that, Isobel. A pledge of love. You are pale, beautiful lady, you are sad. And no wonder. You have sacrificed your youth and beauty to an old man for your country's sake. You have done well; you have a fine Prince to prove it. Now, you are entitled to a little happiness. We will comfort each other, you and I. And I will know you, for always, my friend.'

'Your loving servant, sire.'

'My love.' He stood up, pushed aside the tea things, gathered her in his arms. 'I carried you once before, Isobel. Knew it would come to this. Today is our destiny. Tomorrow, I must leave for Petersburg and face the world.'

'What can I say?'

'No need for words.' He bent to kiss her.

Travelling slowly with the defeated army, the three young men did not reach Petersburg till well after Christmas.

'The Tsar seems to have received a hero's welcome.' Glynde and Jan were entertaining Granville.

'That was before the wounded started limping in,' Granville said impatiently. 'Everyone's waiting now for news of the dead. There's none, of course. It's painful to go out into society, be buttonholed by mothers and wives longing for news I can't give. Frankly, I long for my recall.'

'You're so sure it will come?'

'Yes. Pitt's dying; there's bound to be a change of government. New men, new policies . . . I hope you'll stay on, Glynde, and keep me posted.'

'Oh, I think so. There's not much to call me home. If you'll excuse me, gentlemen? I have a visit to make.'

Left alone, the other two exchanged a long, thoughtful glance. 'Mrs. Richards?' asked Granville at last.

'I'm afraid so. It don't mean a thing, you know. I suspect he really goes there for news of the Princess. The other . . . just happened. If you'd ever seen Mary Richards, you'd under-

134

stand. She's pretty as a picture, and not much more to say for herself.'

Granville laughed. 'You make her sound irresistible!'

'Welcome. At last.' The Prince greeted his wife at the great wooden gate of his country house at Vinsk. 'And Miss Peverel.' He took her hand, very completely his urbane self. 'But where is the child? Where is Casimir?'

'He was not well,' lied Casimir's mother. 'A childhood ailment, but it quite unfitted him for the journey. He will be better at home.'

'From now on, this is your home, ma'am. We will send for the child. My people here must get to know their next lord. You are in looks, my dear. I trust I see you better.'

'Quite better, thank you.' She was looking at the ranks of serfs drawn up almost in military order to greet her. 'You keep your state here, I see.'

'I hope you will find things well ordered. There was a sad lack of discipline when I arrived. Well, when the master's away . . .'

Jenny, following as they walked slowly along the lines of serfs towards the palace doorway, could see what they could not: ingratiating smirks replaced instantly by scowls, and here and there the unmistakable mark of the knout, savagely red across a face that tried to smile. Order had been achieved at a price.

'I don't like it here!' Olga came to her room as she was changing for dinner. 'I wish we had brought more of our own people. They treat us like dirt belowstairs. And their lingo! I had a friend in Warsaw from Lithuania, learned a bit of their horrid language from him. I'm glad I did now. I soon showed them they couldn't sneer at us to our faces.'

'Was that what they were doing?' Jenny had been disconcerted to find the Prince's people speaking a language she had never heard before.

'Of course. I learned a thing or two before I let them know I could understand.'

Jenny was surprised and disconcerted to find that the Princess and her small retinue of close servants were lodged in a wing of the rambling wood-built palace far removed from the

Prince's quarters. Conducting his wife there, later that night, the Prince bade her a stately farewell at the entrance to her suite of rooms. 'You will be fatigued; there will be time to talk in the morning.'

'He's got a mistress, tucked away in his own wing, that's why.' Olga had brought Jenny's breakfast. 'A Jewish beauty he bought from her father years ago when she was a mere child. On a promise of marriage, of course. They're strict, the Jews. He's kept her here ever since, poor girl. I do wonder, don't you, what made him insist on the Princess coming here?'

'So they are talking to you downstairs?' Jenny was too much interested in the information to scold Olga for producing it.

'Freely enough now.' Olga laughed and tossed her head. 'Now I've told them we don't like their Prince Almighty any more than they do. The stories they tell of him would make your blood run cold. He hadn't been here for a while, see. The overseer had got lax; more drinking than working went on, and a merry time had by all.'

'What about the Jewish lady?'

'God, they hate her. She's the one told on them; wrote him what was going on. Must have been. He turned up with no notice given one day when they were drinking his vodka in his dining-hall. The overseer's in Siberia now,' Olga told it with relish, 'his family were turned out of the house into the snow. No one knows what happened to them. No one dared take them in. The Jewish woman spoke up for them, I'll say that for her, but he shut her up in that smooth way of his. "Be grateful it's not your children," he said.'

'She has children?'

'Two boys. Both older than Casimir. Wouldn't I just like to see the Princess's face when she meets them.'

'That will do, Olga.'

'So you see your problem, my dear.' The Prince had joined his wife over breakfast in her boudoir. 'I could declare our marriage bigamous tomorrow, if I so wished. It would inconvenience me too, of course; the Tsar would not much like it. Miriam is from Warsaw, by the way. Our sons are proper little Poles. I'm sorry you did not choose to bring Casimir. It would have been good for him to have two older brothers to knock some behaviour into him.'

'You acknowledge them as your sons?'

'Not as my legitimate sons. Not yet . . . And that reminds me, I wish to hear more of that remarkable visit the Tsar paid you on his way back from Austerlitz. You did not choose to mention it in your letters.'

'You have heard? You know?' She was white as ivory.

'Where you are concerned, my dear, you may count on it that I keep myself well informed. Of course I have heard. Of course I know. And no need to look so whey-faced either. As a husband, I should, I suppose, resent it, but, granted that most unfortunate miscarriage, I can only, as a diplomat, admire you for what you did. At least,' he smiled his urbane smile, and suddenly made her think of a death's-head, 'you are logical in your behaviour. An heir for Poland. And what an heir that would have been.' He stood up, looked down at her with a detachment she found frightening. 'As it is, I think we had best decide to make do with Casimir. At least for the time being.' And on that dubious note he left her.

13

Glynde was walking by himself in the summer gardens one bright June morning when he saw the tall figure of the Tsar approaching. Alexander did not enjoy the unpopularity that had grown steadily through the winter and mostly shut himself up in his summer palace, visiting only his mistress and his wife. Glynde expected to be ignored, but this time Alexander paused beside him with a friendly smile, and head inclined as usual to favour his deaf ear. 'All alone, Mr. Rendel? Where is your young American friend?'

'He's hard at work, sire, arranging for what trade he can.'

'And you, Mr. Rendel, what news have you of your friend Lord Leveson Gower? Is he sad that the peace negotiations between your country and France have come to nothing?'

'I've not heard from him yet, sire.'

'Ah, the mails . . . the everlasting mails. How much we blame on them.'

'Yes.' It was too good a chance to miss. 'Mr. Warrington and I have been hoping for news of the Princess Ovinska, but communication with Vilno seems unusually slow.'

'She's at Vinsk with her husband?' A shade of something flickered across the handsome face. 'If I decide to go west this autumn I must most certainly pay them a visit. Perhaps you would care to accompany me, Mr. Rendel? I miss your friend Lord Leveson Gower sadly, though I must not say so. It is restful to be with someone who does not flatter.'

'I should be more than honoured, sire.'

'Miriam?' An unsigned note had summoned the Princess to this assignation at a corner of the long walk, invisible from the house. 'Forgive me,' she went on. 'I do not know your other name.'

'You know what it should be. He told me he had told you.'

Her hand was cold in Isobel's. 'I have been hoping to meet you like this. Where no one can see. No one must know. I can trust you?'

'Surely the boot is on the other foot?'

'I beg your pardon?' They were speaking French, and the English idiom baffled her.

'I'm sorry. I meant, surely it is I who have cause to fear you?'

'No need. But remember, I love him. You don't.' It was not a question.

'No. I liked him at first. Now, he terrifies me.' She was still holding the other woman's hand, staring at her. 'You're very beautiful.'

'So he thought. Once.' Dark eyes met dark eyes.

'The strange thing is . . . You remind me of someone.'

Miriam laughed, harshly. 'Yourself. We're cousins, Isobel. I grew up on your grandfather's estate at Grodno. His granddaughter. If I was not a Jewess, born on the wrong side of the blanket, I would be a Sobieska like you. Prince Ovinski knew that all the time. Before I did. My parents never told me. Only when I married – thought I married –' she corrected herself, blushing crimson. 'My mother was dead, my father away,' she went on painfully. 'I was so much in love. He said – the Prince – that it was our chance. It had to be in secret because I was Jewish. I'm proud to be Jewish.' The black eyes flashed.

'Yes?' Isobel was increasingly aware of the tie of blood between them.

'I didn't know the marriage service. I never did understand what was left out, but it was enough. I've been his chattel ever since. And I still love him. It's not for you I am doing this, Isobel; it is for him.'

'Doing what?' Isobel looked anxiously down the long walk, recently cleared of late snow.

'He's out hunting. No fear of being interrupted. But you're right to be cautious. Come in here.' She pulled her into an alcove with a rustic bench. Too cold to sit; they stood facing each other. 'Have you sent for the little Prince yet?'

'No. I said he wasn't well enough. That it must wait until the roads dry out after the thaw. That I'd send then.'

'Don't. If he comes, I think he will die. An accident. I don't want the Prince to have the child's blood on his hands. Even for the sake of my own children. Is Casimir his son?'

Once again, black eyes met black eyes squarely. Then, 'No one will ever know,' said Isobel.

'And he's not chancing it. I can understand that. It's like him. He doesn't take chances. I think you should go back to Rendomierz, Isobel.'

'He won't let me.'

'I'll try what I can do. A few jealous scenes, perhaps? They sometimes work.'

'You have no cause.'

Miriam smiled. 'I know. I'm sorry for you, Isobel.' She sounded immensely older.

'Your sons? I'd like to see them. How old are they?'

'Six and four. Michael and Jan. If he wants you to see them, you will. You and I must not meet again, unless he wishes it.' For her, Isobel saw, there was only one 'he'. 'We have talked long enough. Goodbye, cousin. May God protect you and your son.'

'And you, too.' They kissed like old friends, parted, walked swiftly away down their different alleys.

The wood-built palace gave only a feeling of privacy, never the fact. It was three days before Isobel managed to be alone with Jenny out on the carriage sweep which had just been cleared of snow by a sullen army of serfs. 'How they hate us.' She took Jenny's arm to walk up and down on the cleared gravel, and wished she had warned Miriam that the serfs blamed her for the Prince's return. But Miriam probably knew.

'Yes. I wish we could go back to Rendomierz.'

'So do I! I'm going to ask the Prince, the next chance I get.' She poured out the story of her meeting with Miriam. 'I knew I was right to be afraid,' she concluded.

'Yes. But what are we going to do?' She thought about it. 'I think we should send a message to the Brotherhood.'

'The Brotherhood?'

'Casimir is part of their hope for the future. A pawn in the game, at least. They will protect him.'

'Unless they prefer Miriam's sons,' said Isobel.

'You know that's impossible.' Jenny had been thinking about this. 'They are half Jewish, Isobel. You know as well as

140

I do how you Poles treat the Jews. Use them, and abuse them. Oh, we're bad enough in England, but it's only social with us. Much worse here. Poor Miriam is deluding herself about this; as she must have about her marriage. The Prince knows better. Don't let him frighten you with that bugbear, because that is all it is. Do you remember how that Jewish landlord cringed, when we stopped at his inn for refreshments on the way here? Think of him, and ask yourself if someone with even a hint of Jewish blood could lay claim to the Polish crown.'

'You're absolutely right,' said Isobel slowly. 'So – there is no threat. No need to apply to the Brotherhood.'

'But Miriam was afraid?'

'Yes.' Reluctantly. 'She was afraid for the Prince, she said, not for me.'

'And she knows him. Loves him. I suspect she simply does not recognise the depth of his plans. One thing I have learned since we came here, and that is that the Prince is not a rich man. He's land-poor, like our Irish aristocrats. I just hope he hasn't got another heiress in mind. There's a very rich Princess of Courland I heard someone speak of. Rich and young.'

'You mean he would kill me, too?'

'You had not thought of that? Who would inherit your estates if you and Casimir should both die?'

'The Prince, of course.' Her face was white as the snow.

This was not a message that could be sent by Olga. 'Tell Them I must talk to someone myself.' Jenny kept her exchanges with Olga to a minimum.

'You don't trust me?'

'Why should I? But I know you have more sense than to disobey Them. So I can trust you to take my message.'

She met the Brotherhood's messenger a few days later in the Greek rotunda above the ornamental water. The weather had turned mild enough so that it was possible to walk in the grounds without causing comment, and the mock Greek temple provided the perfect site for a secret meeting, since it stood on a little hill with a clear view in all directions. Arriving, on Olga's instructions, as early as she could get out of the house, Jenny thought she was the first for a moment. Then a masked

141

figure appeared in the entrance to the temple's little central chamber.

'Sit down on the bench,' he told her, without greeting. 'Keep watch. Don't look at me as we talk. You are alone here, so far as anyone can see. Now, tell me the meaning of your message. Quickly. You cannot stay here long.'

'No.' After one quick glance, which summed him up as in his twenties, dressed for hunting, an undoubted aristocrat behind the mask, she sat obediently on the bench, scanning the park, briefly summing up her fears for Isobel and Casimir. 'I thought you should know,' she concluded.

'You were right. You have served us well, and we will remember it. I will take counsel with my Brothers. You may or may not hear from us, but I promise you, action will be taken. But, first, one question. Is Prince Casimir the Prince's son?'

'I know nothing to suggest he is not.' Stating merely the facts of the case, she had not raised this question, but had been prepared for it.

'Not really an answer,' he said.

'The best I can give.' It was oddly frightening to carry on this conversation with her back to him. But even if she had been facing him, the mask would have prevented her from seeing his expression.

'You do not trust the girl, Olga, or you would not have insisted on this meeting. Do you wish her replaced?'

'No. I have great confidence in her fear of you.'

'Which I hope you share.'

'There's someone coming,' she said. 'It's the Prince!'

'Then go down to meet him. Don't let him come here, if you value both your lives.'

'I do.' She rose, shook out her skirts, bent to pick a sprig of lavender from the neglected formal garden that encircled the little building, and moved forward to intercept the Prince.

A few days later, he joined his wife in the small parlour where Jenny was reading aloud from *La Nouvelle Héloïse*. 'I have a favour to ask of you, my dear.'

'A favour?' She looked up from her embroidery.

'Yes. I have had a disturbing letter from Warsaw. My fool of a steward there seems to have got himself into some kind of difficulty with the Austrian Governor.'

'He's Polish? Your steward?'

'Yes. Got a lot of mad ideas in his head when the Austrians were defeated back in December . . . Been having meetings in my house . . . Now he's in a great panic, poor fool.'

'As well he may be.'

'Yes. And though he is a fool, he is also a cousin of mine, in some sort. But – I am not exactly *persona grata* with the Prussians. My intervention would do nothing but harm. If you were to go? Your friends the Potockis go on well enough under Prussian rule, do they not?'

'They seem to.'

'And would help you with the necessary approaches? I really would be immensely grateful.'

'I would be most happy.' The Princess put down her work and rose. 'And flattered to be asked. I imagine the sooner I leave the better?'

'If you would be so good. I will send to the Governor of Vilno for the necessary papers today. They should be here by the time you have made your preparations. I am afraid you may find my Warsaw house in some disarray.'

'It would be my pleasure to put it in order for you. It's a long time since I have been in Warsaw. With your approval, I would like to spend a little while there.'

'And get back in touch with your old friends? An excellent idea.'

That was a happy summer. They found the Prince's big house in Saxon Square near Warsaw's Royal Palace in a sad state of disrepair, and his steward in daily terror of arrest. But, whatever his reasons, the Prince had been quite right. The Princess had enough old family friends in Warsaw to intercede successfully with General Kalkreuth, the Prussian Commandant. In fact, he had much more serious anxieties to plague him, since his royal master King Frederick William was busy negotiating with Russia and France at the same time. To sign a quittance for one stupid little intriguer, when asked by a beauty like the Princess Ovinska, was simply a matter of course.

By the autumn of 1806 the Princess had her own salon, where she entertained every Thursday, and had sent at last for the little Prince. Both her husband and the Brotherhood had asked her to spend the winter in Warsaw, and she had been happy to agree. She and Jenny had got more or less used by now to the sight of grey Prussian uniforms in the streets, to the sharp North German bark of command, and Jenny was working hard at improving her German.

They celebrated Casimir's arrival from Rendomierz with an unusually elaborate reception early in October, but though the Ovinski house was now well known for its hospitality, this occasion was not a happy one. People stood about in twos and threes, talking in low voices, hushed at the sight of one of the few Prussian officers who had the entrée.

'What is it?' Princess Isobel asked her friend Anna Potocka. 'Something's happened, I can tell.'

'Come to the window. There has been no hard news for days. No papers. That's always how we know there is trouble brewing. They keep us deaf and gagged, our Prussian –' She smiled over Isobel's shoulder. 'Good evening, Herr von Arnim.' And then, when he had kissed their hands in his stiff, Prussian way, and moved off to where the food and drink were being served, 'It was months before we heard of the deaths of our young men when Napoleon sent the Polish Legion to its destruction on Haiti. And there are still families who have had no news of sons who fought at Austerlitz. But this kind of universal silence always bodes worse news still.'

'And I have just brought Casimir here!'

'Oh, never fret about that. I don't suppose any of it will affect us here; everyone has forgotten about Poland. And it will be some time before your little Casimir is old enough to fight.'

'And thank God for that,' said Princess Isobel, telling Jenny about the conversation afterwards. 'Hasn't he grown, though? And talking like a six-year-old.'

'Yes.' Jenny smiled. 'I sometimes wish his command of language was not quite so good. You should have heard what he said to a Prussian soldier he thought uncivil to me in the street. Luckily the man thought it was funny, but . . .'

'Was the man uncivil?'

'Oh, of course. They hardly know they are doing it. He may even have thought he was paying me a compliment, noticing a plain little creature like me. Words don't hurt. But I'm sorry for the Polish girls, who have no protection whatever. Though mind you,' she smiled, 'I've heard them give as good as they get. Only, I'm afraid it's not always just words in their case. Sometimes I wish we were safe at Rendomierz.'

'I wish we'd get some real news. When did you last hear from England, Jenny?'

'Not since we left Vinsk.'

'Which could mean anything.' They both knew the Prince perfectly capable of opening or keeping Jenny's letters.

There was a new message from the Brotherhood the next day. 'They say she is not to think of returning to Rendomierz. I didn't know she was.' Olga was beginning to assume the airs of a confidante. Jenny did not like the way she referred to the Princess and began to wonder how long she would go on feeling her the lesser evil.

'I wish I knew how they learned we had even thought of it.' She had waited to give the Princess the message until they were alone together in the carriage on the way to the Countess Potocka's soirée.

'Yes. We must be more careful. I don't know a great deal about the Prince's father, who built the house, but I suppose he may have installed some kind of spying system. We Poles don't seem to trust each other much.'

'And with cause,' said Jenny. 'I'm losing count of the number of family feuds I hear about! I do sometimes long for Rendomierz, don't you?'

'Yes. But I think we had best stay here, since both the Prince and the Brotherhood wish it. And it's good to meet so many old friends. I really begin to look forward to quite an agreeable winter. Besides, it's good for Casimir to mix with other children of his own class. He was getting a little spoiled at Rendomierz.' She paused as the carriage drew up outside the Potockis' town house, where Anna Potocka and her husband lived with his parents. 'I'm glad I have no in-laws to share with.'

Entering the crowded rooms, they were at once aware of an electricity in the air. 'Something's happened!' Isobel pushed ahead of Jenny up the crowded stairway. 'Pray God it's good.'

The first greetings over, they looked about for information. 'There's Prince Poniatowski,' Isobel said. 'Warsaw's most eligible bachelor; Anna Potocka's cousin. Mine, too, remotely, but he's related to the last King, like her.'

'The Prince Poniatowski, who fought under Kosciusko? But he's a great hero, surely? And living peacefully here?'

'It was the Russians he fought against; not the Prussians. Besides, he's kin to the King of Prussia.' They had been talking English, now switched to French as the Princess greeted Josef Poniatowski as an old friend and introduced Jenny.

He was a striking figure of a man: dark, handsome, upright, though older than Jenny had expected, perhaps as much as forty, with a carriage that cried out for the uniform he could not wear. 'A young English lady?' He bent over her hand. 'You are not afraid to be here?'

'Afraid?'

'Why should she be?' asked Isobel.

'You've not heard, Princess? Had you not noticed that there are no Prussians here today? They are all packing their traps; awaiting the order to leave. Their King suddenly lost patience and demanded that the French move back across the Rhine. An ultimatum to Napoleon! Madness. He's learnt his lesson already, my poor cousin, in two defeats by Napoleon himself. At Jena; and somewhere else. Napoleon's moving east like lightning. God knows where he will stop. We must hope that it is good news for us.'

'Has Napoleon said anything?'

'About Poland? Not yet. There's talk of Kosciusko coming from Paris to lead a new Polish army of liberation. Pamphlets in his name are being scattered in the north. The people are rising like lions, turning on their oppressors. It's a great moment, Princess. Perhaps the dawn of a new day for Poland.'

'You think the French might come here?'

'If they do not, we will liberate ourselves. But nothing seems impossible to Napoleon.' He turned to Jenny. 'That is why I asked if you were not afraid. The Emperor has not been good to such of your countrymen as he has captured.'

'You think I should send her away?' asked the Princess. 'To Rendomierz?'

He thought about it for a moment. 'Best not, I think. Too late! The Russians are on the move too; the Tsar is treaty-bound to his Prussian friends. They've been slow enough about it, so far, under their ailing old General Kamensky, but they were at Vilno when we last heard of them. Probably much nearer by now. I think it safer for Miss Peverel to stay here in Warsaw than to risk falling into their hands. An army on the march!'

'The Russians may come here?' Isobel was white.

'Of course!' Impatiently. 'Poland's always been the debatable ground between east and west. You may see your husband sooner than you expected, Princess. Though, mind you, I think the chances are that the French will get here first. And if they do,' he turned to Jenny, 'you may rely on me for any help you need.'

A few days later, the last of the Prussians marched away and a strange hush fell on Warsaw. A belated letter from the King of Prussia himself begged Prince Josef Poniatowski to take command of the abandoned city. 'He must know I would rather fight the Russians than the French.' Poniatowski had called to reassure Princess Isobel. 'But I doubt if there will be any fighting. Napoleon is carrying all before him. He has taken Berlin and moved on to Poznan. All Prussian Poland is behind him. If only our late masters had left us any arms!' he exclaimed. 'But we're arming ourselves as best we may. We'll give a good account of ourselves if it comes to it. We Poles are always at our best in an emergency.'

A Russian skirmishing party actually entered the undefended city a few days later, but Warsaw had not forgotten the Russian massacre at Praga and the raiding party soon found the place too hot for them, and withdrew. But a note had been thrown on to the step of the Ovinski house. 'It's from my husband,' Isobel said. 'Unsigned. But I'd know the hand anywhere. He says we are to stay and make the best of things. I wonder just what he means by that.'

'I expect he likes the idea of having a foot in both camps,' said Jenny. 'Prince Poniatowski seems certain that the French will be here any day now.'

'He's a good friend.' The Princess smiled at herself in the looking-glass. 'No need to fret, Jenny. He'll see to it that no one in my house comes to harm.'

14

Napoleon's flamboyant brother-in-law, Prince Joachim Murat, led the French troops into Warsaw that late November afternoon of 1806. Hoping to be their King, he had dressed, he thought, like a Polish nobleman. His green velvet cloak was lined with sable; his matching velvet hat sported white ostrich plumes, his leather breeches were impeccably white. Waiting to greet him, Prince Josef Poniatowski was comparatively austere in his old uniform as Lieutenant General of the Polish army.

'What a striking figure!' said the Princess, looking down at Murat. She and Jenny were watching the procession from the balcony of a friend's house.

'Yes, and doesn't he just know it.' Jenny's tone was dry. 'But the people seem to love him. He's getting a hero's welcome. They all are.'

'They are our friends. We will have one billeted on us, and you will be civil to him, Jenny.'

'Yes, Highness.'

All Warsaw turned out to fête the French. Nothing was too good for the conquering army, who were welcomed as liberators. Festive tables were set out for them in the streets; families begged them to come and live in their best rooms; money and provisions that had been hidden from the Prussians appeared as if by magic and were lavished on them; young men flocked to join the Polish army that Josef Poniatowski was raising.

Prince Murat had accepted what he called the hospitality of the Potockis, who had moved out of their own apartments to give him the luxury he expected. 'Who do you think we will get?' The Princess was adjusting her furs, ready to go and call on Anna Potocka. 'You're sure you won't come, Jenny? Anna always says how much she enjoys talking to you. Your fresh English mind, she speaks of.'

'I think today, and for as long as this French occupation lasts, my fresh English mind is best at home. Do ask Madame Potocka if anything has been heard yet about where the patriot Kosciusko stands in all this. It seems so strange that he's not here, or at least known to be coming.'

'Oh, Jenny, for the love of God stop your croaking!' The Princess pulled up her sable hood. 'They say the Emperor Napoleon himself is coming any day now. This is our day of glory; don't spoil it for me.'

Fortunately, she left the room before Jenny could tell her just how she felt about the arrival of the man she still looked on as the Corsican upstart. She sat for a while, most unusually, hands in her lap, doing nothing. Her own position appalled her. How had she let it happen? She was here, in Warsaw, God knew how many miles from home, in the hands of the French, her country's enemies. Outside in the streets, the rejoicings went on noisily as liberated and liberators drank together, but stories of the other side of liberation were beginning to creep in by way of the servants. A scullery maid had been raped by five French soldiers; the groom who tried to come to her aid was in gaol, lucky to get away with his life.

'Yes?' She looked up as Grucz, the Prince's steward, came timidly into the room.

'It's a French gentleman, ma'am. Says he's to live here. Oh Lord, Lord, what would the master say?'

'He would expect us to receive the man. Show him in, Grucz, and stay, please, while I speak to him.' She rose. One should meet one's enemies standing. Had Giles been standing, when he got his death wound? Or, more likely, bending over the guns he loved?

'Good-day.' She looked the young Frenchman up and down, and dismissed him as small, dark and inconspicuous in a uniform so creased and dirty that she was tempted to refuse to receive him. But what was the use? 'You are come to live here, Monsieur –?'

'Genet, Highness. Paul Genet, most absolutely at your service. And most grateful . . .'

'Spare me your speeches, Monsieur Genet. I am not the Princess Ovinska, as the servant should have told you, but I speak for her. She would wish you made welcome. The steward,

Grucz here, will show you to your apartments. Your wishes, of course, are our commands. You have only to make them known.'

'Thank you, mademoiselle. But to whom do I have the pleasure of speaking? You do not speak French as the Poles do.'

'How should I? I am English, monsieur. Your enemy.'

'*Tiens*,' he said. And then, in surprisingly good English, 'I ask your pardon, ma'am, for being, as you think, your enemy. I hope I can persuade you that we do not make war with women, we French.'

'That's what everyone says.' It was a surprising relief to lapse into English. 'There is a scullery maid here in the house would not agree with you.'

'*Tiens*,' he said again. And then, 'You had best tell me about it, Miss –'

'Peverel,' she said bleakly. 'Jenny Peverel. My brother was killed at Aboukir Bay, but you will not know about that either.' And why in the world had she said that?

'My father died at Aboukir, Miss Peverel. It may not make us friends, but it gives us something in common, just the same. Please tell me about the girl who was attacked by our soldiers. Is there anything that can be done for her?'

'Not much for her, poor Klara, she'll do well enough, as long as there is no child, but her fiancé was beaten and arrested for trying to save her.'

'Do you know where he is held? Never mind, give me his name; I'll see what I can do for him. There have been some regrettable incidents, I am afraid. Soldiers are the same all the world over, Miss Peverel.' He crossed the room to the Princess's own writing-table, perched astride the gilt-backed chair, helped himself to pen and paper and wrote rapidly. 'There!' He handed her the paper. 'That should protect you if anyone else should recognise that English voice and look of yours.'

'Thank you.' Her tone was icy as she stood over him to make sure he did not tamper with the Princess's papers.

'I think you should. You perhaps do not know that our Emperor has announced, in his Decrees dated from Berlin, that any Englishman we capture will be treated as a prisoner of war. He probably did not intend it to apply to ladies, but just the same . . .'

'Your Emperor makes war like a barbarian, sir –'

'War is a barbarous business, ma'am. Anyone who pretends otherwise is a fool.'

'Thank you.'

'And I'm a boor?' Still sitting casually astride, he looked up at her, his smile made lop-sided by a missing tooth. 'Sitting in a lady's presence. Disgraceful. But remember, Miss Peverel, that I am a nobody, member of a citizen's army.'

'You said you served an Emperor.'

'*Touché.*' He laughed, and pulled himself to his feet. 'A thousand pardons, Miss Peverel.' His tone was mocking as he changed to French, the language of gallantry.'Forgive my military barbarism, and be so good as to have your man show me to my quarters. Perhaps I may prove more fit for a lady's company when I have had a bath and maybe even some sleep.' He yawned enormously and she was aware of dirt ingrained in fatigue lines creasing the sallow face. 'But, first, your man – what was his name? I'll write you an order for his release. Have I your permission to sit down again?'

'Of course.' She felt a fool. And then, 'But – you're hurt?' She had seen how he favoured his right leg as he sat.

'It's nothing. A scratch I got at Jena. Nothing that sleep won't cure.'

'When did you last?'

'Sleep? Two days ago? Three? There.' He handed her the release. 'He'll be in the town gaol. You'll forgive me if I don't go myself?'

'I'm ashamed . . . I'll send the Princess's doctor to you. He's Scottish, by the way. Dr. Scott.'

'An ally, for certain.' His tone was still faintly mocking as he made her a deep formal bow, staggered just slightly, and turned to follow Grucz to his own quarters on the floor below.

'What's he like, our gallant officer?' The Princess dropped her sables on a chair and moved over to the big stove to warm her hands.

'Not particularly gallant, and a mere Captain.'

'Well, after all, we can hardly offer the luxury the Potockis do. She's welcome to that Prince Murat! A braggart if ever I heard one. He talked of nothing but the taking of Lübeck. The slaughter! How he rode in at the head of his cavalry through streets running with blood. He didn't spare us a drop of it. Oh, Jenny, I'm glad Casimir is no older! Murat seems to look on himself as the future King of Poland, by the way.'

'Oh?'

'Yes. Talked a good deal about "my gallant Poles". And in terms of such patronage! I was hard put to it not to speak up!'

'Is Bonaparte himself truly coming here? It seems extraordinary that I might really see him.'

'You must call him Napoleon, Jenny, or, better still, the Emperor. Yes, he's coming. A group of dignitaries are gone to Poznan to welcome him, and Murat and Josef Poniatowski have their heads together already about a ceremonial reception.'

Since a great many of Warsaw's chief families had chosen to avoid committing themselves to either French or Russians by awaiting the outcome of the campaign on their country estates, the three deputies sent with Warsaw's official greetings to Napoleon were not of the first rank, and all they got from him were friendly words, no promises. And then, while the triumphal arches were still building on his expected way into Warsaw, he disconcerted everyone by riding in at four in the morning on a spavined horse acquired at the last staging post. News of his arrival at the palace spread like wildfire through the town, but he only stayed four days, consolidating his position, reviewing his troops, demanding more and still more supplies for his exhausted army, which had been living off the starving land since leaving Berlin.

'He's gone to the front,' the Princess told Jenny. 'Prince Josef says he'd hoped to let his troops go into winter quarters, rest them a little, but the Russians don't seem to mind the bitter weather. Where are you off to, Jenny?'

'To Madame Walewska's house. She has a working party today, to make lint and bandages. I promised to help.'

'For your enemies, the French?'

'And for the young Poles who have gone with them.'

'You're going out into the cold?' Paul Genet emerged from his apartments on the main floor as she passed them going down the grand stairway.

'Yes.' She was surprised to see him. 'You're not gone with the army?'

'No, to my sorrow. The doctors have put me on light duties for a while. So, let me have the pleasure of escorting you, Miss Peverel. It is not a time for young ladies to be out alone.' He turned to shout for a servant to bring his outdoor clothes, and Jenny noticed how swiftly and deferentially he was served. 'May I ask where you are going?' He pulled on his big fur hat.

'To Madame Walewska's house. It's just round the corner.'

'To join her working party?' He took her arm as they reached the hard-packed snow of the street. 'Madame Walewska's a great beauty, they say, but in quite a different line from the Princess Sobieska. Will you indulge my curiosity by introducing me to her?'

'If you like. She's a great enthusiast for you French.'

'I'm glad to hear it. I suppose she must be about the same age as the Princess. Both married to much older men. Somebody told me that Madame Walewska was pushed into marriage by her family when she was only sixteen. Nearly fainted during the ceremony, poor girl.'

'I can well believe it,' said Jenny. 'I've met Count Walewski!'

'Well then, your report.' The French Minister, Talleyrand, had accompanied Napoleon on his campaign and was now installed in one of Warsaw's finest palaces.

'I entirely agree with you, sir.' Paul Genet finished his wine and put down the Venetian glass. 'It has to be Madame Walewska.'

'Ah. And why?'

'Many reasons. First of all; there is the Princess Ovinska's claim to the throne of Poland. She's Sobieska by birth, as you know. Her marriage with Ovinski was entirely dynastic; the union of two lines with claims to the Polish crown. And they have a son.'

'If he is Ovinski's son,' said Talleyrand.

Genet laughed and threw out a hand. 'I can see that as usual you know more than I do, sir. Yes, there is that question, but, so far, Ovinski has acknowledged the little Prince. I understand that there are great hopes built on the child.'

'A fortunate thing he is no older. What do you think would

153

happen, Genet, if the Emperor were to declare him the future King of Poland, naming, perhaps, Joachim Murat as his regent?'

'I think all Poland – Austrian, Russian and Prussian – would rise in his name. And I think Murat would probably have him murdered. He counts on the crown for himself.'

Talleyrand smiled his subtle smile and poured more wine. 'I do appreciate your gift for going to the heart of a matter, Genet. So – Madame Walewska it is. She'll cooperate, you think?'

'I'm told she hero-worships the Emperor already. She's a much more likely candidate than the Princess, who is one of those devilish proud Poles I can't abide.'

'Which would make it all the more effective if she were to become the Emperor's mistress. But I doubt if her husband would be so complaisant as Walewski. I don't much like the Russian element there.'

'No,' said Genet. 'And, another thing, the Princess is too tall. She'd tower over the Emperor. Madame Walewska's a little thing.'

'Just as high as his heart.'

'Exactly.'

Russians and French fought a bitter winter campaign through mud and snow those last days of December. The Russians claimed the battle of Pultusk as a victory, but they retreated afterwards and Napoleon was able to return to Warsaw in apparent triumph. And now, at last, he announced a formal reception at the castle.

'The Brotherhood want you to go,' Jenny told the Princess.

'I shall please myself, not the Brotherhood. I long to meet this conquering Emperor who carries all before him.'

But she returned from the reception in a very bad temper. 'He looked us over as if we were a lot of cattle at the market, said something about beautiful women, as he might have said promising fatstock, lavished his one smile on the Walewska, and went back to his politics. And what an insignificant figure of a man! I expected some majesty at least. He's a mere dwarf against Murat or Poniatowski. No wonder he likes to spend his time with that crippled Foreign Minister of his, Monsieur Talleyrand.'

'Monsieur Genet speaks highly of Talleyrand. Says he has more brains than all the Marshals put together.'

'At least he has manners,' admitted the Princess. 'Well – he's one of the old French aristocracy, however much of a renegade. You should hear Napoleon; he still speaks with a frightful Corsican accent. And no dignity! He came hurrying into the room as if the devil were after him, and Talleyrand limping as hard as he could to keep up with him. A pitiful exhibition. And to see our Polish dignitaries fawning on him! It made me sick. He's promised us nothing; does nothing but grumble because his soldiers haven't enough supplies . . . You were right about Kosciusko, by the way. I asked Prince Murat when he was coming, and Murat as good as admitted that Kosciusko asked for promises the Emperor wouldn't give.' She smiled at herself in the glass. 'Then he begged me to forget he'd said it. He'd been charmed into indiscretion,' he said. 'Forget I told you, Jenny, please.'

'Yes, of course.' Jenny could not help wondering if the Princess would have liked Napoleon better if he had paid her more attention, committed an indiscretion or two for her sake. But it did not sound likely in the formidable Emperor of the French.

'Napoleon can't hold a candle to the Tsar,' said Isobel now, thoughtfully, as if, perhaps, her train of thought had been running parallel to Jenny's. 'I really begin to wish we were in Petersburg, Jenny.'

It was Carnival in Warsaw and the town saw a gaiety it had not known since it lost its capital status at the Third Partition in 1795. The Princes of Napoleon's recently established Confederation of the Rhine were there to dance attendance on its founder, and more and more Polish aristocrats decided that Napoleon was a more hopeful patron for Poland than the Tsar and came in from their estates to pay him court.

The season opened officially with a ball given by Talleyrand at his luxurious palace on Honey Street in the old town. 'I wish you could come, Jenny.' The Princess clasped the Sobieski emeralds round her throat. 'It's going to be like the good old days, they say. No expense spared. Provisions and even flowers by courier from Dresden; Napoleon's own Concert-Master Kapellmeister Paër from Berlin.'

'And people starving in the streets.' Jenny held out the Princess's fur-lined velvet cloak for her. 'You know I wouldn't come, even if I were asked. You may build hopes in the French, Isobel, though I am not sure if you are wise to. But either way, they are still my enemies.'

'Including Monsieur Genet?' With a roguish look. 'But I won't tease. Tell me I'm in looks, and I must be gone.'

'You're magnificent,' said Jenny with complete truth. The Princess was at her sparkling best: short dark curls glossy with health, the white Empire dress setting off her tall, elegant figure to perfection, the family emeralds her one brilliant note of colour, if you did not count her remarkable eyes. 'You'll be the belle of the ball,' Jenny prophesied, and wondered privately just who the Princess meant to captivate. She had been both relieved and puzzled to receive no message from the Brotherhood about this important occasion, and was allowing herself to hope that perhaps now the French control of Warsaw was absolute, their power had lessened.

But once again, Isobel returned in a bad temper. 'The man can't even dance! You never saw anything so vulgar and clumsy. And laughing all the time, as if it did not matter in the slightest.'

'I suppose if you are master of half the world, it hardly does. But did you dance with him, Isobel?'

'In a manner of speaking. I was chosen for the quadrille. With Anna Potocka, of course, and Elizabeth Sobolewska and the Walewska. And Napoleon roaring with laughter, and talking through the music and holding the Walewska's hand so long he missed the beat.' She laughed. 'He asked Anna Potocka if she thought him a good dancer, and she told him he danced perfectly "for a great man". Murat can dance, mind you. Compared to Napoleon he seems quite a man of the world.'

'He was one of the quadrille?'

'Yes, he and Napoleon's other brother-in-law Camillo Borghese, and that oaf Marshal Berthier. Elegant company for a Princess of Poland!'

Two nights later, Napoleon himself gave a dinner and concert at the castle. 'I shall stay at home,' announced the Princess. 'I won't go on lending countenance to his vulgar merrymaking.'

'Everyone else is going,' said Jenny.

'We Sobieskis lead, we do not follow. If my ancestor, Jan Sobieski, had waited for a leader before he saved Vienna . . .'

'That was a long time ago,' said Jenny. 'Is it true that Napoleon is bombarding Marie Walewska with messages and gifts, and she is holding him at arms' length? She was certainly looking very pale at the working party this morning. Poor child, she seems so young.'

'And inexperienced. I tell you, Jenny, if she yields to Napoleon, she will become his devoted slave, quite forget the interests of Poland!'

'I see.' Jenny saw a great deal. 'But I do wonder if you are right. Marie could be a powerful advocate, I think, just because she is so gentle and good. The Empress Josephine is gentle, they say.'

'But not good! And if Marie Walewska thinks Napoleon is going to get the divorce that has been talked about for her sake, she's out of her mind. Emperors don't divorce for charming little bourgeoises.'

'She's hardly that.' But she knew the protest wasted. Princess Isobel was not reasonable where Marie Walewska was concerned. Had she really planned to captivate the French Emperor herself?

Not all Jenny's persuasions, not even a message from the Brotherhood could persuade the Princess to go to Napoleon's dinner. Jenny was reading aloud to Prince Casimir, while his mother sat gazing sombrely into her glass, when the front doorbell jangled imperiously two floors below.

'What in the world?' The Princess dropped her glass and they sat silent, listening to booted footsteps on the grand stair.

'Princess!' The door had swung open to reveal Prince Murat, more resplendent than ever in evening-dress. 'I am come on the Emperor's orders to take you to the castle.' He reached down a confident hand to raise her to her feet. 'Your fine young Princeling will entertain me while you change your dress.'

157

'No I won't!' Something about his tone to the Princess had enraged Casimir. 'And I'm not a Princeling either, I'm a Prince of Poland.' For a moment, Jenny was actually afraid he would fly at the handsome Marshal.

But Murat only laughed. 'A fierce young Polish eagle, Princess. You'd best make haste with your dressing, for fear he tries out his talons on me. The Emperor awaits you.'

15

They were taking bets in the salons of Warsaw as to how long Marie Walewska would hold out. 'It's disgusting,' Jenny told the Princess. 'They were even discussing it in whispers at the working party today. She looks hag-ridden, poor girl.'

'The Emperor won't like that.'

'The amazing thing is it doesn't make her any less beautiful. Perhaps, actually, more interesting. She's one of those lucky blondes who can even cry without looking plain. She really has the most extraordinary eyes.' And then, aware of the Princess's fulminating silence. 'You should see her husband! Strutting about as if he'd won some great prize. It's disgusting,' she said again. 'And people calling on her who never thought of doing so before. Men mostly, but some women too. I don't much like high society.'

'Why should you? Or understand it? Even the Walewska's husband and her brother Benedict Lacynski feel she should yield to Napoleon for Poland's sake. What they don't see is that their tool is made of putty. She'll be clay in his hands once she's yielded to him. Forget all about Poland.'

'Not Marie!'

There was a message from the Brotherhood next day. 'They say she is not to think of going,' Olga told Jenny.

'Going where?'

'You didn't know?' Olga was delighted at this evidence of a gradual alienation from the Princess, of which Jenny herself had only been half aware. 'She got a message to her husband, God knows how, saying she wanted to join him in Petersburg. This is the answer.'

'His answer, or theirs?'

'Who knows?' Olga shrugged. 'It's the answer.'

'Did I forget to tell you?' Isobel was casual. 'Monsieur

Talleyrand very kindly said he'd see that a personal message got through to the Prince.'

'Even though France and Russia are at war?'

'You English have such absurdly absolute ideas! For you, on your island, war is war, peace, peace. Here in Europe, it's not like that. Things change ... Relationships change ... Napoleon longs to be friends with his brother Emperor, the Tsar of Russia.'

'That's what Talleyrand says?'

'Yes. When I told him I had actually entertained the Tsar, he was most interested.'

'As well he might be. So – we stay?'

'Of course. My husband is no fool. He and Talleyrand are old friends. Ovinski was in Paris in 1789, when Talleyrand was representing his diocese at the States General. He was still Bishop of Autun then. Lord – what a long time ago! They had the same interests, Talleyrand says, talked the same language.'

'French,' said Jenny.

'Naturally. The language of politics, of Europe . . . I've been stupid. I see it now. I thought my husband asked me to come here because of that message you insisted on sending to the Brotherhood. When you got in such a panic about the Jewess, Miriam. It's not that at all. He thought one of us should be watching Polish interests *vis à vis* France, while the other took the Russian side.'

'And Miriam and her sons?'

'A nothing, a nonsense! One look at the grovelling Jews here in Warsaw showed me what a fool I was to let you frighten me into giving them a second thought. Lucky for them, or I might be compelled to take some kind of action.'

'Isobel!' But a serf was scratching at the door to announce Prince Murat, a frequent caller these days.

'Prince Ovinski is back in Petersburg, did you know?' Jan stamped snow off his padded boots.

'No? Is he? Have you spoken to him?' Glynde folded up his closely written letter to Granville Leveson Gower. 'And the Princess?'

'She's in Warsaw.'

'Good God! In the hands of the French? And Miss Peverel?'

'There too, I suppose. No need to look so anxious. The French aren't barbarians. She'll come to no harm.'

'No harm! Like Pichegru, and d'Enghien and Captain Wright? Not to mention Marie Antoinette and Madame de Lamballe and God knows how many other unfortunate women.' He changed the subject. 'What news of the Richards?'

'He's up to his neck in work, arranging for shipments of arms from England for the Russian troops.'

'It's an ill wind! We'll hear less then, of his grumbling about war being death to trade. And Mrs. Richards?'

'Says he's neglecting her. That we all are.' Glynde was fascinated to see that he was blushing. 'Now that she's ...' he hesitated, 'in an interesting condition.'

'Oh, pregnant, is she?' Glynde was doing rapid sums, hoping he was not responsible. It had been such a brief madness, that. 'How far gone?'

'As if I'd have asked! She is taking it hard, says she longs for Miss Peverel.'

'For Jenny?' How odd to have used her Christian name. 'Oh, of course, I'd forgotten. She saw her through the last time. Well, she'll long in vain, with Miss Peverel in the enemy camp.'

'Unless the Princess manages to rejoin her husband.'

'But that's impossible, surely?'

'Not at all. Not if she wished it, and he allowed it. Because you live in such a small country with such close connections, you British forget how different things are in a large one. It's partly why we beat you, I think.'

'Back to your famous War of Independence?' Glynde laughed and rose to his feet. 'Don't forget we were fighting the French then, too. I must go and pay my respects to Prince Ovinski.'

All Warsaw knew that Napoleon's Master of the Household, Marshal Duroc, fetched Marie Walewska to the castle night after night in a closed carriage and the deepest secrecy, and for a while the Emperor's daytime scowls told Warsaw of her continued resistance. When his public bad temper dissolved into smiles, Warsaw drew its own conclusions.

'I wonder if she gave in gracefully, or if he forced her,' said the Princess. 'It's a miracle she held out so long, with both her husband and her brother urging her on, and all this fine talk of a sacrifice for Poland. I expect she led him on to rape her in the end, and enjoyed every minute of it.'

'Oh, poor Marie,' said Jenny.

'Nonsense! She's going to be very rich, Marie, if she plays her cards right, even if she has no chance of being Empress of the French. And if it lasts. He's off to the front now. Absence doesn't always make the heart grow fonder. We'll miss our soldiers. Even your faithful Genet goes this time. Genet and Jenny, how droll. It means a mule, I believe.'

'No, a Spanish horse. And he's not my Genet, Princess, as you well know.'

'How formal we are all of a sudden! Yes, you do seem to have played the English miss to perfection. I congratulate you!' Her own affair with Prince Murat had been as flamboyant as the man himself, and Jenny could only wonder if she knew that he had first made a very direct approach indeed to Anna Potocka and been as directly repulsed. But then, Anna was six months pregnant, and closely pursued by young Flahaut.

What would Prince Ovinski think of his wife's affair with Murat? Jenny thought, sadly, that it was very likely on his advice. Sometimes, these days, she longed for the quiet of an English country vicarage, the ordered life, the regulated, respectable days. And then, smiling to herself, remembered Petworth House and its troop of illegitimate little Wyndhams. It was class, not country, that seemed to make the difference to one's moral code.

'What's so entertaining?' The Princess's tone was sharp; she scented criticism easily these days.

'I was thinking that Monsieur Genet never suggested I behave like anything but an English miss. Should I be affronted, do you think?' But it was surprising how much she missed those brief, chance encounters with Paul Genet on the grand stairway. Or had they been entirely chance? This was not a thought to share with the Princess. But then, she shared so few these days. Her main concern was to protect Casimir from any hint of what was going on between his mother and Murat. It was not easy and, inevitably, it meant increasing the distance between her and the Princess.

News of the bloody, indecisive battle of Eylau reached Warsaw in mid-February. As at Pultusk, both sides claimed victory, but again it was the Russians who retreated north again and east towards Königsberg. And in Warsaw, Polish families, waiting at full stretch for news of sons and brothers who had joined Napoleon's conquering army, were not cheered by his bulletin about the battle: 'Such a sight as this should inspire rulers with love of peace and hatred of war.'

Paul Genet had brought the news of Eylau to Warsaw. After delivering Napoleon's loving letter to Marie Walewska, he went on to Honey Street, and was ushered at once into Talleyrand's study.

'It's bad news, I gather?' Talleyrand's greeting was informal, direct.

'Technically, a victory. A few more like it, and there will be no French army. The survivors are cold, hungry, out of temper. The Emperor wants everything. Bread, blankets, brandy . . .'

'From here, of course?' Talleyrand was swiftly reading Napoleon's letter.

'Yes. He's not pleased with his "loyal Poles".'

'Thinks they should have done more, does he? Well, he should have promised them more. Give them a cause, a King, they'll fight like lions.'

'I think so, too. But, sir . . .'

'Yes?'

'Forgive me . . . I think we made a mistake.'

'We've made many. Which one? Don't be afraid; out with it, man.'

'Madame Walewska . . . It should have been the Princess. She'd not have fallen in love and forgotten her country.'

Talleyrand laughed and poured wine for them both. 'I expect you're right. Your health! But you know as well as I do that he'd never have looked at her. Your Princess.'

'Not mine, thank God.'

'Like that, is it? Pity. I was hoping to persuade you to be a little in love with her.'

'I beg your pardon?'

'She's beautiful enough; you've lived in her house; it would be a great convenience to me . . . Genet!'

'Sir?'

'You've served me a long time.'

'You made me what I am. I was nothing, starving in the streets of Bayonne, when you found me.'

'So . . . Tell me, is it me you serve, or Napoleon, or France?'

Paul Genet thought for a moment, then: 'France, I think. You taught me to.'

'Good. So do I. Tell me, does Napoleon?'

Once again, Genet paused to think. 'He did, sir.'

'Yes. He's changed. He should have made peace with England, when Fox proposed it last year. For France, he should have done that. But, for Napoleon, it's different now. Do you think he would have dealt so savagely with the Prussians – a great mistake, in my opinion – if he had not found those papers of the King's and Queen's, when he reached Berlin last autumn? Papers that affronted him personally? Napoleon, not France?'

'I don't know, sir.'

'I do. He's beginning to think as Napoleon, not as France. And turning his enemies into those of France. He's not had the training to think like a monarch. Well, how should he have?' He drained his glass. 'I've just put my neck in your noose, Genet.'

'It's safe there.'

'I thought so.' He got up to warm his hands for a moment at the huge stove in the corner of the room. 'A pity you can't find it in you to love the Princess. But there's a young Englishwoman in her train, a Miss Peverel, a serious young woman, I understand. You'll be staying there this time again?'

'I had thought so. But . . .'

'One moment. You're going to say something rash, like the Gascon I thought I'd trained out of you. Pray don't. It would disappoint me. From everything I have learned, and, as you know, I learn a great deal, Miss Peverel is as good an Englishwoman as you and I are French. I believe you have used my influence to protect her from the possible results of her – shall we call it British obstinacy.'

'You know that, sir?'

'My dear Paul – may I call you Paul? – do pray remember that you are by no means my only confidential agent. I have not parted company with the omniscient Monsieur Fouché –

yet. Reports he receives are passed on to me. Of course. He often takes my advice. You should, perhaps, be grateful, but I am very far from expecting you to be.' He laughed. 'Precisely. Pour us some more wine, would you? An admirably steady hand.'

'Thank you, sir.'

'And so, come to that, should Miss Peverel. Be grateful. She is not, quiet creature though she seems to be, without enemies, here in Warsaw. So – you will go there; you will reopen your pleasant acquaintance with her –'

'And?'

'You will be a little indiscreet. You will let slip a casual remark about Napoleon's disgust with his Poles. In the Princess's hearing, if possible, but I don't ask miracles. I think we can count on Miss Peverel's passing it on. And, one other small indiscretion? A word about how Prince Murat's career depends on his wife's influence with her brother? He's not written her, by the way.'

'His wife?'

'Don't pretend to be stupid. No, the Princess. I think she will have recognised that affair, by now, as the mistake it was. And be worrying about consequences? Maybe a delicate reminder that Rendomierz remains neutral territory, so long as Austria stays on the sidelines in this war.'

'You want them to go back there?'

'Yes. And I want you to correspond with Miss Peverel. You'll be relieved to hear that I don't even insist on her answering, so long as she consents to receive your letters. News from Warsaw? Or from the front? She'll be superhuman if she refuses. Don't let her, Genet. Don't let her.'

It was good to be back at Rendomierz. Life in Warsaw had been gloomy after Eylau, with society missing its young men, and hunger obvious in the streets, as Napoleon demanded more and more supplies for his troops. And Jenny had another reason to be glad when the Princess suddenly announced that they were leaving. Something had changed, disconcertingly, in her friendship with Paul Genet. Impossible to tell just what, but something was missing from their old easy exchange.

It had been all the more surprising when he had suddenly

asked, the day before they left, if he might write to her. She thought that she would have said no, but he had chosen to do it in the Princess's presence, and Isobel had answered for her. 'News from the front. Yes, do, Monsieur Genet. Keep us in touch.' It would have been making too much of it to do anything then but acquiesce, and she had let it go in silence, and, afterwards, been a little glad that the matter had been taken out of her hands. She would decide whether to answer him when she had had his first letter, but she thought she would not.

Rendomierz was *en fête* to receive them. Monsieur Poiret had written a 'Welcome Home' cantata for the Princess and trained a group of servants to sing it to her. She listened with the good manners she always displayed in public, thanked him graciously, then announced that she was worn out from the journey and would go early to bed. 'You must be tired, too,' she turned to Jenny. 'Goodnight. Sleep well.'

It felt like a slap in the face. Jenny always went to her room with her to discuss the events of the day and their plans for tomorrow. Now, suddenly, without reason given, she was excluded, useless again. She had never felt so alone. She was ashamed to be glad when Olga came to tell her that Casimir was overexcited from the journey and no one could get him to settle for the night. 'He needs a beating – or a father, that child,' said Olga.

Jenny could not help but agree. Since the disconcerting day when Casimir had flown out at Murat, his mother had tended to keep him at arms' length. More and more, he was being brought up in his own rooms by his own group of servants, and Jenny, trying to make up to him for this, had not found it easy, since the Princess was apt to look on attention to him as neglect of herself. But tonight, the Princess had withdrawn, and Jenny was free to sit with Casimir till he fell asleep, telling him the fairy tales he loved: of the Sleeping Beauty and her Prince; of the dragon that lived under the hill in Cracow; or the one she had learned from Olga of Ivan the Tsarevich, who plucked a feather from the firebird's tail and so gained his heart's desire.

'What's that?' Casimir was sounding sleepy at last.

'The thing you want most.'

'I want to be a Prince, and kill a dragon!'

'Well, you never know.' Jenny eased him down on to his pillow.

The Princess stayed shut up in her rooms, seeing no one but her maid for nearly a week, and life seemed suspended at Rendomierz. On the sixth day, Olga appeared in Jenny's room on one of her usual well-worn pretexts.

'Well, thank God that's over.' She was replacing used towels with clean ones.

'What's over?'

'The Princess's little problem. She didn't tell you? I did wonder. Sent for the wise woman from the village, the night we got here. Surprising it took so long really; old Teresa can usually bring them away in a day. Must have been a tough little thing. Pity really. Casimir could do with a brother.' She moved towards the door, dirty towels over her arm. 'The question is, do we tell the Brotherhood? They won't be pleased. I suppose that's why the Princess kept it from you. Stupid woman; she should know the whole palace is bound to hear.'

'But –' Jenny could not believe her ears. 'Sent for the wise woman, you say? But, how, Olga? No one's been allowed in to see her.'

'You've been here as long as I have, and don't even know that?' Olga became almost friendly on learning how much better she was informed. 'Marta told me. There's a tunnel, built by the Princess's father, leads from one of the guest-cottages to a stair that comes out in that big closet of the Princess's. Very useful.'

'You mean –' But Jenny did not want it spelled out any more. Princess Isobel had found she was carrying Murat's child. Had she at first hoped for a miracle? Murat as King of Poland, and the child acclaimed? And then, what fate for Casimir? Lucky for him that Murat had never said goodbye before he left, never written, made it crystal clear that the affair had been just an affair. 'So,' she said now. 'The Brotherhood? If the whole palace knows, I think we'd best tell them, Olga. You've not heard from them since we came here?' The Princess had announced her departure so suddenly that there had been time only to inform the Brotherhood, not consult them. Jenny understood the Princess's reason now.

167

'No. They'll be angry – angrier still now.' Olga looked frightened and Jenny knew how she felt.

The Princess sent for her next day; nothing was said; the episode was over. But Jenny knew that, for herself, nothing would ever be quite the same. And she grew increasingly anxious as days passed with no word from the Brotherhood.

Early in March a messenger struggled through a blizzard to Rendomierz with the news that the wolves were out and a child missing from the village. He brought the first letters from Warsaw, one from Anna Potocka for the Princess and one from Paul Genet, whose servant he was. Jenny found it oddly disappointing. It seemed hardly worth writing if he was going to say so little.

'Good God! She's out of her mind!' The Princess looked up from her own letter.

'Madame Potocka? Not the baby –'

'No, no. No trouble there, except that it's a girl. It's that fool, Marie Walewska. Imagine! She's gone off to headquarters, bold as brass, to be with Napoleon! Might as well put an announcement in the *Warsaw Gazette!*'

'It must mean public disgrace. Oh, poor Marie!'

'You'd certainly think so. Mind you, it's a deep secret, Anna says, just like those visits of hers to the palace, when he was in Warsaw. Her brother Benedict came for her. A closed coach . . . every luxury . . . they were actually leaving the day Anna wrote. Well, she's very brave, or quite mad. Her husband is bound to cast her off now, and she'll never see that son of hers again.'

'She must be enormously in love.' Jenny could not help feeling a pang of envy. 'Just imagine throwing everything away for a man who could never marry her. The world well lost for love indeed.'

'Or crazy. What does your Monsieur Genet say?'

'Very little. He just wrote to say he was leaving for headquarters at Osterode.'

'Doubtless travelling with the Walewska and her brother,' said the Princess.

'He doesn't say so.'

'Discreet of him. Yes, Leon, what is it?' Her tone held a

mixture of surprise and affront as her chamberlain irrupted into the room, without leave asked or given.

'Highness, the Prince! He's not with you?'

'Why should he be?'

'He's disappeared, Highness. We can't find him anywhere. He was playing hide and seek with Lech, his servant. All over the palace. Lech's in despair. Not his fault, Highness. He'd been confined indoors so long, the little Prince. They were just playing . . . The Prince hid. We can't find him. He's nowhere.'

'Nonsense,' said the Princess. 'He can't have got out of the palace.' They all looked at the windows, lashed by snow. Did they all, like Jenny, think of the little village boy; the wolves?

'Of course he can't. There are men at all the doors. But, where is he, Highness?'

'Where were they playing?'

'Everywhere. No harm, surely? They'd been in the dining-hall, then, Lech says, he ran upstairs, to your apartments, Highness. When Lech went to look for him, he wasn't there. Not anywhere.'

'We'll search again.' The Princess was very white. She must, like Jenny, be thinking of the secret passage that emerged into the closet in her dressing-room. 'Call out all the servants!'

This time, the search was organised, careful, thorough and totally unproductive. Jenny, returning hopelessly for the third time to the main hall from which they all started out, was accosted in French by a man she had never seen before, and realised that he must be Genet's messenger.

'Mademoiselle Peverel?'

'Yes.'

'It's true, the little Prince is missing?'

'Yes.'

'I am so sorry. He is quite small, yes?'

'Four years old.' She would be crying in a moment.

'The poor little one. But, mademoiselle, this palace is well guarded. He cannot have got out of it by accident. Do not be thinking of a little boy running into the forest, eaten by wolves. It cannot be like that at all. This is not a village child, mademoiselle.'

'No. You're right. We should be thinking, not just rushing about.'

'I think so, mademoiselle. And, may I stay? I think my master would wish it. You may be needing a messenger. For Warsaw? For Petersburg? Who knows?'

'You would go?'

'If you would trust me. My master told me that I was your servant, if you needed me.'

'But your errand to Cracow?'

'Oh, that!' He snapped his fingers.

16

'It's an odd kind of victory that calls for such heavy reinforcements,' said Jan as he and Glynde returned from watching the Imperial Guard march through Petersburg on the way to reinforce the Russian army after the battle of Eylau. 'They've been marching past for three days!'

'Yes, I'm afraid it must mean great losses.' Glynde was opening a letter. 'From Granville at last! He thinks the Ministry of All the Talents is done for and the Tories bound to be back in office soon. Then we will see some action.'

'And Granville back as Ambassador? I must leave you, Glynde. I promised I'd look in on the Richards.'

Left alone, Glynde reread his letter carefully, then looked up, surprised, as a frightened servant announced a messenger from Arakcheyev, the Tsar's formidable right-hand man.

'You're to come to the palace,' said the man. 'At once.'

'So late?'

'At once.'

'One moment.' If only Jan were at home. He bent to scribble a quick note to him: 'I've been summoned to the palace. By Arakcheyev. If I do not return, let the Ambassador know.'

'Come,' said the man.

Glynde rang for his valet. 'I've been summoned to the palace. Give this to Mr. Warrington when he returns.' Had he been afraid the messenger might destroy the note?

'Yes, sir. The palace, you said?'

'Yes. Arakcheyev.' He thought the man changed colour. But there was no more time. He followed the messenger out to the closed sledge that awaited them.

He was ashamed to be afraid as he prowled the little receiving room that looked out over the ice-bound Neva. At last the door opened and the Tsar himself appeared, still in the uniform in which he had reviewed his Preobrazhensky Guard. 'Forgive me for keeping you so long! No, no!' He forestalled Glynde's bow. 'No ceremony! This is an informal meeting between old friends and travelling companions. It is hardly the weather for chance encounters on the quay, and you are not much of a courtier, Mr. Rendel. So – the mountain has sent for Mahomet. Tell me, what news have you from Lord Leveson Gower? I miss his honest advice. Can we really hope, do you think, for a change of government in England, and his return?'

'It's possible. I think he might well wish to come . . .'

'Unfinished business? Well, let's hope he does, for whatever reason. In the meantime, are you in a mood to travel, Mr. Rendel?'

'To travel, sire?'

'Yes. I leave, after the anniversary celebrations next week, for Memel, to confer with my friends the King and Queen of Prussia. Can I prevail on you and your American friend to come with me? I mean to travel fast, I warn you. Too fast for the court, which will follow at leisure, if we reach agreement and I decide to stay.'

He's slipping the leash, Glynde thought. 'I should be more than honoured to accompany Your Majesty,' he said. 'But I cannot answer for my friend Warrington, whose affairs may detain him here in Petersburg, though I doubt it.'

'So do I.' Human for once, the Tsar was immensely likeable.

'It's too good to be true,' said Jan. 'He's leaving them all behind and taking us? What it is to be an absolute monarch.'

'You'll leave your affairs, and come?'

'I should just about think I will!'

Since the service that celebrated Alexander's accession and six years of rule inevitably also commemorated his father's murder, it was not an occasion for unqualified rejoicing, but in the circumstances, the two young men thought it best to attend. They met Prince Ovinski outside the church. Glynde thought for a moment that he was going to avoid them, then he changed his mind, pushed his way through the crowd and greeted them civilly enough.

'I hope you have good news of the Princess and your son?' asked Glynde.

'She is back at Rendomierz. She found the air of Warsaw stifling, she says. I begin to hope that if, as I rather expect, the Imperial Court moves west, come spring, it may be possible to arrange a family reunion. I long to see my son, who is everything that is promising, according to his mother.' Was there the faintest hint of irony in his tone? Impossible to tell. 'And you, gentlemen, will you follow the court, if it moves? I think we can expect a great confrontation this summer. An occasion not to be missed.'

'I wonder just what he meant,' said Jan afterwards. 'I must say, I admired the way you dodged the question, Glynde. You're wasted outside the diplomatic service.'

The Tsar was as good as his word. His small cortège covered the three hundred and twenty miles to Riga in a mere forty-eight hours. Two days later, they were in Memel, where Frederick William of Prussia and his Queen Louise were reduced to holding court, since Napoleon's armies had captured Berlin and were threatening Königsberg.

They did not stay long at Memel. Sight of Queen Louise, her health destroyed and her beauty tarnished by misfortune, seemed to clear the Tsar's mind, at least for the time being, of its habitual vacillation. Prussia and Russia signed a new convention at Bartenstein, and all the talk was of battle, of victory.

Emperor and King celebrated Easter together at Bartenstein as the armies massed for the great confrontation. The roads were drying rapidly, but still no word had come from the new English government. 'It's enough to make one want to join the Russian army,' Glynde exclaimed to Adam Czartoryski, who had joined the Tsar's court from his estate at Vilno, where he was occupying his new leisure in reorganising the University.

'Don't do that. I think you would live to regret it. But I agree, it is the greatest pity that your country is not more adequately represented here. And that they have not shown themselves more forward in providing help in this war.'

'If only the change of government had happened sooner! It couldn't have come at a worse time. But tell me, have you had recent news from Warsaw?'

'All of it bad. And not very recent either. Napoleon's bleeding them white for this new campaign, and giving them nothing but promises in return. From what I hear, this is beginning to be noticed, dissension is breaking out. Between Poniatowski and Dombrowski, for instance.'

'And Kosciusko?'

'Sits in Paris and asks for guarantees from Napoleon, like a sensible man. It's horrible to think that when it comes to a battle, there will be Poles serving on both sides.'

'Is it true that the Prussians have conscripted the minor Polish nobles in their territory?'

'The *schlachta*? Yes. It's always the small men who get hurt. Mind you, there is something a little comic about a nobleman who wears his sword while he ploughs his one-acre field. But there's nothing comic about the Bartenstein convention from Poland's point of view. It's the end of my hope for an independent kingdom.'

'I'm surprised you're here,' said Jan.

'I am still the Tsar's old friend. When he wants me, I shall always be there. I think he is going to need all his friends.'

Every chest in the palace had been opened; every closet explored, and still there was no sign of the little Prince. 'It's no use,' the Princess said at last. 'We have to face it: he's been taken.' She had sent for Jenny to her own rooms, from which Prince Casimir had vanished.

'The Brotherhood?'

'I really believe I hope so. You don't ask how.'

'No. Olga told me about the secret passage.'

'Olga knows?'

'Marta told her.'

'So we have to assume that the Brotherhood know.'

'If Olga did? You're right. I had not thought of that. So it is almost certainly they. Surely they'll never hurt him?'

'No, but they'll use him.' The Princess was crying slow, angry tears, something Jenny had never seen before. 'Send for Lech. He must be punished. I'll make him sorry he was born to betray my trust like this.'

'But . . .'

'His instructions were not to let the Prince out of his sight,' said the Princess implacably. 'He'll never disobey me again. I doubt he'll live to. Not after the beating he's going to get.'

174

'But, Isobel. They were playing . . . Safe in the palace, as he thought . . .' Jenny had seen the savage side of the Princess a few times before, and done her best to forget it. 'Casimir loves Lech,' she said now. 'He'll mind.'

'He would, perhaps, if he were here. He's not. Disobedience must be punished, wherever it appears.' Was it a threat? Jenny rather thought so.

In this bitter weather, punishment was administered in the main hall of the palace. Lech, weeping but unsurprised, had bared his back for the knout. Jenny, compelled by the Princess to watch with her from the head of the great stair, winced, closed her eyes as the first savage blow fell, but could not close her ears. Not a sound from Lech, but a shudder of horror among the servants massed in the hall. Lech was much loved.

Another blow; another. Lech let out a kind of animal grunt. I cannot let this happen, Jenny thought. I have to do something. She opened her eyes. Blood streaming down Lech's back . . . the knout rose for the next stroke. She caught the Princess's arm. She had not meant to. 'Highness, no!' She had not meant to speak either, and most certainly not so loud.

The executioner paused in his stroke, looking up in surprised question at Jenny, at the Princess, and Jenny, even in this moment of crisis, found time to be amazed that he had done so.

'Do your office,' said the Princess coldly. 'And you,' to Jenny, 'be quiet if you do not wish to join Lech.'

Jenny opened her mouth, but no sound came. The executioner's arm went up again. The hall was in silence, suspended. And the front door burst open, knocking down the people in front of it, letting in a blast of cold air and a man in the black robes of a monk, his cowl pulled over his face. 'Stop!' He threw back the cowl, revealing a black mask. 'Prince Casimir is asking for the man.' He looked up to address the Princess. 'And for a woman. Olga. If you want the Prince back, you will send them to him.'

'Seize him!' It was almost a shriek from the Princess.

'I do not advise it.' Nobody had stirred. 'Touch me, and you lose your chance of getting your son back. He is only a pawn still, Princess. Expendable. There will always be other pawns. He is on his way to Warsaw already. If you want him, you will go there, too, and await instructions.' He turned to the serf with the knout. 'Untie him.' And then, to the silent group of women at the back of the hall. 'Which one of you is Olga?'

'Here.' She stepped forward, with a terrified glance at the white-faced figure of her mistress, frozen at the head of the stairs.

'Give him your arm. He's faint.' As Olga helped Lech to stagger towards the door, the messenger raised his head to meet the Princess's blazing eyes. 'We look after our own, Highness. Never forget that. You will hear from us when you reach Warsaw.'

Nobody moved. The front door closed behind the three of them.

'We leave for Warsaw tomorrow,' the Princess said at last, quite quietly, and Jenny breathed a sigh of relief. 'Make the arrangements, Leon. And you, all of you. Get out of my sight!'

Madame Poiret tried to take Jenny's arm. 'Come along, dear, and don't worry. She's best alone for the moment, poor lady. She'll be better in the morning; forget it all when she gets the little Prince back. Please God!'

'Yes. I'm so glad he's got Lech and Olga. I'm sure they won't hurt him.' But what did Madame Poiret know about the Brotherhood?

'But they might keep him. His captors. If she doesn't do as they bid. Bring him up as one of themselves. Try and convince her, when she sends for you, that she must swallow her pride and do everything they say.'

'It will be hard for her. And –' Jenny faced it '– I'm not sure she'll send for me.'

'She's bound to blame you. Because of Olga. Because she's angry. Because she's never been crossed before. You must bear it, my dear.'

'Yes,' Jenny said bleakly. 'I must, mustn't I?' She kissed Madame Poiret impulsively. 'Thank you, madame. Now, I think I had better go and look to my packing, in case she wants me to go with her.'

'Oh, she'll want you all right. If only to quarrel with. Be prepared for a hard journey, my dear. I shall pray for you.'

'Thank you.' Alone in her room, Jenny tried to pack, tried

to order her random thoughts, failed in both. Found herself actually missing Olga. If the Princess had given her the chance, she would have told her that she had recognised the Brotherhood's messenger. He was the young man who had met her in the Greek folly on Prince Ovinski's estate. He had been masked then, as now, and she had only seen him briefly, but was in no doubt about the voice, the aristocratic presence, the habit of command. He had asked her then if Casimir was Ovinski's son. Passionately, now, she wished that she had been more positive in her answer. A pawn, he had called little Casimir. Suppose they were to decide he was also expendable?

'Pani.' One of the maids scratching at her door: a welcome distraction. 'Leon says I am to look after you, now Olga is gone.' She came forward, a young girl, fresh-faced, golden plaits hanging to her waist. 'I thank God for you, Pani Jenny.' She bent to grasp and kiss Jenny's hands. 'I am Lech's sister. You risked your life for him, I think.'

'I didn't mean to,' Jenny said, incurably honest. 'I just . . . I'm so glad about Lech. That he's safe. You're his sister?' She smiled at the girl. 'What is your name? You don't look much like Lech.'

'Marylka, pani. No, it's lucky. I think the Princess has forgotten that Lech and I are kin, and no one will remind her. Of that or of anything else. I was a child of the tunnel, you see.'

'A what?'

'You must know about the tunnel, pani? The secret passage to the family apartments? The way the poor little Prince was taken?'

'Yes?'

'You knew about Marta? That she was –' she coloured '– kin to the Princess?'

'Yes?' What now?

'It was not only the Princes who sent for serfs, pani. The Princesses did, too. My father, and Lech's, was chief huntsman. Such a handsome man, until the vodka got him. He's dead many years, rest his soul.' She crossed herself. 'His wife, Lech's mother, was kind to me, brought me up as her own. Well, she was paid for it, so long as the old Princess was alive.'

'The old Princess?'

'The Prince's sister. My mother. She never married. That's why I had to be smuggled out through the tunnel. While she was alive, she was good to me. Had me taught French and a little Russian. Promised me a dowry. Just think, pani! I'm the little Prince's cousin! Poor little man. But they'll be good to him. They told me to tell you so. If his mother does what they tell her. Goes back to Warsaw. Stays there. They'll look after you, too. They told me to promise it.'

'You mean?'

'I told you, pani. I'm to look after you, now Olga is gone.'

They reached Warsaw without a word being spoken between the Princess and Jenny. It was a horrible journey, with the roads beginning to thaw and damp snow falling, and Jenny, banished this time from the Princess's luxurious carriage with its built-in fittings and regular supply of hot bricks, wondered if she would have survived its rigours if it had not been for Marylka's loving care. As it was, she arrived suffering from a heavy feverish cold and longing for her bed. But the Princess had arrived already, and Jenny was summoned instantly to her presence.

'You're to go and fetch him.' Princess Isobel was at her writing-desk. 'Here are the written promises they demand. You are to give them my word on them.'

'Should I know what they are?'

'So they say.' She was hating this. She put a hand on the paper she had just signed. 'Not to try for vengeance. Not to question Casimir about them. Not to harm anyone involved in the business. Which includes you, you'll be glad to hear.'

'Thank you,' said Jenny.

'Don't thank me. Thank them.'

'Where must I go?'

'To the White House, in the grounds of the Lazienki Palace. They will be awaiting you there. With Casimir, Lech and Olga.'

'Olga?'

'So they say. But I won't have her. I don't care what you do, how you do it, but don't bring her back with you. The Brotherhood can find themselves another messenger.'

'Yes.' No need to say they had already done so.

'You're not well enough,' Marylka protested, as Jenny wearily struggled back into her furs.

'I've got to be.'

'Then let me come with you.'

'No, I must go alone. Just one footman, They said.'

'I don't like it.'

'Nor do I. But there will be Lech on the way back. And the footman will be armed, of course.' She had never been to the Lazienki Palace, where once Stanislas Augustus had held court, but knew that it stood isolated in its own gardens. No place for a woman alone. 'They'll protect me,' she said to comfort herself as much as Marylka. 'If they want Casimir to get back safely.'

'I hope so.' She fastened the wadded hood snugly under Jenny's chin. 'You should be in your bed.'

'I wish I was.' She was hot now; presently, she would be ice-cold again.

The Princess's town carriage was awaiting her outside in the street. The footman held the door open for her.

'You?' It was Paul Genet's messenger. 'How in the world?'

'Bribery,' he said cheerfully. 'The master told me to look after you, if you needed it. I reckon you do. I'm well armed, and can use them.'

'Pray don't. You know where we are going?'

'Of course.' He smiled, bowed, closed the door behind her, and jumped up behind.

Too far out of town for easy winter access, the Lazienki Palace and the White House where Stanislas Augustus's mistress had lived were empty at this time of the year, and the snow-covered grounds lay eerily silent in cold afternoon light.

'I shall come in with you.' Genet's messenger held out his hand to help her down from the carriage.

'Thank you. I don't know your name.'

'François, mademoiselle, most absolutely at your service.' He rapped loudly on the door of the square white house. No answer. He pushed it and it swung open, revealing a Dutch tiled hall. 'Is anyone there?'

The air of the house struck cold as Jenny followed him in. 'Lech?' she called. 'Olga?' A wild-goose chase?

'There's somebody here.' He pulled the pistol out of his belt, led the way through echoing empty rooms.

Now she could hear what he had: muffled, distant shouting.

A locked door; no key and the voices from inside. Lech's, she thought, and Olga's. Casimir?

'Stand back from the door,' François shouted. 'I'm going to shoot out the lock.'

'We're clear.' Lech's voice? The shot reverberated through the empty rooms; some plaster fell from the moulded ceiling; the door swung open to reveal Lech with Casimir apparently asleep in his arms; Olga plunging into hysteria. No one else.

'They drugged him.' Lech's whole thought was for the little Prince. 'Promised it would do him no harm. I'm glad you came, pani, it's been cold here.'

'How long?'

'Since yesterday. Oh, be quiet, you!' To Olga. 'What are we going to do with her?' he asked Jenny.

'Did they say anything?'

'No, but they don't trust her, and no more do I.'

'We can't leave her here,' Jenny said. 'It will be dark soon.'

'Serve her right,' said Lech.

'We'll drop her at the edge of town.' François took command. 'If you agree, mademoiselle.' He struck Olga a sharp blow on the side of the face. 'Quiet, you. We won't hurt you. Where do you want to be let go?'

'Near the barracks,' Olga said, and then was silent.

17

Prince Casimir pined for his captors. He had changed from baby to little boy in their hands, and refused to answer to the old pet names Jenny had called him. 'I'm Prince Casimir –' He repelled her embrace and went on in rapid Polish.

'What does he say?' Jenny asked Marylka.

'Bless him! He says he's the hope of Poland.'

The Princess, who had been used to caress her son very much as she did her lapdogs, was repelled by this change in him. 'The hope of Poland, indeed! He'll need better manners if he's to be that. Idiotic to have taught him to say it. I count on you to cure him of it, Jenny. Imagine if he were to come out with it at school.' She planned to send him to Warsaw's military academy just as soon as he was old enough. In the meantime, he played soldiers with the children of the palace serfs. But it was still Jenny to whom he came when the play was too rough and he got hurt, and Jenny who told him his fairy story in bed every night. But now the dragons had to be fiercer, the Princes bolder, and the battles bloody.

The standard Princess Isobel had embroidered was ceremonially blessed, along with many other proofs of the devotion of Polish ladies, early in May, when the new regiments of eager young men marched away to join Napoleon for the spring campaign. And Marie Walewska came back from her stay with Napoleon at his headquarters as quietly as she had gone, though once again the news was around town in twenty-four hours.

Jenny had known it still sooner, having received a visit from Paul Genet, who had joined Marie Walewska's brother Benedict in escorting her back.

'You'll call on her, I hope,' he said. 'News of her return will be out soon enough. What's hard to say is how society will take it.'

'I suppose it depends on her husband.' Jenny felt a moment's revulsion at the abject plight of a married woman.

'No problem there. Welcomed her with open arms. His dearest Marie.' Genet's tone was dry. 'If there should be a child, I think he'll be glad to acknowledge it. Forgive me!' She had blushed scarlet. 'I am treating you as an old friend. You do not talk of these things in England?'

'Do you with your women in France?'

'Only with those we value most. Tell me, how do you go on with the Princess these days?'

'Not well. But better than at first. I've so wanted to thank you, Monsieur Genet, for the services of your man, François. I don't know what I would have done without him.' She had taken it for granted that François would have reported fully to Paul Genet and been amazed at how little she minded this.

'The little Prince is none the worse, I hear.'

'He enjoyed every moment of it! He's changed, of course. He's a little boy now. He needs a tutor, some discipline. He's running wild with the servants' children; bullying them, I'm afraid. It's not good for him.'

'No.' Thoughtfully. He rose. 'I must leave again for head-quarters tonight. Miss Peverel, may I leave François with you? If you should ever need help, for whatever reason, he would find it for you.'

'Good of you, but it's not possible. The Princess . . .'

'Stupid of me. I should have explained. I propose to leave him here in Warsaw, at Monsieur Talleyrand's, to keep me posted of events. Only you will know that it is you he serves.'

'In that case, thank you.' Disconcerting to find herself close to tears.

He took her hand, kissed it. 'Thank you, Miss Peverel, for trusting me. And – do call on Madame Walewska?'

The thaw was general now, and Warsaw was beginning to stink. Since elegant town houses and ornate palaces stood marooned among groups of slum hovels, and only the lucky people close to the Vistula had any pretence of drainage, warm weather brought an instant threat of disease in the overcrowded city. More and more families were moving out to their country houses. The Walewskis had gone to Walewice, the Potockis to Willanow, and Princess Isobel was one of the few aristocrats still in town.

'It's intolerable.' She had come in from her carriage sniffing at a clove orange. 'You still have some means of getting in touch with the Brotherhood? Tell them it will be on their heads if Casimir dies of the typhus.'

'I've told them already,' said Marylka, when Jenny spoke to her. 'They say there will be instructions soon. I don't know why it has taken so long.'

A few days later an elegant town carriage drew up outside the Ovinski house.

'The Prince of Benevento wishes to pay his respects to Your Highness.' Grucz sounded frightened.

'Talleyrand? Napoleon's *éminence grise*? Show him in, then.' Princess Isobel moved to the glass to adjust a curl. 'An unlooked-for honour. You've not met him, Jenny?' The use of her Christian name, rare since Casimir's kidnapping, was encouraging.

'No.' She had not gone into society since the French took Warsaw.

An ugly man, with a limp. That was Jenny's first thought. Then, as he greeted them both and began to talk to the Princess, she revised it. A brilliant man, with the manners of an angel. Did angels have manners? He was apologising to the Princess. A letter from her husband the Prince had been intercepted by mistake, delayed. She must forgive him. He handed it to her, turned to Jenny.

'You must be starved for word from England, Miss Peverel. The *Warsaw Gazette* is hardly noted for its international news. You have a new government, did you know?'

'No! I hadn't heard.'

'The Tories are back in office, under Lord Portland. They are sending Lord Leveson Gower back as Ambassador to Russia. You met him, I believe, at Rendomierz?'

'No, sir.' How did one address Napoleonic Princes? 'He was supposed to come, with the Tsar, but had to wait for a messenger from England. Two friends of his came, a Mr. Rendel and an American, Jan Warrington.'

'Old friends of the Princess's, I believe.'

'Yes.' She felt herself colouring. 'They arrived at Rendomierz the same year that I did.'

'Gratify an old man's curiosity, my dear, and tell me about Mr. Rendel. I knew his parents, many years ago, in France before the Revolution. It makes me feel my age to say so!'

'He never spoke of them.'

'His mother has been dead many years. She was a most beautiful lady . . . Does her son take after her?'

'He's not exactly handsome.' Hard to be casual. 'Fair hair, grey eyes. You know the type of Englishman?'

Talleyrand nodded. 'His mother was a ravishing blonde.'

'And he just misses it.' She indulged herself in the rare chance to talk about Glynde. 'It's almost as if he didn't want to be handsome, didn't want to draw attention to himself. Plays the English fashionable, and all the time there's the hint of steel underneath. How strange . . .' Something was tugging at her mind. 'Who is it he's like?'

'The Tsar seems to have taken quite a fancy to him.' Talleyrand had lost interest in Glynde's appearance. 'He and Warrington are with him again in what's left of Eastern Prussia. You have the advantage of me there, too, young lady. You have met the Tsar and I have not. A great gentleman, they say.'

'Yes.' But the Princess had finished her husband's long letter.

'So many instructions,' she said. 'You've read it of course, Prince.'

'My reluctant duty. You will be glad, I am sure, to escape from the bad air of Warsaw, for the child's sake as well as your own. I leave myself, tomorrow, for army headquarters, and am not sorry.'

'I shall get permission to go?'

'I can promise you that. And the sooner the better. The roads are drying fast; the campaign will reopen soon. A wife's place is at her husband's side, particularly when he is not well. It shall never be said that the civilised French are slower to see this than the Russians. Send to my house tomorrow and you shall have the necessary papers.' He shared his urbane smile between them. 'And my best wishes for a prosperous journey, ladies.'

'He's very sure I'll go,' said the Princess when he had left.

'To Rendomierz?' Jenny had been longing to ask it.

'Idiot! No. To join my husband. He's in attendance on the

Tsar with the rest of the Russian court. I'm to apply for leave to go to Vinsk; leave the boy there; then to headquarters, which are at Bartenstein now; maybe much further west by then.'

'And Talleyrand read all this? And lets you go? I don't understand.'

'How should you? How should a little bourgeoise like you expect to understand the chivalry of the great? Talleyrand's a gentleman, one of the old aristocracy. He knows how to behave.'

'They say he's brilliantly clever.'

'So is my husband, who wrote his letter knowing it would be read. He is very far from well, he says. Too old a man to be roughing it in the wilds.'

'But, Princess, what of the Brotherhood? Remember what happened last time we left Warsaw.'

For a moment, she thought the Princess would strike her. Then, 'Send them a message. Tell them I am ordered to leave.'

'Ordered?'

'It comes to that. Use your wits, Jenny! Talleyrand didn't pay that visit in order to make agreeable conversation with you about Glynde Rendel. He came to give me my orders. I expect you will find that he has dealt with the Brotherhood too.'

And in this she proved entirely right. When Jenny returned to her own room she found Marylka awaiting her with their message, approving the journey. Reporting this to the Princess, she said, 'I don't understand it. And, Princess, what of Miriam and her little boys? Will it be safe to leave Casimir at Vinsk?' This plan went terribly against the grain with her.

'The boys are dead,' said the Princess flatly. 'Smallpox. Poor little things. My husband merely mentioned it in passing. I imagine Miriam has gone home to her family. And good riddance. She had it too,' she explained. 'Caught it doing good works in the village, gave it to the children. Her looks are quite gone.' She paused to admire her own in the glass.

'Oh, the poor creature! Both of them?'

'He'll never forgive her for catching it, giving it to them. If she's not gone, she might as well. She'd make a reliable housekeeper, mind you. At least she's devoted to the Prince.'

'She feels herself married to him,' said Jenny, forgetting herself.

'God give me patience! Will you never even try to understand! Married to him! A little bastard of a Jewess married to the Prince Ovinski! I think perhaps I will leave you behind at Vinsk.'

Setting out a few days later, the Princess travelled slowly north in her usual luxurious state. But on the sixth morning, as she made her leisurely way to her own carriage, the little party were suddenly surrounded by a group of hooded figures who had emerged, silently, from the forest.

No hope of resistance, but Jenny thought no one even intended it. The hooded leader approached the Princess, bowed. 'Highness, you have been travelling too slowly. We are come, with your permission, to escort you for the rest of your journey.'

'You! Who are you?'

'We do not name ourselves, Highness, but we are Poland's friends, yours, and your son's.' And as if to prove this, Casimir now hurled himself forward with cries of glad recognition to clasp the stranger's knee and demand a ride on his horse. 'You can see we are not very terrible,' he looked down a little ruefully at the child, then swung him up in front of him. 'Quiet, Prince, I am speaking to your mother.' And to Jenny's amazement, Casimir relapsed into obedient silence. She watched with awed amusement as he let himself be put down without a word of protest. And felt herself watched in her turn as he came straight to her, ignoring his mother. 'It's my friends, Jenny! Are we going with them?'

It was amazing how much faster they went with the Brotherhood in charge. When the Princess said something about stopping for lunch, her guide simply looked at her. Then, 'You may eat in the carriage,' he told her.

It was a most uncomfortable journey, with the heavy carriage plunging and swaying through deep sand, or lurching over the logs of a corduroy road across the swampland near rivers. When it stuck fast, as it did several times, they all had to get out and everyone but the Princess did their best to help push.

Towards evening, Jenny caught a moment alone with their

186

masked guide. 'Where are you taking us? It's not to Vinsk, or the sun has changed its habits a great deal. And we've crossed a lot of small rivers, but surely the Niemen is a big one.'

'I never said I was taking you to Vinsk.'

'Nor you did. So – where?' She should be terrified, but did not seem to be.

'To the Russian camp, of course. To the Prince. Why waste time going all the way east to Vinsk?' For the first time, she thought he smiled behind the mask. 'I won't go so far as to say that the little Prince would be better with his mother than left behind among servants, but I do think he will be better with you. Who better than a freeborn Englishwoman to train up the hope of Poland?'

'And how ridiculous of you to teach him to call himself that.'

'I'm sure you have cured him. Now, tell me, are you going to oblige me by not mentioning to the Princess what you have noticed?'

'Oh, I think so. It would only make trouble.'

'I'm glad you see that. Never forget that where the future of Poland is concerned, we are absolutely ruthless.'

'Believe me, I won't.' Could it have been he who had so ruthlessly mishandled her, back in the forest at Rendomierz? She did not want to think so, but her eye went down to the ankle that was still a little stiff when it rained.

The journey began to seem endless, and Jenny waited for the inevitable moment when the Princess would realise something was wrong, but one road in this desolate country looked very like another. Their anonymous guide approached her again one evening when she was taking Casimir for a run by the small stream near which they were encamped. 'I've news,' he told her. 'The Russian court has moved from Memel to Tilsit to be nearer the seat of operations. You will be able to reach Tilsit tomorrow. I have sent a messenger to Prince Ovinski, asking him to send an escort for his wife. You have only to wait here for them. Make my excuses to the Princess, when she finds us gone in the morning.'

'You do not propose to stay and face her?'

'Why should I?'

'No reason. But please let me thank you, for all of us.'

187

'For the little Prince, what would we not do? You'll look after him, Miss Peverel. We count on you.'

'Thank you.'

'And, remember, our power crosses all frontiers. We will be watching you in Russia, no more, no less.'

'I wish I understood . . .'

'Don't try, Miss Peverel. If you value your life, don't try.'

When she woke in the morning to find her carriage unguarded, her escort vanished, the Princess was so angry she could hardly speak. And Jenny's explanation did nothing to calm her. 'You knew last night, and did not tell me!'

'I was ordered not to. You may not fear the Brotherhood, Highness, but I do. And with cause.' She had never told the Princess about that savage attack on her, back at Rendomierz, and thought this was the moment to do so.

'They did that to you?' The Princess's hand went up to her own mouth, as if she imagined it disfigured as Jenny's was. 'And you said nothing!'

'Highness, I was afraid. And – remember – in their strange, violent way, they are working for what you want: the freedom of Poland. It is not you or me they care about; it is the little Prince, their hope for the future. I wish I understood why they want him back with his father.'

She thought she began to when they approached the little town of Tilsit later that day and Prince Ovinski rode out to meet them. He had aged almost beyond recognition since she had last seen him only a year before. He had always been an immensely elegant, upright rider. She hardly recognised him now, slumped in his saddle, thin, scaly hands clutching at the reins.

But his greeting for his wife was debonair as ever, and he seemed actually pleased that she had brought Casimir, against his instructions. 'The Prince, my heir.' He said it loudly, making a public statement of it. 'But we must not be dallying here,' he went on. 'I cannot tell you how relieved I am to see you, my dear. It is fortunate you have travelled so fast. There is news. Bad news I am afraid. We have lost a battle at Friedland, not very far south of here. Dantzig has fallen, and Königsberg. My master, the Tsar, has given orders that Tilsit be evacuated; the bridge across the Niemen will be burned this evening. We must cross it first. The Emperor is staying on Prince Zubov's estate and we have his gracious permission to join him there. But we must lose no time. Miss Peverel, may I take an old man's privilege and your place in the carriage? Casimir will be happy to have you travel with him, I know.'

They were almost the last across the wooden bridge that spanned the Niemen and Jenny did not think they would have been allowed to cross if Prince Ovinski had not been with them. Other pitiful wagon-loads of refugees from the approaching French were being ruthlessly turned back, and as the carriage breasted the slight slope of the river, the dull thud of an explosion and a sudden tower of flame from behind them told their own story.

18

'Do you get the impression that the Tsar begins to wish he had not brought us?' Jan waited to ask Glynde in the comparative privacy of their tiny room in the overcrowded stable wing of Prince Zubov's palace.

'Me, most certainly.' Glynde came closer and spoke low. 'And I hardly blame him. British inactivity has so obviously contributed to these new disasters. If we had only sent ships to help defend Dantzig! And a small detachment of troops – 50,000, 30,000 even – might have made all the difference at Friedland.'

'I doubt that,' said Jan. 'The Russian troops fought like tigers, everyone says. It was the command that was so disastrous. But it does seem significant that when they retreated . . .'

'Ran away.'

'Ran away from Tilsit,' Jan agreed, 'the Tsar let Granville go off to Memel instead of keeping him at his side. After all, it is to the Russians not the Prussians that Granville is accredited. It seems extraordinary that when he is here at last to offer the new British government's support he should not be kept at the centre of things.'

'It does make one wonder what may be afoot. Do you know Napoleon refused to see a Polish delegation the other day? Fobbed them off with Marshal Davout. Not a good sign, I think.' He moved away to peer out of the window. 'Someone else is arriving. Where in the world will they find to lodge?' And then: 'Good God! The Princess!'

'Come to join her husband?' Jan crossed the room at a stride. 'The Prince said nothing about it yesterday.'

'He said nothing about anything. No more pleased to see us than the Tsar. She's more beautiful than ever.' Ovinski had appeared and was helping his wife down from the carriage.

'If possible.' They watched in silence as the Prince and

Princess paused in the crowded courtyard of the palace, as if waiting for something, the Princess apparently eager to be gone, the Prince delaying. 'I wonder,' Jan went on as a smaller carriage drew up behind the one from which the Prince and Princess had emerged. 'Yes, by Tophet, it's the boy!'

'And Miss Peverel. She's not changed.'

'The child has.'

'Yes, into a boy, as you say.' The little party moved towards the porticoed main entrance of the palace and disappeared from the two young men's sight. 'I wonder if the Prince sent for them?'

'Surely the Princess would not have ventured on the dangerous journey from Warsaw otherwise?'

'But would he have risked her and the child by doing so?'

'Not to mention Miss Peverel,' said Jan. 'Are we going to brave the Tsar's indifference and join his soirée this evening?'

'I think so, don't you? He has not actually asked us not to.'

'And Adam Czartoryski may have some news.'

'I wonder. The Tsar is not much more friendly to him than he is to us these days. And that's hardly surprising, if it is true that his friend the King of Prussia was negotiating with Napoleon before the disaster at Friedland about a handover of what was Prussian Poland.'

'So much for poor Adam's dreams of an independent, or even semi-independent Poland! If I were he, I believe I'd ask leave to return to the university he is building at Vilno.'

'Abandoning hope? It would not be like Czartoryski. Besides, I think he's genuinely fond of the Tsar, maybe hopes to save him from any too disastrous mistake.'

'Good luck to him,' said Jan.

They met Adam Czartoryski at the entrance to the great hall of the Zubov palace, where the Tsar held his informal evening receptions.

'What's the news, Adam?' Glynde felt a stab of pity at the sight of his friend's drawn face.

'I'm the last to hear it these days.' He kept his voice low. 'But there is talk of a meeting between the two Emperors. If it happens, God help us all!' He looked past them, raised his voice, forced a smile. 'Prince Ovinski, may I congratulate you on the safe arrival of your wife. And here are some old friends of yours and hers.'

'We met last night.' Ovinski favoured the two young men with a curt nod. 'Yes, it is a great weight off my mind that my wife and heir have reached me safely after their hazardous journey. I hope to present Prince Casimir to our master in the morning.' He gave the three of them another nod and made as if to move on.

'May I ask where you are lodged, Highness?' asked Glynde. 'I would like to pay my respects to the Princess.'

'She is hardly in a position to entertain, sir. You must know that we are none of us luxuriously housed.'

He moved away and Glynde gave an angry little laugh. 'The rebuff courteous. Think of Granville's descriptions of how the Queen of Prussia keeps up the spirits of her little court in great discomfort at Memel!'

'She's had long enough to learn the meaning of exile,' said Adam Czartoryski. 'And dealt with it gallantly, though I am afraid it has told both on her looks and her health. But I know my master is still her very good friend . . . I just wish . . .'

'Poor Adam,' said Glynde later. 'How can he wish good for that unlucky exiled Queen of Prussia, when he knows that her good must be Poland's misfortune?'

'We never did discover where the Princess is staying.' Jan never pretended to find the complexities of central European politics anything but tedious. 'A continent run by a lot of cousins,' he had summed it up to Glynde. 'I sometimes think Napoleon is doing them a favour by getting rid of the old, rigid boundaries, and all the formalities that go with them.'

They heard from Granville Leveson Gower next morning, still from Memel. In a quickly scrawled note, he let them know that he had set off a few days earlier in hopes of rejoining the Tsar, only to be informed, after covering fifty English miles of bad road, that the Tsar had moved and was still not permanently settled. He had returned to Memel, to keep up his attendance on the unlucky Queen of Prussia and wait for more certain intelligence.

'The Tsar don't want him,' said Jan. 'He's putting him off.'

'That's about it. There must be some truth in these rumours about a projected meeting with Napoleon.'

Jan laughed. 'Do you remember when you went on insisting on calling him Bonaparte?'

'That was a long time ago. Before all his victories. Shall we see if we can find where the Princess is lodged?'

'Do let us.' For them, still, there was only one Princess.

They found her at last lodged in a gardener's cottage and not liking it much. 'The serfs on my estate have better quarters.' She apologised for their entertainment.

'No matter.' Glynde held her hand a shade longer than he should. 'It is you we are come to see, Princess. And –' he looked about him '– our friend Leveson Gower tells us that the Queen of Prussia is hardly better lodged than this.'

'Really?' The Princess smiled, and his heart gave the old leap. 'Then who am I to grumble? I am only a little anxious for my child, worn out by the perils of our journey, and now forced to sleep in what is hardly a cupboard, with Miss Peverel for company. The Prince builds such hopes on him . . . He means to present him to the Tsar today.'

'The hope of Poland,' said Jan.

'Mr. Warrington,' she turned to him eagerly. 'I do beg you to forget that foolish phrase. I'm sorry you ever heard it, but you must see that now, particularly, when the fate of Europe hangs in the balance, is no time to be saying such things.'

'Only among friends,' said Jan.

'Thank you!' Her smile for him was as ravishing as ever, and Glynde felt a sudden spasm of jealousy. Jealous of Jan? Absurd. 'But as a friend,' the Princess went on, 'I must beg you to be immensely careful what you say. My husband tells me we are on a powder keg here. Anything may happen. Anything!'

'He thinks the Tsar will meet Napoleon?' Glynde asked.

'He is very much afraid so.' She put her hand to her mouth. 'I should not have said that. Forget I did. Please?'

'It's forgotten.' Glynde smiled at her. 'Let us talk of other things. Tell us of your journey, Princess. It must have been fraught with danger, for you and for the child.'

'And for Miss Peverel,' said Jan. 'How is Miss Peverel, Highness? And the child?'

'Both well, thank you. As to the journey – I am sure I do not need to tell you what the roads were like. You must have encountered much the same kind of thing on your way here from Petersburg. I've told my husband that next time I make a long journey I shall be sure to do it in winter, when the roads are hard.'

'I doubt you will be able to wait so long,' said Jan. 'You can hardly intend to stay here much longer than the Tsar does.'

'You're right, of course. And only God knows what he means to do next. Ah,' she turned with obvious relief at the sound of voices outside the cottage. 'Here come my son and Miss Peverel. They went with my husband as far as the palace to see if they could pick up any news. Casimir wanted to see the Tsar's Guard. He's army-mad, you know.'

'At four?' asked Jan.

'Such a well-grown four! You'll see.' She turned, smiling, to the door as it was pushed open, a little timidly, Glynde thought, and Casimir appeared, followed by Miss Peverel. 'There you are, my darling! Give your mother a kiss!' And then, as he hesitated. 'Any news, Miss Peverel? Look! Here are some old friends of ours. I don't need to introduce them, I know.'

'Goodness gracious!' Jenny smiled, blushed and held out a hand to each. 'Mr. Rendel! Mr. Warrington! You are the most amazing travellers. You came with the Tsar, did you?' There was something in her voice, a note of – what?

'Yes,' Glynde told her. 'He was so good as to bring us with him from Petersburg.'

'And now regrets it,' said forthright Jan.

'Understandably.' Jenny's tone was dry. 'Since he has just ridden out, with the King of Prussia, to meet Napoleon on the river between here and Tilsit.'

'What?' Glynde turned on her furiously. 'I don't believe it!'

'No?' She met his angry gaze squarely. 'Go over to the palace, then, and ask where they all are. The Prince is gone too.' To the Princess, 'I think he had hoped to present Casimir to the Tsar, but it was very evidently not the moment. He sent for his horse instead, and has joined the cortège that has accompanied Tsar and King down to the Niemen.'

'Where are they meeting, then?' asked Jan.

'On a raft Napoleon has had built in midstream. Lech told

me.' She turned again to the Princess. 'They worked all night. A raft, with two pavilions. Well,' she smiled, 'huts really. Decorated with Napoleon's initial, and the Tsar's. No sop for the poor King of Prussia. I suppose he will have to wait on the river-bank while his fate, his wife's, and their country's, is decided. And it is beginning to rain, too,' she added. 'That's why Casimir and I came back. They are going to have a damp time of it, I'm afraid.'

'The Prince went, too?' Isobel asked.

'Yes. I hope he doesn't get too wet.'

Nobody said anything for a moment. They had all in their different ways been shocked by the change in the Prince's appearance; all had a vision of him sitting his horse on the bank of the Niemen, getting wet.

'You've hardly told us about your journey.' Glynde changed the subject. 'How did things seem, as you came across Russian Poland? And did you really come all that way without incident?'

Did he imagine a quick exchange of glances between the Princess and Jenny Peverel? 'Nothing to signify,' said the Princess carelessly. 'As to the country; it's bleak of course, and barbarous, and poverty-stricken, but we certainly saw no sign of disaffection, did we, Jenny?'

'We saw nothing,' said Jenny flatly. 'We came on by-roads, Mr. Rendel; camped in the carriages; it was remarkably uncomfortable.'

'It was a great lark,' broke in Casimir. 'I rode ahead with –'

'That's enough, Casimir.' The Princess's voice was sharp. 'Take him away, Jenny. He's making my head ache.'

It was an obvious cue to leave and the two men walked away in thoughtful silence.

The two Emperors conferred all day, and emerged apparently the greatest of friends. 'If only one knew what they had said!' exclaimed Jan.

'They've agreed a peace by the look of things, coming out arm in arm like that. But what it will mean for the world . . .' Glynde turned to greet Adam Czartoryski. 'What news, Adam?'

'The worst! Napoleon has charmed my master into friendship. God knows what concessions he has made. I tremble for the future of Poland.'

Two days later, Napoleon declared Tilsit a neutral zone, and the Tsar and King of Prussia left their crowded lodgings on the east side of the Niemen and moved over to join him there. 'It's unbelievable,' exclaimed Glynde. 'Two weeks ago, they were confronting each other across the savage field of Friedland; now it's all wining and dining and reviewing each other's troops.'

'Which I would like to see,' said Jan. 'Shall we get ourselves a couple of passes to cross the river? You're a civilian after all, no reason why you shouldn't. Sir Robert Wilson went yesterday, disguised as a Russian officer. He told me so.'

'Robert Wilson is a law unto himself!' Glynde laughed. 'But, yes, what's safe for him, British Military Adviser to the Tsar, should be safe enough for two harmless travellers.'

'Do let's go. Something to tell our grandchildren.'

'I don't know. Better not, I think.' Jan's very eagerness increased Glynde's habitual caution. But in the end he gave in, and they joined the crowd crossing and recrossing the river that had been such an absolute barrier only a few days before. They found the little town of Tilsit so crowded that any chance of being noticed seemed remote, and saw several Russian officers of their acquaintance, rather carelessly disguised as civilians, in the crowd that watched the arrival of the Queen of Prussia to join with her husband in pleas for their country.

'Poor lady,' said Jan. 'Everyone knows how she and Napoleon hate each other. Shall we go?'

'Yes. I think we should call on the Princess when we get back and enquire after her husband. Dr. Wylie seems to think the chill he caught by the river the other day quite serious.'

They were accosted just as they were about to step into a boat to be rowed back to the other side of the river. 'Your papers, messieurs, if you please.' The French officer was perfectly civil, but Glynde's heart sank as they handed over their passes.

'Yes, these are quite in order,' said the man. 'So far as they go. You are Monsieur Rendel and Monsieur Warrington, and have permission to cross the river, but what I want to know is just who you are and why you are come.'

'Curiosity,' said Glynde. 'To see your Emperor. We are travellers, sir, tourists; it was an opportunity not to be missed.'

'You were seen standing very close when the King of Prussia greeted our Emperor. There have been rumours of an assassination attempt. You will come with me to my superior, if you please, and explain yourselves to him.'

'But we are unarmed.' Glynde had insisted on this. 'What harm could we have done the Emperor, even if we had wished to?'

'You are unarmed now,' said the officer. 'Having failed in your attempt, you had plenty of chances to get rid of the weapon on your way back here. My men could not follow you closely enough to be sure of this, but they are searching now.'

'And you will find nothing.' Glynde was angry, because he was beginning to be very much afraid.

'So I hope, for your sakes.' His men had closed in round them. 'This way, gentlemen. We are wasting time here. I have not the authority to release you, even if I were inclined to do so, which I am not. You British have a great stake in the Emperor's death, particularly now.'

'But I am American,' protested Jan. 'How would I ever have connived in such a monstrous thing?'

'Tell that to my master.'

Locked in a tolerably comfortable cell on an upper floor of the town gaol, they looked at each other in gloomy silence. 'I am so very sorry,' said Jan at last. 'This is entirely my fault. What do you think will happen to us, Glynde?'

'Nothing to you. Of that I am sure. I wish I felt quite so confident about my own prospects.' He could not help thinking of the English prisoners who had died, mysterious apparent suicides in French prisons. 'If they separate us, Jan, which I hope they will for your sake, you'll speak up for me, won't you? Whatever happens, you'll tell the world I did not kill myself.'

'Of course. But it won't happen.'

Time dragged by, endless, until at last the jingling of keys announced their gaoler, who led them down to a side-entrance, where a closed carriage waited with a small escort of troops. 'You're in luck,' he said. 'He wants to see you at once. I've known prisoners wait days, weeks even.'

'Who?' asked Glynde, but the carriage door slammed on the question.

'If it's Fouché, I hardly call it luck,' said Jan, and they fell silent again, both of them thinking about Napoleon's formidable Chief of Police.

'He lives in style at all events.' Glynde tried for a light note as the carriage drove through a guarded archway into the yard of a town house that was almost a palace. 'No chance of escape.' He was a little afraid his companion might do something rash.

'No. Madness,' Jan agreed.

Descending from the carriage, they saw that the escort had remained at the entrance, leaving just one man to guard them. 'This way, gentlemen.' He led them up porticoed steps. 'My master says you are to consider yourselves his guests.'

'Very civil of him,' said Glynde. 'Who is your master?'

But the man appeared not to have heard the question, as he led the way up a handsome staircase to the main floor of the house. Opening a door, he ushered them in, said, 'The gentlemen, sir,' and left them.

'The very foolish gentlemen.' The slender, grey-haired man who awaited them looked from one to the other, then held out his hand in welcome to Jan. 'Mr. Warrington.' He took a difficult step forward, 'And Mr. Rendel! May I welcome you to what, I must remind you, is technically the soil of France.'

'Declared neutral,' said Glynde. 'Monsieur Talleyrand –' And then, 'I beg your pardon, I should say –'

'No, no. Talleyrand will do very well. My master was so good as to make me a Prince, but I still prefer my family's name, for reasons that baffle even myself.' He had shaken Jan's hand, now held Glynde's, looking him over with eyes that seemed to miss nothing. 'I cannot tell you how delighted I am with your quite idiotic rashness, Mr. Rendel. I have been very much wishing to meet you.'

'To meet me?' Nothing was going as Glynde had expected. Had feared? His hand parted from Talleyrand's reluctantly as he met look with look.

'Yes. I knew your mother, so many years ago that it makes me feel old to recall it, something I particularly dislike. When I learned that Fouché's men had picked you up, risking your life here in Tilsit, I could not resist arranging the meeting.

198

But, forgive me, you gentlemen must be starving. You were presumably on your way home to your dinner, when you were arrested. Quite rightly, if I may say so. Tilsit is no place for an Englishman at this moment.' He took another of his halting steps forward to a table with wine and glasses.

'Please let me.' Glynde anticipated him.

'With pleasure. And then we will eat. Or rather, you will eat while I entertain you with scintillating conversation. I have been dining with my Emperor and the unfortunate King and Queen of Prussia,' he explained, 'or I would have released you from what must have been a quite anxious period of detention long before this. Though I consider that it served you richly right, and will, I trust, be a lasting lesson to you, Mr. Rendel. Mr. Warrington I have no need to scold. As an American, he is free of Europe, though I can think of circumstances in which he might find the freedom more theory than practice.'

'You're right there.' Jan and Glynde exchanged glances, remembering their first meeting, and Glynde found himself wondering, as he poured and passed the wine, if Talleyrand, with Fouché's omniscience at his disposal, did not perhaps know about it, too.

'Your very good health, gentlemen,' Talleyrand raised his glass. 'But bring your wine with you. I have no doubt you have young men's appetites, and propose to let you help yourselves, so that we can talk undisturbed.' He took his seat at the head of a table lavishly supplied with smoked fish and cold meats and gestured them to do likewise. 'Are you Pole enough to enjoy their inevitable salad of beet greens, Mr. Warrington?'

'I'm learning to like it, sir. You appear to know all about us.'

'I have made it my study since you became the Tsar Alexander's good friends. He is a man who interests me enormously; such a chapter of contradictions. Can you tell me, Mr. Rendel, which is the real man?'

Glynde put down his glass and looked at him very straight. 'I would need to know two things first, sir.'

'Yes?'

'Are we guests or prisoners, and, why do you want to know?'

'Two very good questions. To the first, my guests, of course.

To put it on no higher level, I do not intend that anything should tarnish the glow of this meeting between the world's two great men, and, has it not struck you, Mr. Rendel, that the Tsar would hardly be pleased at the arrest of men who have been his constant companions.'

'No.' Surprised. 'It had not, to tell truth. And, forgive me, I am not sure you are right. I think, at the moment, that we represent what the Tsar is turning away from. We have felt, Mr. Warrington and I, that our presence was no longer welcome.'

'Especially yours?'

'Yes.' Glynde was already angry with himself for having spoken so freely. 'You have not answered my second question.'

'Why I want to know? But you must see that, Mr. Rendel. My Emperor and the Tsar are the two masters of Europe; they hold its future in their hands, are planning it now. I am, by the accident that lamed me, and whether I like it or not, a man of peace. I have lived through enough violence for a lifetime, and Europe has lived it with me. Did you see the battlefield of Friedland? No, of course you did not.'

'We've seen enough,' said Glynde.

'To understand what I am saying? Good. Then think. Now, this very moment, these few days, here on the outskirts of Europe, these two men are deciding its future, for years, perhaps, for ever. Anything any of us can contribute to their getting it right is of the most immense importance. My master listens to me, sometimes.'

'Please do not for a moment imagine that the Tsar ever listens to us,' said Glynde.

'But to Adam Czartoryski, perhaps?'

'No longer, I am afraid.'

'Unfortunate. Prince Ovinski?'

'I don't know. Besides, he is ill.'

'Prince Ovinski? Now, that I did not know. I really begin to believe that Poland's star is crossed.'

'Poland's?' Jan had been eating and drinking heartily, leaving the conversation to the other two. 'You care about Poland, Prince?'

'Any thinking man who cares about Europe must consider Poland, Mr. Warrington. If you romantic Poles would only leave tilting at windmills and remember this, we would all go on much better at the conference table, where, in the end, the fate of nations is settled. Oh, I give you gallantry, every time, but where is the statesmanship that should back it? Let me refill your glass, Mr. Warrington, and we will drink a toast. To your Mr. Jefferson: now there is a statesman!' He reached over to refill Jan's glass from the bottle that stood on his side of the table. 'To Mr. Jefferson! A great egalitarian and a great man of peace.'

'Mr. Jefferson!' Jan emptied his glass at a draught, swayed a little, looked across the table to Glynde. 'I don't feel quite the thing. Forgive –' As he turned towards Talleyrand, he began to collapse, in slow motion, his legs giving way first.

'Don't let him fall. That's it.' Talleyrand must have given some signal, for two servants had appeared to gather him up as he fell.

19

'I am so very sorry.' Dr. Wylie rose from beside the Prince's bed. 'I had hoped for a mere cold in the head, an influenza at the worst of it. Believe me, we have done everything we could. Your nursing has been beyond praise.' He looked from the Princess to Jenny. 'But I am afraid we must face it that we are losing the battle. The Tsar my master will be deeply grieved.'

'But isn't there any treatment? What should we do?' asked the Princess, and then, as the doctor shook his head, 'You can't mean . . .'

'He should not have got so wet, and then neglected himself. Keep him warm, keep him as comfortable as possible; let nothing agitate him. There could be a miracle, Highness. In this world, miracles are always possible. But: he should see a priest; understand his state; make his arrangements; see his son?'

'I don't believe it!' But Jenny could see that the very fact that they were talking about the Prince as if he was not there was bringing the truth home to her. 'There must be something we can do!'

'You can pray, Highness.' He turned to Jenny. 'I rely on you to take care of her, Miss Peverel. And to let me know when I am needed.'

'Yes.' Left alone they looked at each other in silence, remembering.

'You met him before I did,' said the Princess at last.

'I thought him the most polished gentleman I had ever seen.'

'And so he –' She stopped. She had almost said 'was'. 'I shall go on believing in Dr. Wylie's miracle, Jenny. But send Lech for the priest.'

Much later, the Prince, who had been semi-conscious all day, woke clear-headed and asked to see the Tsar.

'It's impossible, I'm afraid.' His wife bent over the bed and took his hand. 'He is across the river, in Tilsit, conferring with Napoleon.'

'Who will betray him! As he has us Poles. Used us and cast us aside. Like Marie Walewska, poor child. Will we never learn? Then I must write to him. Fetch pen and paper.' But he was too weak to hold the pen. 'I'll dictate it then.' His fierce gaze travelled round the crowded little room. 'Miss Peverel, you will do me this favour? And you,' to the Princess, 'will sign each sheet when she has written it. It will not be long. Send for Casimir; he should be here, too. And – who is there of the court still on this side of the river, or have they all gone to fawn on the Corsican?'

'I saw young Prince Vorontzov this morning.' Jenny volunteered it into a lengthening silence.

'Let him be fetched. Quickly.' There was no need of the warning. They could all see how he fought for a thread of strength. 'Give me some brandy, my dear, and while we wait for our witnesses, one small request to you.'

'Yes?' The Princess was holding the glass while he sipped from it.

'Miriam. I left her as housekeeper at Vinsk. Let her stay?'

'Of course I will.' The Princess's eyes met Jenny's. 'No need to ask it.'

'Thank you. And – don't think too hardly of me. Ah, here they are. Casimir, come here to me. Vorontzov; it's good of you to come. I shall ask you to witness, with my wife, the letter I am about to dictate to the Tsar.' He raised his voice, not waiting for an answer, and began to dictate so fast and with such certainty that Jenny was hard put to it to keep up with him. He must have been composing it in his head during the lucid intervals of the days he had lain ill. He was the Tsar's faithful and humble servant; these were his last words. He was also a Pole. 'Let me commend your Poles to you, sire. Just give them hope, and they will serve you far better than they have ever served the Corsican upstart. The world needs Poland. Russia needs it; as a protection, as a barrier, a first line of defence. Let me commend to you, too, my son Casimir, to whom I bequeath all my Russian estates, and may I beg you to join his mother, my wife, in watching over his minority. He will serve you, sire, I am sure, as faithfully as I have. I only hope, to more purpose.' He paused as Jenny took a new leaf, began writing frantically to catch up. 'Almost done, Miss Peverel.' The words came with difficulty now. Instructions about his funeral; Casimir was his beloved son; he begged the Tsar's protection for him and his mother: 'My loyal wife. There.' He lay back among the pillows, looked at his wife: 'Read and sign, if you please. There is no time for talk. And then you, Prince.'

Passing the closely written sheets to the Princess, Jenny was aware of her silent, seething rage. And yet, surely, she had got infinitely more than she might have feared. Suppose he had disowned Casimir. Instead, amazingly, he had made him his heir direct, not in succession to his mother, as she must have expected.

The tired eyes turned to her. 'Thank you, Miss Peverel.' A whisper now; she bent close to his ear. 'I know I can trust you to have taken it down, word for word. And to look after –' a straight look from bloodshot eyes '– my son, Casimir. Now, promise to do one more thing for me.' A quick glance showed the Princess still angrily reading. 'That chest in the corner. In the confusion after my death, get rid of its contents for me? I doubt they'll surprise you much.' His mouth tried for a smile. 'It has been a pleasure to know you, Miss Peverel. Thank you, my dear.' He turned back to the Princess as she signed at the bottom of the letter's two pages. 'Now you, Prince?' That done, he reached out a hand to encircle a slightly shrinking Casimir. 'Gentlemen, my son and heir. The hope of Poland!' And fell back on the pillows.

In the chaos that followed, Jenny found it easy enough to open the cedar chest in the corner of the room. Odd to be so little surprised by its contents: the cloak and mask of the Brotherhood, and the insignia that denoted one of their leaders. How long had she suspected that the Prince had been one of the group who interrogated her, that first time, at the hunting lodge, on her way to Rendomierz? There were other episodes that were less easy to understand, suggesting, perhaps, divided leadership in the Brotherhood itself, but there would be time to think about that later. For the moment, she owed it to the Prince – and to the Princess – to get rid of this evidence of his involvement. She sent for Lech. 'There are some old clothes of the Prince's in that chest, Lech. He asked me to get rid of them for him. You'll do it, for me? And nothing said.'

'What have you done to him?' Glynde was on his feet, gazing furiously at Talleyrand, as his servants picked up Jan's lifeless form.

'No harm, just a small knock-out drop in his wine. He'll wake in the morning with a very sore head, and you and I will convince him that he is suffering merely from my strong burgundy. He's an abstemious young man in the general way, I understand. It should be easy enough. There is really no need to go with him, Mr. Rendel. I promise you, word of a gentleman, that my people are going to put him comfortably to bed in my guest-chamber, where you may join him at your leisure.' He had risen, too, and took one of his awkward steps forward to lay a hand on Glynde's arm. 'I beg you to indulge me in this. We have to talk, you and I.'

'I cannot see why.' Still angry, confused and a little afraid, Glynde nevertheless did not feel he could keep the older man awkwardly standing at his side. He moved reluctantly back towards the table, aware of Talleyrand's weight on his arm.

'Thank you.' Seated again, Talleyrand smiled at him. 'Where to begin? I've waited a long time for this day.'

'At the beginning, perhaps? What is it you want of me, sir?'

'Oh, nothing, nothing at all. It is what I owe you that has weighed on me for the last thirty years or so.'

'Thirty years?'

'Rather more, I suppose. How time does pass. Do you remember your mother at all?'

'I'll never forget her. Oh – what she looked like, no. I was a child when she died.' How strange to remember, in this moment of danger, that Jenny had reminded him of his mother, the fragrance of her. 'You met her, you say?'

'Oh yes, I met her.' Talleyrand refilled both their glasses from a new bottle, smiling ruefully at Glynde as he did so, then raised his glass. 'I drink to her memory. Your beautiful mother. I met her in seventy-five. They were in Paris, she and her husband, for the coronation of Louis XVI, poor man, and his unfortunate wife. I was twenty-one, a wild young student, disinherited by my father, because of this leg, thinking the world my enemy. They hadn't made a priest of me, yet. But they meant to, and I knew it. I'm making excuses! Disgusting.' He paused for a moment, sipping his wine.

'But why are you telling me all this?' asked Glynde impatiently. 'What has this ancient history to do with anything?'

'Because the past so often explains the present. A lesson you might usefully learn. And because I'm a coward, I suppose. I hadn't thought I was, but it seems I am after all. You're not going to like what I am about to tell you.'

'Then cut the roundaboutation and tell me. Something about my mother? Nothing you tell me can make me love her less. She loved me. The only person who did.'

'Ah? Your father?'

'Never has. Never will.'

'But he gave you his name.' Elbows on table, Talleyrand met his eyes steadily. 'He had every right not to.'

'What?' He was on his feet, knocking over his glass. 'What are you daring to say!'

'That I loved your mother. The only woman, I think, I ever truly loved. And she loved me. But we didn't talk enough, she and I. Oh, she told me how unhappy she was with your father, of his blatant unfaithfulness since the birth of your brother; what she failed to make me understand, can you blame her, was how totally he neglected her.'

'What are you saying?' Red wine seeped across the damask cloth.

'That I did not see soon enough, how completely she and your father lived apart, what a disaster your birth would be for her. If I had – I wonder – We students knew a great deal, much of it bad. I might have prepared your death for her. I am glad I did not.'

'You're saying –'

'That I am your father. Like it or not, you have to live with it. Personally, I find I like it.'

'Like it! So that was why – is why! You're right; he gave me his name. Nothing more. But I owe him everything. Now tell me what I owe you, Monsieur Talleyrand? Except this shame!'

'Nothing. I have said so already. But I do allow myself to

hope that perhaps, when you have come to terms with it a little, we might be friends.'

'Our countries are enemies. Don't think I shall ever forget it.'

'Admirable, Mr. Rendel. Do you know, I believe I shall indulge myself by calling you Glynde. I hope you now recognise what a gesture it was on Lord Ringmer's part to give you one of the family names.'

'You make me sick.'

'I hope I am making you rethink your entire personal history and then, perhaps, if I have not overestimated you, you will move on from there to consider with me, for a minute or two, the history of the world. Your future, and its.'

'Soft talk!'

'More productive than abuse. And – are you so very much holier than your mother and I were, all those years ago? She was twenty, already neglected, forced to leave her only son behind and come abroad with a husband who made no pretence at loving her. I was twenty-one, with my own misery. We were the greatest comfort to each other. I have never forgotten her. I shall never be able even to dislike you, however much you may find it in your heart to hate me. I see her in you, but I see myself too. What is your father? A country English gentleman with not a thought in his head but of hunting and smuggled brandy, and maybe still a woman or two. And your brother cut straight from the same cloth, by what I hear. They were bound to dislike you . . . Does your brother know, do you think?'

Infuriating to be asked the question that was racking his own brain. But, 'I don't think so,' he said slowly. 'He's never liked me, you're right about that, we're as unlike as chalk and cheese, but – he's a straightforward man – if he had known, I think he'd have showed it.'

'Precisely. Your father's son. Another Whig squire. And you're a diplomat, like me.'

'What makes you think so?'

'My dear Glynde, give me credit for a little common sense and a certain access to information. You've been reporting to your friend Canning since you first came to Europe after Amiens. What other reason could have kept you apparently idle here for so long? And very good letters they are too, the ones I have seen. They have made me quite long to meet you. So, here we are! Two wise old spies confabulating.'

'I'm not a spy!'

'I cry your pardon. Gatherers of intelligence, then. You will find, as you grow older in the business, that the line is a fine drawn one. Now, you are to learn the advantage of having a friend in the enemy's camp. Better than a friend! A father.'

'You're not suggesting we betray our respective masters?' He had not thought he could grow angrier.

'On the contrary, I am suggesting that the better we understand each other, the better we can serve them. To understand all is to be master of all.'

'You'll never master Napoleon!'

'Congratulations! Precisely the conclusion I had reached myself. I'll never master him, but, well enough informed, I may be able to steer him in directions that are equally good for him, and for Europe.'

'You pretend to care about Europe?'

'I do care about Europe. Believe that, or we will never understand each other. I care more for Europe than any of you insular Englishmen will ever do, and understand more of her problems. You have your Channel to defend you; we are all part of each other. I have always hoped to weave Napoleon into the fabric of Europe. Soon now, he'll divorce that poor Josephine and make the marriage he needs.'

'Countess Walewska?'

Talleyrand smiled at him. 'That's not the marriage he needs; it's the one he wants. A very different matter. But when it happens – his dynastic marriage – as I promise you it will, it would be better if it were done with England's blessing. Are you going to tell Canning you are my son?'

The sudden question took Glynde off his guard. 'I don't know . . . I doubt it.'

'A wise doubt. Let it be our secret. It is absolute, so far as I am concerned, and shall remain so. This unusual meeting happened merely because I intervened to protect two young men known to be under the Tsar's wing.'

'Not that we are any longer,' said Glynde. 'He don't much

like the British just now. Look at the way he's treating Gran-ville Leveson Gower.'

Talleyrand smiled his enigmatic smile. 'That's as much a matter of the heart as of politics. You did not know that the Tsar took one of his lightning fancies for Leveson Gower's very good friend, the Princess Galitzin? He was very far from pleased when he heard his rival was returning, my informants tell me.'

'You seem to be better informed about Russia than I am!'

'You should go more into society. Your young friend War-rington is a very good sort of man, I am sure, but has it not struck you that you have let him limit your activities just a little?'

'I suppose I have.' Glynde thought about it. 'You know too much about me! What do you want from me?'

'I like the way you come to the point! I want to feel that when either of us knows something that will advance the cause of peace in Europe, he will share it with the other.'

'So long as it does not prejudice his own country.'

'That, of course. And to show that I mean it, I will give you a piece of news now, to take back with you for your next letter. The treaty of peace between France and Russia was signed yesterday and is being ratified today, at speed. It is all over, for the time being. The Tsar leaves for Petersburg tomorrow or the next day, my Emperor for the west soon after.'

'And the terms of the treaty?'

'Are hard on Prussia, despite Queen Louise's tears. Prussian Poland is to become a Duchy of Warsaw, with Napoleon's protégé, the newly made King of Saxony, for its Lord.'

'Will the Poles like that?'

'Up to a point. But when were the Poles ever satisfied with anything? More important from your British point of view is a secret article of the treaty we have made with Russia.' He stopped for a moment. 'I would advise you to find out what it is.'

'And how do you suggest I set about that?'

'You could try bribing me.'

'Bribing!'

Talleyrand laughed. 'No need to flare up at me; it's a very respectable, old-fashioned approach as between two gatherers of intelligence. And no need to look so shocked either. What is worth having, is worth paying for. I've taken money in my time, as I have no doubt you know, but what I want from you is information. You've been remarkably close to the Tsar now for some years. I've been studying him for two weeks, but not under ideal circumstances. He's fallen under Napoleon's spell for the time being; my master is convinced he holds him in the hollow of his hand. What I want to know is, will it last?'

Glynde thought for a moment. Then: 'I doubt it. He's a great charmer, the Tsar; all things to all men. He bends to his company; hardly knows he's doing it. And – he's been under immense pressure here from his brother and the pro-French party. When he gets back to Petersburg, and still more to Moscow, it will be another story. The Russians don't much like you French.'

'So. He'll change again. That is rather what I thought. That this is not a European arrangement that will last. So we have to be thinking of the next time. By then, I hope to know the Tsar better. That's where I want your help. The story of this escapade of yours, this meeting, is bound to get out. When you next meet the Tsar in one of those chance encounters on the quay, you will give him a good report of me?'

'Without, I take it, mentioning our relationship?'

'Quite so. Just rouse his interest in me, make him wonder a little about me, remind him that I, too, am an aristocrat, unlike those uncouth marshals of Napoleon's. But I'm insulting you with these suggestions; you will know how best to do it.'

'Thank you!' Glynde thought for a moment. 'I can really see no harm in doing that.'

'There is none.'

'And in return?'

'If I tell you the terms of the secret article, how will you get them safely to England?'

'I could go myself.'

'Thus making it entirely obvious that you got them from me. Think again.'

'I could pass them in strictest confidence to my friend Leveson Gower who, I am sure, has his own arrangements for communication with England.'

'Which have not proved very reliable. And, besides, he's not here. But you know Mr. Mackenzie?'

'Of course. A friend of Dr. Wylie's.'

'Among other things. When you leave here tomorrow, you and Mr. Warrington, I shall give you a pass to see more of Tilsit before you recross the river. You will make as many visits to as many ladies as you can scrape acquaintance with. I am sure the two of you will be able to contrive that. And, having crossed the Niemen at last, you will do the same thing on the other side, with the additional pretext of being able to describe your captivity in my formidable hands. And you will make a point of separating from Mr. Warrington in all these houses. I cannot make it too clear to you that my confidence is for you alone. Mr. Warrington is a good enough sort of young man, I have no doubt, but you yourself must be aware of how unfit he is for any diplomatic business.'

'Yes. You're right.' He remembered all the times he had had to bridle Jan's unruly tongue.

'Good. So, by tomorrow night you will have visited as many ladies as possible, on both sides of the Niemen. Then you will seek out Mr. Mackenzie, very much the eager young innocent, and ask him how, in the absence of your friend Leveson Gower, you should set about sending an urgent message to England. Pressed, you will let him get it out of you what the message is, letting him understand that you picked it up, under dubious circumstances, in the house of a lady you refuse to name. He will think you an honest innocent and pass on your message with the scrupulous efficiency for which we professionals respect him.'

'Thank you,' said Glynde drily. 'I take it an honest innocent is how you rate me, too?'

'On the contrary. I rather hope you are growing, as I watch, both in duplicity and in wisdom.'

'And in all this time, you have still not told me the terms of this famous secret article.'

'I have your promise? Of a word to the Tsar?'

'As many as you like.'

'And total silence.' Glynde nodded. 'Yes. Well then, my master has sweet-talked the Tsar into a naval alliance against Great Britain. It is to include France and Russia, of course, and Denmark and Portugal whether they like it or not. All their harbours to be closed to British shipping.'

'Good God!' Glynde took it in. 'It makes Napoleon's Berlin Decrees seem like child's play! It would be death to trade; mean unemployment; starvation; maybe even revolution. And not only in England!'

'Just what I think. And we have had enough of revolution in Europe. I hope your new government has the good sense to take action without delay. And now, it is very late. I think you should join Mr. Warrington, who must, of course, know nothing of this talk. I have been entertaining you with improper stories about Napoleon's marshals.' He proceeded to tell him two. 'And now, bed.' He pulled a rope behind his chair. 'But first, I wish you to meet a young protégé of mine in whom I place absolute trust.'

'Another son?'

'No.' Talleyrand's smile was genial. 'You will doubtless meet my son Flahaut one of these days, and my nephew, young Talleyrand Périgord, for whom I am doing my best to arrange a good marriage here at Tilsit, but Paul Genet is a trusted friend, whom I would like you to trust, too.' He turned as the door opened. 'Ah, Genet, let me introduce Mr. Rendel, with whom I have come to an amicable understanding.' He smiled from one to the other. 'Each of you knows enough to hang me; I do beg you not to compare notes. You have, by the way, friends in common, the Princess Ovinska and her friend Miss Peverel. What is it, Paul?'

'The Prince is dead, sir. Left a letter commending the Poles to the Tsar's benevolence. And leaving all his property to his beloved son, Prince Casimir, the hope of Poland.'

'Good God,' said Glynde. 'I must go to her!'

'Let an older man advise you to do no such thing,' said Talleyrand. 'A house of mourning. And so recent. Is the news out this side of the river?' he asked Genet.

'Not yet.'

'Good.' He glanced at the buhl clock on the chimney-piece. 'Too late for visiting tonight. This piece of news will be your entrée anywhere in the morning. Oh, one more thing, Mr. Rendel. If I should ever be moved to write to you, I shall sign myself merely your friend from Tilsit.'

20

Three rather grumpy young men set off from Talleyrand's house next morning. Jan had the predicted sore head, and was in no mood for paying calls, and Glynde longed to be across the river, condoling with the Princess on her husband's death. He had not been best pleased to learn that Genet was to accompany them, though it was true that this made their entrée much easier, with Genet suavely lying for all three of them. He appeared to be on the best of terms with the French ladies who had followed their Emperor into the wilds, and Glynde was sometimes hard put to it to follow their rapid, idiomatic French. But, more and more, he was aware of something odd, something not quite right in the tone of the inevitable exclamations over Prince Ovinski's death. And why did Prince Murat's name seem to crop up so often among the breathless little sentences?

After the fifth call, Glynde could stand no more, and turned to Genet. 'Many thanks for your company, sir, but I think it is time my friend and I crossed the river and paid our respects to the Princess Ovinska.'

'I was going to suggest the same thing myself,' said Genet. 'I am charged with Monsieur Talleyrand's condolences, and shall look for your good offices on the other side.'

'In fair exchange.' But Glynde, who had counted on leaving Genet behind, was hard put to it to control his irritation. They found the river-crossing busier than ever, and had to wait some time for a boat, which did not improve anybody's temper. The reason was obvious when they reached the Russian side. Everyone was in the throes of packing up. 'The Tsar leaves today,' explained an officer acquaintance of Glynde's. 'The rest of us as soon as we can get horses.'

'Does Dr. Wylie go with the Tsar?'

'Well, of course. He has the Empress Mother's instructions never to leave him. You're not ill, I hope?'

'Lord, no. I was just thinking about Princess Ovinska.' But his mind was quickly registering that Mackenzie would go with Wylie. He must lose no time.

Luckily for him, they found most of the ladies of the court assembled in Princess Ovinska's exiguous parlour making their official calls of condolence before they set off for Petersburg, and she, as he learned from Jenny Peverel, for Vinsk. 'The Prince is to be buried there,' Jenny explained. 'It was his wish. The embalmers are at work now. I shall be glad when it's over.' She was looking exhausted and plainer than ever, her hair severely braided round her head, the scar standing out in her pale face. 'I think the Princess is ready for you now. It must be brief, I am afraid. She intends to speak to everyone.' She led him towards the big chair where the Princess sat enthroned. She was talking fast and seriously with Paul Genet, he noticed with surprise.

'Paul,' Jenny touched his arm. 'Here is Mr. Rendel to speak to the Princess.'

Paul? Glynde looked at the young Frenchman speculatively. Jenny had never used his first name. But now, Paul Genet was kissing the Princess's hand, promising her his master's services if she ever needed them, turning to offer his arm to Jenny, the glow in his eyes telling its own story. No time for that now: 'Princess!' Glynde bent to her hand. 'At last!' So much to say. How to begin? How to say it, here among this crowd of acquaintances? But it was his only chance, and the babble of the crowd gave a kind of privacy.

'At last, Mr. Rendel? You are not, I imagine, referring to the sad death of my husband, the Prince.'

Her tone, and her deep black should have warned him, but he had played this scene so often in his imagination that it went on almost without his own volition. 'At last you are free.' He tried to keep hold of her hand, lost it just the same. 'I have waited all these years, Princess, with burning love, with constant devotion, for this moment when I can say: "Be mine. Be my wife."'

'Your father and brother are dead perhaps, Mr. Rendel?'

'I do not understand you.' He stared at her with amazement and a kind of horror.

'Yes you do. I am asking what you have to offer me, what

214

help in the hard years to come, that I should give up my freedom, my absolute authority. And with my husband scarce cold in his bed. You shock me, Mr. Rendel. But I forgive you as an old friend . . . I am left a great charge, you know. My son, the hope of Poland. His father called him that on his deathbed. You did not know? He has made him his absolute heir. And I am his guardian.'

'And when he grows up —'

'Miss Peverel.' The Princess's cool, autocratic voice drowned his. 'Mr. Rendel is asking to see Casimir before he leaves. Perhaps Lech or Marylka could take him? But pray do not speak to the child of his father's death, Mr. Rendel. He was there, held close in his arm, when it happened. He needs to begin to forget.' She looked past him, held out her hand: 'Mr. Warrington, how good of you to come. You find me mourning among my friends.'

Casimir was in the stables, helping the grooms clean tack, and so obviously and happily absorbed in what he was doing that Glynde merely smiled, patted his head, and paused to watch him for a moment, trying to digest what had happened. His son. But the Princess would never admit it. She had made that ruthlessly clear. Fool; idiot to have approached her so absurdly too soon. But at least now, she knew that he was there, always, waiting for her. And what she had said about his father and brother . . . There was a certain ruthless sense in that, too. If he was to have any hope, he must make himself a man of power for her sake. Memory of his talk with Talleyrand filtered into his mind, bringing a hint of hope. I'll make myself her equal, he thought, a father for a Prince.

He turned sharply at the sound of his own name. 'Monsieur Genet?' He had hoped himself quit of him.

'I am told the Tsar leaves very soon,' Paul Genet told him. 'You will want to take your leave of him, I am sure.'

'Yes.' He waited in silent anger for Genet to propose to accompany him.

'I wish I could join you. Do, pray, say everything that is civil to the Tsar from my master. I still have a word, myself, to say to Miss Peverel.'

'Say goodbye to her for me, would you? Not that she'll notice my absence, so important as she is these days. The Princess's right hand, wouldn't you say?'

'Not always the safest position.' Some curious shade had crossed the other man's face while Glynde was speaking, but before he could try to identify it, Genet turned away: 'Mr. Warrington! Come to pay your respects to the little Prince, too?'

'The hope of Poland? Hey, Casimir, how you've grown! Too big to ride on my shoulder now, are you?' And contradicting the words, Jan tossed him up on to his shoulder for a swift run round the stable yard, the little Prince laughing and hanging on to his curling dark hair.

Something about the spectacle disgusted Glynde. Or was he jealous, because he had not the same gift with children? At all events, he took a brusque leave of Paul Genet. 'Tell Warrington I've an errand to do, would you? I'll see him back at our lodgings. And thank your master again on both our behalfs.'

'I most certainly will. We will meet again, I hope.'

'Some day?' Without enthusiasm.

Hurrying to the palace, he tried to calm his seething thoughts. Madness to have approached the Princess so soon. All his own fault? But what other chance would there have been? Or was the real madness even to have hoped? To have imagined an English gentleman the equal . . . He stopped at the thought . . . Not an English gentleman; the bastard son of a Frenchman. But she could not know that. As for the calumnies he had heard hinted about her, he most absolutely did not believe them. Would not believe them. What she had done in the past, she had done for her country. So – the inevitable question presented itself – what might she do now, for her son? Suppose he were to tell her of his relationship with Talleyrand, the *éminence grise* of Europe? Of the possible influence he might have? And knew the answer as he half formulated the thought. She would laugh, and dismiss him: a nameless bastard. And she a Princess.

He found Mackenzie helping Dr. Wylie pack up his medicaments for the long journey back to Petersburg, and the conversation inevitably started with the Prince's death. 'A foregone conclusion, I'm afraid,' said Wylie, 'but I did not wish to discourage the Princess too soon. We'll be lucky if that's the worst thing to come out of Tilsit. I for one will be glad to see my master safe home at Petersburg.'

'Before the cold weather sets in,' said Mackenzie. 'These country quarters are all very fine in summertime. I shall be glad to be back in my own bed.'

'In Petersburg or in England?' asked Wylie.

'If I could only decide. The chance of the *Astrea* actually at anchor off Memel is a temptation indeed. And to be spared all those miles of rutted road between here and Petersburg. And yet – the pleasure of your company is a great inducement!'

'Thank you,' said Wylie. 'But, for the moment, can I persuade you to do without it? I have affairs that need my attention, if you two gentlemen will excuse me.'

'Let's take a turn in the gardens,' said Mackenzie. 'I long to hear more of this rash venture of yours into Tilsit.'

It was the chance Glynde had been hoping for, and he lost no time in telling Mackenzie the tale Talleyrand had suggested.

'I wish you would name your source, Mr. Rendel,' Mackenzie said at last. 'You must see that it makes my position difficult. And I wish, too, that you would explain to me what inspired you to bring this story to me.'

'Common sense, Mr. Mackenzie.' He was relieved that they were interrupted at this point by Dr. Wylie, with the news that the Tsar proposed to start in half an hour. 'It's time you made up your mind, my friend.'

'I have,' said Mackenzie. 'I'm for England.'

Paul Genet found the Princess and Jenny alone, the last guest gone. 'Forgive me for coming back to trouble you, Highness, when you must be exhausted.' A quick glance from one to the other told him that they had been quarrelling. 'I came to ask if Miss Peverel would take a breath of air with me. This is no place for an unattended lady, I am afraid, until the court goes. I hope you have arranged for an adequate escort for the journey to Vinsk, Princess?'

'So do I! Yes – do get your bonnet, Jenny. A turn in the air will do you good. And I shall be glad to be alone, for once.'

'I'll wait for you outside.' He and Jenny exchanged glances.

'Poor lady,' he said, when she joined him five minutes later.

217

'She's been having an unhappy time of it. To put it mildly. That's a very fetching bonnet, if I may say so.'

'Compliments, Monsieur Genet?'

'You called me Paul earlier today.'

'I know.' She blushed crimson.

'And I know why. It was to tease Mr. Rendel, was it not?' He had taken her arm and led her round the corner of the house to the neglected pleasure gardens. 'Miss Peverel – Jenny – may I speak to you like a brother? The one you lost at Aboukir Bay?'

'You remember that?'

'Of course I do. And telling you that my father died there, too. Which was true, by the way.'

'I never doubted it.'

'Thank you. I am not always truthful. In my way of life, it is not possible, but what I am saying now is God's truth. As I see it.'

'A timely qualification, Monsieur Genet.'

'I liked it when you called me Paul. Whatever the reason. And, coming to that reason, that's what I came to talk about.'

'Like a brother?'

'Like someone who cares for you very much. Worries about you. It won't do, you know.' They had been walking down an avenue of shaggy lime trees; now, at the end of it, moving out of sight of the house, he stopped, turned her to face him. 'He's entirely beglamoured. Even now, he won't get over her.'

'What do you mean?' But she knew.

'Fool of a man.' He said it with complete toleration. 'He proposed today, didn't he? In the midst of the gossiping crowd. And got his comeuppance, as anyone could have seen he would. He's in a rage at the moment, but it won't last. He's under her spell; don't let yourself think otherwise, Jenny. How old are you?'

'Twenty-six.' The big grey eyes met his straight, but through a veil of tears. 'What a very personal question, Monsieur Genet.'

'I'm speaking to you like a brother, remember.'

'A brother would know.' But she was smiling now, an uncertain smile.

'Twenty-six, and never been kissed.' She thought for a mad

218

moment that he was going to rectify this, but he put both hands on her shoulders and held her, studying her, grey eyes meeting grey eyes. 'There's more to life than romantic passion, Jenny. In France, we arrange our marriages; by and large, they work very well.'

'By and large.' She was still meeting his eyes. 'We have arranged marriages in England too, only we don't call them that. My mother married my father, because he was the only man who proposed to her. She was plain, like me, with no fortune, like me. He made every minute of her life a misery. A petty tyrant. I couldn't bear to go on watching it. That's why I came to Poland. Single life has to be better than that.'

'Would your mother think so?'

'This is a very strange conversation.' She thought about it, their eyes still locked. 'I don't know,' she said at last, slowly. 'I absolutely do not know.'

'She has children? How many?'

'Three of us girls, and my dead brother. My sisters are married. I was the failure.' She thought about this, now. 'I had never thought: I believe she hoped I would stay at home.'

'And help her tame the tyrant, your father?'

'I rather think so. Oh, poor mother, how good she was. She never said a word.'

'Was? She's dead?'

'No. But her life's over, such as it was. My father died three years ago, leaving her with nothing. My sisters complain about having to keep her. I don't think I shall ever see her again.'

'There's no place for you there? You're very much alone, Jenny, are you not?'

'I suppose I am.' This conversation, opening up the past for once, brought it home to her. Particularly after the sudden quarrel with the Princess.

'Don't be. Jenny – Miss Peverel –' Formally now. 'I know it is too soon. I know you do not love me. But – tomorrow my master leaves for France, and I go with him. The next day, you go with the Princess to Vinsk. Who knows? We may never meet again. Now is our time. Now is my chance. Say you'll marry me, Jenny, and I swear you will never regret it. Everything shall be as you wish, for as long as you wish. I promise I'll make you love me, in the end.'

Now, at last, she looked away, detached herself gently from his grasp, moved from him to gaze down at weed-infested ornamental water. 'Arranging your own marriage, Monsieur Genet, like a good Frenchman? You pay me a great compliment, but I must thank you and refuse. You seem to have forgotten that we are enemies.'

'But we are not! You know perfectly well that we are not. We're friends, Jenny, the best of friends. We could so easily be more. Say you'll marry me! I'll tell my master. I know he'd help me . . .'

'Do what? Our countries are at war, Monsieur Genet. You're a soldier. Can you imagine presenting me to Napoleon?'

'Easily. He'd like you. I know it. Besides, look at the marriages he's made for his family.'

'That's different, as you well know. There's one law for aristocrats; another for the rest of us.'

'I'm more of an aristocrat than that upstart Napoleon. Before the Revolution . . .'

'Was a long time ago. And this is all beside the point. I'll never marry without love, Monsieur Genet.'

'I'll make you love me –'

'By force?'

'No! Damnation. What is it?' Lech had come running from the lime walk.

'There you are, Pani Peverel. Thank God I've found you. The Princess needs you urgently.'

'What's happened?' She turned and started moving back towards the house, the two men following.

'I don't know. The Tsar came to see her.'

'The Tsar?'

'Yes. Hurry, please, pani!' There was no mistaking his sense of urgency, and she was glad of Paul Genet's arm, helping her as she half walked half ran over the rough grass of the walk. But glad, too, that with Lech close behind them further conversation was impossible.

When they reached the house, she detached herself, held out her hand. 'Goodbye, Monsieur Genet. And I do thank you.'

'I won't give up.' He bent to kiss her hand. 'Remember, I am at your service. Always.'

The Princess was shouting orders at a terrified Marylka. 'There you are at last,' she turned on Jenny. 'Never there when you are wanted. We leave tomorrow. For Petersburg, in the Tsar's train.'

'What?' Jenny could not believe her ears.

'You heard me. The Tsar has been here. He made it a request, but it was one that had to be obeyed. He says the Prince must be buried in the cathedral. It's a great honour.'

'But not what he wanted.'

'He's dead,' said the Princess bleakly. And then, brightening. 'The Tsar saw Casimir at last! He was kindness itself, Jenny. Said all sorts of things. That Casimir must stay for a while in the Ovinski palace at Petersburg. As its owner.'

'For a while?'

'That's what he said.'

'And the Brotherhood?' They had been quarrelling earlier about whether to approach them about the long, hazardous journey back to Vinsk. Jenny had wished to do so, and the Princess had insisted that there was no need.

'Oh, do what you like! Nothing can make any difference to the Tsar's orders. Even They must see that. Send Them a message, if you wish, to say we are going. Just think, Jenny, we are going to see Petersburg!' Something was different about the Princess, Jenny thought; something had changed in her. The shock of her husband's death had passed, and there was a subdued glow about her, an expectation. Of what?

But it made it possible to ask a question she had longed to. 'Did the Tsar say anything about this new Grand Duchy of Warsaw? About how it would affect you, with estates there as well as in Austrian and Russian Poland?'

'He said it would be under French control,' said the Princess. 'The King of Saxony will be the figurehead, but the French will rule. No other Ambassadors are to be allowed. But he promises that people under his protection will be safe under his brother Napoleon. That is one of the reasons why Casimir and I are to go to Petersburg. To make our position clear. He speaks with enthusiasm of Napoleon: a great man, a visionary, with a huge grasp of the future of Europe. And keep a careful tongue in your head. The Tsar don't much like you British.

More talk than action, he says. He's learned it by bitter experience. So – you'll watch yourself in Petersburg.'

Paul Genet loitered to some purpose outside the Princess's quarters, and was able to take the news of her change of plan back to Talleyrand.

'So?' Talleyrand thought about it. 'The Tsar had been to see her in person?'

'Apparently. Talked with her for half an hour alone.'

'Promising great things for the little Prince, no doubt. Did he see him?'

'Yes. Patted his head.'

'He's no fool, Alexander. I see that more and more. I wonder just how he means to use the Princess. Remind me to have a word with Savary about her before he leaves for Petersburg.'

'Savary? You can't mean that he is going as Ambassador? One of d'Enghien's killers?'

'I'm afraid so. I should think he would find it an uncomfortable appointment, would not you? Russian society will hardly welcome him with open arms.'

21

That was the most brilliant autumn season in Petersburg for years. The Tsar had returned to find that the Russian people did not share his enthusiasm for Napoleon. The Treaty of Tilsit had seriously damaged his popularity, and the presence of the detested Savary as French Ambassador did nothing to improve matters. At Tilsit, his brother the Archduke Constantine had hinted at a threat of assassination if he did not make peace with Napoleon. Now, back in his capital, he found the threat looming because he had. But at least he had peace, and a chance to rebuild the army that had been shattered at Eylau and Friedland. Handing this duty to his protégé Arakchayev, who had already revolutionised the artillery, he plunged himself into the social whirl, aiming to charm where he could not convince.

He was a regular visitor at the Ovinski Palace, where the Princess was now established. 'I treat you quite like an old friend.' He had found her and Jenny taking tea in the conservatory Prince Ovinski had had built between his palace and the Fontanka Canal. 'Before I leave for my travels, I want to know how things go on in the new Duchy of Warsaw, Princess, and I am sure you two ladies will know as well as anyone.'

'You are going away, sire?' asked the Princess.

'A small tour in White Russia, to look at some garrison towns: Polotsk, Vitebsk, Minsk. He who wants peace must be ready for war.'

'So far? You are a most intrepid traveller, sire.'

'Too much of the sire, ma'am. It is plain Pan Thaddeus today, wanting news of his Polish friends.'

'There is so little. But I did hear from Countess Potocka the other day. She does not seem altogether enamoured of the new arrangement.'

'No?' He drew his chair closer to hers, holding out his cup for more tea.

'No.' She poured it for him, smiling into his eyes. 'A French army of three thousand men to be supported, after all the sacrifices Poland has already made! And the country more cut off than ever . . . No foreign representatives . . . The King of Saxony shows no sign of coming to see his new Duchy. The French Minister is all-powerful. They are disappointed, I think, bitterly disappointed.'

'Are they so?' It was, Jenny thought, what he had wanted to hear. 'The Countess Potocka,' he said thoughtfully. 'I remember her well. She entertained me most delightfully at Willanow two years ago. A charming young lady. Do pray send her my kindest regards when you next write to her. Tell her I look forward to our next meeting. And you, Princess, may an old friend ask about your plans? Do you mean to honour us with your company here in Petersburg this winter, or do the claims of home call you?'

'To tell you the truth, sire, I have not quite made up my mind. It is hard to decide what would be best for my son, who must be the centre of my thoughts.'

'How long since he has been at your beautiful palace of Rendomierz?'

'Just since the spring.' She and Jenny looked at each other, remembering the desperate return to Warsaw after little Casimir had been kidnapped. 'But we were hardly there for any time.'

'I hope you are not letting him forget his Polish?'

'Oh, no. His servants are all Poles, of course.'

'Quite so.' The Tsar rose. 'Just the same, I wonder if you might not be wise to think about taking him home.'

'To Vinsk, or Rendomierz, sire?'

'Both, surely. Tilsit has ushered in a period of peace and prosperity. We are all to be friends now. Protected by me, your young Prince should be equally at home in Vinsk, Rendomierz or even Warsaw. Not to speak of Petersburg!'

When he had gone, the Princess turned to Jenny, eyes shining. 'You heard him! It was as good as a promise, Jenny. He wants Casimir brought up as a Pole, the hope of Poland. Give the orders to leave at once.' And then, 'But, no. I must take leave of the Empresses, and that takes time to arrange. When the roads have hardened will be best. Maybe after the

Tsar returns from his tour, God bless him. I should be sad not to see him to say goodbye, and thank him.'

'So long as he does not change his mind,' said Jenny. 'He does seem rather to do so.'

'Oh, must you always croak at me, and believe the worst? You British are all the same, constantly making difficulties. And that reminds me, if Mr. Rendel calls again, you are to see him for me. I am tired of having him dawdling round the palace as if he had nothing else to do. Make him see that. Isn't it time he went back to England, anyway? We both knew very well what the Tsar meant when he said he hoped we could all be friends. It's you British who insist on keeping on with this interminable fighting. If only they would come to terms with Napoleon, perhaps we Europeans would be able to settle our own destinies.'

'I wonder if Napoleon would let you,' said Jenny.

'Croaking again! I tell you, I'm sick of it!'

'Then perhaps, Highness, it would be best if I were to make arrangements to go back to England.' The words were out almost before Jenny knew what she was doing. 'With so many people leaving, I am sure I could find someone to go with.'

'What?' This had surprised the Princess. 'You want to leave us? Casimir would miss you.' She was thinking about it.

'I think perhaps it is time I went, Highness. I shall be more sorry than I can say to leave Casimir, but the fact remains that I am British; all the rumours suggest that we will be ordered out any day now. Do you want an acknowledged enemy in your household?'

'Oh, enemy! It won't be like that. We're not going to war, or anything so absurd. It's just that your nation of tradesmen are making life impossible for us.'

'You're sure it is not Napoleon who is doing that? His Berlin Decrees came first, after all.'

'Oh, politics! I'm sick to death of them. Ring for my maid, Jenny, I must go and start making arrangements for my official farewells. You know how long it can take.'

'But about me,' Jenny paused, hand on the bell-pull. 'If I am to go, Highness, I must start thinking about arrangements, too.' It was not going to be easy, either. She had lived luxuriously with the Princess, but the only pay she had ever received had been the ruby necklace Prince Ovinski had given her, so long ago. She would have to arrange to sell it, and hope that it would fetch enough to pay the expenses of her journey. And return home penniless . . . It was not a happy prospect.

'Oh, do as you think best,' said the Princess impatiently. 'If you are homesick, pray don't let me keep you. Casimir will miss you, of course.' She did not choose to say that she would.

'But not for long.' Jenny rang the bell.

The serf who answered it brought the news that Mr. Rendel had called and was waiting in one of the small salons.

'Tell him I'm out,' said the Princess. And then, 'No, you see him for me, Jenny. Perhaps he will help you with your arrangements. You'd like that, wouldn't you? Give him my best wishes for a safe journey home, and bid him goodbye for me. Tell him there is no need for him to call again.' She turned to the maid. 'My furs, Gabriela. I'm going out.'

Dismissed, Jenny made her gloomy way to the seldom-used parlour, where Glynde Rendel had been left to wait. The Princess must have already given orders that he was to be treated as a less than welcome guest.

He was standing, looking out at the bleak garden, where snow was falling idly. 'Highness!' He turned eagerly at the sound of the door, then: 'Miss Peverel,' on a falling note.

'Mr. Rendel. I am so sorry, the Princess has had to go out. She asked me to make her excuses, and wish you well for your journey home.'

'Home? She thinks I am leaving?'

'Perhaps she thinks you would be wise to do so.'

'Kind of her to think about me. It's true; my friend Leveson Gower was approached by someone, just the other day, offering to buy his horses, assuming he was leaving.'

'As if they knew something he didn't?'

'Exactly. The town is so full of rumours it's impossible to be sure of anything. But the Princess –' his tone softened when he spoke of her. 'She must have access to the most reliable information. Such exalted company as she keeps.' He coloured. 'Forgive me, I do not wish to sound like another Petersburg gossip, but it was impossible not to recognise the guest who was leaving as I arrived. No wonder I have been left to cool my heels!' He smiled at her, that heart-twisting smile. 'Do you

226

remember the first time they met? And what a disaster it would have been, but for your quick wits? And hers! I'm so glad she has such a good friend in him,' he went on, careful, Jenny noticed, not to name the august name. 'It's a heavy burden of responsibility she carries since the Prince's death. The little Prince – the hope of Poland – and all his estates. Will she stay here in Petersburg much longer, do you think?'

'No.' Here was her chance to get her unwelcome message across. 'I think she plans to leave quite soon.'

'His advice?'

'I think, Mr. Rendel, you must see that that is entirely her affair,' she said gently.

'Forgive me! I care so much . . . If only I could be of use to her . . . serve her in some way.' His colour was high again, and she actually felt herself sorry for him. 'We were such friends, such good friends, back at Rendomierz . . .'

'Yes.' She smiled, remembering. 'But everything was different there, Mr. Rendel. You must see that. There, she was the *châtelaine*, the mistress of the house. Here, she's a great lady.'

'You feel it, too?' Suddenly she had his attention.

'Yes. In fact, Mr. Rendel, I had it in mind to ask you . . .' She paused, looking for the right words. 'If you should know of an English family, going back, who might need a travelling companion, a governess, anything?'

'You?' Now she had his concentrated attention. 'But you'd never leave her! Not you. Her right hand. Her support. Surely, her friend? You'd never fail her so!'

'Fail?' She could have shaken him. 'It's not quite like that, Mr. Rendel. We British are sadly out of favour here. I think the Princess is beginning to wonder whether she could afford to keep me.'

'Afford? But she's rich beyond measure, beyond comprehension . . .'

Jenny laughed, surprising them both. 'Not that kind of expense, Mr. Rendel.' She looked down at her silk dress, her cashmere shawl. 'The Princess has been kindness itself to me, generous, as to all her dependants.' She thought about it for a moment. 'We must look well, or shame her. But,' she looked up and met his eyes, 'she treats me like the rest of her serfs.

I've never had a penny in salary from her, all the time I've been with her. I have to tell you this.' She had seen how it shocked him. 'Because I need to ask you, Mr. Rendel, if you could bring yourself to help me in selling my only earnings, a ruby necklace the Prince gave me, years ago, at Rendomierz. That has to pay my passage home.'

'But why do you want to go? To leave her?' In his deep concern for the Princess, he was hardly taking in her own predicament.

'Because she thinks it's time I went. Just now, the British connection is an ill-omened one. We have to face it, Mr. Rendel, she is better without us, you and me.'

'Oh.' She watched him, infinitely sorry for him, as he took it in. 'You mean, she wants me to go, too?' He ran a hand through his hair. 'I've been stupid, haven't I? Time I went. And of course I'll help you to a safe way home to England, if that is really what you want; what she wants! But the boy, Prince Casimir, who will care for him as you have done?'

'That does worry me, he's such a promising child! But even his mother doesn't seem to see what harm it does him to be let run wild as he is.' She could not tell him or anyone of her greatest anxiety: the strong, unreasonable dislike Casimir had taken to the Tsar. Or was it unreasonable?

'She has so much on her mind.' Glynde took Jenny's hand, and felt it quiver in his. 'Don't go! Don't leave her. I'm sure, in her heart, she knows how badly she and the boy need you. If I do have to go, I'd be so much happier to know you are still with them. Please?'

'It's not my decision. If she wants me to go, I go.'

'And if she does, I'll help you. She's really out? If I could only see her; try to persuade her.'

'She's really out.' Withdrawing her hand. 'But, Mr. Rendel, she doesn't want to see you. I'm sorry.'

She found Marylka waiting in her room. 'There's a message, Pani Jenny. Lech brought it. Someone spoke to him as he left the cathedral this morning. They say it is time the Princess went home. And took you with her. You weren't thinking of leaving us, pani? They told Lech to remind you and the mistress that their arm is long. If you try to go to England,

228

you'll be stopped as a spy. Were you really thinking of leaving us?'

'It had come up . . . The Princess . . .'

'Is thinking Russian thoughts,' said Marylka surprisingly. 'They're right, pani. It is time we went home.'

The Princess came back from her afternoon round of visits in a thoughtful mood. She surprised Jenny by sending for her at once.

'They all say I am wise to go.' She had dismissed her maid. 'I hadn't quite realised how little the Empress and the Empress Mother like the French. And they say feeling in Moscow is fierce against this alliance; that the Tsar will never be able to hold to it; even if he goes on wanting to. That this is a time when wise people stay at home and keep quiet. Sir Robert Wilson was at the Empress Mother's palace; treated like a dear friend; he's just back with some new message for the Tsar. To England and back in seventeen days, or something amazing like that. An uppish young man, very full of himself, but the Empress Mother seems to like him just the same. I don't know what to think, Jenny.'

It was good to be called Jenny again. 'Princess, I've had a message; from the Brotherhood. They say it's time you went home. And –' she felt herself colour '– They want you to take me with you.'

'Taking a great deal on themselves!' The Princess was predictably angry. 'But of course that was a crazy idea of yours, about going back to England. I can't think what put it into your head. You're part of my family. Mine and Casimir's. We can't possibly do without you, so let that be the end of it, please.'

'Very well.' A brave woman, Jenny thought, would have said something about a salary, but, if so, she was not a brave woman.

Two days later, the Foreign Minister, Count Rumyantsev, declared war on England. A hastily scrawled message from Glynde informed Jenny that he was leaving with Granville Leveson Gower. 'I have spoken to George Richards,' he wrote. 'He promises to look after you, if you feel you must leave, but may I urge you once again to stay. I am so very sorry not to be able to see you, or the Princess again. Please assure her of my enduring devotion and earnest hope that we will meet again.'

'So much for that,' said the Princess. I'll never see him again, thought Jenny. And Glynde, starting out on the long, dangerous journey home, found himself thinking what a gallant companion she would have made. And thanking God she had stayed with the Princess, and his son.

22

England seemed a foreign land to Glynde after his five years abroad. All the talk that winter of 1807 was of Napoleon's new wars against Spain and Portugal. British progress there was of much more interest to the public than anything that had been going on so much further away, in eastern Europe. People asked him polite questions about life in Russia, and then hardly listened to his answers. Nothing the Tsar could do was half so important in English eyes as the fact that the would-be King of France, Louis XVIII, had landed at Yarmouth under the name of the Count de Lille, and been received without much enthusiasm by the British government, itself involved in abortive peace negotiations with Napoleon.

Glynde's old friend Canning was still Foreign Minister, but he, too, was preoccupied with the seething pot of the Iberian Peninsula. And he had been infuriated by Glynde's continued refusal to tell him the source of the vital information about the secret articles of the Treaty of Tilsit that had precipitated British action both in Denmark and in Portugal. It weighed on Glynde's conscience that he had not done so. But to tell Canning that his informant was Talleyrand would have meant telling him of their relationship, and how could he do that? He had held to it that his source had been a lady he must not compromise, thought Canning justifiably angry, and been sad but not surprised when Canning made only vague promises about future employment for him.

Feeling at odds with London society, he went to pay the essential courtesy visit at Ringmer Place, and was shocked at the change in Lord Ringmer's appearance. He had become an old man, and Glynde supposed his son must stay with him out of filial anxiety, but they made an irascible pair, and it was a relief to receive an invitation from his mother's surviving sister.

Maud Savage had moved to Brighton long before the Prince

Regent had made the little watering place popular. She had been the beauty of her family and the gossips had been surprised when she failed to marry. As a child, Glynde had been afraid of her sharp tongue, but when he came back wounded and in disgrace from Valmy, it was she who had taken him in and nursed him back to health. Her comfortable, unpretentious house in Ship Street, with its wide views of the sea, had been home to him from then on.

'It's good to be home.' He had ridden over the downs from Ringmer. 'You've not changed in the least, aunt.' It was almost true. Always small, fine-boned, elegant, she was tiny now, the grey hair white, the blue eyes sharp as ever.

'I won't say the same of you.' She looked him over thoughtfully. 'You've grown up, I believe. Or are growing? Something that brother of yours will never do. How did you find them? He and your father?'

'Not my father.' Had he meant to tell her this?

'Ah? You found out. That's a weight off my mind. I'd been wondering whether it was not perhaps my duty to tell you. In fairness to him as much as anything else.'

'It does explain a good deal. Why should he like me? I have to be grateful to him for letting me take his name.'

'I think you do.'

'But my mother? Aunt Maud, I have to know. How was he to her?'

'Do you need to ask? Irreproachably courteous and unbelievably cruel. I wanted her to come here to me; he would not allow it. If he was going to acknowledge you as his, there must be nothing to suggest otherwise. It killed her, I think, the way he treated her. She tried so hard to live, to endure it, for your sake, but she wasn't strong like me. She was a gentle creature, your mother; she could not bear the quiet unkindness. They called it a wasting disease, but I think it was just misery. I wanted to have you when she died, but of course he would not allow that either. How do he and his son go on?'

'Badly. They are too much alike to be able to live together. I cannot imagine why they do.'

'Of necessity. Can you really not have heard of your brother's marriage?'

'He's married!'

'Disastrously. A run-away match with what he thought was a great fortune. A complete take-in, and to make things worse, the poor girl bore him an idiot child, then lost her own wits. The expense of keeping the two of them shut away, and some extravagances of his own constrain him to live at Ringmer.'

'Dear God! I knew nothing of it. Poor Christopher . . .'

'Well, yes, poor Christopher. Up to a point.'

'What do you mean?'

'That the insanity is on his side, and that I suspect it was his treatment of his wife after the child was born that sent her off her head. I cannot tell you how glad I am that his name is all you can have inherited from Lord Ringmer, Glynde.'

'But you're sure? This is certain?' He could not help thinking of how it might affect him. Suppose the Princess should hear that he came from tainted stock.

'Certain enough for anyone who cared to investigate. You did not know that I was engaged to your father first? I broke it off after I saw him in one of his rages, asked a few questions. Like a proud fool, I went away, kept quiet about my reasons. I sometimes think he married your poor mother to spite me. But that's enough of the sad past. Are you taking in what this means for your future? Like it or not, you are likely to find yourself Lord Ringmer in the end. He can hardly disown you now.'

'No wonder they hate me.' He was thinking of the Princess again, that sharp question of hers. If he went back to her, as Lord Ringmer? But, with a tale of madness in the family?

'It's not easy, is it, Glynde?' Her tone made him wonder just how much she knew, or suspected. 'Pull the bell for me, would you? I tend to drink a glass of something at this time of day, for my health's sake, and I imagine you would not mind joining me.' And then, when he had poured wine for them both. 'Now, tell me about this fairy-tale Princess of yours.'

'Fairy-tale?'

'That's how you painted her in your letters. A creature of fantasy. A rose without a thorn. Poor Glynde.' Her smile was almost more understanding than he could bear. 'Do you love her so very much?'

'How can I help it?'

233

'Your bright, particular star? I'm glad you have come home. You've been mad a little, have you not? Beglamoured?'

'I suppose so.' Reluctantly. It angered him to sense what a fool she thought him for his passion, but how could he tell her the truth of his relationship with the Princess, the grounds he had for his obstinate hope?

'Here's to romance!' She drained her glass. 'A little of it never hurt anyone. But I'll tell you one thing, Glynde, before we start looking about for a good match for you. The person your letters made me want to meet was not your fairy Princess at all, but plain Miss Peverel from the other end of Sussex. I did meet her once, at Petworth House, a very long time ago. A quiet young thing, I remember, but she struck me as having a great deal of sense, and concealing it admirably.'

Glynde laughed. 'Miss Peverel to the life. She is a most inspiring listener. The Princess is lucky to have her for a companion, and as for the little Prince, Jenny Peverel has been the making of him. All Europe may be grateful to her one day.'

In the end, the Princess went to Rendomierz. She paused long enough at Vinsk to celebrate Christmas and see Grucz remarried to one of his numerous poverty-stricken cousins, and Jenny, who had refused him three times on the journey, breathed a sigh of relief. 'I need you with me,' was all the Princess said about it. 'Rendomierz is going to be a dead bore after Petersburg. I mean to spend most of the winters in Warsaw, of course.'

'In Warsaw? Under the French?'

'Why not? We're all friends now. And Casimir must grow up among his fellow Poles. Must know and be known. I've written to Anna Potocka to ask how things go in the Duchy these days. Her father-in-law's in the government after all. And you might write to Marie Walewska. They say she's still likely to be well informed.' She gave one of her quick glances to the looking-glass. 'A pity it's Davout in charge of the army there, not Murat, or another of our old friends. Baron Vincent, the French Minister is a nothing, they say, but a nothing in absolute power. It will be interesting to see how the government of the Duchy goes on. They've problems enough, by what one hears: food, money, an occupying army.' She put her hand to her mouth. 'Forget I said that! Josef Poniatowski says they are liberators. He begins to think highly of Marshal Davout, he tells me. A man who believes in the future of Poland. And Josef has great plans for our own army.'

'He's still in command?'

'Of course he is. Who else?'

When they got to Warsaw at the end of March, they found it quiet enough, with families still reeling under late news of the fates of sons and brothers who had fought in the summer campaign. Anna Potocka was in heavy mourning, having just returned from her great aunt's deathbed at the family palace in Bialystok. 'Madame de Cracovie was one of the last of the great Polish ladies,' Isobel told Jenny. 'She was King Stanislas Augustus's sister, Josef Poniatowski's aunt. All Poland will mourn her.'

'What does Countess Potocka say about things in Bialystok under the Russians?' Jenny asked. 'How do they go on?' Though the *Warsaw Gazette* was closely controlled, she had heard rumours of Russian reprisals against serfs who had joined the advancing French army.

'Oh, well enough! To tell truth she did not say much about it. She certainly had no trouble getting there and back. Oh, yes, she did mention something about a steward who had been sent to Siberia. Served him right, I have no doubt, but she seemed to miss him. But she told me one thing that will surprise you. Do you know where your friend Marie Walewska is?'

'No. I knew she was from home.'

'She's in Paris, would you believe it! What it is to be monarch of the world! He sends for her half across Europe, and she goes to him as meek and public as you please! Not presented at court, you understand. Well, how could she be? But living in the greatest comfort in the Rue de la Houssaye; seen at the Opéra; dressed by Leroy. I wonder where it will all end.'

'So do I,' said Jenny.

When she heard, at the end of the month, that Marie had returned to Warsaw, she made haste to call, urged on by the Princess. 'She's to be recognised still, it seems. Davout has let it be known, through that wife of his who thinks herself so important because her brother married Napoleon's sister. You call on the Walewska, Jenny, I have better things to do.'

'Jenny!' Marie came towards her with open arms. 'I am so very glad to see you safe. I wondered so much about you, at the time of Tilsit. You are well, you are happy, you go on as always with the Princess Ovinska?'

'Yes to it all.' Jenny returned the embrace with enthusiasm. 'And all the better for seeing you!' She held her off at arms' length. 'Anyone can see you have been to Paris! I would not have thought you could be more elegant. Be ready to be heartily disliked, dear Marie, by all the Polish ladies.'

'Not including you! But you know how much he cares about dress.' For Marie, Jenny had learned, there was only one he. 'I've scolded him many times for the sharp things he says to ladies whose costume does not please him. So of course I made an effort. And Monsieur Leroy, the great designer, was so good to me!'

'No wonder,' said Jenny. 'He must have enjoyed himself. The Princess will be wild to go to Paris, too, when she sees you. But, Marie, if you were enjoying yourself so much there, why did you come back to sad little Warsaw?'

'My home, Jenny. And for the best of reasons. He had to go away. This trouble in Spain is becoming almost serious, he thinks. He's gone to see to it himself. He'll soon show those boorish Spanish peasants the error of their ways. But Paris is nothing to me without him there, so of course I came home.'

'And the Count, your husband?' Greatly daring, Jenny asked the question.

'I haven't seen him. Don't propose to if it can be avoided. But you must see, Jenny, the changes in our law at Dresden last summer.' She coloured. 'They are going to make a great difference.'

'The Code Napoleon, you mean, as it now applies in the Grand Duchy? I'm sure it is an admirable thing that there should be a proper code of laws at last here in Poland, but I'm afraid I'm stupid; I don't quite understand . . .'

'No, why should you? There does seem to have been some delay in publishing the details here, and of course there is no reason why it should concern you.' Marie smiled, her colour still high. 'But, Jenny, divorce has become a possibility here for the first time. I wonder if that is why he would not let me risk scandal by going to Dresden last year. He thinks of everything!'

'You can't mean?' Jenny took it in with amazement. 'That he might divorce the Empress? And you the Count?'

'He loves me. He truly does. And then, oh Jenny! Just think what I could do for Poland!'

'Marie!' Now she was afraid for her friend. 'I do beg of you to be careful . . . not to hope too easily . . .'

Marie surprised her with a quick kiss. 'I love him,' she said, as if that settled it.

After that, there was no more to be said, but Jenny went away very thoughtful.

Warsaw was in a ferment as more and more details of the constitution Napoleon had dictated for the new Duchy gradually became known. This took some time, since the great landowners still controlled the day-to-day government and were far from enthusiastic about many of its provisions.

'They say Napoleon has freed the serfs, but I can't believe it.' Lech had found Jenny and Marylka trying to make Casimir concentrate on a reading lesson.

'Freed us?' Marylka jumped to her feet. 'Oh, Pani Jenny, do you think it's true? And, what will the Princess say?'

A little silence fell as they all thought about it. Then, 'Mother will be angry,' said Prince Casimir. 'But don't worry, Marylka. If she won't free you, I will when I'm grown up.'

'Oh, the little love.' Marylka hugged him. But he had been right about his mother. She returned to the Ovinski Palace a little later in a flaming rage, and sent for Jenny.

'Have the slaves heard?' was her first question.

'Yes, Highness.' No use pretending not to understand.

'Then tell them this. I have been talking to Marshal Davout. He has the full details of this fine new constitution. They are free to leave, tell them, and go where they please. But I am just as free to hold on to their land if they do so. They leave without a penny and without a hope. They'll be back soon enough! Marshal Davout's a gentleman, by the way. Why did no one tell me? I begin to think I shall be able to deal with him.' She smiled at herself in the glass.

News of Napoleon's setbacks in Spain and Portugal was slow to reach Warsaw, where the press was tightly controlled. Jenny heard the first hints from Marie Walewska who had come to town for a few June days. 'To cheer myself up,' she explained. 'Paris begins to seem like a dream, and he writes nothing about another meeting. He's got so much on his mind. This revolt in Madrid! Idiotic creatures; can't they see how lucky they are to be rid of their mad King and that wretch Godoy!'

'A revolt?' asked Jenny.

'His messenger told me. Joseph Bonaparte has been made King of Spain. Apparently the *madrileños* don't like it! They actually took to the streets; fired on the French soldiers. Thousands of Spaniards were killed. They've learned their lesson. But it's no wonder my poor Napoleon writes in such haste. He never troubles me with bad news. You'll not tell anyone, Jenny? He wouldn't like it.'

'No one but Isobel,' said Jenny. 'You know you can trust her.'

'Trouble in Spain?' Isobel pounced on the news. 'I thought Davout looked preoccupied yesterday. He said something about being busy with new troop dispositions. Do you think Napoleon is asking for reinforcements from here? I wonder what the Austrians would do if the French army here were much weakened.'

'The Austrians?'

'Are waiting their chance for revenge, of course. Like the Prussians. Naturally, they want to recover the land they lost to the new Duchy of Warsaw. Haven't you noticed how much more trouble there is now at the frontier between Austrian-held Rendomierz and the Duchy? They're watching each other, French and Austrians. Each waiting for a chance to strike. And, when it happens, maybe it will be Poland's chance at last.'

'Why, Isobel, you're becoming a politician.'

'I must, for my son's sake. Call on Marie again tomorrow, Jenny, and see what else you can find out. Ask her whether it is true that Talleyrand is in disgrace.'

'I thought his new position was a promotion.'

'So did I at first. Now, I'm not so sure.'

'I'll certainly ask Marie, but you know her, she's no politician.'

As Jenny expected, Marie knew nothing about Talleyrand, but she had had some more talk with Napoleon's messenger. 'He says that it's the British who are stirring up the trouble in Spain.' Marie put her hand to her mouth. 'Oh – I quite forgot.'

'I'm glad you don't look on me as an enemy.' She thought about it. 'I'm not sure I don't feel as much Polish as British by now. England's so far away . . .'

'Poor Jenny!' Marie reached out to take her hand. 'Do you hear from home at all?'

'Home? What is my home, I wonder? No – I've not heard since we left Petersburg. My family aren't great correspondents. Well, my sisters have the children . . . That was my last news. Another niece and another nephew. I'm afraid I'm not much use as an aunt.' She did not choose to explain that even this news had come in a friendly letter from Lady Egremont. But she had had no answer to her own reply, which was hardly surprising, granted that a state of war now existed between England and both Russia and the new Duchy of Warsaw.

'Dear Jenny.' Marie pressed the hand she held.

'Is it true that the Tsar is off on his travels again?' George Richards had met Jan Warrington on the English Quay one misty September morning of 1808. The two men were better friends than ever since Jan's intercession with the Tsar had made it possible for George and his wife to stay on in Petersburg when the other English left the year before.

'I believe so. He's off to Königsberg in that famous open calèche of his, to see his friends the King and Queen of Prussia, and then on to Erfurt to take council with the Emperor.'

'Napoleon? I hope he's taking a long spoon!'

'It's not for lack of warning if he doesn't! The Empress Mother and the Princess Catherine both hate Napoleon like the plague. But I'm told the Tsar just listens to them, and smiles that gracious, remote smile of his, and says nothing.'

'I wonder what he thinks.'

'If we knew that, George, we'd be rich men, you and I, or on the way to being.'

George smiled. 'We're not doing so badly as it is, since we formed our own Anglo-American alliance.'

'Long may it last.' He and George had discovered that by pooling their interests they could use British or American ships' papers as suited them best, and were doing very well indeed, despite Napoleon's Berlin Decrees, the British Orders in Council and a resultant American embargo on trade with both England and France. 'I just hope that this meeting of the Emperors does not portend more fighting.'

'Not in these parts, surely? The Tsar is busy wresting Finland from the Swedes, and Napoleon's got troubles enough of his own in Spain and Portugal. He just wants to make sure of his position here in the east, I expect, while he's occupied elsewhere.'

'I expect you're right.' Jan tended to defer to George on matters of politics, as he had been used to do to Glynde.

News of the Emperors' proposed meeting at Erfurt reached the Princess at Rendomierz, where she had gone for the summer to avoid the stinking streets of Warsaw and to let the little Prince get back in touch with the Austrian part of his future estates. News of the technical liberation of serfs in the new Duchy of Warsaw had inevitably caused unrest all over what had once been Poland, and Jenny thought the Princess's move a wise one as she watched the serfs crowd round to kiss and bless their little Prince. And, fond though she was of Marie Walewska, it had been a relief to leave her, still pining in vain for a summons from her imperial lover.

'They've done nothing!' They had driven out to visit the model village the Princess was building south of Rendomierz. 'I'll have the hide off them! What happens when I go away?'

'They stop work, I'm afraid. Or rather, they go to work on their own land.' In her heart, Jenny could not blame them. 'You're going to have to find a replacement for Leon, I think, Highness.' This was no time for informality. 'I'm afraid he has grown old and lazy.'

'Useless! When I think how well things go on at Vinsk.'

'You owe that to Miriam. It was a lucky day when Grucz handed over to her. She really seems to care for your interests.'

'Not mine,' said the Princess drily. 'Casimir's. Is it not strange?' And then: 'We've a guest!' As their carriage emerged on to the final sweep of the driveway they could see a dusty calèche being driven away towards the stable yard. 'I wonder who it can be, travelling so light and fast.'

'Like the Tsar,' said Jenny lightly. 'Do you remember?' And was surprised to see the Princess blush crimson.

But it was Paul Genet who awaited them under the portico. 'Highness! Forgive my dust; I could not but wait when I saw your carriage approaching. And Miss Peverel.' He had kissed the Princess's hand; held Jenny's for a long extra minute. 'It is good to see you both in such looks. I am the bearer of a letter, which must be my excuse, from my master, the Prince of Benevento.'

'Talleyrand?' said the Princess. 'I am delighted to see you, Monsieur Genet. Leon! There you are at last. Take Monsieur Genet to the guest village. He will dine with us, of course. And the letter?'

'Here, Highness.' He paused for a moment after handing it to her. 'And the little Prince? How is he?'

'Growing like the green bay tree, Monsieur Genet. And, I have no doubt, at this moment playing soldiers with the village boys. He leads them, of course.'

'Of course.'

'Come along then, Jenny.' The Princess paused impatiently on the stair. 'I know you are as impatient as I am to hear what the Prince of Benevento has to say.' Safe in her room, she broke the seal impatiently, scanned the short letter. 'Well!' She read it again more slowly. 'He takes a good deal on himself,' she said at last.

'Yes?'

'The Emperors are to meet at Erfurt. Napoleon and the Tsar. Soon now; the beginning of October. Talleyrand thinks I should be there. And Casimir.'

'I wonder why?'

'To pay our respects to the new Duke of Warsaw. He says. The King of Saxony, stupid. Erfurt's in his territory. Do you English know no geography at all?'

'Well, not much, I'm afraid. But now I begin to understand what They meant.'

'They? The Brotherhood? A message from them?'

'Yes. Marylka gave it me on the stairs. They just said you were to go.'

'Naturally, I shall go.' She was rereading the letter. 'Pity. The Tsar is going by way of Königsberg; will keep well north of here. It would have been good to entertain him again, but as it is . . . Give the orders, Jenny. Monsieur Genet can escort us. With him, we'll have no trouble with the petty tyrants at the frontier posts.'

'I'm so happy you are coming.' Genet spoke quietly to Jenny under cover of Monsieur Poiret's variations on a theme of Haydn's. 'It's more than good to see you. I've been anxious . . . The news from Petersburg . . . You ran into no difficulty there? I'm glad you did not choose to go home.'

'I thought of it. It was *sauve qui peut* for a while there. But I think I am glad I stayed. Well – you've seen Casimir.'

'A most delightful child, and he needs you.'

'I really think so. But, Monsieur Genet, I wanted to ask you – are you sure he should come to Erfurt? Such a long journey, and maybe dangerous?'

'Talleyrand thinks so, and I have the greatest respect for his judgment. And, seriously, I do not think the journey will be dangerous. It will all be French-controlled territory, you know, once we leave Austria. And – you called me Paul when we last met.'

'That was at Tilsit. Best not here, don't you think?' Her smile deprived the remark of its sting.

'You're right as always. But – I'm sorry. I want you to know that nothing else has changed. I am your servant, always, to command.'

'Thank you.' She turned away, swallowing a surprising hint of tears, to join in the applause as the music ended.

23

The ancient city of Erfurt was *en fête* for the two Emperors. The Kings of Bavaria, Saxony, Westphalia and Württemberg were all there to do them honour. Only, very noticeably, the King of Prussia and the Emperor of Austria were absent; uninvited.

'What do the Austrians think of this conference?' Jenny asked Paul Genet as they started on the last lap of their journey.

'Ask my master,' he told her.

'Shall I get the chance to?'

'I think you can count on that.'

In fact, Talleyrand was their first caller in the house Genet had found for them just off the Wilhelmsplatz. 'Princess!' He kissed her hand. 'I cannot tell you how grateful I am to you for taking my advice and coming.'

'I have to thank you too, sir, for finding me this delightful house. I am most infinitely obliged to you.'

'I had hoped to place you in that position. The truth is, Highness, that I have a favour to ask of you.'

'Yes?' She was instantly on her guard.

'One I think you will find it no hardship to grant. You are an old friend of the Tsar Alexander, are you not?'

'I like to think so.' Cautiously.

'So it would be natural for him to call on you, when he learns that you are here in Erfurt.'

'Why, yes, I would hope so.'

'Conferences are hard work, Highness. All the talk, all the careful negotiations, the public appearances, the inevitable pretence. The participants need to be able to relax in the evening, when their day's work for the peace of the world is done. May I venture to suggest that you keep open house, so long as the conference lasts?'

'I can see no harm in that,' said the Princess slowly. 'Can you, Jenny?'

'It will cost a great deal,' said Jenny bluntly. Sometimes, with the new demands made by both French and Austrian overlords, she worried about even the Princess's finances.

'I am sure that need be no problem.' Talleyrand smiled his charming smile and something twitched at the bottom of her mind. 'But I am grateful to you, Miss Peverel, for raising the point. It shall most certainly be taken care of. And now, am I to see this young Prince, of whom I hear such fine things? You'll bring him, Princess, to see the ceremonial entrance of the Emperors tomorrow? I have arranged places for you in the Wilhelmsplatz, where you will be able to see and to be seen. I think the boy would enjoy it.'

'I am sure he would. You are kindness itself, Prince. Fetch Casimir, Jenny.'

Returning with the little Prince, Jenny found the Princess flushed and sparkling, and wondered just what compliments Talleyrand had been paying her. The brief encounter between the old and young Princes went off well enough, but confirmed Jenny's impression that children were not much in the old diplomat's line. Which made his insistence on seeing the child even more interesting.

On the surface, the meeting between the two Emperors went brilliantly. Napoleon had had to hurry to get to Erfurt first, but had been in time to meet Alexander outside the city. They rode into town side by side, to the roar of artillery and the clangour of bells, Alexander towering over his older companion, the crowd shouting, '*Vivent les empereurs!*' From then on, they spent their days together, talked incessantly, dined together in the company of the attendant Princes and Kings, and went on to Erfurt's handsome city theatre, where Napoleon had installed thirty-two actors from the *Théâtre Français*, with the great Talma at their head. When Talma appeared as Oedipus and gave Molière's line: 'The friendship of a great man is a favour from the Gods,' Alexander stood up in his place and shook Napoleon's hand, while the whole audience applauded.

'A *coup de théâtre*, though I do say so,' Alexander told Talleyrand at the Princess's house later that night. After the official ceremonies were over, he usually dropped in there. 'To relax among my friends,' he told her. And Talleyrand was inevitably there too, the blond young head and the grizzled one close together against a background of music. The talk with Napoleon was official and public; the talk with Talleyrand secret and confidential. Napoleon wrote home to Josephine that he was pleased with Alexander: 'If he were a woman I think I would make him my mistress.' And Alexander wrote to his sister Catherine that: 'Napoleon thinks me a fool, but he who laughs last, laughs longest.'

Catherine herself was one of the subjects to be discussed. Napoleon had let it be known that he was ready to divorce Josephine and make a dynastic match. His marriage with the Tsar's sister would consolidate their relationship as nothing else could. But Catherine was a strong-minded young woman of eighteen and anti-French like her mother. Alexander hedged. Perhaps his younger sister Anna, when she was old enough? Altogether things went less smoothly than Napoleon had expected.

'He threw his hat on the floor, and trampled on it,' Alexander told Talleyrand.

'And what did you do, sire?'

'I smiled at him. "You are violent," I told him. "And I am stubborn. Anger will gain nothing with me. Let us talk, let us reason – or I will go away."'

'And what happened then?'

'He pulled himself together. We went on talking.'

'I think you have crossed your Rubicon, sire. And he does not even know it. It is not many who keep their heads, when my Emperor loses his.'

'Your Emperor?' asked Alexander.

'I speak for France, sire. The French people are civilised; their sovereign is not. The sovereign of Russia is civilised; his people are not. The sovereign of Russia must therefore be the ally of the people of France.'

The charade continued. The two Emperors went to a ball given by Alexander's sister at Weimar, where Alexander danced with his mother's niece, Catherine of Württemberg, now married to Napoleon's brother, Jérome, the ruler of Westphalia.

'Which used to be Polish Silesia,' said the Princess, learning of this. And then, greatly daring, to Talleyrand: 'What are your plans for Poland, Prince?'

'Immense, Highness. Europe needs Poland. An outpost of civilisation, a barrier state between France and Russia. Why do you think I wanted you here? And your son? Your promising son.'

'Well, it's over.' Talleyrand called on the Princess the night after Napoleon had seen the Tsar off on his long journey home to Petersburg.

'Well over?'

'I hope so. Time now to be thinking of the future. I know I can count on you to see to it that my promising young friend Casimir keeps up his education, his languages particularly. I'm glad that you were able to persuade Miss Peverel to stay with you when the British left Russia; her influence on the child seems admirable. There are to be new peace proposals, by the way, from both France and Russia to Great Britain, but I doubt anything will come of them.' He turned, smiling as Jenny approached them. 'Miss Peverel. I was just telling the Princess how glad I am that her promising child is in your hands.'

'I thank you, sir.' This was too good a chance to be missed. 'I shall miss him when he goes away.'

'Away?'

'I thought of sending him to the Military Academy.' The Princess flashed an angry glance at Jenny.

'An admirable plan in the normal way of things. But, Highness, which one? School him in Warsaw, you alienate the Tsar; school him in Russia . . . Well, you're a woman of sense, Highness. You know what follows. And as for Austria . . . You had not thought of starting your own school? I have heard great things of your philanthropy; that model village of yours; surely it would be possible to collect some other boys in the same position as young Casimir; educate them together? The whole world knows of your namesake Princess Isabella Czartoryskia's collection of antiquities; why should not Princess

246

Ovinska's school for the noble young be spoken of in the same breath?'

'I? A school?'

'Well, hardly you personally, Highness.' His tone deprecated the very suggestion. 'But with the proper assistance? Suitable tutors? In languages, in the military arts, of course, but also in history . . . in politics . . . And as to the housekeeping side of it – for of course, you would hardly wish a seminary for young gentlemen under your own roof – dare I suggest that Miss Peverel would be the very person to look after that? I have not, alas, had the pleasure of seeing Rendomierz, but Paul Genet described it to me with enthusiasm. Could you not establish your young gentlemen, Princess, in the guest village, where he stayed in such luxury? Then they would be near enough to feel the civilising influence of your court, but not too close for comfort.'

Inevitably, Jenny's eyes met Isobel's, both of them thinking of the tunnel, but: 'A most interesting idea,' said the Princess slowly. 'It's quite true, I had wondered – such an enthusiast as he is – what would happen if I enrolled Casimir in either a French or Russian-dominated military school.'

'I was sure you would have.' Talleyrand knew as well as Jenny that the thought had never entered her head. 'So, is this not the answer?'

They stopped in Warsaw on the way back from Erfurt so that the Princess could begin to plan for her school. They found the town ablaze with rumours. Davout, whom the Poles had gradually learned to respect, had been ordered to Breslau by Napoleon, but before he left he had watched the departure of three newly enrolled regiments of Polish Lancers for the long march through Europe to join Napoleon's army in Spain.

'We miss Davout,' Marie Walewska told Jenny. 'He was a hard man, but one could trust him, and I liked his wife. Everything changed when she came here to join him. I'm sorry they are gone, but I think he and Prince Poniatowski understand each other at last. Things will go on better now, and I believe our sending so many soldiers to join the French army has helped our finances, though I cannot pretend to understand why.'

'No more can I,' said Jenny, 'but I am glad to hear it. There seem to be the most extraordinary stories abroad. About forged Prussian coins and I don't know what. To listen to them, you'd think money was worth nothing.'

'Oh, you mustn't believe what you hear in Warsaw,' said Marie. 'They don't understand my Napoleon. Look at the way they grumble about the Polish estates he has given to his Marshals. Can't they see this gives them a stake in the country? Must make them care about it?'

The Princess returned from Anna Potocka's with another batch of gloomy stories about Polish finance. 'But Anna says it's all nothing but rumour. Of course it's a pity the King of Saxony doesn't choose to spend more time here, but things will come about, she is sure. Mind you,' she removed her furs and handed them to Jenny, 'I think she hopes for a Kingdom of Poland at last, with her father-in-law for King.'

'She can't be serious?'

'If she is, she's a fool. Adam Czartoryski or my cousin Josef Poniatowski have better claims, and more sense than to think of it. I saw Josef, by the way. He says it's a tragedy Davout's been called away. I told him we had no need of Frenchmen when we have him for Minister of War and Commander in Chief. Oh, he has a young cousin he wishes to enrol in our school.'

The school throve. By the spring of 1809, ten little Polish noblemen were learning Latin and Greek, French, German, English and Russian, in the intervals of their more serious exercise with miniature lance and sword, on horseback and on foot. They were a wild enough lot, each used to being the lord of his own universe. Jenny did her best to instil good manners, helped in this by Casimir, who had a kind of instinctive courtesy, the good manners of the heart. It never struck her that he had learned them from her.

She had been surprised and surprisingly wretched – she could admit it to herself now – when Paul Genet took leave of her at Erfurt without another word about how things stood between them. That he had looked miserable, too, had been her comfort on the slow journey back to Rendomierz, when they missed his useful presence at every stage. And yet, she thought, sorting little boys' socks, she was being ridiculous. If he had said anything, she would have refused him. It was just that she had been so sure he would say something.

She folded the last pair of socks and rose to her feet at the sound of shouting outside. The little boys had just finished the day's drill in the improvised yard outside the Turkish bath, and were coming shouting up to their houses to change for their lessons. They were always noisy at this time of day, but today, surely, they were noisier than usual.

'War. It's war!' Casimir was inevitably the leader, and, she was afraid, getting a little more spoiled as a result.

'What's this about war?' She caught him alone later.

'Everyone's talking about it! Ask Lech!' He was hurrying to join his friends, and she let him go with a sigh. She was beginning to wonder if Talleyrand's idea of a private school had been such a good one after all. The other little boys were even less biddable than Casimir, and the rather random group of tutors the Princess had managed to assemble were hard put to it to get any learning into them, let alone manners. She must talk to the Princess about it when she went over in the evening, and urge once again that one of the tutors be put in authority over the rest. And not the Master at Arms.

But when she paid her regular evening visit, after the little boys were in bed, she found Princess Isobel full of the war news. 'The Austrians have attacked the French; it must mean that they expect help from the Tsar.'

'But how can they? He and Napoleon are still allies, surely?'

'I'm not so sure. When I was in Warsaw the other day, Josef Poniatowski told me he thought the ties between them were stretched to breaking point. It's public knowledge now that Napoleon is planning to divorce his wife; looking for a royal marriage. And the Tsar has just married his sister Catherine to the Duke of Oldenburg.'

'Yes,' said Jenny doubtfully, 'but surely there is more to an alliance than that?'

'He entertained the King and Queen of Prussia royally at Petersburg after Christmas. You can hardly call that friendly to Napoleon. And that newcomer Minister of his, Speransky, is busy putting the country on a war footing, Josef says. The Tsar's cultivating the Muscovites, too. Do you know, he had never been there since his coronation? Now, he's made his new brother-in-law Governor at Tver, between Petersburg and Moscow; refurbished Catherine the Great's palace there for the married couple. He's planning something. I wish I knew what it was.'

'I wonder if he does,' said Jenny. 'But is Napoleon really thinking of divorcing the Empress Josephine?'

'Yes, and not for your friend Marie Walewska.'

'Poor Marie. I wish I could see her.'

'Well, you can't,' said the Princess. 'Remember the Brotherhood's message.'

'Yes. It does sound as if they expect trouble.' The Brotherhood had told Marylka that no one should leave Rendomierz.

That was a bitterly cold spring, and they stayed frozen up at Rendomierz, with no more news, but an increasing feeling of tension in the air. Jenny had learned to respect the curious way in which not so much news as a phantasm of news travelled among the serfs. When Lech urged her to persuade the Princess not to let the little boys out of sight of the palace, she did not question his reason.

News, when it came, came drastically. Prince Poniatowski rode up to the palace one late May morning at the head of a battle-stained detachment of the Franco–Polish army. 'I'm glad to find you safe, Princess.' He was eating like a man who had not seen food for days. 'I've been afraid for you, since Warsaw fell.'

'Warsaw?'

'You've not heard? The Austrians took it. They launched a dastardly attack, both east and west, just when Napoleon was occupied in Spain. They'll regret it! He has rolled them up in the west; will be in Vienna any day; but here in Poland – I insist on calling it that – we have the Russians to contend with as well as the Austrians.'

'The Russians?' asked Jenny, greatly daring. 'But are they not allied to the French?'

'You'd not think so if you saw what they are doing. That is why I am so relieved to find you safe, Princess. Golitzin, the Russian Commander, seems more interested in suppressing us Poles than in fighting the Austrians.'

'He would not suppress me,' said the Princess.

'Probably not. But, if I may give you a cousin's advice, don't count on that Tsar of yours too absolutely. He changes like the moon. Though I hope he will join me in seeing that you are protected. You and your treasure house of Poland's future. May I see your little boys? I have another cousin among them, remember, as well as Casimir.'

'Why, of course. They will be beside themselves with joy. We have the greatest trouble in making them study anything but arms these days, do we not, Jenny?'

'Yes,' said Jenny. 'I wish you would speak to them, Prince. Tell them that there is more to life than warfare.'

'Only when the war is done, Miss Peverel.'

But he did speak to the boys before he rode away next morning, and to some purpose, Jenny thought. At least they applied themselves to their language studies after that. But it was hard to settle to anything, with rumour piled on rumour. The next news they had of Poniatowski was that he was laying siege to Austrian-held Cracow, but in the end it was to the Russian Golitzin that the Austrians yielded.

'As if they were allies already,' said the Princess bitterly. 'With us Poles for the grist between the two millstones, as always.' But she had a new glow to her these days, Jenny thought, as if life had become immensely interesting.

24

The little boys had spent the winter re-enacting the desperate Polish charge that had captured the Spanish valley of Somosierra for Napoleon, when his advisers thought it impossible. Now, in July, they were playing at Wagram, where he had finally defeated the Austrians. An armistice followed; the Austrian Archduke Ferdinand evacuated Warsaw, and the Princess went there at once. Jenny wanted to stay at Rendomierz, where she now felt her duty lay with the little boys, but the Princess was adamant, Jenny could not quite understand why.

She began to do so when they reached Warsaw, found the Ovinski Palace less damaged by its Austrian occupiers than they had feared, and learned that Marie Walewska was rumoured to be on the point of leaving for Vienna.

'Go and call on her,' said the Princess. 'If she is really going, she will need a chaperone. Tell her, tactfully, that I would be happy to fill the position.'

'You, Isobel?'

'I trust that she will understand what a concession it would be.'

'You want so badly to go to Vienna?'

'Use your head, Jenny. If anyone has come gallantly out of the war, it's my Cousin Josef and his Polish army. Look what they have done! And would have done much more if the Russians had not intervened. They must not be forgotten this time, among the shuffling compromises of the great powers. They deserve their reward. Remember that gallant charge at Somosierra!'

'That mad charge. Three of the little boys lost kinsmen there. I hardly dare face my friends here in Warsaw, and their mourning.'

'For such noble deaths? One should rejoice.'

'Suppose it was Casimir.'

'Fiddlestick,' said the Princess.

Jenny found Marie Walewska in the throes of packing. Her face was flushed; her eyes sparkled. 'Yes, I'm going to him! He wanted me sooner; the minute he reached Vienna; but there was no way I could get there, with the Austrian troops still here. Now! I cannot wait to see him, to see him triumphant. Oh, Jenny!'

'I am so glad.' Jenny put the Princess's offer as succinctly as she could.

'Kind of her!' Marie flushed crimson. 'But no need. My husband's niece and her husband go with me, the Wittes. Josephine Witte is a good friend of mine. You must know about her; she had one of the first divorces under the new law.' Her colour rose. Was she thinking of a possible divorce for herself, and the marriage that might follow? 'Do tell the Princess that I would be delighted if she felt like joining us for the journey. And you too, dear Jenny.'

But Jenny did her best to dissuade the Princess from going. 'No good will come of it, I am sure.'

'Nonsense,' said Princess Isobel. 'My cousin Josef urges it. He has great hopes of this peace conference, but cannot be there himself. Now Talleyrand is in disgrace with Napoleon, Poland will need all her friends.'

Travelling fast, the little party reached Vienna in four days. Marie's old friend Duroc had found her a house at Mödling, about ten miles from the palace of Schönbrunn, where Napoleon had established himself, but quiet Marie had contrived to make it quite clear that she did not expect the Princess to stay with her. Jenny thought she had got a little tired of Isobel's talk of her great ancestor, Jan Sobieski, and his heroic march to save Vienna, and did not entirely blame her. But it left them with a problem about lodgings, since the city was crowded to overflowing. The owner of the hotel, where the Princess usually stayed, merely shrugged his shoulders. 'Highness, you should have sent in advance. It desolates me to have to refuse . . .' He had come out to her carriage, and stood bareheaded in the hot July sun. 'But I have a letter for you,' he went on quickly, fearing, as Jenny did, an explosion. 'It was left with me some days ago.'

'Paul Genet.' The Princess was reading it rapidly. 'Obliging of him! He has taken the liberty of getting me an apartment in the Landstrasse. We'll do well enough there. Thank you, my man. Tell the coachman to drive on, Jenny.'

Surveying the luxurious first-floor apartment, Jenny could not help wondering about its Austrian owners, presumably turned out to make room for their conqueror's friends. 'Talleyrand may be in disgrace,' said the Princess with satisfaction, 'but he is evidently far from powerless. This will do very well.'

The apartment was soon a meeting place for the young Polish aristocrats of the Polish Lancers, who were quartered near Schönbrunn, and they crowded into the Princess's box at the theatre and the opera, competing for her attention, telling Jenny their stories of death and glory at Somosierra, when they could not tell the Princess. There was a rumour going around that the new Duchy of Warsaw was to gain territory from Austria under the terms of the peace treaty, and they made no secret of their conviction that they had earned this.

Paul Genet had been out of town when they arrived, but came to call ten days or so later, and Jenny was surprised how pleased she was to see him. It was good to be treated as a person in her own right again, not just an appendage of the Princess.

Isobel thanked Genet very graciously for the apartment and asked civilly after Talleyrand. 'I am only sorry he is not here in person. We miss him sadly. Tell him so, when you write.'

'I certainly will, Highness. And he has specially charged me to ask after the progress of your young Prince, and his schoolfellows.'

'Admirable, of course. But Jenny can tell you about that better than I can. If you will excuse me, I must get ready for the opera. I am joining Madame Walewska in her box tonight, so I'll have no need of your company, Jenny. You will entertain Monsieur Genet for me.'

'I'm sorry,' he said, when she had left them. 'You expected to go?'

'No matter. It's only Salieri. But, it's true, I always enjoy seeing Marie Walewska. She's so happy! It does one good just to be with her. She glows with it. And isn't it amazing how she goes on in society?'

'She's powerfully protected,' he said drily. 'Long may it last for her. Did you know that Napoleon delayed his entry to Schönbrunn because the Archduchess Marie Louise was lying ill there?'

'No. Unusually civil of him, surely?'

'That's what I thought. Tell me about the group of young Poles who share their attentions between the Princess and Madame Walewska? What do you think of them?'

She thought about it for a moment. Then, 'Frankly, anything I say will be unfair to them.'

'Promising! Why?'

'Because they treat me like a thing; like the Princess's waiting-gentlewoman. Which is what I am.'

He laughed. 'Admirable. I know just how you feel. So – granted this totally unreasonable prejudice of yours, tell me what you think of them.'

'I wish they didn't compete and quarrel all the time among themselves. You should see them, around the Princess, debating points of precedence, the military added to the dynastic. I find it childish, Monsieur Genet, and not hopeful for the future of Poland.'

'Would you be very much surprised if I told you that Napoleon himself is said to have made very similar remarks?'

'It's so sad,' she said. 'I often think Lech is worth ten of them. He really cares for his country, and for the Princess as representing it.'

'Which she deserves?'

'I work for her, Monsieur Genet.'

'Forgive me. Now, you are to tell me about the little Prince. How, truly, do he – and the school go on?'

'This is for Talleyrand?'

'Naturally.'

'Then tell him that I am worried. I'm glad to have this chance to say it. In theory, the school was a brilliant idea . . .'

'But in practice?'

'It's just making matters worse, I think. The masters fight among themselves, and for the boys' favour. Because the boys are their future masters, don't you see? Specially Casimir.

255

Just imagine yourself a struggling tutor, disciplining him, the possible future King of Poland? I've tried to say this to the Princess. To suggest that she needs an outsider. A headmaster, I suppose? Someone who is afraid of no one. Impossible, of course.'

'Very interesting,' he said. 'Thank you, Miss Peverel. I'll most certainly tell my master.'

In England, news of Napoleon's defeat of Austria seemed less immediately important than events nearer home. All the talk was of the Duke of York who had had to resign as Commander in Chief after the parliamentary enquiry into his mistress's sale of commissions in his name. 'Duke or darling,' said the wits, tossing coins. General Moore had been killed at the evacuation of Corunna, and Arthur Wellesley's triumph in Portugal had been thrown away by the ridiculous terms of the Convention of Cintra, negotiated by his successors. And this summer's Walcheren expedition had been a disaster from start to finish.

With so much to concern him nearer home, it was hardly surprising that Canning had found no employment for Glynde. But he began to hold out hopes in the summer of 1809, detecting, he said, a hint of slackening in Russian hostility to England. Then, in September, he fought a duel with his political rival Castlereagh and lost office as a result. Granville Leveson Gower resigned too, and with them went all Glynde's hopes of employment.

'It's bad.' His aunt always faced facts. 'I am so sorry, Glynde. Just glad that you are here with me to face it.'

'And so am I! I begin to think you're my only friend.'

'At least you can count on me.' She smiled at him. 'Up to a point. It struck me, when I heard the news of Canning's duel, that a good aunt would catch a tertian fever, die, and leave you her heir. You are, of course. But,' again her heart-warming smile, 'I don't propose to die even for you, dear Glynde.'

'I should think not indeed.' He felt better already. 'I'm not even going to let myself wish my father and brother would.'

'No, barbarous. And besides, to decline into a landowner,

so dull,' she said. 'But I think I must ask it – your funds, Glynde?'

'Out of tune,' he groaned. 'I'm rolled up, aunt. It's all over with me. Nothing for it but to join the army and let the French oblige me with a bullet through the head.'

'That's no way to talk.'

'Forgive me! But wherever I look I see nothing but disaster. We're even at odds with the Americans now; Napoleon is isolating us, slowly and surely. It's a glum lookout.'

'But we're still free. I wish we would hear what happened to your Princess Ovinska and the little boy when the Austrians took Warsaw and the Poles went on the rampage through Galicia. And to Jenny Peverel.'

'I'm sure they will have been unharmed.' But he had lain awake, night after night, trying to convince himself of this. 'The Princess has cousins everywhere,' he said now. 'And of course she would protect Miss Peverel. The Tsar himself is her friend; she will have been quite safe either at Rendomierz or further north in her other estate in Russian-held Lithuania. She has her own army of serfs to guard her; all devoted both to her and to the little Prince. But just the same I'd give a good deal to have news of her. It's extraordinary how little one hears about what goes on in what used to be Poland.'

'You cannot love her still, Glynde, after all this time?'

'I think I shall love her always.' How could he explain it? 'There will never be anyone like her. I cannot imagine marrying. Oh, I suppose in the end – I don't like to speak of dead men's shoes – but if I should find myself succeeding as Lord Ringmer I might feel called upon to marry some well-bred young person – you're laughing at me, aunt?'

'I was feeling a little sorry for the well-bred young person. I confess I rather hope she refuses you when you come to the point. I wish I could meet this Princess who has cast such a spell on you! And that you could see her again, come to that. Seriously, Glynde, it makes me sad to see you creating an idol for yourself and falling down before it. Just think what a good marriage could do for you now.'

'Money in my purse?' He smiled at her lovingly. 'Don't think I haven't seen you trying. All those charming young grand-daughters of your friends we have entertained of late!

257

With not a word to say for themselves! Ribbons and laces, and young Betty as Hamlet! And dear mama watching our every movement.'

'You're spoiled, Glynde, that's what's the matter with you.' She shook her head at him. 'Now, let us sit down and be realists. Not the army: you and I know you are not strong enough. I didn't nurse you through that wound of yours to have you throw it all away. Not the church. Not marriage.'

'Debtors' prison,' he said savagely. 'My only future.'

'You're not . . .'

'In debt? Not yet. I'm not that much of a fool, but in the end, I am bound to be.' He took an angry turn round the room, came back to stand looking down at her, his face setting in lines she had not seen before. 'If it were not for the chance of inheriting the title, aunt, I'd throw the gentleman to the winds and go into trade. I could make money. I know it. I've watched my friends, Richards and Warrington. I've as good a mind as theirs, and better connections, though you wouldn't think it to look at me now. But how can I drag the prospective title through the dirt?'

'Glynde! There's something else, something I've been wondering whether to tell you, to add to your troubles.'

'Yes? What now? Let's have it, aunt.'

'It's your brother's wife. They say she's dying.'

'And he'll remarry! So – no dead men's shoes after all. Then I really had better look about me. Thank you for telling me. It makes things simpler in a way. No estate. No title. No responsibilities.'

'Mr. Rendel?'

'Yes?' Walking down the Steyne a few days later, Glynde stopped at the sound of his own name.

'I've a letter for you, mister. From a friend a long way off. Worth half a guinea to you, is it?'

'But how –?'

'No questions, mister, no trouble. Half a guinea and you gets it.'

'Oh, very well!' Savagely, he wondered what would have happened if he had not borrowed some money from his aunt that very morning, the first time he had been forced to do so.

'Treat it gentle, guv. It's come a long way by the look of it. I'd take it home out of the wind I reckon if I was you.' He exchanged the tattered letter for the half guinea Glynde held out and disappeared smartly down one of Brighton's narrow lanes.

His aunt was out paying calls and he went straight to his room and opened the letter, sure that many other people had done so before him. Creased, stained, barely legible, it was dated from Vienna, in August. Just the place-name and date. The Princess's hand? He had thought so, reading the superscription as the letter was held out to him, was now sure of it. 'You will know my hand,' she wrote. 'I dare not sign this. A good friend of yours promises to get it to you. I need your help. Come to us. I ask it as your old friend.'

And a postscript in a hand he did not know: 'I have undertaken to get this to you, be responsible for your journey. You will not regret it. Destroy this letter. Be ready. Wait where you are for instructions. Tell no one. Your friend from Tilsit.'

Talleyrand. The agreed phrase. My friend. My father. But can I trust him? Of course not, but that was not the point. He had heard of the extraordinary scene in which Napoleon had insulted Talleyrand and deprived him of office. Talleyrand had taken it with his habitual *sang-froid*. Could this letter be a result? It certainly opened up the most extraordinary vistas. But, infinitely more important was the fact that Isobel needed him. Wanted him? 'And what have I to lose?' He said it aloud.

About to destroy the letter, he hesitated. Tell no one? He owed it to her to tell his aunt. And Canning? He was less certain of this.

'I wonder what they want of you,' said Maud Savage thoughtfully, having read the letter and its postscript. 'It seems quite extraordinary. And – did you know that Talleyrand and the Princess were on such terms?'

'They certainly knew each other; that's of course. There was a young protégé of Talleyrand's dangling round Miss Peverel. Genet, his name was.'

'Good gracious,' said Maud, amused. 'And there was I thinking Jenny Peverel had turned old maid, doomed to lead apes in hell.'

259

'She well may. She doesn't seem to care what she looks like, or what one thinks of her.'

'Fatal!' He had an uncomfortable feeling that she was laughing at him again. 'But none of that is to the point. You cannot seriously be thinking of going, Glynde? An invitation endorsed by Napoleon's right-hand man? You risk being taken for a traitor. May risk being one, for all you know.'

'No. Talleyrand's out of office, remember. Napoleon kicked him out last winter. If he wants me there, I am sure he has a reason for it that is not to my disadvantage.'

'Nor to his, I take it.'

'That's of course!' Fantastic thoughts were crowding through his mind. Even far off here in England, he had heard rumours about the Princess and Murat, the Princess and Davout, even the Princess and her cousin Josef Poniatowski. He had refused to believe them, still did. But just suppose that her headstrong great lady's behaviour had allowed her to be compromised . . . Suppose she needed a husband, one she knew she could trust? He had made up his mind. 'It's hard to see how the summons could possibly come, aunt, but if it does, I shall go. After all, what have I to lose?'

Much to Jenny's relief, the Princess decided to leave Vienna as soon as the Treaty of Schönbrunn was signed. Calling on Marie Walewska to say goodbye, she found her in tears.

'It's the shock,' Marie explained. 'But he's safe, thank God!' And then: 'You hadn't heard? A mad young German tried to kill him. They caught him just in time – a savage knife hidden in his "petition". Jenny, just think, he might be dead!'

And the world a safer place. But Jenny did not say it, aware that Marie had more to tell her. It came tumbling out. 'Tell no one; no one in the world. Particularly not the Princess. I'm . . . oh, Jenny, I'm so happy! And he's so pleased! Nothing's good enough for me! I'll be lucky if I ever get to Paris, so surrounded as I shall be with doctors, with care, with cherishing. Jenny, do you understand what I am saying?'

'Of course I do.' Jenny kissed her. 'And no wonder the Emperor is so pleased. His first child!'

'Yes.' Marie laughed. 'You'd think no one had ever been in

this situation before. It's lucky I'm an experienced mother. Oh, Jenny, just think what this may mean.'

'Dearest Marie; don't hope too much.'

A courier caught up with the Princess's carriage on the second night of their slow journey east. He was taking the details of the Treaty of Schönbrunn to Warsaw and was happy to stop and drink the Princess's health while he told her about it. Jenny, who had been making arrangements for the night, rejoined them to find the Princess rewarding him munificently.

'It's great news,' she said. 'The beginning of what we have prayed for. Western Galicia has been ceded by Austria to the Duchy of Warsaw. Just think, Jenny, Rendomierz is on the way to being Polish at last.'

'French,' said Jenny.

'Oh, don't be such a voice of doom, Jenny! It will make no difference to you. And for us, I am sure, it is the first step. I knew it was worth my while to go; it's not for nothing I've done my best to entertain all those old diplomats; to speak to them of my country, of Poland. Oh, my goodness!' She clapped her hand to her mouth, looking, Jenny thought, both appalled and amused. 'But what will happen to him?'

'To whom?'

'Did I not tell you? No, I do believe I quite forgot to. Do you remember that lightning visit your friend Genet paid us in August?'

'Why, yes?' Jenny remembered it well.

'He wrote that I must tell no one,' the Princess said now. 'Talleyrand, I mean. You didn't think I could keep a secret so well, did you, Jenny? And one that concerns you, in a way, such a friend of yours as he has always been.'

'Who? I do not understand you, Highness.'

'Who but Mr. Rendel? It was Talleyrand's idea; a brilliant one as his all are. He's a good friend to me, and to Casimir. He had heard – he who hears everything – that all was not entirely well with my school. It was his suggestion, do you remember, in the first place?'

'Yes, I remember.' Where could this be leading?

'He said he had heard about the problems. Had thought about it. Decided what was needed was a strong hand at

261

the top of the school; an undivided command. He made a recommendation that surprised me at first, until I had time to think it over. Then, of course, I could see the sense of it. Who better than an Englishman to oversee the education of a future constitutional monarch?'

'An Englishman? Who?' But she was afraid she knew.

'Who but Mr. Rendel? Such a good friend to us all. Talleyrand took a great liking to him when they met at Tilsit, Genet told me, has followed his career since he was back in England. He's had a hard time of it, poor man. His friend Canning did nothing for him; and now Canning's out of office himself after some crazy duel. He's had nothing to do, poor Mr. Rendel, but dangle at the apron strings of some spinster aunt or other.'

'Glynde Rendel?' Jenny took it in slowly. 'You must be out of your mind, Isobel. I can sooner imagine Napoleon turning priest than Mr. Rendel turning schoolmaster. He'll never come. Besides, how could he?'

'Monsieur Talleyrand very kindly promised to see to all that.' The Princess still looked guiltily mischievous. 'Will you have a small bet with me that Mr. Rendel comes?'

'No,' said Jenny uncompromisingly. 'Not unless you tell me in just what terms you invited him.'

'The briefest possible, of course. A letter that was to pass through so many hands. Oh well, if by any chance he has been so foolish as to misunderstand it, we will just have to do our best to make it up to him.'

Jan Warrington had called on Mr. Harris, the American Consul at St. Petersburg, to be presented to the first American Ambassador, Mr. Adams. Hurrying home along the quay, he held his mittened hands across his face to keep off the biting February wind. Enough snow had fallen to make the going fairly safe, and he was finding his way almost without the use of his eyes, when, as he reached his own house, a figure loomed towards him out of the gathering dusk. A footpad? A beggar? The secret police?

'Jan! It's me, Glynde. Don't say anything. You know my voice? Take me in with you.'

'You here? You're mad! Stark staring mad.' But he rang a peal at his own door, stood aside to usher the muffled figure in ahead of him. 'Come up to my room. We'll look after ourselves.' He dismissed the hovering servant.

Removing his own fur hat and wadded coat, he was relieved to see Glynde revealing an immense, obliterating growth of beard. He also recognised his friend's haggard exhaustion. 'You're worn out. Food first, or sleep?'

'Something to drink? You're not going to turn me in?'

'Don't be an idiot. I owe you this, for Cracow.' He opened the bedroom door to shout down instructions for a hot toddy, soup. At once. Turning back to Glynde, he saw him clumsily trying to take off his heavy duffel coat. 'God! Your hands. What have you been doing, Glynde?'

'Working my passage. Not precisely what I expected, but it has been an interesting experience. I'm filthy, Jan, disgusting. I should have a bath first.'

'Nonsense.' But Jan was beginning to smell him. 'Something hot inside you first of all. When did you last eat?'

'If you can call it eating. No questions, Jan, till my mind's clear? For old time's sake. For hers, if you like.'

'The Princess? You're on your way there?'

'Where else? You'll help me?'

'It depends why you are going. But I'll most certainly not betray you. You can count on that.'

'I knew I could. What are you going to tell your servants? Can you trust them?'

'Of course not. Have you any papers?'

'None. We were wrecked in the Gulf. Those damned pirates of islanders . . . They took everything I had. Would have killed me, I suppose, only they were short of manpower. Put me to work instead. A galley slave? I jumped ship in the end; damned lucky to be alive . . .' His words were beginning to slur, his head drooping forwards towards the empty soup bowl.

'You're an American,' said Jan loudly. 'An American to whom all this happened. Remember that, Glynde, if you remember nothing else.'

'An American. Of course. Thank you, Jan.' The savagely chapped lips, smiling in the tawny forest of beard, gave the first real hint of the old, charming Glynde Rendel. Then, before Jan could leap up to catch him, he fell forward with a great clatter of broken crockery.

He slept for twenty-four hours, during which Jan did a great deal of thinking. Summoned to his bedside at the first hint of his waking, he smiled down at him. 'I am glad to see you better, Cousin Clancy. We've been anxious about you.' His hand, lightly on Glynde's was a warning.

'Cousin!' Glynde smiled sleepily. 'I thank God for you, Cousin Jan.'

When he next waked, he proclaimed himself better, demanded a bath, but refused to be shaved. 'I think I like myself as a caveman. The spit of Granpa, wouldn't you say, Cousin Jan?'

'So who am I? If you've got that far? And I do thank you from my heart for getting there so quick.' Glynde was sitting across the fire from Jan in his study, his beard neatly trimmed, his hands bandaged.

'A Polish American adventurer.' He laughed. 'You look every inch the part. I'd never have thought you had it in you. I've told Harris you're my cousin. He's our Consul,' he explained. 'He'll tell Adams, the new Ambassador. They'll want to see you, of course, when you're strong enough. Lucky you've never met either of them.'

'A Pole.' Glynde was enjoying this. 'But, my voice, Jan, my accent. Where am I from in your United States?'

'Difficult, isn't it? I decided you were a second cousin of my mother's; your family emigrated at about the same time as hers did. I'd have made it New England, only Adams is from there, you'd never fool him, so it has to be the south. The wild hinterland of Georgia. By the time they check up on you, we'll have you safe away to Vilno. I can manage that; you'll be on your own from there. If you're sure you must put your head into the lion's mouth. You do know that Rendomierz is in French hands now? Part of Napoleon's new Duchy of Warsaw?'

'I didn't when I left England. Too late to fret about it now. Have you news of the Princess, Jan?' Eagerly.

'Not much, since the Richards finally went home last year, but one does hear, of course. She was at Vienna last summer, intriguing for the Poles. Close friends with Poniatowski, they say.'

'And you, Jan? Do you still have hopes for Poland?'

'Czartoryski is back at the Tsar's side. That has to be good news for Poland. But we know nothing here of what really goes on in the Duchy of Warsaw. Frankly, that's one reason why I'll gladly help you get there. You'll promise to write and tell me how things are?'

'If you can find me a safe channel.'

'Oh, I can do that. There are great advantages about being in my way of business. Merchants have to be in touch with the world. You won't mind going to Vilno disguised as one?'

'Delighted! And glad to see you such a success, Jan.'

'No thanks to you British! But we won't start that old argument about your policy on trade, though it will be a miracle if it doesn't come to war between our countries, sooner or later. If you should find means of writing home to England, you can tell them I said so. For what that's worth!'

'A good deal, I should think.' He did not choose to reply to Jan's hinted question about his means of communication with England. Jan had changed, he thought, in the years since he had last seen him.

'Time I kept my appointment with Mr. Adams.' Jan stood up. 'And told him the dramatic tale of my cousin who came to study business and got wrecked on the way. Let's just go through it again. It's all solid, I take it,' he said, when they had gone through the lists of dates and names of ships. 'I must congratulate whoever arranged it for you. They did a good job.'

'Yes.' Again he ignored the hinted question.

Jan returned from visiting Mr. Adams full of the news he had heard there. 'Would you believe it?' He broke into speech as his man was helping him out of his coat. 'Napoleon's to marry! That assassination attempt has taught him he's mortal!'

'Who?'

'A slap in the face for the Tsar! There was talk after Erfurt of a proposal for the Grand Duchess Catherine. Well, she's safely married, but there was still the Grand Duchess Anne.'

'It's not her?'

'No. He is to marry the Archduchess Marie Louise of Austria as soon as the arrangements can be completed.'

'Good God! After Austerlitz; after Wagram! What will the Tsar do, do you think?'

265

'Arm,' said Jan. 'But he's doing that already. It's a consignment of guns you'll be accompanying to Vilno. But you'll be taking good news to the Princess, if she's not heard it already.'

'Oh?'

'The news of the Austrian marriage. Much better for Poland than a Russian alliance would have been. I happen to know that the French Ambassador, Caulaincourt, had agreed, on Napoleon's behalf, that in return for the Russian match he would undertake that the Kingdom of Poland would never be restored, the word Poland erased from history. Tell the Princess that if she repines over the Austrian marriage.'

'But that's not good news for Poland either.' Glynde was thinking how much Jan seemed to know.

'What is!'

25

The Princess insisted on going to Warsaw for the carnival season of 1810, but Jenny stayed behind. They had found the little boys badly out of hand when they got back from Vienna, the tutors quarrelling among themselves and the children taking advantage of it. Only their gymnastic and military studies seemed to be pursued to any advantage. Herr von Stenck, the Master at Arms, was a strict disciplinarian when he was not keeping the boys spellbound with tales of his own exploits fighting the Russians under Kosciusko in the nineties.

Casimir, still the ringleader, had been delighted to see Jenny, and by persuading him, she managed to get some sort of attendance at lessons, despite the obvious scorn of other little boys whose own fathers could neither read nor write. A firm, male hand was certainly needed. She did not know whether to fear or to hope that Glynde would really come, but could not help hoping.

The Princess returned at last full of news. 'The Emperor's to be married.' In her own room, she was letting Jenny help her out of her furs.

'Napoleon? Not –'

'Not to Marie Walewska, be sure. No, it's the Austrian Archduchess Marie Louise. The poor Walewska's nose is quite out of joint; she came creeping back to the Duchy and – would you believe it – is about to bear what they call her husband's child, at his house. I do wonder just what bribes persuaded old Walewski to that!'

'Oh, poor Marie!' Jenny remembered that autumn's golden hopes.

'Poor Josephine, come to that. I don't suppose she much likes being divorced. But now Marie's proved him potent, Napoleon's mad for an heir; a dynasty. Well, he needs it. Just imagine what would happen if he were killed in one of his desperate victories. That brother of his, Joseph, couldn't even manage Spain, still less all Europe. The empire would fall apart in no time without him. Which might not be a bad thing for us Poles,' she went on thoughtfully. 'But my cousin, Josef, is still convinced Napoleon is only biding his time to do us justice.'

'He thinks Napoleon will keep better faith with Poland than he has with Marie Walewska?' asked Jenny bitterly.

'The Emperor needs his Poles.' She changed the subject. 'What's this I hear about Casimir being beaten for neglecting his studies?'

'He said he wouldn't learn Russian, Princess. That it was the language of tyrants.' The Tsar's language? 'It was a very small beating. I'm afraid he's boasting about it. It's hard to know what to do for the best with those boys.'

'Time Glynde Rendel got here.'

'You've heard something?' If only her heart would be quiet.

'Not a word. But he'll come. And the sooner the better. Anna Potocka is going to Paris for the great wedding. She asked me to go too. There is money owed to her husband's family for occupation expenses. They have asked her to go and see if she can get it for them. Innocents! She didn't take much persuading. Her adored Flahaut will be there, won't he? Dear me,' thoughtfully, 'do you remember what exciting times those were in Warsaw, when the French were first there? Everyone will be in Paris for the wedding! I've half a mind to go with Anna, if Mr. Rendel would only get here and take charge of our problem boys for us.'

'I hope you're not thinking I would go too?'

'You'd rather stay behind and help Glynde Rendel look after the boys? If he would just get here!'

'Pani Jenny?' Marylka was waiting for Jenny in the little house she had made very much her own, with books on the shelves Lech had built and brilliantly coloured rugs, woven by the village women, on the floor.

'Yes? You're out late, Marylka. What is it?'

'I wish I knew! The village is full of rumours. But nothing from them.' She and Jenny never mentioned the Brotherhood by name if they could help it. 'Has the Princess heard anything?'

'If she has, she's not told me. But what are the rumours?'

'Something about Vinsk, pani. About Miriam, the woman who manages it for the Princess. There is talk that she is coming here. And – she has enemies – that they will attack her on the way.'

'But nothing from Them? That's very strange, surely.'

'That's why I came to you. In case it is Them. Because there's something else, the reason why she's coming without leave. There have been two strangers at Vinsk. Come from Petersburg, perhaps? She's bringing them here, they say. But the word in the village is that they'll never arrive.'

Jenny's blood ran cold. Glynde? Could it be? By way of Petersburg? Head in both lions' mouths? But, possible. Jan Warrington was still there, after all. She hurried over to the palace to tell the Princess. 'But why would the Brotherhood want to stop them?' she concluded. 'Not that I have ever really understood their motives.'

'I think they change,' said the Princess. 'Josef Poniatowski said something to me in Warsaw. About a German society, the *Tugendbund*. Very secret. Very deadly. And no friends to Poland. I did wonder if he was trying to warn me of something.'

'That they've taken over? It would be easy, wouldn't it, with all that secrecy?'

'Fool of a woman to start off without consulting me,' said Princess Isobel. 'Send for Wysocki, Jenny. Have him waked, if necessary. We must send out a party to meet them.'

When he married the Princess, Prince Ovinski had ordered the building of staging houses at comfortable intervals on the journey between his estates at Vinsk and hers at Rendomierz, and Miriam's pretext for her winter journey had been to make sure that the ones under her authority were fit for use. She gave out that she was going only as far as the border between Russian Lithuania and French Galicia.

'But I wonder how many people believe her,' said Jan to Glynde the night before they started.

'Or believe that you are going along for the pleasure of her company.' Glynde had been surprised and delighted when Jan announced his firm intention of accompanying him to Vinsk, explaining that it was what he would do for a real cousin. It turned out to be a journey he had made many times before,

269

and Glynde had watched with interest as Miriam greeted him as an old and valued friend. Or something more? Miriam must have been a beautiful woman, he thought, before the smallpox ravaged one side of her face; was still a handsome one, with a surprising air of command. The Vinsk estates had prospered under her management and Jan had helped and advised her through the problems of turning her trade away from bankrupt Prussia towards central Russia. The waggons that brought consignments of arms westwards towards the frontier were loaded with priceless cargoes of furs for the return journey, and Jan acted as her agent for their sale in Petersburg.

'If all Russian estates were managed as well as Vinsk, the country would be a very different place,' he told Glynde as they settled for the night on the third day of their journey south.

'I wonder if the Princess knows how lucky she is,' said Glynde, and then, quietly: 'Has it struck you that we are being followed?'

'Followed? Good God, no! What makes you think so?'

'Hard to say. Instinct, if you like. Bird noises, and the lack of them. Just by one man, I'd say, or I'd have given the alarm sooner. But I think we should take it in turns to watch tonight. I rather wish our hostess had chosen to bring a larger escort.'

'I doubt there are that many she can trust so absolutely,' said Jan. 'This secret way she knows, avoiding the border posts, is not something to be confided to any Tom, Dick or Harry.'

'Or David or Benjamin, come to that. Interesting about the powerful Jewish network that seems to exist right across the frontiers.'

'Remember how the frontiers change. And be grateful for the network. The border between Russia and French-held Poland's hard to cross these days, with both sides arming and neither side admitting to it. Much better to take Miriam's way through the woods.'

'If we get that far.' They took it in turns to watch that night but it passed peacefully enough, with a new fall of snow to blanket sound.

It made the going slower next day, and Jan, helping Glynde

to push Miriam's sledge out of a hole, chose his moment to mouth, 'You were right. There is someone.'

Back in the sledge when they had cleared the obstacle, they broke the news to Miriam. She took it calmly. 'Just one, you think?'

'Certainly not more than two.'

'Two would be enough. One to keep with us, the other to summon the rest of the gang.'

'Robbers?' asked Jan.

'Or someone who doesn't wish your cousin to get to Rendomierz. But that gets us no further. As we don't know why the Princess wants you so badly, Glynde, we have no clue as to why anyone should wish to stop you. But I think we should assume they do and keep good watch.'

'You must go back at once,' said Jan.

'Impossible. Or – if I go back, we all do. I gave my word that I would tell no one of the secret way. I have to show you.'

'But we can't go back,' said Glynde.

'I agree with you. It would only make the next try more dangerous. We must do nothing to let it seem we are expecting an attack. So, the element of surprise is reversed. Whoever they are, they will want it to seem a mere affair of robbery with violence.'

'Mere?' asked Glynde.

'They happen all the time. Or it could be a band of Cossacks, of course, got out of hand. That happens, too.'

'We should never have let you come,' groaned Jan.

'Nonsense. Do you think it is only men who can risk their lives for Poland? Oh, gallant to die in the field of battle! Woman's part is different: lonely, but taking no less courage. And, it's a strange thing, but since I lost my own boys, I can't help loving the little Prince. He has my whole allegiance. He and Poland. If the Princess needs you, so must he. And Poland. So – we go on.'

'And the man who is following?'

'We'll have to deal with him. Or them. That is my affair. They shall not learn my secret path. Nor, I warn you, will you, though I lead you along it. It's not something one learns by one experience.'

'You mean, you have taken it before?' asked Jan.

271

'When I was young; many times. You forget that there has never been real peace here in my lifetime. And for us Jews . . . Never . . .'

Four members of the escort vanished next morning. Glynde and Jan exchanged glances, said nothing. They did not comment either on the fact that Miriam was forcing the pace. Whips cracked, men shouted and swore, horses squealed as the sledges struggled forward over newly frozen snow. Today, the forest was closer to the track, looming dark and vast on either side.

'I'll never get used to the immensity of it,' said Glynde. 'No wonder this has always been a land of violence, when an outlaw can vanish into the forest and live off it as long as he pleases.'

'Or so long as he can do without salt, and a few other of the essentials of life,' said Miriam drily. 'Even outlaws need friends. We're going to spend tonight with a band of them,' she went on. 'I'd been meaning to warn you. We're in the district of Bialystok now; do you know what that means?'

'No,' said Glynde. 'I seem to have heard the name, but . . .'

'Why should you know or care? At Vienna last year, Napoleon gave Bialystok to the Tsar, just like that. For doing nothing!'

'I heard about it, of course,' said Jan. 'They said in Petersburg that it was a bride gift for the Tsar's sister.'

'A bride gift drenched in blood,' said Miriam. 'Imagine what happened to the men who had risked their lives to support the French against the Russians three years ago. Oh, there was fine talk in Vienna about no reprisals. Tell that to the men of Bialystok. You'll be meeting some of the lucky ones tonight. The ones who saw vengeance coming and got away into the forest. The wisest of them brought their wives and children with them. It's a hard life, but it's life.'

'You can't mean –' Glynde was horrified. 'But the Tsar is a man of peace; deeply religious; he can't have intended –'

'What the Tsar intends, and what happens at the ends of his empire are two different things,' said Miriam bleakly. 'Remember who stand at his side: the martinet Arakchayev; the shark Speranski. What does he hear from them? That things are quiet in Bialystok, his new province. Quiet! The quiet of death. Remember this tonight, gentlemen. It is a great concession on the part of this group that they have agreed to receive you. Listen, and say nothing.'

As dusk was falling, they left even the semblance of a track behind. A man had emerged, silently, from the great darkness of the forest, to guide their little party. Voices hushed; they could hear the creak of runners on snow, the crack of a branch giving way under its load.

'Have you noticed that our four strays are back?' Jan asked Glynde quietly as Miriam spoke to their new guide.

'Yes, looking pleased with themselves. I take it we are no longer being followed.'

The outlaws' camp lay low, in the hollow carved by a tributary of the River Bug, black forest close around it. 'Little fear of their smoke being seen,' said Miriam. 'You will be welcome, for my sake. And for my sake, be careful what you say.'

'I'm afraid I'll say nothing to the purpose,' Glynde told her. 'Since I speak no Polish, no Lithuanian, only Russian.'

'I'd not speak that.'

But they were made immensely welcome and dined lavishly on river fish, venison and bear steaks washed down with the strongest vodka Glynde had ever tasted. 'They certainly have friends in the village,' he said sleepily to Jan as they fell on to the beds made of fresh fir branches.

What waked him? Still pitch dark. A sense of danger. Instant. Immediate. He rolled over. Roused Jan. 'Quick! Wake up! Something's happening.' And while Jan grumbled slowly awake, he was rousing the other men in the big hut.

Outside, a hint of dawn light in the air, the outlaws hurrying to accustomed places at the stockade. The leader silently handed him a gun. 'They must have surprised our lookout. Can you use it?'

'Yes.' He had always been a brilliant shot. Now, peering down the sights of this unknown weapon, he saw the light was just beginning to seep into the clearing. Mist and snow made everything strange, fantastic, a scene from a tale of witchcraft. But ahead, something moved. His finger on the trigger was instinctive, automatic. A dark shape fell forward into the snow, vanished. After that, it was just a mad repetition. Miriam, handing him a loaded gun; another movement, another shot, another death?

It seemed to go on for ever; was probably over quite soon. His right hand was stiff and ice cold; Miriam was chafing it. 'They're on the run. They didn't expect such a reception.'

'Who?'

'Ah.' She smiled at him brilliantly. 'If we only knew that! Lucky for all of us you are such a good shot, Mr. Rendel.'

'Lucky your friends stood firm. Tell me, Miriam, can you believe this is a coincidence?'

'No.' She met his eyes squarely. 'I agree with you. But, I promise you, my men took care of our two followers.'

'So, there was another?'

'I think so. And I am sure they will try again. We are moving off at once. Find Mr. Warrington, would you, and tell him?'

Jan was binding up the wounds of one of the outlaws who had been hit by the random fire of the attackers. 'All I'm good for,' he said ruefully. 'I'm no shot! If it had come to hand to hand, I hope I'd have given a good account of myself.'

'Thank God it didn't,' said Glynde. A scream, suddenly cut short, from outside the stockade. 'They must be finishing off the wounded.'

'Kinder than to leave them to a slow death in the snow.'

'I suppose so.' Rejoining Miriam, he found her deep in talk with the chief outlaw. 'They were Poles,' she turned to him bleakly. 'They'd been told we were Russians.'

'Who by?'

'That's the question, isn't it? And so many possible answers. By someone who hates one of us, that's sure enough. You, or Mr. Warrington, or even me. Enough of my people at Vinsk would be glad to be rid of me. We'll probably never know, but we're taking no chances. We're starting at once, leaving the others to move their camp. I lost two of my men, I'm sorry to say, but my friend here is lending me two.'

'He's a good friend to do so.'

'We all help each other these days.'

Except when you are accidentally killing each other. But he kept the thought to himself, brooding silently as they started out over trampled, blood-stained snow, about the disastrous muddle that was Poland. Might his son, got so strangely, really prove a rallying point? Hard to believe, but something infinitely worth fighting for.

Miriam's secret road took them among the foothills of the River Bug and was rough going indeed. 'It makes what's gone before seem like child's play.' Glynde was helping Miriam across the channel of what must be a stream in summer, now frozen solid under a treacherous layer of new snow. 'It's gallant of you to bring us.'

'I'm enjoying it! My father brought me up as the son he never had. We used to do this journey together. When I grew up, it was hard to turn into a woman. Took a while to see I could still fight his fight for Poland.'

'He fought?'

'Metaphorically. Being a Jew, he was not eligible for the army. He fought with his wits; with his money. There are more ways of winning a battle than charging the enemy's guns, Mr. Rendel.'

'Yes, but first you must decide who is the enemy. And who your friends. Don't trust the French too far, Miriam. May I call you that?'

'What else? It's all the name I have. It's liberating, being Jewish, Mr. Rendel. And – thank you for your warning – I trust the French only a little more than I do the Russians. But I hate them a great deal less. Does that answer you?'

'Completely.' It was a silencer too.

They were back on what passed for the main road two days later when they saw a mounted party approaching. There was a moment of intense anxiety as they rode nearer across the waste of snow, then: 'It's Wysocki,' said Glynde, who was riding beside Miriam, while Jan brought up the rear.

'That's a relief.' Miriam turned to him. 'Mr. Rendel, before we meet them, may I give you a word of advice?'

'Do.'

'Trust no one,' she said.

Warned by an advance messenger from Wysocki, the Princess sent for Jenny. 'I shall receive him in state. He deserves it after coming so far, and through such dangers. Imagine their being attacked in that wild border country, and his saving them by

275

his sharp shooting. Did you know he was such a shot, Jenny?'

'No. Why should I? But he fought at Valmy.'

'All those years ago? Fancy that! Best tell Casimir. He must be there when I receive Mr. Rendel, and I want no nonsense about his welcome. It's to be enthusiastic, tell Casimir, and if you can't count on the rest of the little boys, keep them away.'

'You mean to receive him publicly as your son's tutor?'

'Well, of course. That's why I sent for him, after all.'

But did you tell him? She could not ask it. Instead: 'But, Princess, do you mean to receive him publicly as Mr. Glynde Rendel, or under whatever alias he may have used for his travels?'

'His dangerous travels.' The Princess obviously liked this idea. 'I shall receive him as Mr. Rendel. He comes, after all, with Monsieur Talleyrand's blessing.'

'Monsieur Talleyrand is in disgrace with Napoleon.'

'Nonsense. Your news is out of date. The Austrian marriage was always Talleyrand's project. With it, he'll be re-established. He's too clever a man for Napoleon to do without for long. And anyway, I told Stanislas Potocki and my cousin Josef that I'd sent for an Englishman to see to my son's education, and they both approved the idea. Better than any other nationality, they said, in the circumstances. A stroke of genius, Josef called it. Characteristic, he said.'

And what will Mr. Rendel say? Poor Glynde. Jenny kept quiet.

26

The Princess received them in her mirrored entrance hall, as she had the Prince all those years ago, and Glynde was torn between thinking this the best of omens, and wishing that there had been a chance to tidy himself, to remove the disfiguring beard. It was all happening too fast, too publicly. Hands helped them out of furs and wadded coats as they moved forward to where Isobel stood on the fourth step of the wide stairway, a gleaming figure all in white, with a sparkle of diamonds.

'Miriam!' She came down to meet her, kissed her ceremonially on both cheeks, with just a perceptible moment of hesitation at the pockmarked one. 'This has been gallant of you. I thank you, for myself and for my son. Casimir, make your bow.'

So far, all Glynde's attention had been for Isobel. Now he was aware of Jenny, standing a little back and to the right of the stair's last twirl of gilded balustrade, the boy beside her. A handsome child, well grown for his age, he had the Princess's brilliant dark eyes under the close cap of thick, curling black hair. He was stepping forward now, very much in command of himself, to greet Miriam in French as fluent as his mother's.

'And my two good friends!' The Princess held out a hand to each. 'Mr. Rendel, Mr. Warrington, welcome back to Rendomierz. I cannot tell you what pleasure it gives me to see you here. And after such dangers encountered for our sakes! Casimir, you will not remember Mr. Warrington and Mr. Rendel, but they are old friends. Good friends of your father. If only he were here today.'

There was a little murmur among the crowd around her as those who understood French crossed themselves. While the boy made his bow first to Jan, then to himself, Glynde was very much aware of Jenny's hovering presence just behind him. She had changed, he thought, more than the Princess had. She looked smaller, her face thin under the neat crown of braided hair. Every inch a governess, poor girl. And she looked anxious, too, presumably concerned over her charge's behaviour.

The Princess was handsomer than ever, even more the great lady than he had remembered her, immensely in command. Now she was bringing Jenny into their charmed circle. 'You'll not have forgotten my beloved Miss Peverel,' and so on to the rest of her little court, grouped on either side of the grand stairway. Bowing, greeting old and new faces, saying the proper things, he began to feel like a figure in some masquerade, or fairy-tale ballet. Had he come all this way, risking death at sea, the Tsar's secret police, the savagery of the other night's attack, only for this?

But what else had he imagined? Had he really expected her to hold out both hands to him, greet him as her lord? Absurd. She had sent for him and he had come. Later, there would be time to talk. And now she was putting an end to the oddly formal little scene: 'You must be exhausted, all of you. You too, Leon, but before you rest yourself, I know you will see our valued guests safely to their quarters. We will meet again for dinner. Casimir,' her voice was suddenly sharp, a note Glynde had not heard before, 'come here.'

Through all the business of the introductions, Glynde had been aware of Casimir's eyes upon him: a steady, somehow disconcerting scrutiny. The boy had been moving forward, about to speak to him, when his mother's command stopped him. Just behind him, Jenny Peverel looked more anxious than ever. Something was up, but what? Fantastic, mad to imagine that any hint at a possible relationship between him and Casimir could have got out here at Rendomierz. He had looked in vain for any trace of himself in the boy, was glad of the strong likeness to the Princess.

Leon Wysocki was speaking to him. 'Yes,' he agreed, 'let's go.' Time to talk later, when he looked and felt himself again. 'I'm for the Turkish bath, aren't you, Jan?'

'I most certainly am.' Jan was a complete pirate with a week's growth of beard and dark curls beginning to spring wirily back after their long confinement under a fur hat.

As Wysocki led them up the street by the stream, Glynde automatically turned towards the house they had occupied before. The house with the tunnel. His blood stirred. Perhaps the Princess was waiting to send for him tonight.

'No, Excellency, not that one,' Wysocki shepherded them forward. 'The Pani Peverel lives there, now she is in charge of the boys. I am afraid it will be a little further for your Excellencies to get to the bath. The boys have the first houses in the street, you see. They and their tutors.' And as if to confirm this, they heard a great howl of childish mirth from the house they were passing.

'Boys?' asked Glynde. 'What boys?'

'But, Excellency!' The man looked entirely astonished. 'The little boys! Her Highness's school.'

'A school? The Princess?' Glynde's amazement mirrored Wysocki's.

'Her Highness will doubtless tell you about it herself.' Something odd about the man's tone? 'But here is your house, Excellencies. And Jadwiga awaiting you. I hope you will find everything to your satisfaction.'

'A school?' Glynde faced Jan across the living-room of the little house that was the duplicate of the one they had occupied before. 'The Princess running a school?'

'You can bet your boots that Jenny Peverel really runs it,' said Jan. 'We'd better get shaving, Glynde, if we're to be fit for the Princess's dinner table.'

'Yes. You're right.' He was impatient to get to his own room. Dismissing the voluble Jadwiga, he paced it eagerly, looking for the remembered signs of an entrance to the tunnel. And finding none.

When they reached the Princess's salon, they found her as they had before, leaning on the big pianoforte, listening to Monsieur Poiret play Haydn. It might have been a replay of the scene eight years ago except that Jenny Peverel was there instead of Marta, still looking anxious, but surprisingly elegant in demure grey satin. And Jan had surprised him by appearing, formidably handsome, in formal evening rig of breeches and silk stockings. Jan had changed; no doubt about that. In the old days, Glynde had been the unquestioned leader of the two; now, from time to time, he was disconcerted to feel that Jan

279

was – what? Bearing with him, perhaps even patronising him a little?

He had known that there would be no chance to speak to the Princess before dinner, and the meal seemed interminable. He had forgotten what social trivialities the Poles talked in public, and caused a frisson down the length of the table by asking the Princess how she found life under French rule after the long Austrian domination.

'It's a change, of course,' she told him lightly, while Jan flashed him a reproachful glance from beyond her. 'But you have been living in Brighton, Mr. Rendel, you must tell us about this country palace your Prince of Wales is building for himself there. It's something quite out of the way, I understand.'

Thus firmly directed back into normal conversational channels, he exerted himself to be entertaining about Prinny's Brighton fantasy. 'But my aunt says he has done wonders for the town. She asked me to remember her kindly to you, by the way, Miss Peverel,' he leaned across to where Jenny was sitting on the other side of the table.

'Good of her to remember.' Jenny flushed and smiled, and he thought with surprise that she was becoming better looking as she grew older. 'We only met once, when she was staying at Petworth House. I remember her well. A formidable lady. She did not speak much, but when she did, everyone listened.'

'That's my aunt.' He smiled at Jenny warmly. 'Sometimes she even frightens me.'

'And what news of your family in America, Mr. Warrington?' The Princess half turned away from Glynde to ask the question. 'How do they endure your being away so long?'

'My father does so very easily, Highness, now he finds me useful to him in his business. My sister used to complain she missed me, but she's a married lady now, with children; I hardly hear from her. Out of sight, out of mind, you know.' He sounded philosophical about it. 'I flatter myself I am something of a European now.'

'Or an Asian perhaps? After so long in Russia.'

'Petersburg, Highness, not outer Mongolia. And – always – a Pole. I think my friend, Miriam, will speak for me there.'

He looked across to where she sat, relegated, almost below the salt.

'No need. I never forget you are my kin. And nor should you. Enough of this "Highness". Call me cousin, Jan.'

'I thank you, cousin.' He raised his glass to toast her. They had reached the dessert stage, and hothouse fruits were being piled on the table. 'Is young Casimir not to join us? I long to make his better acquaintance. And his fellow pupils? Wysocki tells us you have founded your own school, for the boy's sake. A most enlightened move, if I may say so. It goes on well?'

'Not altogether.' Her eyes met Jenny's across the table. 'We have found that the young have a disturbing tendency to sink to the lowest level. Casimir must grow up a Prince, first among equals. But it doesn't seem to be working out like that. They lead each other on, I am afraid. They need the firm hand of one reared in truly democratic principles. Of someone they must respect on every count. A soldier, a statesman, a man of both war and peace. I hope I have found him for them. How can they but respect someone who has braved such dangers to come to us here? And who better than an Englishman to guide the training of a democratic Prince?' She turned, at last, to Glynde, who had been trying not to believe what he heard. 'Mr. Rendel, you came when I sent you my plea. Tell me that you are not going to fail me now. And Casimir.'

A tutor! A private tutor. He had risked his life, clear across Europe, to be appointed bear-leader to his own son. Not just to his son, to a parcel of boorish little Poles. For a few moments, he was beyond speech. Perhaps as well? He raised his eyes, as if at a summons, and met Jenny Peverel's, anxious, pleading. Advising? He had been a complete, an absolute fool, and she somehow knew it, understood. Was warning him? Yes. If he threw the Princess's offer back in her teeth, what would happen? What would she do? It was a cold and sobering thought. The Princess was absolute mistress here, under the French. His enemies. He had put his head into the lion's mouth indeed. The lioness. The woman he loved, would always love. And their son. The hope of Poland.

The silence had gone on too long. He met the Princess's eyes. 'You do me great honour, Highness. But I confess you have taken me most absolutely by surprise. Before I decide to

281

undertake this onerous and honourable task, may I have the privilege of discussing it with you alone?'

'If you feel the need.' The Princess had expected instant capitulation. What a milksop she must think him. Well: what a milksop he had been. It had taken the life-or-death decisions of his appalling journey to teach him he was a man. Now he must conceal it.

The Princess rose gracefully to her feet, and he saw for the first time the slight thickening under the flow of her dress, the tiny map of lines below the chin shown him in profile. She had been living hard, while he ate out his heart for her in England. All the rumours he had heard and and discounted fluttered about him, bat-winged. Murat? Her cousin Poniatowski? Davout? He was drowning in his own poisoned thoughts. Rising as she did, holding out his arm, he met Jenny's eyes once more across the table, read the renewed warning in them and hoped he had flashed back a message of thanks.

Alone in her study, the Princess turned to face him. No suggestion that they sit. She meant the meeting to be brief. 'Yes, Mr. Rendel?'

'Isobel!' She had lain in his arms, night after night, meeting fire with fire. He knew every inch of her, knew what pleased her. If he could only touch her.

It must have shown in his face. 'No, Mr. Rendel.' Without actually moving, she seemed to withdraw from him. 'It is "Highness" now. We are engaged in a great enterprise, you and I. We are to bring up a King for Poland. A King whom everyone will accept. It is a heavy charge, a great responsibility, and nothing shall interfere with it. Besides, think of the future, yours and mine, standing behind the throne, giving wise counsel for the peace of Europe.'

'You truly think it possible? You have grounds?'

'But, of course. You know on whose advice I sent for you, surely? I had thought he would have told you more. I am sorry if there has been any room for misunderstanding, but I suppose he did not dare risk anything in writing, placed as he is.' She held up a warning hand. 'We'll not mention his name, if you please, but we know of whom we are speaking.'

'Yes.' But what had Talleyrand told her?

'He is playing an immensely dangerous game. I was at both

Erfurt and Vienna. He is walking a tightrope between the two Emperors in the firm belief that in the end they will understand each other, agree to a balance of power in Europe. And for that, Poland is essential. Do you begin to understand? Poland with a King who is on good terms with both France and Russia, but not tarred with either brush, and whom even England can approve.'

'It would be a miracle.' But, despite himself, he was engaged, interested . . .

'A miracle we all need. And – miracles don't just happen, Mr. Rendel, they must be worked for. That is what you and I are going to do, together.'

'How soon do you expect your miracle? The chance of it.'

'Who can tell? Not too soon, I hope, or Casimir won't be ready. I warn you, it's no sinecure I am asking you to take on. He's a spirited child, and the others are little tearaways. They egg each other on. We Poles don't bend the neck easily.' She was proud of it.

'No.' Amazing to find himself becoming engaged in this extraordinary project. 'He knows why I've come, of course. I thought he was taking a great interest in me.'

'Looking for chinks in your armour,' said Casimir's mother. 'He's army mad, they all are. You'll have to share them with the military instructors.'

'My problem, of course, being that I cannot tell him for what he is being trained. Why it matters so much.'

'To be a Prince of Poland. That's enough, surely.'

'Like all the others, who care more for their estates than their country?'

'Not all of them. Think of my cousin Poniatowski, think of Adam Czartoryski.'

'They do rather sum up the problem,' he said. 'One all for the French, the other all Russian.'

'So Casimir must be all Pole.'

'And to achieve that, you have sent for an Englishman!'

'Who better? And – the right Englishman.' Now, she seemed nearer again, leaning a little towards him, with a waft of scent, heavier than what she used to wear. 'We'll be his mentors,' she said. 'You and I.'

Now? In the future? A bribe? A promise? She was right, of

course. If Talleyrand really thought Casimir a possible answer to the problem of Poland, nothing must threaten his claim to be both Sobieski and Ovinski. And yet: 'The tunnel?' he asked. 'We may need to confer.'

'The tunnel is closed. We will confer publicly, you and I. And have done so, this time, for long enough.' She held out a white hand heavy with rings. 'I am more glad than I can say, Mr. Rendel, that you agree to take on this heavy charge.'

He thought she meant him to kiss it, took it instead and shook it warmly, finding it oddly limp in his grasp, the hand of a woman who did not do very much. 'I shall try to bring him up as a democratic Prince,' he said, and wondered if that was a threat or a promise. 'It won't be easy.' Still holding her hand, he turned to lead her towards the door. 'I had better go back and start.'

'But you'll say nothing about the future,' she hung back for a moment. 'To anyone, to Jan Warrington . . . I don't entirely trust him. He seems remarkably thick with the Jewess, Miriam.'

'They've been making money for you, the two of them. And, no doubt, for themselves, too. But I agree with you about Jan. He's changed.' He had meant to say more.

'We've all changed.' The Princess let him lead her back to the supper-room; the first time, he thought, that he had taken the initiative between them.

'So you've agreed to do it?' Jan moved eagerly across the room to meet them. 'I'm delighted to hear it.' He sounded more than a little surprised. 'You must promise to let me know how you go on. I take a great interest in young Casimir. Miriam says she will see to it that your letters get through to me.'

'Indeed I will,' she was on Jan's arm, smiling at them both, a beautiful woman still if you looked at the right side of her face.

'Thank you. Of course I'll write, Jan. And you must send me all the news of Petersburg. But now I must have a word with Miss Peverel, who knows, I suspect, better than anyone, just what I have agreed to take on.'

'You're going to do it! I'm so glad.' Jenny's smile was

brilliant with relief. 'He needs it so badly. But . . . I was afraid . . .'

'As well you might be.' He smiled back. 'Would it have been the oubliette, do you think, if I'd refused? I'm sure there must be one somewhere in Rendomierz.' Disconcerting to realise that he was not entirely joking. 'You'll have to show me how to go on. I'm counting on you for that. The duties of a pedagogue are a closed book to me, I'm afraid. If the Princess were to ask for qualifications, she'd be grievously disappointed. I never had a tutor. My father sent me off to school when I was in short coats.'

'Poor little boy,' she said. 'Of course I'll help in any way I can. What's needed, really, is a firm hand, someone Casimir respects. You come with great advantages: a soldier, a traveller, an English aristocrat.'

'Not much of one,' he told her. 'My brother's wife is dying, Miss Peverel. He'll marry again as soon as she does, get himself an heir. I find myself, all of a sudden, a man quite without expectations.' What in the world had made him tell her that?

'I see.' She took it in. 'I am so very sorry.'

'Don't be. I don't like myself very much just now, but at least I am my own man, for what that is worth. I had thought of going into business, maybe with Jan Warrington. Why should I blench at dwindling into a tutor? And one with such interesting prospects.' His tone was savage.

'One must live, Mr. Rendel.'

Something in her tone caught him up short. 'Forgive me! Now I really am ashamed. You've gone through it all, have you not?' He was remembering the first time they had met, when she had found herself marooned in the stable yard, butt of Cossacks and servants, and how gallantly she had borne it.

'And still am.' She raised suddenly brilliant eyes to his. 'So – I'll give you a word of advice, Mr. Rendel. Name your terms to the Princess. A house, independence, a salary . . . You'd best consult with Miriam and Mr. Warrington about that. But – get it in writing, signed and witnessed.'

'You mean –' This was an entirely new thought to him. 'You?'

'I have been here eight years, Mr. Rendel, and these are my total earnings so far.' Her hand touched the necklace she wore.

'Be warned by me. And for God's sake, don't speak of it!'

'Monstrous! No – of course I won't. And, Miss Peverel, nor you of what has happened to me. Shameful enough to have thought of dead men's shoes . . . to have imagined myself Lord Ringmer. It's done me good to tell you, but you're the only one. May it remain like that?' How easy she was to talk to. What an admirable listener.

'It most surely will. I was going to advise it. I'll never understand the Poles. At least I've reached the point of knowing that! But, I do think it might make some difference, not perhaps to Casimir, but to the little devils his schoolmates.'

'Little devils? Strong words, Miss Peverel.'

'Wait till you meet them.'

They were little devils. They were proud and ignorant, and proud of their ignorance. Each one of them had grown up a small tyrant, monarch of all he surveyed, subject only to the authority of his father. The idea of cooperation, of working together towards a common goal was totally alien to them. Force was the only argument they recognised, so force it had to be. Glynde learned more about Poland and its problems in the next few months than he had in all the time he had spent before at the Princess's court, and in all the reading and thinking he had done about Poland since.

Casimir would have been the worst of all – because of having had no father – if he had not had Jenny. You could reason with Casimir, and if you interested him, he would listen. And he was passionate about Poland. Tell him of hope for Poland, and he would listen almost for ever. The problem was to hold the balance steady. French domination was visible all around them: in the taxes paid to support the occupying army, in men marched away to join it, mourned as gone for ever by their families. The Duchy of Warsaw, bankrupted by war and occupation, was paying its debts in men for Napoleon's army, now more and more deeply engaged in the Spanish peninsula. There might be glory to be found with the French armies, but there was also death, and with the man of the family gone, the family starved. Dead soldiers pay no pensions.

Casimir, in and out of peasant houses at Rendomierz, was very much aware of this. But then, there were peasant families,

too, who had lost breadwinners to the Russian armies generations back, or, more recently, at the massacre of Praga, or
when French and Russians clashed along the Vistula. Hatred
of the Russians was ancestral, engrained; hatred of the French
was comparatively new, just being learned, hardly yet recognised because they were providing glory, too.

'The trouble is –' As so often, Glynde had taken his problem
for discussion with Jenny Peverel. 'I can't get them to think
as Poles. They are either against the French, or against the
Russians. Their only union lies in hatred. It just depends
where they are from, who they hate.'

'And Casimir?'

'Ah, he's different, thanks largely to you. I have great hopes
of him.' Of course Casimir was different. His son! How strange
it all was, and how frustrating that he could not possibly tell
Jenny about Casimir's democratic heritage.

While he fought his first battles with the little boys, the weather
was growing perceptibly milder. The thaw would come soon,
and anyone who wished to travel, must do so. Miriam and
Jan only stayed three days, and he was glad to see them go.
He had still told no one about the Polish émigré he had quietly
visited for language lessons in Brighton, letting them all assume
that he was as ignorant of Polish as he had been on his first
arrival eight years before. He had felt guilty at first at letting
Jan go on interpreting for him, but when they had reached
Vinsk, the deception had paid off handsomely. In French
and Russian, Jan and Miriam were good friends and trading
partners; in the few phrases of Polish they allowed themselves,
they were obviously lovers. It had been anxiety, not accident,
that had kept him restless on the night of the attack in the
forest, but it had been lucky for them all.

His intention, on reaching Rendomierz, had been to warn
the Princess at once. But nothing had been as he expected. It
had gone horribly against the grain with him to follow Jenny's
advice and ask for a firm contract from the Princess. But her
reaction, when he did so, had been illuminating.

'A contract! Between friends?' She had not tried to conceal
her anger. 'I thought you my friend, Mr. Rendel.'

'I thought more than that of you, Highness.' If she wished to take this as a threat, she was welcome to do so. 'But if I have dwindled into your son's tutor, the labourer must be seen to be worthy of his hire. I'll get no respect from that bunch of rapscallions you choose to call your school unless they see me in an assured position; gentleman among gentlefolk. I need an estate from you, preferably one so close to Rendomierz that I can run my school in my own grounds. This arrangement of yours, with the boys living luxuriously in different houses, and all the rivalries it gives rise to, has been a disaster from the start. I had a word with Wysocki this morning. He tells me there is a small house and a big barn down closer to the Renn; just the other side of the pleasure gardens. It belonged to Marta, he tells me, she gave it up when she went into her convent. What could be more suitable? I'll live in the house, the boys can play at being Spartans in the barn; we will be out of your way, but happy to pay our respects to our Foundress and Commander when she so desires.'

'You've got it all worked out, then, you and my steward between you?' She was hesitating between surprise, amusement and fury.

'Why, yes, Highness. I thought best to lose no time, since if you are really going to Paris with Madame Potocka, you will want to take advantage of the frozen roads as far as Warsaw. If I am to do any good here, I must have my position secure before you go. And you will doubtless wish to be able to make a favourable report to our mutual friend whose ingenious idea the whole thing was.' He was almost tempted to tell her of his relationship with Talleyrand, but that would be the act of a coward. And anyway, the reminder that he was in a sense Talleyrand's man should be enough.

'Paris?' she said thoughtfully. 'I doubt I could get there in time for the Emperor's wedding, but the celebrations should prove interesting. And there is quite a Polish colony there, by what I hear from Anna Potocka. Send for Wysocki, Mr. Rendel. We had better finish what you two have taken upon yourselves to start.'

'I do congratulate you.' Jenny had been amazed and delighted to see an army of serfs set to work in the barn. 'It will be much better than what we had here; I'm only sad you'll be so far away.'

'But, Miss Peverel, you are coming too! You cannot imagine I have any idea of doing without you. You are to have a suite of apartments on the ground floor of the barn, with a room for Marylka. My idea is that the two of you will be absolutely responsible for the boys' physical well-being, while I try to knock some sense into them!'

'And the Princess has agreed to this too?'

'With enthusiasm. So —' he held out his hand '— is it agreed? You and Marylka will temper the monastic simplicity I plan for my boys?'

'Representing the gentler sex? A grave responsibility.' She put her strong little hand in his. 'Gladly, Mr. Rendel. And the Princess?'

'Goes to Paris, or so I devoutly hope.' It surprised him to hear himself say it.

'Stay a little longer, Jan.' Naked in his arms, the first night at Vinsk, Miriam put up a loving hand to touch his cheek. 'I've missed you so, all these nights we've been apart.'

'And I you! To be so near, and unable to touch you!' They had made love passionately at first, then more gently, now were comfortable together in the friendly aftermath. 'But it went well, don't you think?'

'Better than I could have imagined possible. I never thought he'd do it, did you?'

'He must have been having things harder than I knew in England. Do you know, I actually found myself feeling sorry for him.' He kissed her, laughing. 'How surprised he would have been, if I'd told him I was expecting him when he turned up on my doorstep in Petersburg! Or, before that, when I got him into Talleyrand's clutches at Tilsit. Ignorant, innocent Jan, the simple American, outsmarting him all the way! He, the great British aristocrat, friend of Ambassadors, so good to the poor American. Watching my tongue for me! And now he's head tutor of a boys' school in the depths of Poland. Not at all what he expected!'

'He took it admirably.'

'Yes, didn't he! I felt a brute, when the Princess sprang it on him like that. I suppose that's the other side of the aristo-cratic coin. They do have good behaviour drilled into them.'

'Which he will do to Casimir.'

'Yes. He'll make a Prince of him. And a man.'

'A great gentleman, like himself.'

'In a moment, my love, you are going to make me jealous.' He pulled her to him, laughing.

For a man with a broken heart and hopes destroyed, Glynde found himself remarkably busy and cheerful. The Princess had given him *carte blanche* before she took the long road for Warsaw and Paris, and work on the new school-building went on apace. He had moved into the manor house, known for no good reason as the cottage, as soon as the Princess made it over to him, so he was on hand to direct the alterations to the barn that was to be his school. On Jenny's advice, he had asked for Lech as his servant, and was amazed to find himself, all of a sudden, master of a thriving household, where his every wish was law.

He still had one overriding anxiety. There had been no message from Talleyrand, and so he had no means of communi-cating with him. The instructions he had received in England had been precise. He was to get himself to Rendomierz, arrange his own channel to Petersburg, and then wait for Talleyrand to supply the westward link in the chain. Then – as Talley-rand's man had told him – 'accidentally' met on Brighton beach, where the sea would mask their voices, Talleyrand would have his line of communications clear, all the way from Paris to Petersburg.

He had his eastward link, by way of Miriam and Jan, but had no idea to what extent he could trust them. He had been almost tempted, before they left, to admit his knowledge of Polish, challenge them to explain their relationship, but what he thought were wiser counsels had prevailed. But he desper-ately needed to let Talleyrand know of this new hazard. Which brought him up sharp against another problem. How far could he trust this unknown father of his? The short answer was: not at all. Urging him to accept the Princess's amazing invitation, Talleyrand's man had said nothing about the reason for it. He had been left to make his idiotic mistake, to risk his life, a modern Quixote, all across Europe to a Dulcinea who merely wanted him to run a school. The fact that he was enjoying this enormously was neither here nor there. He had been shamelessly used, and would not forget it.

It was the little boys who brought the first news that something had happened in the forest somewhere between Rendomierz and Warsaw. 'They don't much like to talk of it in the village,' Casimir told Glynde, 'but there are men missing. They can't hide that. Mama will be angry when she hears. We're short-handed enough as it is after that last draft went for soldiers. I don't know how we're going to get in the harvest.'

'We'll all have to help.' Glynde was both touched and impressed by Casimir's small assumption of authority. 'I shall declare a school holiday. But – you mean there has been fighting in the forest?'

'And no one will speak of it. Can I tell the boys about the holiday, Mr. Rendel?' He was eager to be away; fighting in the forest was nothing new to him.

'Yes, of course.' Left alone, Glynde thought for a while, then went out to the stables, where he could be sure of finding Lech at this time of day. 'Saddle two horses,' he told him. 'There's something I need to look at.'

'Yes, Pan Rendel.' A look of total comprehension on Lech's calm face.

They started out with Glynde in the lead, but as soon as they were safe into the dark of the forest he slowed to let Lech come up beside him. 'Now, what's this about fighting in the forest?'

'I was hoping for a chance to tell you. Trust the little Prince to know what is going on!' He looked about him nervously, as if the trees might have ears. 'It's the Brotherhood. There's been dissension among them for a long time. There was a meeting, between here and Warsaw, at a hunting lodge. It came to blows, to deaths. I'm glad to say that the Poles won.'

'The Poles? The Brotherhood? What are you talking about, Lech?'

The man looked appalled. 'You mean, you don't know?' His face closed. 'You'd best ask the Pani Peverel.' And he would say no more.

27

'The Brotherhood?' 'A hunting lodge south of Warsaw?' Glynde had called on Jenny to ask her what Lech had meant. 'They kidnapped you and took you there? You must have been terrified!'

'Yes.' She looked at him, faintly amused, over her glass of wine. 'I was frightened at the time. Well – I still am, of the Brotherhood. But I think this has to be good news about them, Mr. Rendel. I have thought, for a long time, that they suffered extraordinarily from divided command. It would be so easy, don't you see? All that dressing up, that disguise, those masks. Prince Ovinski was a member. While he was alive, I thought they veered between the French and the Russian side, but that could not explain the attack on you on your way here. I would have thought only the Prussians would want Casimir to grow up a little fool.'

'The Prussians! There's a secret society there called the *Tugendbund*; it started in East Prussia, I believe, at Königsberg when the court was there. You think they might have managed to infiltrate your Brotherhood?'

'Not my Brotherhood,' she said drily. 'Though, it's true, they have intervened in my favour in their time. But I can't say my heart is going to bleed much over any deaths among them, on whichever side. I wonder if it is the French or the Russians who are in control now.'

'You don't imagine it could be the Poles?'

'Never the Poles!'

Two days later Marylka brought her the Brotherhood's first message for a very long time indeed. 'I am to tell you that they have set their house in order and that we are under their special protection. If you ever need their help, you have only to let me know. And they have re-established their secret courier service, both to the west and to the east.'

'And what in the world would I be needing a secret courier for?'

'They seemed to think that the Pan Rendel might.'

'Oh, they did, did they?' And then, 'I suppose you aren't allowed to tell me how you would get in touch with them.'

'No, pani.' Marylka looked frightened.

'Frankly, I'm just as glad not to know.' It had been the most enormous relief to leave the little house by the stream, where she had always been aware of the secret tunnel, blocked off it was true, but still there. 'Mr. Rendel must know about this. I'll see him after school.' And then, as Marylka still lingered, 'What is it, Marylka? Is there something else?'

'Yes, pani. I had news of Marta the other day.'

'From the convent? Is she happy?'

'Happy! She's a drudge, Pani Jenny; starving for a crust. The endowment that was promised with her was never sent. They put her into the kitchen to earn her keep. She asked me to speak for her. We're kin, of course, in a backstairs kind of way. But, pani, I dare not. Besides, it would do no good.'

'No,' said Jenny thoughtfully. 'The question is, do I dare?'

'I thought, perhaps, you might have a word with Pan Rendel? The Princess listens to him.'

'When she's here.' But it was true that the Princess had given Glynde an absolutely free hand in his arrangements for the boys in his charge, and, so far, they were working out wonderfully well. He had formed them into what he called his band of Knights Crusaders, training for some mystic unspecified future purpose, their leader chosen weekly by a parliament of the whole group on the basis of reports from masters and boys alike. Casimir was often, but by no means always, the leader and Jenny had been amazed at how well he took his occasional demotions, and had said so to Glynde.

'Oh, I think he is beginning to understand,' Glynde had told her. 'He's a rational being, that boy.'

Looking for Glynde now, she found him in the boys' big common-room telling them stories before bedtime. Seeing her hesitant at the door, he smiled an apology across the spellbound heads and ended his story: 'So the Prince George killed the dragon, and took the kingdom, and married the Princess, and they lived happily ever afterwards.'

'But, sir,' a hand went up. 'How did he kill it? With his lance?'

'No, his sword, idiot!'

'But there's a picture in the chapel at home, with his lance in its mouth –'

'Silence,' said Glynde, and got it. 'You may ask the Master at Arms, with my compliments, what he thinks the best method for killing dragons. Personally, I believe I would favour a long lance, because of the fire he breathes.'

'Or a pistol? Better still?' suggested Casimir eagerly. 'Or do you think that would be cheating?'

'I think that would depend on what the dragon had done,' said Glynde. 'Perhaps you should discuss that with Father Ignatz, Casimir. Now, make your bows to Miss Peverel, and off to bed with the lot of you. Marylka will be waiting.' He smiled at Jenny. 'Come and join me by the fire, and tell me what I can do for you.'

'It's something Marylka told me.' Jenny settled in her usual chair. 'Do you remember Marta?'

'The Princess's companion? Of course I do. Lord, what a long time ago.' He was grateful for the heat of the fire, masking the rush of colour to his face. It was Marta who had fetched him to his assignations with the Princess. But it had also been Marta who had lured Jenny Peverel into what he now realised must have been an ambush by the Brotherhood. 'What of Marta?'

'Marylka has heard from her. She's starving, a penniless drudge in her convent. Her endowment was never sent. She begs for help, for a word said to the Princess.'

'And you and Marylka have chosen me to bell the cat?'

'Well.' Surprised. 'If you want to put it like that. I'm sorry! I'm telling my story back to front. I was so distressed to hear about poor Marta.'

'Poor Marta, who got you ambushed by the Brotherhood?'

'Oh! You worked that out?'

'I'm not entirely a fool, Miss Peverel, though I do sometimes seem to behave like one. So what is the front of your story?'

'A message from the Brotherhood. Marylka brought it. They say they have got their house in order, and we are under their protection. And that they have re-established their secret courier service, both to the east and to the west. They seem to think that would interest you.' She smiled her friendly smile. 'There's a good deal you haven't told me, is there not, Mr. Rendel?' She got up and walked over to open the door and make sure that Marylka and the little boys were all safe upstairs. 'You're really a secret agent of some kind, are you not? I do devoutly hope it is for the British that you work?'

He looked at her strangely. 'Frankly, Miss Peverel, so do I.'

'He ate nothing but artichokes.' Anna Potocka had dined in state with the Emperor and new Empress at Saint Cloud, and summoned the Princess next morning to hear all about it. 'As fast and untidy as you please. And hurried us through our dinners so that the poor little Empress never even got her ice! Sometimes I almost feel sorry for that girl. I'll tell you someone else I was sorry for. Your old friend Davout, on duty as Captain of the Guard. Do you remember the royal airs he used to put on in Warsaw? Now I was the honoured guest, and he was just part of the retinue. I gave him my very friendliest smile as I passed him on my way into dinner. Have you seen him?' she asked casually.

'No, not yet.'

'I thought not. Playing the family man, like his master. And your other old friend, Murat, busy being King of Naples. Sad for you. Napoleon was kindness itself to me last night. He said he did not think I should trouble myself too much about this ukase of the Emperor Alexander's, this threat to confiscate the estates of absentee landowners. No hurry about packing my bags, he thinks. I told him I must await my husband's permission, of course. Lucky you, to have no husband to defer to.' She did not mean this, as both of them knew.

'All very well for Napoleon to talk.' Isobel ignored Anna's last remark. 'But suppose we don't return to our Russian-held estates, and they really are confiscated, as the Tsar threatens. I'd never forgive myself.'

'No.' Thoughtfully. 'In fact the estate near Vilno is your son's, is it not? I suppose you could send orders for him to move there.'

'Without me? Never.' She was interrupted by a page, announcing the Prince of Benevento.

'Monsieur Talleyrand,' said Anna. 'He will know what we should do for the best.'

But first Talleyrand had to hear all about last night's party. He was such a good listener that Anna remembered more of the conversation. 'It was all hints,' she said. 'There was talk of the Indies. As if Napoleon meant to get there by way of Russia. Someone – I'll leave you to guess his name – asked me what I would like brought back from there. "From Moscow or Petersburg?" I asked him, playing the innocent.'

'And what did he say?' asked Talleyrand.

'Oh, he turned it off with a joke about the Pyramids, but everyone seemed to be sure in their hearts that war with Russia is inevitable. So what should we Poles do for the best?'

'It won't come,' said Talleyrand comfortably. 'But on mature consideration, I believe you ladies might be wise to pay some heed to the Tsar's threats. It is never wise to flout a monarch's wishes. And if enough of you great families who hold lands on both sides of the border show yourselves able to cooperate with both France and Russia, it must help put an end to this mad talk of war.'

'You really think it is mad?' asked Isobel.

'Dear lady, I am sure of it. Now may I have the pleasure of seeing you home?'

Outside: 'I don't care about Anna Potocka, but I think you should go,' he told her. 'Though I am sorry to have to advise it, when your presence here gives such pleasure to your friends. But, perhaps, a brief visit to Vinsk, to show the young Prince to his people? There will be no difficulty about crossing the border, I can promise you. Oh, by the way, I heard an interesting bit of news about your Mr. Rendel the other day. His father is dying, his brother ill, too. Your head tutor may suddenly find himself Lord Ringmer. I leave it to you, Princess, to decide whether to tell him of this, which is merely a rumour, come by underground channels from England. It would be a pity if he were to decide it was his duty to abandon his interesting charge and risk his life trying to get back to England.'

'Lord Ringmer? His brother is still childless then?'

'Yes. There was some tragedy. A huge estate, I believe. A

barbarous district, mind you, Sussex. The worst roads in the country, but full of possibilities.'

'How very interesting.'

'I thought you might find it so.'

'How he has grown!' The Princess ruffled her son's dark hair. 'And more handsome than ever! I couldn't bear to stay a day longer than necessary in Warsaw! Have you been minding your books, Casimir?' She turned to Rendel and Jenny without waiting for an answer. 'I can see I have to thank you both for excellent care of my son.' She smiled at Jenny. 'Talking of sons, I heard in Warsaw that your friend Marie Walewska is actually taking her little by-blow to Paris to meet the Emperor his father, despite the rumours that the Empress is pregnant. Poor Marie, will she never learn?'

'Oh, poor Marie indeed. What will happen to her?'

'And the child! Suppose this is the last straw and Walewski disowns him after all. One could hardly blame him. Oh, Jenny, that reminds me, an old friend of yours gave me his company from Paris. I am sure you remember Paul Genet. Yes,' she saw Jenny's colour rise, 'I can see you do. Well, he's coming tomorrow, having finished his business in Warsaw, to stay with us until it is time for us to move, and then accompany us to the frontier, to make sure that we have no trouble there.'

'The frontier, Princess?' asked Glynde. 'What move?'

'Fool that I am!' The Princess put a dramatic hand to her brow. 'Can I really have forgotten to say? But you must have heard of the Emperor Alexander's ukase?'

'News from Russia is hard to come by, Highness,' said Glynde. He had had only one letter from Jan since he had left, and it had merely established the line of communication, said very little. 'What is this ukase?'

'Owners of estates in Russia must return to them, or they will be confiscated. I have been advised to take Casimir to Vinsk for a short visit, to let him see his people. You'll enjoy that, won't you, my darling?'

'To Russia? No!' He pulled away from her. 'They're murderers, mother! Devils! Do you know what the Cossacks did to Karol's family? Shall I tell you?'

'I think not,' said his mother coldly. 'Jenny, will you take

Casimir away and talk some sense into him, while Mr. Rendel explains to me what kind of history he has been teaching his charges? I can see it's more than time I took Casimir to Vinsk,' she went on, as Jenny removed him, still protesting.

'Not history, Highness,' said Glynde ruefully. 'It's life. It was perhaps a pity there was not more chance to investigate the backgrounds of the boys you chose for Casimir's companions.' It was the nearest he thought it safe to go to an actual reproach. 'I knew Karol was a very unhappy child; I only learned the reason the other day when we were, in fact, studying history, and I thought I would enliven the lesson for them by a description of the Tsar's visit to you here. It was too much for poor Karol. He suddenly came out with the whole horrible story of how his home was sacked by the Cossacks three years ago, before Eylau. His nurse hid him in the cellar, but he heard what happened to his family; heard his mother and sisters scream, saw their bodies afterwards. I hope you were not thinking of taking the whole school to Vinsk, Highness. Casimir is a reasonable boy. I think I will be able to persuade him that it is his duty to go and see for himself. But I do not think it would be wise to take the others. Most certainly not Karol.'

'No. I see. And I see that I have more to thank you for, Mr. Rendel, than I had quite realised. Believe me,' she moved closer to him and held out her hand, 'I do.'

Paul Genet arrived two days later with the news that Marie Walewska had actually left for Paris. 'She's a brave woman, one has to recognise that.'

'Or a little mad,' said the Princess.

'Maybe just deep in love.' Genet's look aimed this remark at Jenny, who felt herself blushing, and felt Glynde Rendel seeing this. Genet turned to Glynde. 'May I ask to see this interesting school you have established for the young Prince, Mr. Rendel? I hope the fact that we are officially enemies need not affect us here. In fact, it's possible that I may be able to give you news of England more recent than any you can have had.'

'I should be most grateful. I've had none since I got here; not much since I left England, and that's a long time ago now.

Is the King truly mad yet? The Prince of Wales Regent and the Whigs in power?'

'No to both, though it seems impossible that it can be long before the King is officially declared mad. How this will affect the country's government remains to be seen. Would there be time, do you think, for me to see your school before the Princess's dinner hour?'

'Why, yes, if you wish to. The boys will be at their military exercises.'

'Most interesting,' said Genet gravely. 'Do you teach them Russian strategy, or French?'

'Polish, Monsieur Genet. If you will excuse us, Highness?'

'They don't seem to like each other very much.' The Princess turned to Jenny after the two young men had left. 'I do hope they don't actually come to blows.'

In fact, the two young men were seated comfortably enough over glasses of wine, having made a fairly summary tour of the little school and briefly watched the little boys at their drill. 'I have a letter for you from my master.' Paul Genet reached into the pocket of his coat.

'I hoped you had.'

'And another, which he hopes you will be able to get through to Petersburg for him.'

'So he still hopes for peace?'

'Yes.'

'But you're less sure?' Glynde gave him a quick look.

'Sometimes our hopes deceive us. Tell me, Mr. Rendel, do you believe that if the Prince of Wales becomes Regent he will send at once for the Whigs and make peace with us?'

'I've always assumed so, but I have an aunt, lives in Brighton, knows the Prince as I do not. She's not so sure. This is a very strange conversation.'

'Between two enemies? But I have it on my master's authority that you agreed to risk your life, coming here, because his messenger convinced you that your being here would further the cause of peace.'

'Among other things,' said Glynde.

The autumn days were beginning to draw in. If they were to get to Vinsk before rain made the roads impassable, they must start as soon as possible, and Jenny and Marylka were busy from morning to night with preparations for the journey and arrangements for the diminished household that would be left behind. To Jenny's relief, she, Marylka and Glynde were to accompany the Princess, but she was less happy about Isobel's decision that the Master at Arms would be left in charge of the school. It was true that he was both the oldest of the masters, and the highest in rank, but he was also almost as passionate a Russian-hater as little Karol, for very similar reasons.

'Can you not persuade the Princess that it is a dangerous choice?' she asked Paul Genet. 'She seems to listen to you.'

'To my master speaking through me. And I am not sure that even he would be able to persuade her to fly in the face of Polish considerations of rank. Miss Peverel,' he had found her sorting linen in the school-house, 'you have been at work all day; the sun has come out; take a turn in the gardens with me. You look after everyone else; never think about yourself.'

'Not a very interesting subject.' But she was glad enough to put on bonnet and pelisse and walk down towards the ornamental water with him, remembering, as they went, the day when Casimir had nearly drenched the Tsar with water from the joke fountains. She found herself telling Genet about this, which seemed comic enough now it was all safely in the past.

'Good God!' he said. 'And what would have happened to you, Miss Peverel?'

'To me? What should have?'

'You'd have been the scapegoat. This was Austrian territory then, so it wouldn't have been Siberia, but I don't like to think . . . I've never seen the Princess really angry, but I've heard things . . .'

'Yes.' She remembered the day the Princess had had Lech whipped. It had very nearly been her own turn then.

'Miss Peverel.' They were standing side by side now, looking down at autumn leaves, golden in the dark water. 'Have you thought how close Rendomierz is to the new border between French-held Poland and Russia?'

'I'd be a fool if I hadn't.'

'And you're no fool, thank God. I'm going to tell you

something I've told no one else; not even Mr. Rendel, though he asked for my opinion. I told him my master's. Talleyrand still believes there is a chance of peace between France and Russia. Miss Peverel, I don't agree with him. And still less, now I'm here. You must be aware of it too.'

'There are rumours,' she said reluctantly. 'Of Russian armies building up beyond the border . . . Well, this journey the Princess must make tells you something of how the Tsar is thinking.'

'Yes. Vinsk is close to the frontier too. On the other side. You'll be safer there. A little. Never forget, you're enemy to both France and Russia. What safety for you anywhere, if it does come to war? And, I tell you, if it comes, this is going to be no small skirmish, but war to the death.' He turned to face her, took both her hands in his. 'Jenny, you know I have always loved you. Marry me; let me take you out of this; home to France with me; where you will be my wife; safe. My master promises us a livelihood.'

'Ah,' she said. 'You have Talleyrand's permission now, which you did not have last time we met.'

'That's true. I longed to speak to you at Erfurt; he saw it; he sees everything; told me if I did, I was no man of his. Well – without him, I'm nothing. I could not have supported you. Now – yes, I have his leave, his blessing.'

'I wonder why,' she said thoughtfully. 'He's a strange man, your master. We all dance to his tune. But – I'm sorry.' She realised he had misunderstood her, leapt into hope. 'Not I; not to this tune. You do me great honour, but I cannot marry you, now or ever. I must just take my chance, here on the dangerous frontier. But I do thank you for asking me . . . thinking of me . . .'

'How can I help it? Jenny, think again. I do truly love you.'

She smiled at him. 'Truly, but within the limits of your master's permission.'

'It's true.' It was almost a groan. 'Oh, Jenny . . .'

'Miss Peverel, Monsieur Genet.' She turned away from him to walk back to the house.

28

The Princess travelled in slow comfort, spending her nights in the lodges her husband had had built, where servants, sent on ahead, had lit fires and prepared lavish picnic meals for the party. When they passed through a village and the peasants came trooping out to kneel in the dust while their mistress drove by, Jenny was appalled by the contrast between their rags and the Princess's luxury. It was something one tended to forget in the oasis of Rendomierz, with its model village and well-dressed servants.

'I'm glad we have the Brotherhood's blessing for this journey,' she told Glynde Rendel as they enjoyed the last warmth of a fine October day and waited for the *bigos* to heat. 'Otherwise, I confess, I'd be a little anxious.'

He laughed. 'Not half so anxious as I would. When I think of the last time I came this way! But I confess I'm glad we have your friend Monsieur Genet to see us across the border. That's a very remarkable man.' He had seen how Genet devoted himself to Jenny's comfort, and drawn his own conclusions.

'And with remarkable power behind him,' said Jenny drily. 'You have met Monsieur Talleyrand have you not, Mr. Rendel?'

'Yes – at Tilsit. Were it not for him, I think I might still be languishing in prison there. I have the greatest respect for him.'

'Oh, yes,' said Jenny. 'Such charm – and so frightening. I just wonder if anyone ever dares tell him the truth. Or – no, that's not quite what I mean. Whether, just because he is so immensely cleverer than anyone else, he may not misunderstand the truth when it is told to him. Am I making any sense at all?'

'Why, yes, I rather think you are.' It was a disconcerting idea to Glynde.

And he was still more taken aback when she went on: 'It's the strangest thing, but something keeps reminding me of him on this journey. Almost as if he were here with us. Do you think Monsieur Genet might be related to him in some way?'

'One of his natural sons, you mean?' Glynde surprised her with a harsh laugh. 'Anything's possible, Miss Peverel. That he is a very favoured follower is not in doubt at all. He has a great future before him, that young man. I spoke to the Princess about Marta,' he went on. 'I'm afraid with little success. She made her bed, the Princess says . . .'

'But she was promised an endowment –'

'The promises of Princes! Gossamer.'

'You see all this,' she said, surprising herself. 'And still –'

'Love her.' It was almost a groan. 'I cannot help myself. I adore her.' He could not tell Jenny Peverel how it had all started. 'Always will. Do you know, fool that I was, when I received her message, last year, in England, I thought . . .' He stopped; it was too painful; he could not tell her.

'Of course you did.' She paused for a moment. 'As she intended you to think.'

'So I came.' He was facing it with himself as well as with her. 'And find myself her son's tutor. And,' now his laugh was gentler, more recognisably his, 'am surprised to find myself enjoying it very much. It's a terrible thing to be without occupation, Miss Peverel.'

'Yes,' she said. 'I can imagine, though it's not something that has ever happened to me.'

'No, indeed. I remember with what loving respect George Richards always spoke of you. But, Miss Peverel, I'm trying to say something to you, as an older brother might. Will you bear with me?'

'Of course.' She turned a little away, to screw up her eyes against the sunset glow in the west.

'I'm – anxious for you. Marta's case could so easily be your own. The Princess is a great lady –'

'But greatly unconcerned about the fate of her servants?'

'Exactly. Besides, anything could happen here, between France and Russia. Now the frontier has moved, Rendomierz as well as Vinsk is too close to the front line for comfort.'

'I know.'

'I think Paul Genet truly loves you. Everything he does and says goes to prove it. Even the Princess has seen.'

'Yes.' And been surprised, thought Jenny, that when she is in view, anyone else can be noticed. But this was hardly something to say to Glynde Rendel.

'Why not take him? You're more than a mother to Casimir. Just think how happy you would be with sons of your own.'

'Little French boys? Little enemies of England? You don't know me very well, do you?' She was grateful to have found this solid ground. 'You do not seem to be arranging to leave this frontier you tell me is so dangerous.'

'Of course not. My duty is here; the Princess; the boy –'

'And you love her, though you warn me against her.'

'Always.'

'It's cold.' The sun had sunk behind the dark edge of the forest. 'The *bigos* should be ready.'

'Yes. We'd best go in.'

Jenny was glad that they had Paul Genet with them at the frontier. She and Glynde Rendel had both done their best to cure Casimir of his flaming hatred of Russia, but both were anxious as to what might happen if he should imagine any insult to his mother. But everything went smoothly, so that they were saying their farewells to Paul Genet almost before they expected.

'God bless you,' he held her hand for a long moment. 'If you should ever need me . . .'

'Thank you.' But would Talleyrand let him come? She thought she had had her chance, and lost it. For a little while, she felt very lonely. So far, the Princess had invited one or other of the two young men to join her in her luxurious travelling carriage each day. Now, inevitably, Glynde Rendel was with her all the time, while Jenny did her best to answer Casimir's steady flow of questions about everything he saw that was strange and new. She was surprised to find how much she missed Paul Genet, who had always been at hand to help her down from the carriage, or to guide her over the lumpy road, or just to answer Casimir's questions for a while.

'Let me ride with the Prince today, Pani Jenny?' Marylka

caught up with her as they shivered their way to the carriages through the first light fall of snow. 'You look worn out. It's very comfortable in the *kibitka* once you get used to it, and you won't have to talk.' She tucked Jenny in among a pile of furs. 'Try and get some sleep. You don't look well to me.'

'I don't feel it! Thank you, Marylka.' She let herself drift off into a light, feverish doze as the awkward carriage bumped its way over the rough road.

She woke suddenly, rigid with fright. Shouts, curses, the crack of a whip up ahead. The *kibitka* had stopped and the driver was shouting at his horses.

'What is it?' she leaned out of the half-open carriage to ask him.

'Russian troops, pani.' He spat. 'They want us off the road, but how can we? And no room to turn the horses either. They should have sent someone on ahead.'

'So should we, I suppose.' She looked at the dark, impenetrable forest on either side of the track. They had met no one so far in this interminable journey; it had occurred to none of them as a possibility. They were likely to pay for it now. She could hear the Princess's voice ahead raised in anger, and then, her blood chilled, Casimir's. The *kibitka* was lower than a carriage; she managed to get herself out of it without help and down onto the rough log road. Half walking, half running over the uneven ground, she made her way forward to where Casimir was standing, head tilted defiantly upwards at the Russian officer who looked down at him, amazed, from his big horse.

'Don't speak to my mother like that! She's a Princess!'

'Like all the other women!' But for the moment the Russian was amused by his small challenger. 'And who are you, my fine princeling?'

'The Prince Ovinski!' The boy's chin went up still further. 'On my way to my estates at Vinsk. Out of my way, you boor.' To Jenny's relief, he was speaking French, not Polish. His mother leaned out of her carriage to intervene, but the officer was still merely amused.

'Such a bold little Prince.' And then, thoughtfully. 'Ovinski, eh? One of those damned Poles? But you'll maybe know Prince Czartoryski.'

305

'Our cousin.' Now the Princess did intervene. 'And a good friend of the Tsar's.'

'Again, they say.' But his tone had mellowed. 'I'm from Vilno myself, Highness.' Jenny was relieved to hear him use her title. 'Czartoryski's been there for a while, founding a university for fools who want to study. He's back in Petersburg now. The Tsar sent for him. Any cousin of his . . . Trouble is, I've got guns back there. Can't turn them easily. We'll just have to clear ourselves a passing place. You put your people to work that side, Highness, we'll deal with this.'

The clearing work took a long time, and longer still for the convoy to pass their little party. 'Did you count the guns?' Glynde asked Jenny that night. 'I did. It doesn't look like peace to me.'

'And you're glad?' Something in his tone had alerted her.

'I have to be, and so should you, as an Englishwoman. Napoleon has got to be stopped. If he's not, he means either to conquer us or starve us into submission. He's still building ships. Nelson's victory at Trafalgar held him for a while, but he's been hitting us as hard as he could in our trade ever since. You have no idea of how things are in England. The price of bread going up and up; bankruptcies by the hundred; unrest among the labouring classes who always feel these things hardest. And, as bad as anything else, it's making trouble between us and the Americans. They don't like our navy's powers of stop and search, and you can hardly blame them.'

'Oh,' she said. 'I see. I wondered why things weren't so easy as they used to be between you and Mr. Warrington.'

'Me and Jan?' She had amazed him. 'What in the world makes you think that, Miss Peverel? We're the oldest and best of friends, he and I.' But afterwards, thinking it over, he found himself just a little wondering about this, and disconcerted to be doing so. 'Tell me,' he went on now. 'Does Marylka maintain her links with the Brotherhood here on the road? I'd very much like to send messages both east and west if it's possible.'

'About the guns? I'll ask her.'

Marylka confirmed that they were being escorted by the Brotherhood, who would certainly start messages on their way in both directions, and Glynde sat down in his cell-like room in their stopping-place that night to try and work out what he was to say, and to whom. The westward message was easy enough. Talleyrand must be told the Russians were arming the border. His own instructions, back in England, when he got in touch after his amazing encounter with Talleyrand's messenger, had been precise. 'He's playing a deep and dangerous game,' he had been told. 'Do whatever he tells you, keep us posted, and leave the rest to us.'

The eastward message proved more difficult. The seed of doubt Jenny had planted in his mind about Jan had grown apace. He had noticed a change in Jan himself, but had merely thought he had grown up, failing to draw the conclusion that now stared him in the face. The French and Americans were old allies against the English. Why had he never thought of this in connection with Jan? Had he let himself take his friendship too much for granted? Looking back over their relationship, he saw everything differently. At Tilsit, it had been Jan who insisted on crossing the Niemen, delivering them into Talleyrand's hands. Just suppose this was no accident. And then, what followed? If Jan was working with the French, he would very likely have been warned of his own arrival in Petersburg. In which case, it was no wonder that everything had gone so smoothly. So where did that leave Jan as a link in his chain of communication with England? The link he had been so pleased about. The answer was obvious. He had given it when he told Jenny Peverel of the growing threat of war between America and England, and had entirely failed to listen to himself. Fool. Idiot.

This was getting him nowhere. And all the time the answer was staring him in the face, provided by the Russian officer in that alarming moment of confrontation. Adam Czartoryski was back in favour with the Tsar. He would write to Jan, carefully, but he would write to Adam, too. He had always supported the British alliance and would certainly have means of getting in touch, if he thought fit. But, remembering the Tsar's secret police, Glynde made this letter, too, a very careful one.

It proved unnecessary. When they reached Vinsk, they found Adam Czartoryski himself standing with Miriam on the doorstep to greet them. If he was surprised to meet Glynde in the Princess's train, he hid it well, but Glynde rather thought he was not surprised. As always, no real news could be exchanged while they were surrounded by servants, and their late dinner was taken up with an exchange of gossip. Czartoryski was newly come from Petersburg and was able to bring the Princess up to date on the latest scandal from there as well as from Vilno, where he had spent a week. He also talked at length about his university and the trained minds it would supply. 'We so badly need an administrative class in Russia. I believe they are trying to fill the same need in the Duchy too, is that not so, Princess?' And then, without waiting for the answer she might find it difficult to give, 'I have messages for you from my master, the Tsar. A word alone, if I may?'

'Why, of course.' She coloured becomingly and rose. 'If you will excuse us?' To the others. 'But you're not riding back to Vilno tonight, Prince, surely?'

'I must. My time is not my own at the moment.'

'You really are about the Tsar's business?' She faced him in what had been the Prince's study, felt all over again how strange it was to find herself absolute mistress here. So long as Casimir was a child. What a curious thing to be thinking. She smiled at Czartoryski. 'So, what is this serious errand from the Tsar?'

'Two of them, in fact. The first, to find out how your little Prince goes on, and I see I can give an enthusiastic report. My master will be glad to hear he is so well attended. That was a stroke of genius, getting my old friend Rendel to act as tutor. My master asks to be remembered warmly to you.' He paused.

'Most generous.' She was blushing again.

'And some advice.'

'Advice?'

'Yes. He bade me tell you that he looks upon himself as father-in-God of all his subjects, among whom he is happy to number you, since your marriage to his much regretted servant Ovinski.'

'Yes?' They had been standing so far, now she moved over to settle gracefully on an upright chair, gesturing him to do the same. 'He is kindness itself,' she went on mechanically, fixing him with an enquiring glance.

'And, therefore, grandfather to your son, the little Prince Casimir, in whom he takes an immense interest.'

'Ah?' she leaned forward a little.

He took a new tack. 'It is three years since the Prince's tragic death.'

'Almost three and a half.'

'Quite so. In the normal way, my master says, he would be urging you to remarry, to give the boy a father, would indeed have urged it long since.'

'We spoke of it once, back in Petersburg.'

'So? He did not tell me. He is delicacy itself, our master. A man of feeling. I often think that we are more fortunate than we understand. See how he has protected his sisters from the crass advances of the Corsican.'

She raised her head and looked him straight in the face. 'So now there is a pregnant Austrian Empress.' She threw it at him. 'An heir expected to the empire Napoleon has carved out for himself.'

'Which changes everything,' he agreed. 'I'm glad you see that, Isobel. I may call you Isobel?'

'I don't see why not. You do not propose to call me anything else, I take it.'

'Not wife, you mean? Quick of you. No. His message to you is simple, and hard. For the boy's sake, he thinks it best you do not remarry. Russian or Polish, Prussian or Austrian, no marriage you could make would do his future anything but harm.'

'A Frenchman?' She smiled at him. 'An Englishman? An American even?' And then, holding out a hand, 'No, no! I'm teasing you. Can you blame me? It's hard on a woman to be condemned to celibacy for her child's sake. But you may tell your master that I am grateful from my heart for his advice. Which only confirms what I had decided for myself a long time back.' She smiled. 'No need to tell him that. Tell him I am his loving servant to command. And tell me what he promises for Casimir.' Her tone had changed completely and he suddenly felt, strangely, as if he was dealing with a man, a fellow diplomat.

'Promises?' he said, as if to a fellow diplomat. 'Nothing. But I am instructed to hold out hopes. My general errand is to find out what support there would be here, in Lithuania, as well as in the Duchy, if the Tsar our master were to offer a Kingdom of Poland.'

'In exchange for support against the French? And who for King?'

'Ah, there's the crux of it. For the moment, himself. Who else, in this moment of crisis.'

'Crisis?'

'Best admit it. Napoleon talks peace, but his acts deny it. Acts speak louder than words.'

'They most certainly do.' She smiled at him. 'Do you remember coming to Rendomierz with the Tsar, and how he raised all our hopes? And dashed them to the ground at the last moment. I doubt he can afford to do that again. There are Poles in Paris now would be in Petersburg, if he had spoken out.'

'Straight words. I am to repeat them to my master?'

'If you wish. You'll be going to Pulawy, of course? Your father seems content enough in the Duchy as it now is.'

'I look forward to seeing him. And hope that we can persuade Josef Poniatowski to pay us a visit there.'

'Bold of you! But a mistake, I think. He's committed, heart and soul, to the French.'

'And you are not?'

'I'm committed to Poland. French or Russian, I'll support the one that gives us a clear promise.'

'And if neither does?'

'I shall be in trouble. So shall we all. If you'll take my advice, you'll not speak to Josef Poniatowski. Or, speaking, will remember that whatever you say will go straight back to Napoleon. Poniatowski is his man. If I'm sure of anything, I'm sure of that.'

'But I have the Tsar's orders.'

'Our absolute master.' She shrugged. 'Tell me, how long must I stay here at Vinsk in order not to hazard my estates?' She corrected herself: 'Casimir's, I mean.'

'I am sure our master would be happy to have you leave as soon as you wish, so long as you are ready to join your voice to mine in the Duchy.'

'In favour of a Kingdom for Poland? Of course. But in the

meantime, what am I to do for the best? I'm responsible for my son's welfare; for his estates. From what you say, war may break out any moment. All my estates – all our estates lie in the debatable ground. It was only by the goodness of God, and the kindness of my cousin Josef Poniatowski that no disaster struck us at Rendomierz in the last war. Marie Walewska has taken her son to Paris, I hear. Should I take Casimir there? Or to Petersburg?'

'Don't think of it! Your duty lies here, where your estates are.'

'All very fine.' Isobel was describing the conversation to Jenny after he left next day. 'He says my duty lies here, but here in Russian Vinsk, or home at Rendomierz?'

'Don't you think the fact that you call Rendomierz home is your answer?'

Isobel smiled. 'I must confess I had forgotten how uncomfortable life is here in this ramshackle wooden building. I think you are probably right, Jenny. We'll plan to go back to Rendomierz before spring. No chance of even that wild man Napoleon opening a campaign sooner.'

'No. And don't you think he'll probably stay in Paris for the birth of the Empress's child? Everyone says he is a most devoted husband. Poor Marie . . .'

'Nonsense! I wouldn't mind a house in Paris. You wouldn't believe what a life of luxury she leads. And surrounded by the cream of the young Polish officers. Even the hero Kosciusko has called on her, they say. And she's friends with all those sisters of Napoleon's.'

'Poor Marie, just the same,' said Jenny.

They were back in Rendomierz for the spring and the news of the birth of Napoleon's heir, the little King of Rome. Warsaw emulated Paris in its rejoicings, and the Princess lost no time in going there to join in the festivities. Glynde and Jenny were glad enough to be left alone with the problems of the school. The months spent under the domination of the elderly, irascible Master at Arms had left their mark on the little boys, and it was going to take some time to get them back into line. In Casimir's absence, the Russian-hater Karol had become their leader.

'I almost wish we had taken him with us!' Jenny said to Glynde when she had finished mopping Casimir up after one of his frequent and bloody fights with his rival.

'I don't. What would have happened, do you think, that day we met the Russian convoy?'

'Attempted murder? You're quite right. We might none of us have survived. I thought it was touch and go at the time.'

'So did I.' Curiously, they had never discussed it. 'I wish we could get rid of young Karol.'

'The Princess won't hear of it. I put it to her before she left for Warsaw. She says Casimir must learn to fight his own battles.'

'A pity he's half a head shorter than the enemy. But he'll manage,' said Glynde comfortably. 'I have great confidence in Casimir. Tell me, Jenny, did you get the impression that Miriam was as eager for us to leave as you and I were?'

'Lord, yes.' She laughed. 'I was beginning to be afraid the Princess might notice. She did say once that she had forgotten how uncomfortable that wooden palace was. I was hard put to it not to burst out laughing and tell her that none of the stoves drew properly and there was a remarkable number of strange new draughts from windows and doors that used to be perfectly weather-tight before.'

'But you didn't?'

'No. I've got some sense. Did you hate it there as much as I did?'

'Quite as much, I should think. I'm sure you never woke up in the morning to find that your window had mysteriously come open a crack in the night and everything was freezing around you.'

'No! Did you? And still you didn't tell the Princess?'

'Of course not. I wanted to leave just as badly as Miriam wanted us to go.' He had stopped writing anything but the merest trivialities to Jan. Fortunately, Adam Czartoryski had given him what he said was a totally reliable address in Petersburg, so he was now sending his information there in the elaborate code that had been worked out for him by his Foreign Office contact. Aunt meant the Tsar, or Russia. Uncle meant Napoleon, or France. And so forth. He could write what was apparently a family letter and convey a remarkable

312

amount of international news. But he had had no answers to any of the letters, whether sent by the east or by the west.

'I wish I would hear from England,' he said now.

'You've still had nothing?'

'Not a word in all the time I've been here. It's over two years! I know my aunt will have written.' The man from the Foreign Office had undertaken to get her letters through, though warning that it would take time. 'Have you heard anything?'

'No, but I hardly expect to.'

'I'm sorry.'

29

'You're here at last!' Miriam welcomed Jan formally, then led him swiftly to her own rooms in their separate wing, talking all the time. 'I thought you'd never get here! But I didn't dare send until she had actually left; there was always the chance she would change her mind.' She laughed. 'I think Glynde Rendel was beginning to suspect something towards the end, and I'm quite sure Jenny Peverel was, but she's got more sense than to say anything. It took a week to make the house habitable again after they did go!'

'You weren't afraid a serf might say something?'

'Lord, no. They know when they are well off. It's odd to remember how they hated me at first. Oh, I'm not pretending they love me now, but they know me for the lesser evil. It does make one think, Jan. If only the Tsar, or Napoleon, or anyone would give them the chance to live like human beings, they'd take it with both hands. Just look at the difference, since I've been treating them like reasonable people.'

'I'm looking at you, my love.' Safe in her room at last, he was slowly, lovingly undoing buttons down the front of her silk tunic. 'It's been too long!'

'Much too long.' She was helping him now, impatient as he. Their clothes fell in a heap to the floor. 'I've missed you so!'

'And I you. You're so beautiful.' He was kissing the remaining pock marks on her cheek, gently at first, then hungrily, his lips travelling her body as it arched to meet his.

'Much too long,' he said again, an uncounted length of time later, when she lay at last, relaxed in his arm. 'I love you, you do know that?'

She smiled up at him. 'You do contrive to give me that impression. I love you, too. I didn't know what the word meant, before. I'm – grateful to you. I'd not have missed it for anything.'

'Don't talk like that.' He kissed her again, almost angrily. 'As if it was something passing, something that would end.'

'But it is.' She touched his lips with a finger. 'I've always believed in facing facts. It's something we Jews have to learn early in life, if we are to survive. Don't think me shameless, Jan, if I take this happiness with both hands. I'm making the most of it. While it lasts.'

'It's going to last all our lives. Our lives together. If only I could marry you now, take you back to Petersburg with me, but we need you here. What is it? What's the matter?'

'Did you say marry?'

'Of course I did.'

'But, Jan, you can't, you mustn't. You know about me.'

'That you were married before, in your own eyes, and God's. And that I love you. But, forgive me, I'm ashamed. I should have asked you.' He caught the hand that was now playing in his black curls and held it to his lips. 'Pani Miriam, will you do me the great honour of becoming my wife?'

'Oh, Jan!' She lay quiet for a moment. 'You've made me so happy. But I mustn't. Your family, your father, your sister. What will they say?'

'They'll say: "Welcome to America, Mrs. Warrington." They'll love you, Miriam.'

'If I could only believe that. But, Jan, a Jewess, an ugly woman with a past.'

'A beautiful woman, with a tragic past. And, I promise you, love, it's different for Jews in our United States of America. We're going to have sons, Miriam, you and I. Don't think I ever forget the boys you lost. I've loved you most of all when I've seen you so good to Casimir. And, do you know, I don't think it has ever struck the Princess what a heroine you are being.'

'I'm not a person to her. Just the Jewess, Miriam. But Jenny knows. Jan, when war comes, what's going to happen to Jenny.'

'I worry about her. But it may not come, love.' He settled her more comfortably in his arm. 'It's time we talked business, you and I.'

'Yes.' She snuggled against him, her dark hair brushing his chin. 'Tell me all the news, I'm starved for it.'

'It's none of it good. But none of it quite so bad as I feared. Napoleon and the Tsar are both talking peace in loud voices and arming as fast as they can. But I don't think it's going to come to blows, not for this year at least. The Tsar won't start the war. I believe that. He may alarm Napoleon into starting it; he won't strike the first blow. But, my darling, will you promise me something? I deeply believe that nothing will happen this year, since neither Emperor is ready, but if it should by any wild chance . . . If you should hear that the French are massing beyond the Niemen, you'll pack your things and come east at once, to Petersburg, and me?'

'Leaving the Princess's estate, and all her serfs, exposed in the front line?'

'What do you owe the Princess?'

'Nothing. But to the serfs I owe a great deal.'

'Yes,' he said thoughtfully. 'I was thinking about that. There was an ear at the Princess's keyhole, was there not?'

'Not the keyhole exactly, but, yes, of course.'

'And none, here, today?'

'No. These are my private apartments. I had the spyhole blocked up. I've got a letter for you, by the way, from Glynde Rendel, written the day they left. He sent another one to an address Czartoryski gave him; I thought it best to let it go.'

'I'm sure you were right. I'd trust your instinct before I did my own.' He read the letter quickly. 'This doesn't tell me much that I didn't know already. Of course the Russians are arming along the border; they'd be mad not to.'

'Jan!'

'Yes, my darling?'

'There's so much secrecy; so much mystification. Sometimes, this last winter, I've been worried, frightened . . . Jan, it is Poland we are working for, isn't it?'

'Of course it is! Poland herself again, a free country, free to trade with the world. With ports on the Baltic and a clear way down to the Black Sea.'

'And freedom for all?'

He smiled down at her lovingly. 'You really care about your serfs, don't you? Yes, in the end, I'm sure of it, but it's not something that can be promised at this stage. We'd lose so much support from the nobles. It's hard enough keeping them together as it is.'

'Yes, I do see that. What I don't understand is why you don't trust Glynde Rendel more fully. Granted you're on the same side.'

'But are we? That's something I haven't told you, love. Everything's changed in England. The old King's declared mad at last, and his son is Prince Regent. God knows what will happen next; very likely a Whig government that will make peace with Napoleon. And then, what hope for Poland?'

'Our only hope a war that will destroy more homes, more farmland, kill and starve more thousands? It's horrible, Jan.' She shivered in his arms.

'What's worth having, is worth fighting for.' He pulled her closer. 'You're cold, my darling.' His hand played loving music on the delicate bones of her spine.

'No, Jan, I'm afraid.'

'Don't be. I'll look after you. Always. Believe that?'

'I do.' She smiled up at him, as he bent to kiss her and they plunged back together, everything else forgotten.

At Petersburg, they dedicated the huge new Cathedral of Our Lady of Kazan that mild September of 1811, on the tenth anniversary of the Tsar's accession to the throne, and everyone was there for the three-and-a-half-hour service. Jan went to watch the brief parade of troops that preceded it, and met the American Ambassador, John Quincy Adams, on his way to the new Cathedral.

'I'm glad to see you back.' Adams paused to greet him. 'Tell me, what is the news from the border?'

'Not good.But not desperate. No war this year, I think. But is it true that Napoleon made the Russian Ambassador, Prince Kurakin, another of his scenes on the occasion of his birthday?'

'So I hear. Madness. If he thinks to frighten the Tsar into submission, he much mistakes his man. Are you coming to the service?'

'No, alas, I do not qualify for admission.'

'I'm not sure whether I should absolutely condole with you,' said Adams drily. 'But duty calls . . . Come and see me, Mr. Warrington, and tell me more about how things go on at

Vilno, and at Drissa, where I believe, there are fortifications being built.'

'Yes, though I cannot for the life of me understand what purpose they are intended to serve. But, if you have a moment, tell me, Mr. Adams, is it true that the French are stopping and searching our merchant ships more drastically than ever?'

'I am afraid so. I have tried in vain to explain to Count Lauriston that there is no way we can prevent the British from using our colours as camouflage, but that I, personally, can vouch for the *bona fides* of the American ships that make the dangerous journey here to Kronstadt and Petersburg.'

'And what did Lauriston say to that?'

'Nothing to the purpose. He's a mouthpiece for Napoleon, no more. Caulaincourt was worth ten of him. And his master understands nothing about the realities of trade, how should he? I hope you have no vessels bound this way before the freeze-up. Frankly, there is no way I can guarantee their safety. And we both know how long, and what a struggle it takes to release a cargo once it has been confiscated by the French.'

'I do indeed. But, Mr. Adams, I've had no English news since I got back. Has the Prince of Wales, now he is Regent, not turned out the Tory government he hates and sent for his old friends the Whigs? And will that not mean they make peace with France, and everything is changed?'

'Ah, you've not heard.' He looked over to the imposing curved colonnade of the Cathedral, where people were still pushing their way in. 'I've a moment still. The Prince Regent has surprised everyone. Wrote a civil letter to Mr. Perceval, the First Minister, telling him he felt he owed it to his father to keep the Tories in office. His Whig friends are furious, I understand.'

'So it's business as usual?'

'Yes, the war goes on. Lord Wellington is still giving the French as good as he gets in Spain.' He looked quickly around to make sure there was no possible English speaker within earshot. 'I've even heard rumours that there are feelers out again between here and England, despite the state of war that technically exists between the two countries. So it may be all change again one of these days. But for goodness' sake keep that under your hat, Mr. Warrington.' He moved away a few steps, turned back. 'Oh, two other pieces of news that will interest you. Lord Granville Leveson Gower is married, and Lord Ringmer is dead. Isn't he father of a friend of yours?'

'Yes. His brother succeeds, and he will be next in line. Thank you for telling me.' He went back to the little house on the English Quay that he had once shared with Glynde Rendel and wrote a long letter to Miriam.

The second *Sejm*, or Parliament, in the history of the new Duchy of Warsaw was to be held that winter of 1811, and the King of Saxony came to open it with traditional pomp, and hear the swearing-in of the new members for the six departments acquired from Austria two years before. 'If I was only a man,' said the Princess, as she left Rendomierz to attend the ceremony, 'I would be among the nobles there.'

She reached Warsaw early in September, a few days before the King, and went straight to call on her friend Anna Potocka. They had a great deal to talk about. Anna had been at the Potocki estates in Russian-held Bialystok that summer, just as Isobel had been at Vinsk. 'Do you think it has done any good?' she asked. 'You saw Adam Czartoryski did you not? What hopes does he hold out of tolerance from his master the Tsar?'

'He wants us all to commit ourselves. Cousin Adam says Alexander is just waiting until he is sure of us before he announces a Kingdom of Poland.'

'I seem to have heard that one before,' said her friend. 'And anyway, how can we? My father-in-law is president of the Council of the Grand-Duchy. You've no idea how busy he is with the preparations for the *Sejm*! It's going to be the most brilliant winter we've seen in Warsaw for years. You'll stay for the great opening in December, of course?'

'Oh, I think so. And you?'

'I'm insisting. My husband wanted to pack me off to the country for the good of my health, but I told him I'd go into a decline.'

'Your health? Anna . . . you don't mean?' A quick look at her friend's elegant figure in the revealing empire-line dress.

'Yes, I do! In January. And, Isobel, I'm sure it's a boy this time. Did I tell you about the prophecy I had from the sorceress?'

'Yes, several times.'

'It's all happening, just as she said. An heir at last! You can imagine how I am looked after! But, talking of sons, how does that school of yours go on? And your little Prince? A pity he'll be grown up when mine is ready for schooling.'

'Oh, Anna, don't take it too much for granted! By the way, what is the news of Marie Walewska?'

'Still holding court in Paris. Her little boy has his nose right out of joint of course since the birth of the King of Rome, but she don't seem to mind it too much. All the young Poles gravitate to her house when they are on leave from Spain, and crowd into her box at the opera. She's been presented at court now. That I would have liked to have seen. Graceful Marie and that stiff-necked little Empress, who never can find the right thing to say, or doesn't care to try. Not that there really can have been a right thing for that occasion. They say the Emperor is a devoted father.'

'To both boys? It's odd to think that a year ago the whisper was that he would never have a child.'

'Yes. I wonder if Marie is glad she proved he could. What an odd way to change the future of the world.'

'And her own. Think of the difference to her. Someone was telling me that old husband of hers is facing bankruptcy.'

'Aren't we all! The French seem to think Poland is made of gold and grain.'

'And men,' said Isobel. 'If I lose many more serfs, either here in town or at Rendomierz, I really don't know how I shall contrive to go on. But tell me about the new French Minister here, Monsieur Bignon. What is he like?'

'My dear, a social disaster! No manner at all. A dyer's son I believe, one of Napoleon's jumped-up nobodies. He comes at you like a cavalry charge, and then can think of nothing to say, but "What are you doing in that little corner?" As if one was some poor little social outcast. At least he's not saddled with a frump of a wife, like some of them, but his being unmarried makes his entertaining an odd enough business.'

'He does entertain, though?'

'Oh, yes, everyone! Be sure you get invited. And let me warn you, my father-in-law and I both think there is more to him than meets the eye. The Council are delighted with him, I believe. He really understands business, they say. And is formidably well informed. If I were you I'd make a point of telling him you keep two enemy aliens in your household. He's bound to know!'

Isobel met the French Resident at the theatre a few days later, and was grateful for Anna's warning. Brought to her box by Josef Poniatowski, the Minister of War, he seemed indeed the insignificant little man Anna had described, with no conversation, nothing to say about the play they were watching. But his eyes were formidably intelligent as he asked if he might do himself the honour of calling on her next day. 'For a quiet word, Highness? You have been travelling, I understand. I long to hear about it.'

She received him alone, and actually found herself wishing she had not left Jenny behind in Rendomierz. Absurd. An Englishwoman; an enemy. She sometimes found herself wondering, these days, if it might not be the part of wisdom to get rid of Jenny. But how? And could she manage without her?

They talked for a few minutes about the play, the stifling weather and the bad summer that had meant one of the worst harvests ever. 'You have found it so on both your estates?' he asked. 'You are not long back, I understand, from the Ovinski estates near Vilno.'

'Some months,' she hedged. 'And not my estates, my son's. I feel it my duty to make sure they are kept in good shape for him.'

'I did hear a rumour that the little Prince had come out as quite a fiery young Russian-hater. Some incident on your journey to Vilno?'

'You heard about that?'

'Highness, you would be wise to believe that I hear everything. If you will also believe that anything you tell me will be treated with the strictest confidence, I hope we will go on very well, you and I. You have two enemy aliens in your household, I understand.'

'My tutor and my companion are both British, it's true. I hardly look on them as enemies. Miss Peverel has been with me for almost ten years. And Mr. Rendel . . .' She paused.

'Was recommended to you by Talleyrand himself.' He

laughed the grating little laugh. 'Does that induce you to trust me, Highness?'

'That you know? That he told you? Yes, I suppose so. So, where does that leave me, Monsieur Bignon?'

'It leaves you what you have always been, a most beautiful lady, a great Princess.' His compliments were even more awkward than his laugh, and she was beginning to let herself comfortably despise him, when he concluded 'And one with sufficient hostages to fortune, so that she had better be most scrupulously careful in her behaviour.'

'Is that a threat?' She made it light, but she was frightened, just the same.

'No, Highness, a friendly warning. You have estates – you and your son – too close to the border for comfort. If trouble should come, you will have need of all your friends.'

Glynde and his aunt had agreed to number their letters to each other, so when he received one from her at last, towards Christmas of 1811, he knew how many had failed to reach him. This one had taken nearly six months and had been so much handled on the way that it took him hours to decipher. But her first bit of news leapt from the page at him. She was writing to break the news of his father's death – and his brother's remarriage. She had had only one letter from him, she said: his fourth. 'I am so very glad you are finding the running of your school such an absorbing experience.' She said nothing whatever about the Princess, but ended by sending very kind regards to Miss Peverel.

'What other news?' asked Jenny, after condoling with him on his father's death.

'We agreed to be very careful. But she speaks of her neighbour in the big house down the road – the Prince of Wales of course – and his Regency. He's taken over running the family business, she says, but decided to keep on the old staff. And then there's something I still haven't quite made out. Here, where she's crossed it. Something about an old friend? Your eyes are better than mine; see if you can read it.'

'I'll try.' As she took the letter, their fingers brushed, and she was silent for an instant, fighting the turmoil his touch always roused in her. She moved a little away from him, towards the light, grateful that he never noticed. 'I don't wonder you found it difficult. Lord knows how many hands this letter has been through. Let's see . . . Something about her neighbour – the Prince Regent again, I suppose – hoping to make up an old quarrel. What on earth is this? A performing bear? A quarrel about a bear?'

'Or with a bear? Russia, of course. If the Tsar really means to fight Napoleon, peace with England would be a very logical first step. I suppose we British are to be paymasters again. Bless your sharp eyes.' He took the letter back from her, not noticing how her hand avoided his. 'Do you realise, Jenny, that would mean we no longer had enemies all round us?'

'It would certainly make a change for the better.' Drily. 'But, surely, you will have to go home now?'

'I think not. My aunt does not suggest it. The period of mourning would be almost over by the time I managed to get there, and the rejoicings for my brother's marriage, too. I suppose I might arrive in time to stand godfather to the heir, but, frankly, I'd rather stay here, where I'm needed. Besides, I couldn't afford the statutory silver porringer and case of port.' He laughed. 'And that's a deuced ungrateful thing to say to you, who saw to it that I'm a landed gentleman here. But when even the Princess grumbles about her finances, who am I not to emulate her? Having an estate has brought home to me just how savagely the French are bleeding this country.'

'Well, yes,' she said. 'But don't forget you're bleeding yourself, too. I ought not to take the income you give me.'

'Your tiny salary? Try to stop!'

'That's all very well, but I want you to halve it, please.'

'Halve it? Why?'

'Marylka told me the other day. That you have arranged to pay Marta's endowment to her convent for her. It's wonderfully good of you. I'm so glad . . . But I want to share it.'

'I'll wring Marylka's neck!'

'Please don't. It wasn't her fault. You know she's the soul of discretion. It was just bad luck. Mind you,' she smiled rather mischievously, 'I'd have known something was up sooner or later, by the different way the servants treat you. They used not to like you overmuch, did you know? They do now.'

'I suppose they thought I was a puffed-up nobody, giving himself airs.' He caught her eye. 'And so I was!'

The *Sejm* was finally opened by the King of Saxony on December 8th, and the moment the ceremonies were over, the infighting began. 'My father-in-law says it's just like the good old days,' Anna Potocka told the Princess. 'He's just waiting for someone to flourish his sabre! All the old quarrels; all the old factions! They can't even agree a budget, still less this new code of law.'

'It's unbelievable,' said the Princess. 'Here we are, surrounded by enemies, with the threat of war growing from day to day, and all the *Sejm* can do is grumble about past abuses and niggle about money for the army. I sometimes wish I'd been born a man!'

'To join in the politicking? Don't be absurd.'

'No. To make my own way in the world. Live as I please.' She sighed. 'I believe I'll go home to Rendomierz for Christmas.'

'A very good plan. There's nothing like Christmas at one's own fireside. Besides . . .' Anna paused. 'May I speak to you like an old friend?'

'Of course.' But Isobel's lips tightened.

'You must have felt it, as I do. Things are changing here in Warsaw. The King may be tolerant, as you say, but the Queen's not. We're all to be purer than snow from now on. Seen to be!' She paused, twisting the rings on her left hand. 'You've not quite understood, I think, my dear, what a difference the loss of a husband makes. Even to a Princess.'

'What are you trying to say?'

'I wish you'd remarry, Isobel. That's the way to live as you please. And stop the dull Queen's mouth. It's a pity your Cousin Josef is so heart-and-soul devoted to Henriette de Vauban.'

'And her husband,' said Isobel bitterly. 'They all live together, merry as grigs, in that palace of Josef's.' She picked up her gloves. 'So, who do you suggest, since you are being so helpful?'

'No need to fly out at me. I'm not the Queen! But, seriously, love, I had thought . . . Now he's to be a British Lord . . . That charming young Englishman, Mr. Rendel? Such a romantic story. Risked his life to come to you; adores you, by all I hear; he'd make the very pattern of an obliging husband.'

'Like yours?' But Isobel kept the thought to herself, and went home, furiously thinking, deciding nothing.

30

'I'm thinking of going to Paris.' The Princess summoned Glynde to her side after dinner one wild March day, when it seemed that winter would never end. He did not want it to. There had been a change in the Princess since she came home for Christmas, a new gentleness, a tendency to consult him almost as an equal. Sometimes, mad hope had surged up in him, and sometimes he had seen Jenny looking at him thoughtfully.

'To Paris? Is that wise?' He took her arm to guide her to the far side of the piano, where Monsieur Poiret was performing a noisy Beethoven sonata.

'You think Petersburg would be wiser? You know as well as I do that no one tells us anything here. I went to see Monsieur Bignon when I was in Warsaw for the carnival, actually managed to get him alone for a minute, asked his advice. Wasting my breath! He wouldn't even admit there's a chance of war. So how could I ask him where would be safest for Casimir? For all the little boys? It's a terrible responsibility I have, Mr. Rendel.'

'But will you get better advice in Paris? And may your going there not be misconstrued at Petersburg?'

'A woman going to study the fashions? To see her old friend Marie Walewska?'

'Whose house is full of young Poles on leave from the French army in Spain. That won't do you much good at Petersburg.'

'What will? The Tsar's said nothing! Neither to us here in the Duchy, nor up in Lithuania. Vague talk about a kingdom, about reviving the Constitution of 1791. Never anything definite. Do you know what I told Adam Czartoryski last summer?'

'No.'

'I reminded him of that time – Lord, how long ago – when the Tsar came here. Do you remember? And how we hung on his words? He promised an announcement, over dinner, the day before he left. And then a messenger came from his beloved Queen Louise, and off he went. No announcement. Nothing. Well, this time he's not even promised one. So – I am going to Paris, to the lion's mouth, to see what Napoleon has to say. He visits Marie Walewska, of course, to see the child. I shall speak to him of my son. He's a father now. He'll surely understand.'

'I hope so. You will go and see Monsieur Talleyrand too?'

'He'll come and see me.'

'Her mind was made up,' Glynde told Jenny next day. 'No use trying to dissuade her. And, truly, I believe it might be for the best.'

'The best for her, at any rate. I'm so confused! What ought we to be wishing, you and I?'

'Not victory for Napoleon, that's one thing certain. The question is, can he stop now, or will he have to be stopped? If only there was any news! But the Princess seems to have learned nothing in Warsaw.'

'No. It's frightening how totally a whole people can be kept in the dark. If Bignon won't say anything even to the Princess . . . I wish you'd hear from Jan Warrington.'

'So do I. But with preparations at such a height on each side of the border, it's hard for messengers to get through, even the Brotherhood's. What does Marylka say?'

'She's frightened. She thinks there has been trouble among Them again.'

'I suppose that stands to reason. If the Princess can't make up her mind what line to take, how should They?'

'They are surely better informed.'

'If They can trust their informers. Every third person is probably a spy these days. Or a double spy. I do hope you are immensely careful what you say.'

'I say nothing to anyone but you. Well, there's nothing to say, is there? We're here; we're helpless; we've Casimir to think about. I believe I do hope the Princess gets to Paris and gets some clear guidance at last, one way or another.'

'Either from Napoleon, or from Talleyrand, you mean?'

'I suppose that's just what I mean.'

* * *

'Paris?' Anna Potocka was dandling her son, who had been born in January. 'You won't need to go that far. Bignon tells me the Emperor sets out for Dresden any day now. All the crowned heads of Germany are to meet him there.'

'Which means war?'

'So we all hope! The war that will make this Duchy a kingdom! You've no idea what a winter of hope this has been, Isobel. The Duchy is an armed camp now. Have you seen the uniforms in the streets?'

'And heard some stories from the serfs about the way some of our "allies" behave. As if we were an occupied country, not a friendly one. Didn't I hear something about a Westphalian officer using your mother-in-law's carriage for his butcher's order? Returning it reeking with blood?'

'A misunderstanding,' Anna shrugged. 'Monsieur Bignon soon dealt with that for us. Of course, there are problems, with food and forage so short after last year's terrible harvest. We landowners are going to get a magnificent price for our grain, when we do decide it's time to open our barns. You're going to need it, aren't you, my dear, after the way the taxes turn out to hit the new estates of 1809 like yours. But it's in a good cause. Our army is magnificent! Young men find their way across the frontier every day, by tricks, by bribes, to join in the great fight against Russia.'

'We've not seen many of them down in our part of the world.'

'I did hear that Volhynia is proving less active than Lithuania. It will all change when our Polish army crosses the border. Then they'll come out in their thousands, the Polish Cossacks we need. How can they before? Those who are at all suspect are already being forcibly moved east. Wolodkowicz, the hero of Kosciusko's war, has been taken to Smolensk. Lucky for you that your son is so young, or you would be subject to the Tsar's threats, too. Anyone with a son or brother in our army is liable to have his Russian estates confiscated. Did you hear about Dominic Radziwill?'

'No?'

'He couldn't stand the pressure, left his Vilno estate, came here to Warsaw, offered to raise a squad of 200 cavalrymen. He's a Colonel in our army now, but his Russian estate's been confiscated.' She looked at the ormolu clock on the chimney-piece. 'It's almost time for my working party. Will you join us in our work, my dear?'

'What work?'

'Making bandages, of course. Bignon says it's the most touching thing he ever saw, all of us aristocratic ladies at work for our country's good. Have you seen him yet? Or is he too busy with his beautiful Laure?'

'Laure?'

'You've not heard? Her husband's Poniatowski's aide-de-camp. She and Bignon have been having the most outrageous affair ... The rumour is she's going to get one of these new-fangled divorces, like Marie Walewska.'

'Marie's really divorcing the Count?'

'So they say. Well, poor old man, he's nearly bankrupt, and Marie's a rich woman now, in her son's name. Napoleon has given little Alexander all kinds of lands and titles. I suppose his mother doesn't want the old Count to get his hands on any of it. Or his creditors.'

'Not very pretty.'

'Very practical. I believe she's coming to her own estate at Kiernozie any day now. She could hardly go with Napoleon to Dresden, granted he'll have his wife with him, but she'll be about just the same. And don't say you don't find that very pretty, Isobel.' She smiled down at her son and tickled his chin. 'Isn't he a beauty? There's a lot to be said for marriage. All very well for Marie Walewska; she's powerfully protected; she can afford her divorce.' She bent to kiss the baby. 'You didn't bring your family with you? I quite long to meet the future Lord Ringmer.'

'His brother has remarried,' said Isobel. 'I learned quite by chance, the other day.' She rose. 'I'm afraid you will just have to do your best to defend me against wagging tongues. I have never had any intention of remarrying. My son is my entire life.' She smiled down at the little Potocki. 'Prince Casimir has immense prospects, remember.'

Back at home, she was still seething from this conversation when Monsieur Bignon was announced. 'My dear lady,' he took her hand with the remembered lack of grace, 'you should have summoned me when you reached town, instead of staying here in your little corner and leaving me to learn of your presence from others. You are going to Dresden, I believe.'

'Yes.'

'A long journey for a beautiful lady who just needs the advice of a friend.' She discovered with surprise that he still had her hand. 'Let me be your friend? Let me advise you, Princess?' He raised it to his lips.

'I should be most grateful.' She pretended not to be aware what was happening. 'I need to know what to do for the best for my son. Is he safe at Rendomierz?'

'Are any of us safe, anywhere?' He pushed back the loose sleeve of her dress, his lips moist as they moved up her arm. 'You ask me to read the omens for you, Highness? There have been plenty: comets and portents, signs in the heavens. Fools believe in them. I believe in the star of Napoleon. Stay at Rendomierz, you and the Prince your son. Be happy, be safe, be my friend?' His hand was pushing its way now through the light fabric of her dress towards her breast. 'I will watch over you and yours, I promise you, gracious Princess.'

'For a price?' She had never missed Jenny so much. 'Excellency,' she pulled away, deepest irony in the use of his title. 'Your price is too high. As one of the merchant class, you will understand that.' She tugged at the bell-rope. 'I will wish you a very good day.'

After he had gone, she was angry with herself, with him, with Anna, with everyone. She had made no secret of her passionate affair with Murat; had not needed to. Now, just because that old man, her husband had died, she was the victim of malicious tongues, a prey to vulgar creatures like Bignon. Who had not even really wanted her. Intolerable. Disgusting. She still felt those clammy, clumsy lips on her upper arm. He had promised her safety, at a price. She actually wished now she had refused more gently. Would she have acted differently if Anna Potocka had not told her about Laure? And what were his promises worth anyway?

She was glad to be distracted by a servant who announced Monsieur Genet. 'The very man.' She greeted him with an enthusiasm that surprised him. 'You come from Dresden? I

330

am just packing up to go there. Tell me I am wise to do so.'

'No, I'm from Paris, with a message for you from Talleyrand. He's been spared the round of speechifying that's due to break out at Dresden; sent me ahead to prepare the way for him here.'

'Here?'

'Yes. This is absolutely for your ears only. We are private here?'

'Entirely.'

'My master expects it to be official any day: he is to take over from Monsieur Bignon.'

'Talleyrand Minister here? But that must mean war.' She paused, frightened at her own conclusion. Napoleon would only have plucked his most able Minister out of disgrace for a very good reason. Because he meant to go to war and needed a firm hand in Poland, which would inevitably be headquarters, supply base, everything.

'It looks like it,' said Genet gravely. 'I have received my master's permission to rejoin my regiment, which is already at Poznan. There are great events in the making, Highness, and I could not bear to sit them out as an idle administrator here.'

'Hardly idle,' she said drily. 'Administrators, able ones, are just what the Duchy needs.'

'Which is doubtless why my master is coming here. Making order out of chaos has always been his genius. The Polish battalions are on their way back from Spain; you are going to see stirring times here, Princess. No need to go to Dresden.'

'You don't advise it?'

'I hardly see the purpose of it. Madame Walewska is packing up, ready to come home, did you know?'

'I heard something about a divorce.'

'You are well informed. The Emperor plans to leave the Empress behind in Dresden, to see her family. He is sure to come on here to Warsaw, granted the inducements, both romantic and practical. Why not wait here, Princess? Prepare to entertain him on your own ground. And your old friends in his train. Oh – there's something else my master bade me tell you. He has had recent information from England. That

331

delightful man, your tutor, is likely to find himself Lord Ringmer any day now. His brother's a very sick man, and his new wife has left him. A remarkable change in Mr. Rendel's fortunes. A tidy estate, and a title that goes back to the Norman Conquest. Older than yours, Princess?' He changed the subject. 'How is the little Prince? And Miss Peverel?'

'Well, both of them. Should I move my household here, Monsieur Genet? Did your master say anything about that? Rendomierz is dangerously exposed if it should really come to war.'

'Not the kind of war Napoleon makes. He is surely planning one of his sudden attacks. Straight into the heart of Russia, taking everyone by surprise, maybe – if fate is kind to him as usual – capturing the Tsar himself, as he so narrowly missed doing at Austerlitz. Then, imagine the scene of reconciliation, the brotherly peace negotiated, as at Tilsit, and perhaps our armies free for the conquest of the Indies.'

'Is that really how he is thinking?'

'He is sure to be thinking grandly, as always. And all the strategic planning, as well as all logic suggests that the attack will be well north of here, across the Niemen, spearheading straight towards Petersburg or Moscow, so your family should be safe enough in the south. Better there than here in Warsaw, which is bound to be the centre of affairs and appallingly overcrowded as a result. You know what it is like here in summer at the best of times: no place for a child. And by next winter, who knows, perhaps it will be all over and you will be crowning a new King.'

'Napoleon himself?'

'I'd not think so. One of his brothers perhaps?'

'And my son?'

'You know he's too young, Highness. He is the future, and who can predict that? But keep him safe.'

'At Rendomierz, then, not Vinsk?'

'Dear God, yes. I'm afraid Vinsk really may be in the front line. I think you would be wise to send a message to your people there, couched in the most general terms, warning them to be ready to evacuate if need be. You know how the French army marches, living off the land it conquers. I'd not want my worst enemy to be in the way when Napoleon unleashes it upon Russia.'

'But, surely, Russian-held Lithuania? He'll treat that as Polish, as friendly?'

'Hungry French soldiers don't make such distinctions. It's why things have gone badly for us in Spain. The British really seem to try to supply their armies – or to pay for what they take. Will you tell Mr. Rendel about his improved prospects?'

'I think not. After all, there is no way, at the moment, that he could get home to England, and I need him here.'

'Yes. My master said I was to consult you about this. Mind you,' he was preparing to take his leave, 'if it really does come to blows between us and the Russians, they may patch together a peace with the British. But I'm sure you're wise not to distract Mr. Rendel with information that's no use to him. And, in the end, maybe he will find himself both Lord Ringmer and confidential adviser to the future King of Poland.'

'Who knows?' She held out her hand for his kiss, forgiving him everything else he had said that she had not liked.

All up and down the long, indeterminate border between Russian and French Poland the tension mounted, with more and more troops massing while vital installations were moved back, away from immediate danger on the frontier itself. Jan Warrington, arriving at Vinsk from Vilno late in April was surprised and relieved to find that an armed Russian camp had sprung up across the tributary of the Niemen on which the palace stood.

'I'm happy to see you so well protected,' he told Miriam. 'They've given you no trouble, I hope.'

'Nothing to signify. The commanding officer sent a very civil message when he arrived. A promise of protection for the Princess Ovinska and all her possessions. In fact, the Brotherhood had warned me of their coming, and told me I had nothing to fear. Jan, which side are the Brotherhood on?' They were in each other's arms, safe in the privacy of her room, but even so she spoke in a low voice, straight into his ear.

'Poland's. I hope.'

'You've said that before.' She thought his voice had lacked conviction. 'Are you sure, Jan?'

'Almost.' He owed her the truth. 'The trouble is, can they be sure? Can anyone? It's hard to believe what's happening. The two masters of the world, talking peace, preparing for war, and all for – what? No reason given. There's more cause for us Americans to fight the British than for Russia to fight the French. But – I've not told you –' a swift kiss explained the omission '– the Tsar is at Vilno.'

'What?'

'Yes. He got there a few days ago – a routine review of his troops, he calls it. I managed to get myself into his train, as an observer for Mr. Adams, who stays behind in Petersburg, as does the French Ambassador, much against his will. Maybe just as well for his peace of mind. He'd be surprised how the Tsar is contriving to charm his Polish Lithuanian nobles into loving submission.'

'He's succeeding?'

'He most certainly is. All he needs now is to proclaim himself King of all Poland, and they are his, body and soul.'

'And then?'

'That's the great question. If one could only trust him! But you know how he changes, vacillates . . . It will be all loving enlightenment, I think, so long as the emergency lasts, and then the Russian machine will roll over the new kingdom, and it will find itself just another province, subject to the full bureaucratic tyranny of Holy Russia.' He kissed her thoughtfully. 'What do you hear from the Princess?'

'Nothing for a long time. The border's a desperate gamble these days; the Brotherhood warned me not to try to use the secret way. But the mere fact that she remains in the Duchy, despite all the Tsar's threats, surely means that she still feels the little Prince's best hope, and Poland's, is with the French.'

'And so do I. I won't pretend I'm the passionate enthusiast for Napoleon I once was, but he does give his own form of democratic government to the countries he dominates – and French law. Imagine the Tsar allowing his Polish subjects their *Sejm*?'

'I can't,' she agreed. 'Jan, I'm ashamed, but I'm afraid.

The last message I got from the Princess warned me to have everything ready for flight.'

'I'm glad she took so much thought for you. But you should be safe here, with the Russians encamped across the river, and the Tsar at Vilno. I'm more anxious for the Princess, and the little Prince at Rendomierz. General Tormassov is assembling a Russian army down south, beyond the Pripet Marshes. It's bound to attack the Duchy if war does break out.'

'And Rendomierz would be in its line of march? I must get a message to the Princess; warn her.'

'I think you should. And the Brotherhood's messenger can take a letter for Talleyrand for me.'

'Talleyrand?'

'I saw the French Ambassador in St. Petersburg before I left. He's heard that Talleyrand is back in favour and bound for Warsaw.'

'Isn't that very strange?' she asked.

'After all his hopes for peace? Yes, very strange indeed, but a brilliant move on Napoleon's part. Talleyrand will unite the Poles of the Duchy as no one else could.'

'Maybe even persuade Napoleon to name a kingdom and a King for Poland before the Tsar does. If he wants the kind of universal support he'll need, a mass uprising of Poles on both sides of the border and a Polish Cossack screen for his army, I think he had better. Proclaim a kingdom and the trickle of men across the frontier would become a flood. You'll tell Talleyrand that, when you write? I'm sure it's important.'

'Such a charming strategist.' He nibbled her ear lovingly. 'I'll most certainly remember to mention your views to Talleyrand.'

But the Brotherhood's messenger never reached Rendomierz.

Lingering on in Warsaw as filthy snow began to melt, the Princess was relieved to find that her rejection of Bignon's advances had made no difference in his behaviour to her. She thought a great deal about the curious message Genet had brought her from Talleyrand, and, while she thought about it, delayed her return to Rendomierz. Time enough when she got there to decide whether to act on his hint, and Anna's, and

335

marry Glynde Rendel before he became Lord Ringmer. It was an idea to make the blood race. Her first man, and she had never forgotten him. Memories long repressed welled up in her. That first night, when he had understood what she wanted of him. He had picked her up, stronger than he looked, carried her to her room. And then . . . Her colour rose. Her own hand thoughtfully touched her breast. It had been one of the hardest things she ever did, closing her door to him when the moment came. Casimir's father? And he adored her, would be her devoted slave. And, if the very worst should happen, a haven in England. Baroness Ringmer?

In the meantime, life in Warsaw was brilliantly interesting. Society was at fever pitch, expecting war, victory, and a free Poland. Isobel even found she enjoyed the working parties, where noble ladies made bandages, scraped lint and exchanged gossip. All of them seemed to have husbands, sons or brothers in the swiftly expanding Polish army, and she was disconcerted to find herself tacitly relegated to an older generation. She had long since stopped wearing mourning for her husband. Why should she be treated as a widow, on the shelf? Could she actually be regretting that she had snubbed Bignon? Her thoughts, when she returned from the cheerful working parties, turned more and more to Rendomierz, and Glynde Rendel, the future Lord Ringmer, though he did not know it. But he might learn, any day. She gave her orders, at last, for the journey home, and the horses were ordered, the packing almost complete, when Bignon called on her.

'I've come to say goodbye, cruel lady.' She rather thought he was teasing her.

'Goodbye? You had heard then, that I am leaving for Rendomierz?'

'Why, no. It is I who will soon be leaving. My replacement is on his way.'

'Monsieur Talleyrand?' It was out before she could stop herself.

'You knew? That's interesting. No, not Talleyrand, though I too had looked forward to his coming. The Emperor has changed his mind. Talleyrand is still in Paris, Monsieur de Pradt comes here as Minister in my stead.'

'Who?'

He laughed his dry laugh. 'You may well ask. He's Bishop of Malines, for what that is worth. The Emperor has perhaps taken into consideration the importance of the Church here in Poland. It's the only explanation I can think of for the change of plan. It's a disappointment, I confess. But, you, Highness, you are really leaving us?'

'I cannot bear to be separated from my son any longer.'

'Most understandable. Most creditable. You have not thought of bringing him here to Warsaw?'

'Would you advise it?'

'An armed camp, as the city is becoming? Even here in your beautiful house one is aware of the crowd outside. I do not believe I would venture to advise you one way or the other. It would be an interesting experience for the boy to see the soldiers of so many nations, but maybe overexciting, for him and his schoolfellows.'

'You don't imagine we will be at risk at Rendomierz?'

'At risk? My dear lady, what an absurd idea.'

31

The spring was late in 1812, with green hardly showing until May, and when the Princess finally returned to Rendomierz early in June it was to waterlogged fields and blossom blasted on the fruit trees.

'It's good to be home.' She smiled at Glynde Rendel who had come forward to greet her with the steward, Leon Wysocki, as she alighted from her carriage.

'It's good to see you here, Highness.' He took her hand to help her alight, aware of a change in her. 'More beautiful than ever, if I may say so.'

She laughed, pleased. 'New clothes, Mr. Rendel, straight from Paris.' She had worked hard for the compliment, now put her hand on his arm in a gesture that was a little more than friendly. 'But where is my son? Where is Casimir?'

'He has his own greeting for you. I thought you might prefer it indoors. The air is cold still; you should not be lingering out here after your journey.'

'Always so considerate.' She smiled up at him as she had not for years. 'Then by all means let us go in and see what Casimir has prepared for me.' She had taken off her gloves and her hand was warm on his. 'And here is my good Jenny.' She greeted her more as a servant than as a friend, and he was surprised how it irked him.

The boys, drawn up just inside the door, burst into song at sight of the Princess. 'Dombrowski's March!' She smiled when she recognised the tune, listened with obvious patience as they sang the vigorous stanzas that had resounded in Italy, in Egypt, in Spain, wherever the Polish army had done Napoleon's heaviest work for him. 'And Poland always shall be free,' she sang the last lines with them, and got a resounding cheer. 'But you've changed the words?' Bending to kiss Casimir.

'I wrote them myself.' Proudly.

'Playing at poet?' A hint of disdain in her tone as she turned to Glynde. 'I trust he has not been neglecting his military studies?' And again the intimate smile. 'I am sure I can count on you to have kept the balance even. You'll dine with me, of course. Jenny can see to the boys. Take them away now, Jenny, their chatter is giving me the headache and I'm sure they ought to be drilling or something.' She bent once more, smiling, to Casimir. 'Wait till you see what I've brought you from Warsaw.' And then, relenting under his eager gaze: 'Real uniforms for you and your troop! I hope they are going to be big enough! Now, off you go with Miss Peverel and leave me in peace.' She turned away to greet the rest of her little court, grouped at the foot of the great staircase, then declared herself exhausted and announced that she would see them all at dinner. 'Till then, Mr. Rendel,' she paused on the stair. 'Oh, I quite forgot to tell Jenny. I've messages for her from an old friend of hers, Paul Genet.'

'He was in Warsaw?'

'On his way to the front. Monsieur Talleyrand has given him leave to rejoin his regiment. I hope Jenny will be impressed by his gallantry.' She laughed. 'It was a great disappointment. We quite thought Talleyrand was coming as Minister to Warsaw, and then the Emperor changed his mind at the last minute and sent a nobody called de Pradt. Thinks he's a squire of dames; a flow of talk that would drown you. And treats Marie Walewska as if she were royalty. I will say for her, she was so embarrassed she withdrew to the country. But it's not made him any friends among the ladies. Bignon, whom he replaced, seems brilliant in comparison. I wish Talleyrand had come.'

'Did Genet bring messages from him?'

'Nothing to signify, why should he? Talleyrand too thought he was to come himself. It's been one disappointment after another. We were sure the Emperor would come to Warsaw, use it as his headquarters, tell us his plans for Poland. Genet told me to expect him. You can imagine the preparations that we made.'

'And what happened?'

'He sent Count Narbonne to the Tsar at Vilno with the most peaceful proposals, and got a stony answer back. And set off at once, but for Dantzig, not Warsaw. Such a disappointment for Marie Walewska!'

'For all Poles,' said Glynde. 'If he had intended the kind of promise you hoped for, Napoleon would have gone to Warsaw to make it in person. He's hedging his bets. I wonder if that is wise.'

'It's certainly caused some heartbreak. The second time we've prepared to give him a great welcome and been disappointed. Has there been any news from Vinsk?'

'Not for a long time. The border is almost impassable these days.'

'Except for mad young Lithuanian Poles, who risk all to join our army. I need your advice, by the way. I have to name a delegate to the *Sejm* that is to be held this month. That's what I came home for. Someone I can rely on. Leon Wysocki, do you think?'

'He'll certainly do what you tell him.'

'Which is what counts. Oh me, it's all a heavy responsibility, and I am tired. I'll see you at dinner.' She climbed slowly, gracefully up the great staircase, aware of admiring eyes on her elegant back.

But Glynde had turned instantly away to hurry after Jenny and the boys. He found Jenny alone, taking a short cut across the pleasure gardens. 'They're at their drill?'

'Yes.' Smiling. 'The Master of Arms was not at all pleased that he had not been summoned to greet the Princess. I'm afraid he is going to take it out on the poor little things.'

'Casimir won't stand for unreasonable bullying.'

'No. I think he frightens Herr von Stenck sometimes.'

'I'm delighted to hear it! I've got a message for you.'

'For me?'

'The Princess remembered it a bit late. From Paul Genet. He called on her in Warsaw, and asked to be remembered to you.'

'Such a serious message! But what was Paul Genet doing in Warsaw?'

'Announcing Talleyrand's coming as Minister.'

'Talleyrand? That's good!'

'It would have been. He's not come after all. The Princess says Bignon's been replaced by a nonentity. And, something else, something that worries me. They all expected Napoleon in Warsaw, to make his headquarters there.'

'Yes, of course.'

'He's gone to Dantzig instead. Do you think that even now, at this eleventh hour, we could persuade the Princess to take Casimir across the border, get him to Vilno to swear homage to the Tsar?'

'You're not serious?'

'Never more so. You must see what this means. Napoleon's avoided Warsaw because he intends to let the Poles bleed their lives away for him, promising them nothing. He's done it before, and they've stuck to him, but I think this may be once too often. I've talked a good deal to Herr von Stenck this winter. He's a martinet, but he's no fool. Strategically, I think he's sound. And he says that if Napoleon really means to invade Russia he's going to need two things: the common people on his side, all through what was once Poland, and a screen of Polish Cossacks, who know the country. And he won't get either of those without declaring himself.'

'A Kingdom of Poland, you mean? Something for them to fight for?'

'Exactly. And meanwhile the Tsar is at Vilno. I wish we'd have news from there!'

'So do I!' She smiled at him. 'If you're going to be in time for dinner, you ought to be changing your dress.'

'Devil take it, so I should!' And then, 'Forgive me. I do treat you like an old friend, do I not?'

'Well, we are.'

The Princess drove her new French maid distracted, changing her mind several times before she finally settled on a low-cut white dress. 'How do I look, Denise?'

'Madame is exquisite as always.' Privately the girl thought the *ingénue* effect a mistake. 'Some jewels, perhaps?'

'My new pearls.' She had bought the pearl choker when she sold off the hoarded grain from her barns.

Joining her little court in the salon, she knew a moment's doubt, not of herself but of Glynde. He had always looked his best in evening-dress, but now, contrasted with the elegant young blades of Warsaw, he seemed just faintly shabby, a hint

341

of rust about the black breeches, the suggestion of a crease to the well-tailored coat. She must get him some new clothes before she burst the story of their long romance on Warsaw society. No. That would not do. Not their long romance. Nothing must cast the slightest doubt on Casimir's paternity. She smiled and held out her hand.

'Welcome again!' He could not kiss hands as the young Poles did. 'You look a queen tonight, Highness.'

'Always so gallant! You are admiring my pearls? More suitable for a widowed lady than emeralds or diamonds, do you not think?'

'They must have cost a fortune.'

'Oh, no! I got them for nothing from poor Princess – I'd best not mention her name. But her son is in our army, her Russian estates have been confiscated. It was doing her a real kindness, she said, to buy them from her.'

'These are sad times, Highness. Will you indulge me with a few moments private talk after dinner?'

'As many as you like. I need to talk to you, too.' Could her new approach be working already? Had it taken so little to bring him back to her feet?

But when the long meal and all its toasts were over, and they were alone, he went straight to business. 'Highness, I've been thinking about the news you brought. I don't at all like the sound of it. Do you think that even now you should perhaps move your family to Vinsk?'

'Are you mad? Right into the path of Napoleon's army! I've already warned Miriam to be ready for anything. But she will be safe enough. My presence and Casimir's in the Duchy guarantees her safety from the French, and the palace's.'

'But what about yours? And Casimir's? The Russians are arming all along the border. Remember the troop we met, going to Vinsk last year? Suppose they send a southern army, below the Pripet Marshes? Herr von Stenck thinks it likely. The Tsar has good German advisers, he says.'

'But you know the Tsar. He won't listen to them. The very fact that Napoleon has gone north to Dantzig will concentrate his mind up there. Anyway, this is all idle talk. How can you imagine me so base, Mr. Rendel, as to consider turning my coat now, when the die is as good as cast.' She smiled. 'It is your anxiety for me that speaks, and I thank you for it.'

'Anxiety for Casimir too. I don't like to think what would happen if the Russians really did come here to Rendomierz. You know how he feels about them still.'

'And yet you suggest I take him there?'

'Yes. To learn they are just people, like the rest of us. If not to Vinsk, then to Petersburg, Princess, to the Ovinski Palace there. Safe in the heart of Russia.'

'Nothing of the kind! You know how Napoleon moves! We'd find ourselves engulfed in the tide of the triumphant French army. Having proved ourselves traitors to their cause: the cause of Polish freedom. Have you gone a little off your head, dear Mr. Rendel? Or are you beginning to think of ways of getting home to England?'

'Why in the world should I do that? Thanks to your goodness, Highness, I am a man of means here. There I'd be a pauper. Besides, here I have an occupation I enjoy; there I'd be an idle young man about town all over again. Highness!' He crossed the little room to where she stood, half turned away to look out of the window at drizzling rain. 'You aren't trying to suggest that you wish to dispense with my services?'

'Good God no! Never that!' She turned to him, suddenly an eager girl, both hands outstretched. 'How could you possibly imagine such a thing!'

'I'm relieved! And you will forgive me for taking the liberty of an old,' he paused, 'friend, and giving you bad advice out of a full heart?'

'Of course. Specially now you admit it is bad advice. But I'd forgive you anything, Mr. Rendel, you must know that. As the old friend that you are. Anything.' He had not meant to take her hands, found himself holding them as she smiled up at him.

'I thank you from my heart.' Bending to kiss the smooth little hands that lay so snug in his, he had a sudden vision of Jenny's strong brown fingers. 'Then forgive me now, Highness, if I take my leave. I promised Casimir I'd see their new uniforms tonight.'

'Deserting me for my son?' Playfully.

'For my duties.' He smiled, bowed and left her.

*   *   *

343

'You'll go to the ball at Zakret?' Miriam asked Jan, who was still dividing his time between Vilno and Vinsk.

'I must. If only I could take you with me! There will be no one to touch you there.'

'Not even the little Countess Tysenhaus the Tsar has taken such a fancy to? You're a shameless flatterer, Jan.'

'I love you.' Kissing her fingers. 'The Tsar can have his little girls. When are you going to marry me, Miriam?'

'If you still want me to; the day we sail for America. You know that such a marriage would be a disaster for you here. I have to take your word for it that it would not be there.'

'Will not be there.' But in his heart he knew she was right. As an unattached young American, he had the entrée everywhere in Russia. Married to Miriam, Jewish housekeeper to a Polish aristocrat, he would be an outcast. 'I wish we could marry today and start home tomorrow!'

'But we can't.' She did not make it a question.

'If there was only any news! Nothing from across the border since Narbonne left for Dresden. To see the Tsar riding about the countryside and dancing with the Polish ladies, you'd think this really was just a normal visit. And now this ball! And nothing from the Brotherhood?'

'I'm beginning to be afraid the last messenger I sent failed to get through.'

'The Princess won't have had your warning? Have you sent again?'

'Not yet. I hate to risk a man's life unnecessarily. There are so few, now, that one can trust. I have kept hoping to hear.'

'Send again, Miriam. Today. The one thing I do know is that there is a Russian army operating in the south. I'd never forgive myself –'

'You care so much about the Princess?' She was looking at him thoughtfully.

'Idiot!' He bent to kiss her. 'It's the child. It's Casimir . . . And Jenny Peverel. I'd not like her to come to harm. Nor my old friend, Glynde Rendel.'

'I thought you disliked him.'

'For a while. Ridiculous. I'm ashamed of it now. Do you know how much you have changed me, love?'

'For the better, I hope? Jan! If you're going to this ball, it's time you left.'

'And I must go, my darling. Promise me that if you're worried about anything, you'll send to the Russian camp.'

'I promise.' But she knew they would take no notice. 'Come back soon, Jan.'

'You know I will.'

His officers were giving the ball for the Tsar at Zakret, the country house he had just bought from General Bennigsen, in order, as he charmingly said, to be truly a citizen of the Vilno district. There had been a moment of complete catastrophe when the temporary dance-room, built for the occasion, collapsed because of faulty construction, killing one workman. But, 'Only one serf,' had been the general, relieved conclusion. And no need to cancel. The weather was hot, they would spread carpets on the lawn and begin the ball out of doors. After all, in June, there were only a few hours of darkness, and a full moon.

Arriving late, Jan was glad to find Adam Czartoryski in the crowd of people watching the Tsar open the ball by treading a polonaise with his Generals' wives on the carpeted lawn. The air was heavy with the scent of orange trees in tubs, light cloud masked the full heat of the setting sun. 'Your master wins all hearts,' he told Adam in the English they always used.

'And so he should.' Adam smiled as the Tsar returned Madame Barclay de Tolly to her husband and led out the young Countess Tysenhaus. 'I hope he breaks none. That child is only sixteen. Her father favours the French, I understand. Well,' Jan was aware of his wry smile, 'so does mine! These times try us all. I want to speak to you.' He took Jan's arm and led him clear of the crowd to a terrace, from which they could see the last glow of the setting sun on the ornamental cascades of the Vileka River. 'We had a report on you the other day,' he said when they were out of ear-shot.

'A report on me?' Jan managed a tone of innocent surprise.

'Yes. A dangerous Polish spy!' Could Adam's tone really be

faintly mocking? 'And the associate of others. Is she so very beautiful, your Jewish lady?'

'I love her.'

'Then should you have involved her in your affairs?'

'But –' He stopped. How much did Adam know?

'We've a long file on you.' Adam might have read his thoughts. 'Dating from Tilsit, when we began to think a little about you. Such an odd episode there. Don't say anything. It's not one we wish to know about. But I have been instructed to advise you that you might find the climate of your United States of America more healthy for a while. Particularly now, when the chance of war between your country and England seems to increase daily.'

'You're telling me to leave?'

'I'm giving you a word of friendly advice, for your own good. I'd lose no time, if I were you. Get out, Jan, and if you really love your Jewish lady, take her with you. But look, they are serving supper.' Serfs were placing little tables laden with food around the carpeted dance-floor, and people were already gathering round them. The huge moon had risen to outshine the illuminations. Holding out his glass to be refilled, Jan saw a servant speak quickly into Adam's ear.

'I must leave you for a moment. Stay here. I may need you.' Adam stepped back into the crowd and disappeared.

Food and drink were having their effect. Voices rose, laughs were louder, music playing somewhere nearby was lost among the joyful babble. Jan stood alone, draining his glass, brooding over Adam's terrifying revelations, feeling more alone than ever in his life. He had been watched since Tilsit. Idiot. Fool. Who would he have implicated? Who would he not? That missing messenger. Miriam. Glynde. Jenny Peverel. A servant was about to refill his glass. 'No!' He threw it to the ground. Miriam. No time to lose. Marry today and leave tomorrow. He turned, looking about for the quickest way out of this perfumed garden and found Adam Czartoryski once more at his elbow.

'The French are across the Niemen.' Adam's voice, speaking English, was a thread of sound against the background of music and laughter.

'Across?'

'The Niemen. It's started. Hell is open. And Vinsk is in their line of march. It's to be secret still. The Tsar will dance this evening out. But . . .'

'Thank you, Adam.'

Riding through the moon-drenched night, Jan did the same desperate calculation over and over again. A day's hard ride to Vinsk. Half a day from Vinsk to the frontier. And the French were across it already. He should never have left Miriam exposed there. But he had thought the French still far off in Prussian Poland. Had the Tsar known they were just across the Niemen? And, knowing, agreed to dance the night away, safe to the east of Vilno? Thinking back, as he guided his horse along the well-known tracks, he was sure that Adam had known how near the French were. It explained the note of urgency in his advice.

And the Tsar wanted the French move kept secret still. Would let his Polish Russian subjects stay ignorantly in their homes to be engulfed by the French advance. He was glad that his shortest way to Vinsk avoided Vilno so he did not have to decide whether to lose precious time giving the alarm there. But when he stopped at noon to bait his tired horse at the hovel of an inn he always used between Vilno and Vinsk he asked the obsequious landlord eagerly for news.

'News? None, lord. They took my son, my Benjamin, for the army! Now I've no one to send to Vilno. How can I go myself and leave the womenfolk alone here?' As they talked, in the mud-floored main room of the inn, Jan had been aware of women's voices in the loft above; now a dark-eyed girl in her early teens leaned down to ask something in Yiddish, and he remembered being aware on previous visits of a whole troop of little girls in attendance on the brother who had been taken away.

'You'd best get your family out of here,' he told the man, paying for the horse's miserable fodder. 'The French are across the Niemen.'

'The French! May the Lord of hosts protect us. And you, too, lord! You're going to Vinsk?'

'I must!'

'Then go carefully, and God be your guide. Poles and Jews alike will be nothing but corn between the millstones from

347

now on.' And he turned away, to shout in desperate Yiddish to his wife and daughters.

Riding on, Jan was not sure whether to be glad or sorry that he was so easily taken for a Polish nobleman. It had seemed safer, over the years, to dress like a Russian when travelling and he could even speak Russian well enough now, but here in Polish Russia his appearance and fluent Polish made him accepted everywhere as native. Urging his horse on, he thought about what the landlord had said. Jews and Poles, ground alike between the millstones. Had he been mad to assume the Russian army would protect Miriam and Vinsk? And had she known it, and let him go?

The sun was setting in splendour ahead of him and he had to slow his pace partly to favour his exhausted horse, partly to pick his way along the rutted road with eyes dazzled by almost horizontal rays. Not far now. Another hour if the moon rose unclouded, but he must not risk a fall that might lame his horse. He spoke to it, gently, urgently, trying to convey his own sense of crisis. They were old friends after all.

The last crimson segment of the sun vanished below the dark fringe of forest ahead and he had to slow his pace still further in the suddenly diminished light, grateful that he was within the Vinsk estate now, where Miriam saw to it that the roads were well maintained. The moon was up behind him. Why had the afterglow not vanished from the west?

Fire. A wooden palace, burning. Miriam. His horse was making heavy weather of the climb that led up to the watershed of the Vin. At the top there was a cleared place where he and Miriam sometimes rode in the evening, for a breath of air and a wider view of the sunset. Miriam was a woman of great good sense. Whatever had happened, she would have done the wisest thing. He must believe that, hold on to it, while he thought about the French, the Russians, the grinding millstones of war.

There. He was at the top, looking down on an inferno. The palace, all its outbuildings, blazed fiercely in the gathering dusk. Impossible to make out from this distance whether anyone was fighting the flames, and no time to waste looking. His anxiety must have communicated itself to his horse which plunged willingly into the dark of the forest on the downhill slope.

Presently he could hear the crackle of flames, the crash of falling timber. But no screams, no shouts, no hint of human life. He was praying, under his breath, as he emerged from the forest at last into a great, empty, flickering desolation.

Leon Wysocki was appalled when the Princess told him he must represent Rendomierz at the *Sejm*, and begged Glynde Rendel to intercede with her for him. 'She will take your advice, lord.'

'I doubt it.' Glynde's tone was sharp. There had been something in the man's tone he did not like, confirming as it did the speculative glances of which he was increasingly aware. He even caught Jenny's considering eye on him from time to time, and minded this most of all. But what in the world could he do or say? Ten years ago, he had paced his room, night after night, longing for the summons that did not come, aflame with love for the Princess. Love? Passion. And that had worn away, somewhere in the years between. Mary Richards had helped, meeting his hunger with her own, and there had been other women, here and there, some remembered with pleasure, some forgotten on purpose. And now, here was the Princess, visibly older, though as handsome as ever, paying public court to him. No other way to describe it. But what did she want? What did she intend? And how could he stop her without insulting her beyond forgiveness? He had long since given up trying to convince himself that there was no truth in the talk of her affairs with Murat and Davout. But they were men of power. What in the world could she want with him? And how could he convince her that it was not available for her, whatever it was? He would be glad when she left for Warsaw.

Wysocki had, of course, agreed to represent Rendomierz at the *Sejm*. The Princess's servants did not refuse her orders. And as a reward, she had arranged a fête for him on the day before they left for Warsaw. 'In the garden, of course,' she told Glynde. 'That way there can be no loss of dignity in our all sitting down together. We'll make what you English would call a picnic of it. How well I remember picnics in the park at Petworth House. Such an easy, delightful, English occasion.

When this war is over, and Poland free, I think I will go and stay with my friends there. Maybe send Casimir to an English school? You would approve of that, I am sure, my wise counsellor.'

'An admirable idea. I am sure Casimir would profit by the rough and tumble of English schooling.'

'And you will be there to show us how to go on. What happiness to throw off the burden of my position for a while, and just be an English lady. Yes, Jenny?' Impatiently.

'It's about the invitations, Princess. You never did decide who should be asked.'

'Everybody! This is to be Liberty Hall. I've not entertained in state since the Tsar came, and your quick wits saved us all from disaster, Mr. Rendel.'

'Miss Peverel's rather. Casimir wants to sing Dombrowski's March to the crowd, Highness. All of them in their new uniforms. Do you think it would be wise?'

'I think it would be admirable. Make sure that the uniforms fit, Jenny. I have been telling Mr. Rendel that I plan to take Casimir to England when the war is over. You'd like that, would you not?'

'Oh, yes!' Jenny blushed brilliantly with pleasure. 'To see my sisters! My nephews and nieces! Oh –' She had almost said Isobel; restrained herself: 'Highness, do you really mean it?'

'If I did not, I would not have said it. But Mr. Rendel is looking glum. What is the matter, wise counsellor?'

'First this war has to be won, Highness.'

'Croaking again! Just because you British used to be allies of the Russians, you seem to think that the young Tsar will carry all before him. I tell you, he's a straw to every wind that blows. And to every lady that smiles. Did Jenny ever tell you about the time he came here on his way back from defeat at Austerlitz?'

'No.' He could not but be interested.

'Such a performance.' Tolerantly. 'Come to the door, like any traveller, asking for shelter, in a shabby old greatcoat, and hat pulled down over his eyes. Do you remember, Jenny? Of course I spotted him at once; pretended not to. He likes to play out those charades of his. All he wanted was a cup of tea, he said, and quiet. We played his game to a nicety, did we not, Jenny?'

'Oh, yes.' Why was she blushing? 'I remember he stayed the night in the end.'

'And has been goodness itself to me since. When the Prince died there was nothing for it but a state funeral in Petersburg. To show how he honoured his old friend, and his old friend's wife. But he's a squire for every dame, that man. Changes with the wind, and his ladies. Napoleon made mincemeat of him before; he'll do it again. And this time, I hope Monsieur Talleyrand will be at the peace table to see that justice is done to us Poles.'

'I hope so too,' said Glynde. 'Tell me, Highness, is everyone in Warsaw as sure of victory as you?'

'Naturally! It would be an insult to the Emperor to think otherwise.'

She meant the fête for Wysocki to give her a chance for a new approach to Glynde Rendel, who was being so obtuse about her delicate advances. She understood it, of course. He knew himself so infinitely beneath her; had trained himself, over the long years, to keep his passion in control. But with wine flowing, her moment would come to let him guess at his happiness.

It was disappointing that many of her neighbours had already gone to Warsaw for the opening of the *Sejm*, but there were enough guests to applaud the boys' singing of Dombrowski's March and walk through the pleasure gardens as the sun set and the moon rose. On Glynde's advice, she had countermanded the wine that was to have flowed from the fountains.

'You see how I value your wise counsel.' She had found him beside one of the innocuous fountains after the boys had sung their song and the rest of the formal entertainment was over.

'I try to think what is best for you, Highness. I am sure at this time of crisis you had better be seen spending your money on necessary stores than on ostentation.'

'Ostentation?' She fingered her pearl choker, remembering what it had cost her, then smiled and held out her glass to a passing footman. 'You still don't entirely understand us Poles, do you, Mr. Rendel? And who can blame you! But, don't you

351

see, this extravagant party, which I hope you are enjoying,' she gestured to the footman to top up Glynde's half empty glass, 'this party is a public declaration of my confidence in Wysocki. Poor man, I'm afraid he is anxious enough about his first venture into politics! I had him for too long this morning, wanting reassurance about the part he is to play at Warsaw.'

'Yes, he told me.'

'I'm delighted to hear it! I hope you helped him to clear his mind of the absurd quixotries he had been harbouring.'

'You mean his odd notion that he should give his vote according to the facts of the situation as he finds them rather than on instructions received from your Highness before he even left home? I'm afraid you must blame me for that absurd idea, Princess.' He drained his glass. 'I have had it on my mind that I should say this to you. We have talked a great deal, Wysocki and I. If he shows signs of understanding what a democratic parliament is all about, I think you should blame it on me rather than on him. Or even on Napoleon!'

'Napoleon?'

'Yes. As an Englishman I hate and fear him, and you should never forget that. But as a democrat, I have to respect what he is doing here, in Europe. Wherever he has taken that conquering army of his, he has left law and democratic government. Look at the difference between Rendomierz and Vinsk. Here you are served by free men; there by slaves. That is what will make the difference, when it comes to war.'

'That's what you told Leon?'

'Of course. Let the free Poles rise and show their brothers in Russia what freedom means, and the victory is yours.'

'Victory?' she said thoughtfully. But if it was indeed Glynde Rendel who had carelessly talked Wysocki into his astonishing moment of resistance it was more than time she brought him to heel. 'Mr. Rendel; Glynde. It is so long, so very long since we talked, you and I. Give me your arm. Let us take the yew walk where I once had to faint for the Tsar's benefit. We can be private there, and you can explain this odd advice you seem to have been giving my poor muddled Leon.'

'Odd, Highness?' What else could he do but take her arm?

'Odd indeed. You know how I care for my serfs. The villages I have built, the schools I have founded, the chances they have. Well, look how they have flocked into the army, shaved their beards, become men. And have I stopped them? Never!'

'No.' He did not add, but could you have?

'It's gone far enough,' she said. 'If this mad idea Bignon seems to have favoured of a universal Polish rising, of master and man off to fight Russia together . . . If that should really happen, it would be the end of Rendomierz, the end of civilisation.'

'It might mean victory over Russia,' said Glynde.

'At such a price? You, as a member of a landowning family, must know how many people – call them serfs, peasants, what you like – it takes to run an estate. I remember the people at Petworth House . . . the keepers, the beaters, the men in the fields. They may not have been serfs, but they were not much different. And we need them, we landowners, you and I!'

'You, Princess. Not I.'

'By birth you are. By breeding. That is why we have always understood each other so well.' They were in the dark yew alley now, moonlight above, shadow all around. She paused, pulling gently back on his arm, turning to face him, her eyes raised to his. 'Glynde! Do you remember how we understood each other?'

'Remember?' His blood throbbed with the message her flesh was giving to his. 'Highness, how could I forget?' Moon mad? He was pulling her into his arms. All those years . . . He was a young man again, pacing a room; waiting for a summons that did not come. And now: 'Isobel!' He bent, found her lips awaiting his, met them. Felt the passion of her response. And knew, too late, that he felt nothing.

'At last! Oh, Glynde, after all these years!' She drew away a little to smile up at him. And at that moment a boy's hand pulled the lever that controlled the joke fountains and they were suddenly drenched from either side.

32

Reaching Vinsk at last, Jan found the fires dying down. The moon showed nothing but desolation. 'Miriam!' His voice sounded strange against the last whispers of the flames and the great silence beyond. 'Miriam!' he called again, knowing it hopeless. Palace, outbuildings, stables: everything was reduced to the same dark rubble. His only comfort was the silence. No screams, no groans, human or animal. No horrible smell of burned flesh. Occupants and animals alike must have been out of the place before it was set ablaze. But to what fate?

No hope of an answer here. He turned his horse along the familiar track to the village and paused at the corner to look across the valley at the Russian camp. And there, too, was nothing but darkness and silence. Not a camp fire burned. The whole detachment must have marched during the few days he was away. Forward, to confront the French? Fool, idiot to have relied on their protection for Miriam.

Where was she now? Reaching the village, he was relieved to find its hovels still standing, but here again there was nothing but silence, no cackle of hens, no smoke from the chimneys. Had Miriam had notice of disaster and taken her people to safety? But where? He had come some way along the Vilno road and seen no sign of their passage. Above him, a nightingale sang, making the moonlit scene more lonely still. But he must make sure. He dismounted, tethered his horse where it could get an illicit meal from the thatch of one of the hovels, and made his way to the hut of the village's headman. His knock on the door sounded harsh in the silence. The nightingale stopped singing. Nothing else.

He stood there in the moonlight, facing disaster. Miriam had vanished into the vastness of Russia. Was dead? Or so savagely treated that she had crept away to hide? Where was the nearest convent? Would its nuns accept her? A Jewess. And how should he find it? He must find her. He must know.

354

If she was alive, he would marry her, whatever had happened. It was all his fault.

If she was alive she would not have gone without leaving a message for him. Suddenly he was sure of that. Even if it was only goodbye. Could he have missed it, back at the palace? He did not think so. Here, surely? He knocked again on the headman's door, shouted against the enveloping darkness. 'It is I, Jan Warrington, looking for Miriam, looking for my wife.' Strange that it should be so difficult to shout into this alien darkness, but he repeated it, over and over again, walking up and down the village street, pausing to listen.

Nothing. No sound. No movement. It was past midnight now, and he and his horse had been travelling for almost twenty-four hours. Sheer exhaustion made up his mind for him. He settled his horse for the night in the noisome lean-to that passed for the headman's stable, ate the last of the food he had so casually taken from the feast at Zakret, wrapped himself in his cloak and fell asleep on filthy straw.

Sunshine slanted on his face. But it was not this that had waked him. Outside, someone was whistling Dombrowski's March, very low – a whisper of a whistle. He peered through what passed for a window and saw a boy walking down the village street, looking nervously, eagerly, this way and that, whistling as he went. He was in the usual rags of a serf; his haggard face showed the tracks of tears.

'Here!' Jan opened the door. 'I'm here!'

He might not know the boy, but the boy knew him. 'Lord Jan!' None of Miriam's serfs had ever managed the name Warrington. 'Thanks be to the Virgin and all her angels. She said you'd come today.'

'She?'

'The lady.'

'She's safe?'

'Safe?' The boy hurried to join Jan in the hut and close the door. 'With the Russian wolves on one side, and the French on the other! But, yes, she is alive. With Them. I'm to take you to her.'

'Thank God!' He bent to pick up his cloak.

'No, no. Not now. Not till dark. The French are everywhere. Foraging, marauding, murdering. They killed my father.' He spat. 'He was telling them we were their friends, offering to share everything with them. And they shot him. Just like that. They've no friends now. Not among us.'

'But the lady, Miriam, what happened to her?' Recognising the boy's sick exhaustion, he pulled him down to sit beside him on his cloak, a friendly arm around him. 'I am so sorry about your father. There will be a vengeance, I am sure of it.'

'So long as I live, no Frenchman is safe. I swear it!' Having said this, the boy took a deep breath, as if he felt better. 'As to the lady, may the Virgin care for her, even if she is a Jewess! If it was not for her, we'd none of us be alive today. First it was the Russians, see? They came at dawn, demanding every horse in the stables. Why? the lady asked. What was the need? They belonged to the Princess. He spat at her, the Russian officer, said he did not take questions from Jews. Said she was lucky they were in such haste. She asked again, why the haste? He struck her, lord, with his whip, across the face. She'll bear the scar until she dies. "That's how I answer you scum of Jews," he said. They took every horse and pony, all the food they could find. But they were in great haste. I speak Russian,' he said proudly. 'The lady's sons were my friends, they taught me. You know about them, lord.'

'Yes, I know.' Did he remember often enough?

'And I'm just a boy. I pretended to help with the animals. At least it made it better for the horses, having a friendly hand on the bridle, and nothing would have made any difference. I listened to what they said to each other. The French are across the Niemen. The Russian army is retreating, on the Tsar's orders.'

'Retreating?' He could not believe it.

'That's what they said. That's what they did. My cousin watched them go back to the other side of the valley, the way to Vilno. He told the lady. That's when the trouble started.'

'More trouble?'

'There's been no end to it. When the Russians had gone, the lady stood there, blood streaming down her face, said it would be the Princess's wish that the French be welcomed as friends. Gave her orders for it. She even had French flags, the tricolor, that she and the other women had made in secret;

said they were to be hung at the great gate. She would receive the French there, she said.'

'Brave!'

'She's a lion! But, there are some among our people have never liked being ruled by a woman, and a Jewess at that. Kin of the old steward the Prince sent to Siberia years ago. They said it was every man for himself now. With the war begun, you see, they had only to join the army, shave their beards, be free men if they survived. When the lady spoke of their duty to the Princess and the little Prince they just laughed. It began to look very ugly. We were all out in the courtyard, shouting at each other, her friends gathering around the lady – not many men, but we'd have died for her. That was when the French came. They were upon us before we knew. No flags! No welcome!' He was shivering convulsively, and Jan pulled out his flask and gave him a few precious drops of brandy. 'That's good!' He wiped his mouth with a filthy hand, tears trickling down his cheeks. 'It would have made no difference. They were savages. Hungry savages. The lady tried to speak to them, in French, tell them we were friends – as she had planned – that the Russians had taken the horses. That made them angrier still. They wanted food, forage for their horses, drink, of course. We did what we were told. Except my father. After they killed him we obeyed. What else? Rushed about, fetching what the Russians had missed. There was plenty; they'd been in such haste. They ate like pigs, those French, in the courtyard, as if they'd not had food for days. And drank. Some fool showed them where the cellar was; the lady had pretended there was nothing but small beer. Her face was bleeding all the time, blood soaking into the front of her gown. She took no notice. Served them. Went on trying to talk to them in French. There was one, a sergeant, I think: the boss.' The boy was crying freely now. 'He listened to her for a while; sitting on the mounting-block, at his ease; she stood by him, speaking, pleading, the blood still flowing. Lord, he laughed. He threw away his tankard, stood up, tore her dress off her. There, in the yard, in front of us all. It was like a signal. The lady had tried to keep the other women close to her. My mother was there, my little sisters. Some of our men tried to protect them, and were struck

357

down. I'm a coward, like the others. I hid my eyes and listened to them scream.'

Jan was shaking too. He drank, silent and deep, from the flask and passed it to the boy. 'But they're alive?'

'By God's goodness. There was commotion at the gate, suddenly; another party of Frenchmen rode in. A real officer, medals and a sash. He shouted something. Furious. It all stopped. Just like that. The lady got up from the ground, very slowly, as if it hurt her to move, mother-naked. I'm sorry!'

'No. I have to know. She's alive.'

'Oh, yes. The officer said something, wrapped her in his cloak. The other men were letting our women go. They're all alive. For what it's worth. My mother won't speak. My sisters won't stop crying.'

'Life is worth a great deal,' said Jan, working it out, slowly, in anguish, for himself. 'You must tell your mother and sisters that. So then what happened?'

'They all rode away, taking everything: food, forage, all kinds of treasures from the palace. We had hardly time to speak, to think, to try to imagine what to say to them, to each other, while the women were indoors, finding clothes to cover their nakedness. I noticed it first!' He was proud of this, and it helped him. 'The smell of fire! As they were going, the first Frenchmen must have set it, angry at being denied their pleasure. It was everywhere. And all the palace wood-built. There was not a hope, not a chance. That was when the lady came out, wrapped in furs, as if she would never be warm again, the blood running more slowly from her face, and took charge. No hope of fighting the fire, she said. We would all come here, to the village. But when we got here, it was empty. The French had been here too. They had all fled, and who can blame them? At least they didn't bother to fire it. While we were standing, wondering what to do, one of Them came out of the forest, masked and cloaked. You know about Them, lord?'

'Yes, I know.'

'So did the lady. He had come for her. She talked to him a little, then turned to us. There was a safe place, she said, in the forest, for those who wanted to come, but the life would be hard. She was so white that the wound across her face looked like . . . looked like . . . Was there a saint, lord, who got such a wound? She had a duty, she said, to tell us, that if we came, we would be throwing in our lot with the French: "The ones who are true friends of Poland. Like those who rescued us." We must not judge all Frenchmen by a few villains, she said. But any of us who did not wish to come were free to go our own ways. She promised us this, on the Princess Ovinska's authority. Of course I went with her, and my mother and sisters. Most of the women, some of the men. I'll take you to them tonight.' His voice was dwindling as he gave way to shock and exhaustion. 'Were there saints, who were raped and saved their people? If she is not a saint, she is most certainly a hero. I think we'd all be dead, were it not for her.' And then, more sleepily still, 'The Frenchman who saved us knew her, I think.'

He slept all day while Jan sat beside him, cold to the heart. At first he just sat, absorbing the full horror of it, but then, gradually, made himself think. He would need his own mind crystal clear if he was to persuade Miriam that they still had a future together. Making himself face it all, he saw that his own presence at Vinsk would almost certainly have made no difference. Except that he would be dead. The French soldiers who had savaged Vinsk must have been entirely out of control. What had happened to Napoleon's Grand Army, his disciplined, devoted troops? And what would happen to them if they moved on into Russian Poland like this, undisciplined, ravaging, making themselves hated? How many Poles would go on supporting them? He was facing not just the personal disaster of what had happened to Miriam, but the collapse of all his hopes, of all he had been working for.

In a way, it made everything easier. Towards evening, he sighed, allowed himself one tiny sip of brandy, and went out quietly to forage for food. The boy would be hungry when he woke. They shared raw beet leaves and a crust of mouldy bread and started as soon as the moon rose, Jan leading his tired horse. There seemed nothing left to say, except, 'How far?'

'Two hours, if we don't lose the way.' The boy's name was Michael. 'I was named after the lady's older son. He'd be a man now. The poor lady . . . Will she kill herself, do you think?'

'No!' Explosively. After that, they were silent for a long while as they penetrated more and more deeply into the forest.

At last, Michael paused at the top of a slight rise. 'Nearly there,' he said. 'Wait here, till I come back.' And went ahead, whistling, very softly, Dombrowski's March.

It must have been a castle once, when Lithuania was rich and free, and its owner had been affluent and foresighted enough to build it of imported stone. Its walls bulked huge in the moonlight and when they had passed through a narrow entrance they found themselves in what felt like a thriving village. It was good to hear sounds of life again: a child cried, a dog barked, they could smell meat cooking. And strangely now, for the first time after all the day's anguish, Jan felt his eyes fill with tears. He turned, put a hand on Michael's shoulder. 'Don't forget,' he said, 'it's life that matters.'

'Thank you, Lord Jan. Here is your way.' He flung open a door. 'I must go to my mother.'

Firelight, the smell of food stronger than ever, guttering tallow candles, and a tall man waiting quietly to greet him. 'Mr. Warrington,' he took a step forward, holding out a hand, speaking English with a French accent, 'I am more sorry than I can say.'

'Genet?' He could not believe it.

'Yes. I've been Talleyrand's liaison with the Brotherhood since Erfurt. We've worked together, you and I, all this time.'

'You and I and Miriam. How is she? Where is she?'

'Asleep. I made her take laudanum. Nothing she and you could have said to each other tonight would have done any good. If it is any comfort to you, the sergeant who allowed the attack on Vinsk has been shot. You must understand that I meant to get there first. I hope you can forgive me.'

'Can she?'

'Yes. She's . . . she's a great lady, Mr. Warrington. She should have been a Princess.'

'The boy, Michael, thinks she's a saint. Will she marry me, do you think, Genet?'

'That's what you want? I'm glad. I can't say more than that I hope so. Anything I can do . . . But, forgive me, my time is short. I have to be back in camp by morning. I need to know what you mean to do. So that I can give the Brotherhood their instructions. This is their Vilno headquarters. You'll not try to see anything, learn anything?'

'I most certainly will not. What I want to do, Genet, is simple. I want to marry Miriam and take her home to America. There, nobody need know anything of this, except that she is a heroine. We've been lovers – I'm sure you know this – for years. If there is a child, it will be mine. And I shall love it, because it will be hers. Anyway, it may be mine. So . . . it is only to persuade her.'

'I hope you can. We'll be sorry to lose you.'

'I'd be sorry to go if I did not think our cause lost already. What's happened to the French army, Genet? How could what happened this morning have happened? What hope for Poland?'

'None, I think. That's why I'm not even trying to persuade you to stay. When he crossed the Nieman, Napoleon told his troops they were entering hostile territory, entering Russia. That explains what happened at Vinsk. So much for the hopes of Polish Lithuania. I think, now, that I'm glad my master Talleyrand is not in charge at Warsaw. I'm afraid it's going to be one long heartbreak, with gallant Polish blood still shed in vain.'

'And you?'

'I'm in the army now. This is my last appearance as a member of the Brotherhood. Tomorrow I march with my regiment on Vilno, on . . . Who knows? Petersburg? Moscow? To the end of the world? It feels a little like that. But first I will tell the Brotherhood to see you and Miriam safe on your way to Warsaw and so to Paris and your United States.'

'By Warsaw?'

'Of course. To all intents and purposes you are in France now. Will you do one thing for me?'

'If I can.'

'When you get to Warsaw, send to Rendomierz, warn the Princess not to stay there. There are rumours of an army in the south of Russia; Rendomierz is dangerously near that border.'

'Miriam has sent a warning already, through the Brotherhood. She is afraid it did not get through.'

'All too likely. But if, as I hope, you find them already in Warsaw, say something to Miss Peverel for me.'

'Yes?'

'Tell her I shall love her always.'

Their eyes met for a long moment. 'You think things are as bad as that?'

'I hope you persuade Miriam to go to America.'

'You mean it?' She held herself tight, and straight, and still, her eyes huge in the white face with its scarlet slash across the pockmarked side.

'You know I do. I can't do without you, Miriam. I was a boy when we met; you made me a man; don't fail me now. We'll go home to America; Genet is arranging it for us. After today we will never speak of what happened yesterday again.'

'If there's a child?'

'It could be mine. I'm glad Father Stefan came with you. He says he'll marry us today.'

'Today?'

'We must leave tomorrow. Miriam, let me decide this for you? For us. Please?'

'If you wish,' she said listlessly. 'I don't matter. Nothing matters any more.'

33

Glynde and the Princess reached the end of the yew walk breathless and soaked to the skin. She was incandescent with rage, aware of white muslin clinging too revealingly, carefully trained curls plastered against her skull. Jenny and von Stenck had seen what happened, awaited them there in anxious silence.

After the first explosion of rage, the Princess told Jenny to get rid of the guests while von Stenck hunted the culprit, 'Who gets a beating, if it's my son himself.' Her voice had changed with her appearance, its beautiful low notes strident with fury.

Acutely aware himself of the fool he looked, Glynde could only sympathise with her, while he thanked God, and the prankster, for his own reprieve. But he was horribly sure it would turn out to have been Casimir. 'Not a beating, Highness,' he pleaded. 'As your fellow sufferer let me speak up for the guilty party. If, as I fear, it is one of my bad boys, let me beg for some sophisticated punishment, something to make him feel foolish, not angry.'

'After he made idiots of us! On any other subject, Mr. Rendel, I will listen to you.' Her tone drew one of Jenny's quick, perceptive glances. 'But on this I must be the judge. Now, goodnight. We'll talk in the morning.' The words held a promise that appalled him.

Water was running down his neck to which the cravat clung sodden. 'Yes – in the morning.' She would be calmer then. 'Remember, you and Wysocki must leave for Warsaw tomorrow.'

'Not until I have seen justice done. And talked to you.'

She meant it as a promise; he felt it a threat. No hope of sleep that night. He paced his room to and fro, to and fro, desperately trying to think how to extricate himself from this predicament without disaster. Could the Princess really mean marriage? No other interpretation fitted the facts as they had presented themselves since she last came home to Rendomierz. To marry her would mean luxury, wealth, and total submission to his wife. Fresh from the fatal embrace in the yew alley, she had still dismissed his plea for the joker without even pausing to consider it. That would be how they would go on.

If he had loved her, would he have risked it? Probably. The mad young man who had paced his room like this ten years ago would certainly have done so. That desperate, long lost young man had revived, for a fatal moment, last night. But the kiss had done for him. Had the Princess really not felt the deadness of his response? Or did she not care? Could she want a husband so badly?

He longed for Jenny, for Jenny's cool, wise counsel, but in this predicament, how could he ask her for it? On the other hand, he and she must put their heads together, as responsible for the little boys, to try and save the culprit – Casimir, he was sure – from the ultimate affront of a public beating. Casimir must have seen, and resented, his mother's changed attitude to his tutor. Who could blame him for what he had done? But how turn the Princess from her determination of vengeance?

Towards dawn, having found no answers to any of his desperate questions, he threw himself on his bed, fell suddenly asleep and awoke to a sense of disaster. Strong light penetrated the room; it must be very late. He pulled the bell-rope angrily.

'Why was I not called?'

'The Princess gave orders you were not to be disturbed, lord.'

A roll of drums outside. 'What's happening?'

'The Prince is taking his beating.' The man looked frightened. 'In public; in the courtyard. Everyone there to see.'

It was all over by the time Glyndë had pulled on his clothes and hurried to the school-house. The little boys were there, very quiet, pretending to read Virgil under the anxious eye of their classics tutor.

'The Prince?' Glyndë asked him.

'Upstairs. Miss Peverel is with him. He hasn't spoken a word. The Princess wants you at the palace at once.'

'Thank you.' But he turned to the stairway, not the door. Casimir must come first.

He was lying flat on his face on the bed, his naked back

364

showing a savage criss-cross of stripes. Jenny, sitting close beside him, had contrived to get hold of one outflung hand, which lay listless in hers.

'Thank God!' Her eyes met Glynde's in a wordless appeal. 'It's Mr. Rendel, Casimir, come to hear that you took your punishment like a man. As he did,' she told Glynde. 'Not a whisper; not a whimper.'

'Who did this?' Glynde had not thought he could be angrier.

'The Princess had trouble finding anyone,' Jenny was glad of the chance to say this. 'But there's always someone with a grievance.'

'I'll kill him,' Casimir spoke for the first time.

'A serf? Under orders?' Glynde made his tone merely reasonable. 'You should save your fire for people worthy of it. I hope you look on me as your equal, Casimir, and are ready to fight me when you are old enough. I am sorry your mother took action without consulting me. You must see that this is a matter between men, between you and me. It was me you meant to make look a fool, and you most certainly succeeded. You owe me the satisfaction of a gentleman, but I'd be twice a fool if I demanded it now. So, look to your weapon training. When you are of age, wherever you are, wherever I am, you owe me the meeting, and I count on you not to fail me.'

'When I'm sixteen!' Casimir sat up suddenly, his face showing, despite himself, how it hurt him. 'You promise?'

'It's you who must promise. I am the challenger, remember, and I say it will be with pistols.'

'But you'll be married to –' he hesitated, could not name her, '– to the Princess. A man cannot fight his stepfather.'

'I? Married to your mother? What crazy servant's talk is this? I thought better of you, Casimir. Your mother is a Princess, quite out of my star. I'm your tutor, had you forgotten?'

'But . . . But Karol said . . .'

'Karol says the Russians eat babies, which you know very well you found untrue when we went to Vinsk.'

'They did kill his family.'

'Just because that is true, you don't have to believe every lying tale he makes up. Casimir,' somehow without a word said, he had changed places with Jenny by the bed, 'fate has made you a Prince and a leader of men. It is a great responsibility, and if you are to lead them, you must understand them. Think about Karol a little; think if he does not go out of his way to make trouble for you. He was sitting in your place in the classroom just now. Do you think, if you were not here, the boys would choose him for their leader?'

'Not if I have anything to say about it!' He was off the bed now, reaching for a clean shirt. Then, with it in his hand, he paused for a moment, looking at Glynde. 'Sir,' it came hard, 'I begin to think I owe you an apology.'

'Spoken like a Prince! May I, then, with some relief withdraw my challenge? You're a better shot than me already, and you know it.' He laughed. 'I'm only sorry you weren't there to see what a drowned rat I looked when I emerged from that joke alley of yours.'

'And my mother, too.' Venom in this.

'You'll apologise to her, I hope, now you understand . . .'

'She had me whipped in public.' He shrugged into his shirt, wincing as he did so, and left them to hurry downstairs.

Alone, they exchanged a long look, then, 'God bless you,' said Jenny, 'that's half the battle.'

'And God help me in the other half.' He had been feeling his way so far. 'What am I to do?'

'You'll have to tell her what you have just told him.' She did not pretend not to understand, and he was grateful. 'She won't like it.'

'You've seen?'

'Everyone's seen. Hence poor Casimir's trouble. Thank God she's leaving for Warsaw today.'

'And I must tell her first. She sent for me, come to that.'

'And you're keeping her waiting? That's not going to help.'

'Well.' He thought about it. 'In a way. I've burned my boats, after all, with what I said to Casimir. No harm in showing I'm not her poodle. But how to do it without making it such an affront that I'll have to go?'

'That she'll dismiss you,' said Jenny, drily.

'I don't care for myself,' he protested, 'but there's Casimir. What's happened to him today could mark him for life.'

'Will mark him for life. Yes, I'd be sorry to see you go, for his sake.'

'I don't intend to go, but how –' They thought about it for a moment. 'There's one thing. If you'd do it; if it's not asking too much. For Casimir's sake; for mine, if you like; I really do not want to find myself a landless, useless man again . . .' He paused.

'Yes?'

'Would you –' He bolted at it. 'Would you agree to having been secretly engaged to me?'

'To what?'

'To having been engaged – oh, for some time. In secret.'

'No,' she said. 'You're not thinking straight, Mr. Rendel. That way, we would both be dismissed. At once. And Casimir can't do without us. You'll have to do better than that.' She looked at him with faintly scornful sympathy. 'I suggest a hopeless passion for someone in England. And I also suggest you go to her without more delay.'

'Yes. Forgive me.'

'You have my deepest sympathy.'

'You remind me of my aunt.'

'Thank you.' Her mocking tone echoed in his ears as he hurried downstairs and across the pleasure garden to the palace.

'At last.' The Princess was awaiting him in the Chinese salon and he was not sure whether he was glad or sorry to see that she was already angry. 'You have taken long enough.'

'I had to see Casimir. He is my pupil, Highness. I am sorry you did not consult me before having him publicly beaten. He has forgiven me, but I doubt he'll forgive you.'

'A child forgive his mother? Nonsense! I hope I have not been mistaken in you, Mr. Rendel. That the honour I propose doing you has not gone to your head already. We must understand each other better than this.'

'We must indeed. I hardly dared believe, last night, what you seemed to be saying, but if it is true, if you really thought of honouring me so far beyond my deserts, Highness, I have to tell you, humbly, and from a deeply grateful heart, that it is not an honour I can accept.'

'Tell me what? Are you out of your mind?'

'No. Trying to be sane for both of us. It would not do, Princess. Such a marriage would make laughing stocks of us both. What Casimir did last night would be just the beginning. You know better than I what the Polish aristocracy are like; and the Russian come to that. With me for his stepfather, Casimir could say goodbye to his chance of the Polish crown.'

'Casimir, Casimir! Still harping on him! I am offering you my heart, Mr. Rendel, and you talk of nothing but my son!'

'My son, too, remember.' He had never thought to find himself saying this to her.

'Yours! What in the world gave you that idea?' The anger that had brewed while she waited for him suddenly engulfed her. 'Any fool can see he is Jan Warrington's.' And then hushed, hand over mouth, the gesture of a child that knows it has erred beyond forgiveness.

'Jan Warrington?' They stood silent, facing each other, taking in the full implications of what she had said. Then, 'God, what a fool!' He was thinking of the nights, all those years ago, when she had not sent for him, pleading one excuse or another. She had been hedging her bets, and sleeping with Jan too. And she was right, of course. He had looked in vain for any likeness to himself in Casimir, only blind confidence had prevented him from seeing Jan in him. Everything was different. Everything was changed. And what he felt, amazingly, was a great sense of liberation. He smiled at the Princess. 'So much for that,' he said.

'I wouldn't marry you, Mr. Rendel, if you were the last man on earth.' She had never looked so plain, her white face patched with red on the cheekbones. 'Be so good as to pull the bell for me. It is more than time Wysocki and I set out for Warsaw. You'll continue as Casimir's tutor, of course. Make him see the error of his ways.'

'I'll be happy to.' He was breathing great breaths of liberty. 'You'll see him before you go? Make it up with him?'

'I'll let it be seen that there is no truth in the rumours that made him indulge in his deplorable jest.'

'And send Karol home? I'm sure he made the trouble. Take him with you to Warsaw, Princess, hand him back to his relations.'

'No. I've had enough of your advice. Enough of your company. It's more than time I left for Warsaw.' She turned and led the way back to the main hall.

Wysocki was awaiting her anxiously among the usual crowd of attendants. 'The carriages await your Highness,' he hurried forward to greet her. 'If we are to reach Warsaw in time . . .'

'Always thoughtful, Pan Wysocki.' She held out her hand for his surprised kiss, turned back to Glynde, every inch the great lady. 'As for you, Mr. Rendel, I count on you to make up for your past neglect by seeing to it that that ill-conditioned son of mine comes to some understanding of his own bad behaviour. Which I blame on you. I shall hope for better news of my school when I return from Warsaw, or we will have to think again of the position, however lowly, that you occupy in it.' She looked past him to where Herr von Stenck was standing beside Jenny. 'Master at Arms! You will be in charge here while Pan Wysocki and I are absent.' She swept her little court with her piercing gaze, making sure that her point had gone home. Then, 'Pan Wysocki, we must go. We have important duties to perform in Warsaw, you and I.'

'Tell me all the news.' The Princess had hurried to visit Anna Potocka.

'Not much. Mind you, there's some wild talk going round in the *Sejm*. I hope your man knows his place.'

'So do I.' Isobel had not meant to say this. 'But my tutor, Mr. Rendel seems to have been talking a lot of wild, British democracy to him. He actually imagined he was going along to listen and base his decisions on what he heard. I trust I have disabused him of such notions.'

'He's not the only one. My father-in-law says there's been some fiery talk of a national uprising.'

'A Polish revolution?'

'It could come to that.' They exchanged silent glances, both thinking of famous beauties gone to the guillotine in France. 'But my father-in-law is hopeful,' Anna went on. 'He says the new Ambassador de Pradt is clay in their hands. And if the *Sejm* shows signs of getting out of hand, they'll just dissolve it.'

She called next morning to announce that the *Sejm* had indeed been dissolved, much to everyone's surprise. 'They've sent messages of support to Napoleon, and authorised a council to govern in their absence. That cipher de Pradt will be all-powerful, in fact.' She laughed and made a little face at

Isobel. 'What's this story I hear about your bad boy Casimir? You've not caught cold from your drenching, I do hope.'

'Not the least in the world.' Isobel had passionately hoped that the story would not get about. 'Silly child,' she went on. 'He'd taken some wild idea into his head about my meaning to marry his tutor.' She laughed, with an effort. 'Not the poor young man's fault, that's for certain. He was scared out of his wits at the very idea!'

'So you won't have to get rid of him?' Anna went to the heart of the matter.

'Lord, no. In the main I think he is doing well enough by Casimir. What a dead bore the story has got out here in Warsaw, but I'm grateful to you, my dear, for letting me know it has. The question is, what to do to stop people's tongues? Of course,' she exclaimed. 'Why did I not think of it sooner? I'll marry him off to the governess; that will take care of everything.'

Napoleon was already installed at Vilno when the deputation from Warsaw reached him. The Russians had withdrawn without a blow struck, and he was in the palace, where a week before the Tsar had entertained his loyal subjects. Now they all danced attendance on Napoleon. Paul Genet, arriving still enraged from what had happened at Vinsk, found that this and other equally barbarous episodes were being shrugged off as fortunes of war. And when the deputation from Warsaw arrived, Napoleon listened to them courteously, but gave them a cool answer that promised nothing. Instead of making one unified Kingdom of Poland from Lithuania and the Duchy, he was setting up an independent state of Lithuania, with Bignon as his representative.

'It's history repeating itself.' Genet called on Bignon the day Napoleon received the Polish deputation. 'I was in Warsaw with Tallyrand in 1806. Lukewarm promises; no real commitment.'

'And the Tsar just the same!' The two men were old friends, having met often at Talleyrand's house in Paris. 'One does have to be sorry for these Polish nobles, forced to fawn first on one Emperor, then on the other. I'm so very sorry about what happened at Vinsk.'

'You've heard?'

'You've not exactly been keeping quiet about it, have you? A mistake, perhaps, if you are hoping for a career in the army.'

'You're right of course. But, frankly, I'm not sure now that I am. I feel it my duty to serve in this campaign, but, when it is over I think I shall ask Talleyrand's help towards a place in civil life.'

'When it is over,' said Bignon thoughtfully. 'Tell me, has the order been given yet for the advance?'

'You know as well as I do that it hasn't. The army's in bad shape, Bignon. There's more than what happened at Vinsk to prove it. Dysentery is killing as many men as a battle would, and the way here is strewn with dead horses . . . It's one thing to let an army live off the land in central Europe, where the land is rich, but here it is simply madness. You'd have thought he'd have learned that in the campaign before Tilsit.'

'Yes, but he won that one,' said Bignon, and the two men exchanged a long, thoughtful glance.

'Will you do something for me?'

'If I can.'

'When you write to de Pradt, ask him to make sure the Princess Ovinska is warned of the danger to Rendomierz. I'd not want her and her family to suffer what happened at Vinsk.'

'I'll certainly write to de Pradt, but I should warn you, he and I are not on the best of terms.' He laughed. 'Odd that I should have found myself urging the Emperor not to dismiss him outright. Napoleon is enraged,' he explained, 'because the *Sejm* was dissolved after three days. He had expected them to lead a patriotic war, but the aristocrats are afraid of revolution French-style and persuaded him to get rid of the parliament before it went too far. I managed to convince the Emperor that getting rid of de Pradt would only make matters worse, but nothing will persuade him what a disaster this Dutchman is that he is naming Governor here in Lithuania. He's a man who learned despotism in Java, and even I, who pride myself on getting on with most people, must confess to finding him impossible. Oh well,' he got up and refilled their glasses, 'let us earnestly hope that August finds our master at Moscow, negotiating a more durable Tilsit with the Tsar.'

371

34

Casimir's back healed fast, but as soon as it was better he picked a quarrel with Karol and was found by the Master at Arms beating him almost to death in the empty drill hall. It was unfortunate that the Princess chose the next day to pay a flying visit to Rendomierz. Both Casimir and Karol had black eyes, and Jenny had found it necessary to separate them in the dormitory for fear of more fighting. Hatred sparked between them. 'What in the world shall we do?' she asked Glynde, when news of the Princess's arrival reached the school.

'Say they are both ill? Maybe suggest it's infectious?'

'Admirable! Then she will never visit them.' Hurrying across the pleasure gardens in hot July sunshine, they reached the palace as the Princess's carriage drew up in the forecourt and she emerged, very elegant in another Paris dress.

'Where are my bad boys?' She looked about the carriage sweep where they were usually drawn up to greet her.

'Highness,' Glynde moved forward. 'Two of them are ill. Miss Peverel is not quite sure that the trouble is not infectious. We thought it best . . .'

'Quite right. I'm glad you had so much sense, Mr. Rendel. Or should I thank Miss Peverel?' Smiling at Jenny she nodded dismissal to the Master at Arms, who was hoping to lead her into the palace, in his role as commandant in her absence. 'I have something to say to you, Mr. Rendel, Miss Peverel. In the small salon, I think.'

The small salon had been the Prince's study, and had been little used since his death. It made the summons seem even more strangely formal . . . Glynde and Jenny exchanged anxious glances as the Princess led the way towards the remote salon, throwing an order over her shoulder as she went for champagne and glasses.

'What in the world?' whispered Glynde, hanging back.

'Hush,' said Jenny.

'Sit down, both of you.' The Princess had enthroned herself in the Prince's huge chair. 'I am thinking of going to Spa,' she told them as a servant arranged wine-cooler and glasses on a marble-topped table. 'My doctor advises it. Nothing serious,' she waved aside their expressions of concern. 'He says I have been carrying more of a load than any woman should be expected to bear. I am to leave Casimir behind.' She answered the question before they could ask it. 'Worry about him is part of my trouble, the doctor thinks. I am to concern myself about nothing but my own well-being. I have sent a message to Miriam, putting her in absolute charge at Vinsk. The question is, how am I to leave things here? In the ordinary way, I would have handed over to Wysocki, but, frankly, after the way he conducted himself in Warsaw, I am not sure I dare. Madmen the lot of them; bonnet over windmill and off to the wars! I don't want to come back to Rendomierz and find all my serfs gone. So I'm going to put you in control here, Mr. Rendel.'

'I'm honoured. But Herr von Stenck won't like it.'

'My people don't like taking orders from a Prussian. They have grown to respect you, somehow, and they love Jenny. Pour the champagne, Mr. Rendel. We are going to drink a toast to something that I have seen and you have not. To my deputy –' The cork exploded and Glynde filled three glasses. She raised hers: '– and his charming wife. Mr. and Mrs. Rendel!'

'No!' Jenny put her glass down and rose. 'We are your servants, Highness, not your serfs. I know I can speak for us both when I tell you your suggestion is absurd.' She had never looked so nearly handsome, Glynde thought, her colour high, her eyes sparkling with unshed tears, which she would not let fall. 'Mr. Rendel and I are old friends,' she went on steadily. 'If we have never thought of marriage in all the years we have known and respected each other, it is too late to start thinking of it now.'

'There's gossip in Warsaw.' The Princess took a long draught of champagne. 'I'd thought to have spared you this, Jenny.'

'Gossip!' Jenny dashed an angry hand across her eyes. 'I expect there has been gossip for years.'

'Indeed there has. And no wonder. I always lied for you

373

and denied the stories about you and Paul Genet.' She raised an imperious hand. 'Don't interrupt! Absolutely your own business, I told Anna Potocka, none of hers nor mine. But now! To be taking money from Mr. Rendel. Your reputation, such as remains, can't stand it, Jenny, and nor can mine as your employer. Something has to be done. I urge you both to think again.'

'Highness!' Glynde was on his feet, furious, about to say something absolutely disastrous.

'No.' Jenny put a silencing hand on his arm. 'Let me explain.' She turned back to the Princess, chin up. 'Highness, when you sent for me, all those years ago, you promised to look after me.'

'And so I have. Look at you!'

'You have been lavish, Highness.' She looked down at her sober cambric dress. 'I hope my appearance has not disgraced you. I have never been cold in winter, nor hungry. But I have earned no wage. I have been able to put nothing by for old age, or for when you no longer need me. When Casimir grows up, perhaps. Your husband gave me a chain of rubies, once. It is all I have earned from your house in the years I have served it. Oh – I think you would never let me starve. You are too proud for that. But, I am proud too. So – when Mr. Rendel very kindly offered me a salary out of the estate you gave him, I was happy to accept.' She was blushing now, but her eyes met Isobel's steadily.

'You'll take his charity, but you won't marry him?'

'Not charity, Highness,' Glynde interposed. 'A well-earned wage.'

'Which I should have paid! Is that what you are saying?'

'I suppose it is.'

'I see.' She looked savagely from him to Jenny and back. 'You made a bargain with me, Mr. Rendel, when I asked you to take on Casimir. You held out for an estate! I do find myself wondering who put you up to that! And now she won't marry you! Well, I'm not sure that I blame her! Not even with your expectations!' She drained her glass, threw it at the wall and swept from the room.

They stood for a moment, gazing at each other. Then: 'Just what did she mean by that, I wonder?' Glynde raised his glass in salute, drank to her. 'You're braver than I am. Thank you.'

'This may tell you something. I didn't have a chance to give it to you before.' The blush had faded, leaving her chalk-white. 'Marylka has heard from the Brotherhood. She stopped me in the hall. This letter for you, and a warning.'

'Warning?' He was eagerly tearing open the letter from his aunt, which looked as if it had been to the end of the world and back.

'There's a Russian army, somewhere to the south. They don't know which way it's moving. It might be making for Warsaw, this way. No one should leave the palace.'

'Good God!' He had hardly heard her. 'I'm Lord Ringmer! My father and brother are both dead. His wife has no hopes of a child . . .' His voice was suddenly quiet. 'I own half Sussex. Marry me?' Now what in the world had made him say that? 'You and Genet,' the Princess had said. His mistress?

'Handsome of you.' A strange little smile. 'But the answer is still no. I'm so happy for you! We don't need to pretend, do we, you and I, about your father and brother. You'll make an admirable landlord. But how will you get there?' Stick to hard facts. She had refused him twice in five minutes. There would be time to think about that later.

'Lord knows! Besides, how can I leave Casimir? Now, when he is so unhappy. Good God!' He saw it all. 'The Princess must have known.'

Their eyes met. 'Oh dear,' said Jenny. 'I suppose she did.'

To her delighted surprise, he was laughing. 'It was going to be Queen Cophetua and the beggar-man. And then, what a delightful surprise, the beggar-man would have turned out a frog Prince. Or at least a frog Baron!'

'You're mixing your fairy tales.' She was laughing, too. 'But I see just what you mean. I wonder how she knew.'

Glynde thought he knew the answer; recognised Talleyrand's hand in it. Had he hoped to have a grateful son in place behind the future King of Poland? 'I don't know what to do.' And then, at last, remembered the Brotherhood's message. 'A Russian army, you say, to the south? How far?'

'They didn't say. Just urged we go back to Warsaw.'

'You should have told her.'

'How could I? Not then! But we must, at once.'

'We?'

'Please?'

Emerging from the secluded salon, they found the palace in uproar. 'What's going on?' Glynde asked Madame Poiret, who was standing at the bottom of the grand stairway, looking distraught.

'The Princess has left again for Warsaw. Everything she needs for Spa is to be sent after her. She's put Herr von Stenck in charge. I've never seen her so angry. Oh *mon Dieu*, what is going to happen to us all?'

Jenny and Glynde exchanged a quick, appalled glance. Then, 'We'd best go at once to von Stenck,' said Glynde. 'Fetch Marylka? He may take some convincing.'

Jenny nodded, knowing him to be right, and hurried off to look for Marylka. The two of them found Glynde with von Stenck and Wysocki in the room the Princess used as her office, all talking angrily at once. Glynde had found the other two already at loggerheads, with Wysocki refusing to hand over his keys, but they united in derision at his news. 'A Russian army to the south!' von Stenck shouted. 'So you're a strategist now, as well as a snivelling tutor! I tell you, we're going to have some discipline in this place, now I'm in charge. You!' He rounded on Wysocki. 'Keep your damned keys, if you must! I don't want to be troubled with your paper-work, but remember, the Princess will expect an accounting when she returns. As for you,' to Glynde, 'back to your charges, and if they are really infectious, keep away from the palace. Which goes for you too.' To Jenny. 'We've had enough of you fawning British, creeping and making interest with the Princess for all the world like a couple of crawling Jews. I'm in charge now! Get back to your duties.'

'You'd best listen to Marylka first,' said Jenny quietly. And something about that very quietness got her a hearing.

'Lords, it was my brother, Lech, brought the message. He's not a fool. He doesn't make things up. He saw the Cossacks himself; had to hide for his life on his way here.'

'You're crazy,' said von Stenck. 'Where was he coming from?'

'The Princess's village, lord, to the south. That's where he lives since he married. The Brotherhood's messenger came there. Told them to take what they valued and hide in the forest.'

'And have they?' asked Glynde.

'Yes, lord. And Lech has gone back to see to his wife. Please God he gets there.' She crossed herself; raised her head to look the three men directly in the face. 'The villagers had the sense to do as they were bid.'

There was a little silence, then Jenny spoke. 'The school is between here and the village.'

'And Lech nearly met Cossacks on his way here?' Glynde asked Marylka.

'Yes, lord.'

'Then there's not a minute to be lost. I'll fetch the boys, von Stenck, while you see to the defence of the palace.' Suddenly they were two soldiers, reckoning the odds. 'If it can be defended?'

'Against flying bands of Cossacks? Yes. Against a whole army, not a hope.'

'Then let us devoutly pray it is only flying bands of Cossacks. Miss Peverel, you'll organise the women? Do exactly as von Stenck bids you?'

'Of course. But –'

Their eyes met. 'You know I must go.'

'Go carefully! It will help no one if you are taken. And come back safe!'

Leaving the house by way of the stable yard, Glynde made his way swiftly through the shrubberies that masked the stables. It was late afternoon now and long shadows fell slantways. Above him, a late lark sang. Everything seemed normal, under the hot westering sun, until he stopped for a moment to listen, and his blood chilled. He had heard that sound before, many times, the Cossack 'hurra', the rush of their horses' hooves. Very near. Too near?

He ran the length of the yew walk, keeping to the shadowed side, dived across the open space by the ornamental water, through another shrubbery, and came out to the side view of the school, pausing there a moment for breath. He could see the boys now, drawn up outside the schoolhouse, on their ponies, glorious in the uniforms the Princess had brought them. Casimir was speaking to them, obviously giving them their orders. Behind him, the classics tutor was pleading, begging, cajoling. Casimir took no notice. Glynde could not hear what they were saying, was helpless himself, too far off to get their attention. He watched in spellbound horror as the Cossack 'hurra' grew louder and a group of them swept round the turn of the drive, their savage figures stark against the light.

Miriam went through the strange, swift marriage service as if in a dream. She hardly spoke on the journey to Warsaw, but did, docile as a child, whatever Jan said. For the first few days, the going was hideous, with signs everywhere of the French army; ruined houses, crops destroyed and the bodies of horses abandoned beside the road, already beginning to stink. 'It looks more like a retreat than a victorious advance,' Jan said, and got no answer. If she would only scream, cry, curse he would feel better about her. He had seen, from the first, that even his touch was intolerable to her, and held himself carefully aloof, but her silence was worst of all. 'I am going to tell you about my family, and my home,' he announced on the morning they left the spoor of the French army behind and plunged into virgin forest. 'And America, so you will know what to expect.' He pretended not to feel how she mutely rejected this, and went on to describe the big plantation house outside Savannah, the detached slaves' quarters, the great sweep of the river almost encircling the house. 'My sister lives not far away, you'll love her, and she you. I know it.' He had not realised how homesick he had been until he started talking about it. Even in the face of her continued silence, it was easy to go on, to talk of his father, of the nephews and nieces he had never seen, the friendly social life of the thriving town.

But she had still not spoken except for an essential yes or no when they reached Warsaw at last. 'I'm going to take you straight to the Princess's house,' he said as they crossed the Vistula. 'And, remember, all that happened to you was a bad fright.' He felt her shudder. 'A very bad fright, Miriam. Paul Genet promised me he would tell everyone that he arrived just in time. So, for both our sakes, and for the child's, if there should be one, try to behave as if that was really all that happened. What is it?' She was shaking her head.

378

'No child,' she said.

'Thank God.' He was relieved, too, when they reached the Ovinski Palace and learned that the Princess was at Rendomierz, though his first act was to send an urgent messenger warning her of the danger of the advancing Russian army. The expurgated story he told of the destruction of Vinsk was dramatic enough to get Miriam the sympathetic attention of the women, who carried her off and put her to bed while he went to pay an essential call on de Pradt.

He found him ostentatiously busy, and only the note Paul Genet had scrawled for him got him admission. At first, de Pradt refused to take him seriously. 'An army in the south? Nonsense. Everyone knows the Tsar is involved in Turkey still, and he'd never divide his main army. A tale of a cock and a bull.' But he looked frightened. 'I'll report it to Schwarzenberg who commands the forces here in the Duchy, but I have no doubt he'll think no more of your rumour than I do. As to Vinsk, naturally, I'm sorry to hear about it, but you know the old saying about the omelette and the eggs. Lucky for Princess Ovinska that her Rendomierz estate is in an altogether safer part of the country. Talking of the Princess, there have been the most extraordinary rumours going around about her, here in Warsaw. Imagine! That she might be going to marry her son's tutor. A nobody of an Englishman. And that her son was so outraged by the prospect that he let fly with some joke fountain or other and drenched the pair of them. Together they were, mind you! Which does give one a little to think.'

'I never heard such nonsense,' said Jan roundly. 'Well, I've given my warning as I promised Genet, now I must set about making arrangements for journeying to Paris with my wife.'

'I must congratulate you.' His tone was dry. 'The Princess Ovinska's Jewish stewardess, you said?'

'My wife, sir.'

The Cossacks had stopped shouting. They paused, resting their horses, staring at the line of boys, who sat their elegant little ponies easily, resplendent in their Polish uniforms, one of them carrying the eagle standard Jenny had made. Glynde, watching, helpless, still had no breath to hold.

379

Casimir pushed forward a pace, raised a hand in greeting and challenge: 'I am the Prince Ovinski. What are you doing on my land, and what can I do for you?' He had spoken in his fluent Russian and Glynde breathed a long sigh of hope.

'Let us pass,' said the Cossack leader. 'We don't fight with children. Put your toy swords away; tell us where your horses are stabled and maybe we'll let you keep those pretty little ponies, and your Polish chicken, good for running away!' His contemptuous gesture was for their flag.

'We don't run.' Casimir held on to his temper. He was playing for time, Glynde realised, must have sent a message to the palace and was doing his best for his friends. 'But — your being here — it's war then?'

'It's war, young cockerel. Our little father the Tsar is going to teach you snivelling Poles a lesson you won't forget.'

An outraged stir among the boys. Casimir's hand went up to quell it; too late. A shot rang out. Karol? 'Damn you!' As he spoke, the leader swayed, fell in slow motion from his horse and his men screamed their war cry and charged.

Glynde was praying and cursing under his breath. He saw Casimir kick his pony forward, sword gleaming in evening sun, and go down like corn to the sickle. Tears streamed down his face. He took one last, helpless look at the mêlée, which was almost over, boys down everywhere before that swift professional onslaught, and turned to run for his life. For Jenny's. For all their lives. For what Casimir had tried to save.

Herr von Stenck had been busy. Every carriage in the stables had been fetched, formed into a barricade eked out with odd bits of furniture from the house. There were marksmen ready at the downstairs windows. Not enough of them.

'The boys?' Von Stenck was directing operations at the front of the house.

'Dead.' Glynde was hardly aware of his tears. 'Not a chance. The Prince was holding them, but young Karol fired on their leader. I had to watch . . . nothing I could do but come and warn you. They may be busy for a while sacking the school. Or they may come straight here.'

'Is it true you're a crack shot?'

'I've killed a pheasant or two.'

'We need a man in the church tower. It commands every side. The Prince's sporting guns. You can use them?'

'Yes. The women?'

'Making bandages. And ready to pass us ammunition when it begins.'

'You got a message off to the Princess?'

'At once. But whether she gets it . . .' He turned to hurry away.

Glynde stood for a moment, facing their desperate case, saw Jenny come running from the palace door.

'You're safe!' she exclaimed. 'But – where's Casimir? The boys?'

'Dead.' He took both her hands in his. For comfort. His, or hers? 'I couldn't save him. All of them . . .'

'Dead? The little boys? The hope of Poland.' Silent tears ebbed from her eyes.

'I could do nothing. Too far away. Had to watch it; leave them to their fate.' He must not tell her about the part her eagle had played. 'I'll never forgive myself; never forget it.'

'But it may save the rest of us.' His wild look frightened her. 'If you break down, we're all lost, I think. The serfs trust you as they don't von Stenck.'

'Thank you.' He released her hands, reached gently to wipe away her tears. 'You're right. No time for tears. Come round with me and talk to them? No need to take my place in the tower until we see them coming. Von Stenck knows his business; he's placed his lookouts well.'

They found him arguing furiously with a group of outdoors men whom he had ordered to destroy the Princess's beloved orangery. 'It's got to go.' He turned to them, 'But the fools are frightened of what the Princess will say.'

'You're right, of course. It would provide cover from the shrubbery right to the palace. Have you explained to them?'

'Explained! To serfs! Anyway, I don't speak their damned lingo!'

'Miss Peverel, make them understand?' Glynde took von Stenck's arm to draw him away and was rewarded a few moments later by the crash of breaking glass.

The sentinel's shouted warning came just as he was beginning to wonder if night might not save them at least for the time being. He turned to Jenny. 'Come and load for me? You know how?'

'Of course.'

They reached the narrow parapet of the tower just as the Cossacks emerged from the shrubbery beyond the ornamental water, and Glynde was glad to see that they were riding, as before, in a solid mass, loaded with what must be booty from his house and the school. He breathed a prayer for the tutors, the servants . . . Not hopefully . . . But nothing could have happened to suggest to the Russians that the palace might be defended. Hoping this, he and von Stenck had agreed to hold their fire to the very last moment for maximum effect on the swift-moving targets. He waited, holding his breath, until the Cossacks had cleared the yew walk and swung round to take the palace from the front. His first shot and those of the other defenders sounded almost at the same moment. Four Cossacks slumped in their saddles and one horse fell under its rider. He took the second gun from Jenny and fired again as the attackers massed on the drive in front of the house. Another volley of shots from the defenders. Two more horses down, and one man. So far, the leader had escaped. The one Karol had hit, he wondered, or another? He took careful aim, fired, and got him. That did it. The rest of the depleted band conferred hastily, turned and fled back the way they had come, taking their wounded with them. With one last shot, Glynde got the rider of a dead horse as he tried to leap up behind one of his fellows. 'I hope he's only wounded,' he told Jenny, handing her the rifle. 'We need to know what to expect.'

'We most certainly do.' She was sitting on the heavy slates of the church roof, her grey dress filthy with dust and oil, a great smear across her face where she had wiped it with a blackened hand. She look up at him. 'You killed – how many?'

'I don't rightly know.' He reached down a hand to pull her to her feet. 'Or care. We're safe for the moment, I think. We'd best get down before it's too dark to see.'

'Look!' She was pointing south to what he had unthinkingly dismissed as an afterglow from the sunset. 'Fire! The school. Your house!'

'My books!'

382

'Everything. Do you think there is any hope Casimir is still alive?'

'We have to face it. None.' There had been no time, before, to tell her what had happened. Now, as they made their way cautiously down the spiral stairway in the half dark, he described the moment of disaster when Karol fired on the Cossack leader. 'I think Casimir might have held them. After that, there was no hope. If only . . .'

'Oh, I know,' she said. 'So many ifs . . . Now it's all over. All our hopes . . . You'll go back to England now, won't you? Take me with you?'

'I intend to,' he told her.

Reaching Warsaw still in a very bad temper, the Princess was more surprised than pleased to find Jan Warrington and Miriam installed in her house. It was Jan, greeting her at her own front door, who broke this to her. 'You did not meet my messenger?'

'No.'

'I'm sorry to have to tell you. Your palace at Vinsk has been destroyed.'

'Destroyed? But why? Who?'

'French stragglers.'

'Brutes! Completely?'

'I'm afraid so. I got there next day. It was burnt out. The survivors had taken refuge in the forest. I managed to find Miriam . . .'

'I should never have left her in charge. A woman! A man would have defended it, kept better watch! I'll never forgive her, never! Where is she? Why is she not here to greet me?'

'She's ill, Princess. It's been a terrible shock to her.'

'It's a terrible shock to *me*! My poor Casimir, his main estate. And all those serfs! They're gone, you say? Into the forest?'

'Many of them died trying to defend themselves. And your son's palace. But it happened too fast; no warning; no reason to expect it.'

'Where were the Russians?'

'Gone. The Tsar withdrew his army when Napoleon crossed the Niemen. But, Highness, if you have not had my messenger, best send another. There's talk at Vilno of a Russian army in

383

the south, commanded by Tormassov. If it comes here, against Warsaw, Rendomierz will be in its line of march.'

'Dear God! Rendomierz too. And my son. Casimir! I must go to de Pradt, to the government, to Schwarzenberg, get them to send help!'

'But first send for your son.'

The wounded Cossack refused to speak. Von Stenck wanted to torture him, and he and Glynde were arguing furiously about this when Lech arrived to report the village destroyed, but the villagers safe and back there, trying to pick up the pieces of their lives. There was more news from the Brotherhood. The Russian army was still in Volhynia, on the other side of the border, it was only its Cossack screen who were operating here in the Duchy. 'No one knows which way they are going to move, whether for Warsaw or north to join the main army.'

'So what do we do?' Glynde had interpreted for von Stenck, who was proud of speaking no Polish. 'Which is more dangerous, to stay here and defend the palace, or to try and get through to Warsaw?'

'The Princess would wish the palace defended.'

'I suppose she would.' He cared nothing for the Princess or her wishes. How strange it was. All he wanted was to get Jenny Peverel to safety. And himself? He had a future now, in England, a whole hierarchy of responsibilities awaiting him there. There had been time, in the quiet watches of the night, to decipher all of his aunt's closely written letter. It told a sad story of an estate gravely neglected by two sick men, who cared nothing about its heir, or its tenants. But then, why should they have considered him? He was surprised that they had not tried to invalidate his claim. He could only think that when it came to the point, he must have seemed a less undesirable successor than the remote cousin who was the next heir. No wonder his aunt urged him to come home as soon as possible. All very well, but how?

He found Jenny trying to comfort Lech, who had taken the news of Casimir's death hard. 'We have to think what's best to do.'

'Yes.' She had been crying again, but managed a travesty of a smile. 'What can we do?'

'Stay here and help defend the palace; try to get to Warsaw; or try to join the Russian army.'

'The enemy?'

'You're forgetting, and no wonder. They are not our enemy. I imagine Britain and Russia are allies again by now; sure to be, with the French across the Niemen. And, don't forget, I have many good friends in Petersburg and in the Russian army. I don't know Tormassov, it's true, but we're bound to have friends in common. If we could only get to him, our troubles would be over.'

'It's a big if.' She thought about it for a moment. 'Too big. I've been a fool. I should never have asked you to take me with you. I hadn't thought what it would mean. By yourself, you might manage to get across country and find Tormassov. With me, you'd not have a chance. It would mean death for you; worse, as they say, for me. Forget I asked you. Go without me. And God go with you.' She would never have a chance to tell him that the Princess had lied in her hints about her and Paul Genet. Better like that?

'No.' He turned to Lech, who had been listening without understanding, and spoke to him in Polish. 'Lech, we can trust you, the pani and I?'

'Till death, lord. We were all the little Prince's friends.' He crossed himself. 'May he rest in peace.'

'He died gallantly. Now, tell us —' He looked quickly round to make sure they could not be overheard. 'The Brotherhood — does it still have links across the border?'

'In Russia?' He spat. 'God rot them! But, yes, lord, I expect so. They have always had connections everywhere.'

'And you are still in touch with them?'

'I can be.'

'Then ask them if they can help us across the border. To the Russian army. It's not safe here for women.'

'It's not safe for anyone,' said Lech. 'But you're right, lord, we peasants can hide in the forest. We've done it before; we'll do it again. But, the Princess?'

'Our duty to her died with the Prince,' said Glynde, and got a strange look from Lech.

'You saved my life once, Pani Jenny,' he turned to her. 'I owe it to you. You want to do this mad thing?'

'Yes, Lech, I do. If you can help us . . .'

'I can try. But, pani, will you take Marylka with you? My sister.' He said it proudly. 'There's no life for her here; not with her blood. It's all right for me; I'm a man; men make their own lives. I'd meant to speak to the little Prince about her, when he was older, when he could understand. But now . . . Take her with you, pani. Find her a life in your England where you are all equal. And I'll help you.'

35

The news of Casimir's death broke Miriam's icy calm. 'Oh, the poor little boy.' Tears streamed down her face at last, and Jan, in a shock of his own, was still relieved to see them. She reached out half blindly and took his hand. 'Your son,' she said. 'Your promising little son.'

'You knew?'

'Anyone who loved you both would have known. He was so like you, Jan.'

'You'll have to give me another.' He had her in his arms now, crying quietly. 'A little American, my darling. Soon.' She was beginning to shake again. He leaned across her and blew out the light, then, very gently, very lovingly, as so often before, began to take off her clothes.

The Princess went from blind rage through hysterical tears to a cold calm that was more frightening still. Jan had whisked Miriam away from the first crisis, so they knew no more until next morning, when they emerged to find her, all in black, issuing a string of orders to a messenger. Von Stenck was to hold Rendomierz for her or never cross her path again. 'As for my son's tutor and governess, who have so signally failed in their duty, they may consider themselves dismissed as of this moment and lucky to get off so lightly. I do not wish ever to see either of them again.' She looked up and saw Jan in the doorway. 'I leave for Spa today. You will be so good as to make other arrangements for yourself and your –' she allowed a significant pause: 'wife.'

'Isobel!' He could not part from her like this. 'You must let me say how sorry I am. How I grieve for him!'

'You?' She looked at him coldly. 'What business is it of yours? Goodbye, Mr. Warrington.'

* * *

Her messenger reached Rendomierz safely and found the palace still in a state of defence. The rumour was that Tormassov's Russian army had moved north towards Brest Litovsk, and no more had been seen of its marauding bands of Cossacks.

'So much for that.' Glynde received the Princess's message almost with relief. 'It leaves us free to go,' he told Jenny, 'as soon as the Brotherhood can arrange it. Frankly, though von Stenck will miss me as a rifleman, I think he'll be glad to see me go as a divider of counsels.'

'You mean you give him good advice he doesn't want to take! I'd noticed that, too. Have you had any luck in selling your estate?'

'No. Nor am likely to, I'm afraid. Nobody believes the Princess won't confiscate it.'

Jenny smiled. 'Sensible of them. I'm surprised she didn't say so by her messenger.' And then, sobering. 'Poor woman. I forget that we've had time to get a little used to Casimir's death. Only think of the shock to her!'

'The end of all her planning. But talking of plans, if I can't sell the estate, what are we to do for funds for our journey? No use thinking von Stenck will advance us anything, granted the tenor of the Princess's message. What are you doing?' She was reaching into the low-cut shoulder of her calico dress, and his blood stirred, surprising him. Paul Genet's mistress.

'Our funds. Here!' She must have released a fastening; now showed him the long, gleaming string of rubies that had hung hidden under her dress. 'Don't you think, doled out carefully, one at a time, they might see us safely to England?'

'Good God! I should say so! But I thought you'd lost them, with everything else, in the Cossack raid?'

'I thought it best everyone should think so.' She was tucking them carefully back as she spoke, and once again a strange little thrill ran through him as she pushed down the fabric of her dress to reveal a shoulder white against the brown hand that fixed the jewels back in place.

He laughed, to conceal a profound sense of shock. What was happening to him? 'How glad I am I insisted you join me in this venture! But you'll need to think of a new hiding place.'

'Oh, why?'

'Lech brought a message today. The Brotherhood advise

that you and Marylka disguise yourselves as men for the journey. Will you mind?'

'Marylka might. But not if Lech tells her to.' She was digesting the fact that the Brotherhood were now getting in touch with Glynde direct. 'Sensible, I can see. We'll put our minds to it.'

Rumours came thick and fast. Tormassov had been beaten by Schwarzenberg somewhere in the north near Brest Litovsk, and was retreating southwards, thus renewing the threat both to Warsaw and to Rendomierz. But more important to Glynde was the news that Tormassov was on his way to meet another Russian army now moving north under Admiral Chichagov, since peace had been signed between Russia and Turkey.

'I know Chichagov,' Glynde told Jenny. 'I met him years ago in Petersburg. He's a strange man, hot-headed, unpredictable. But he loves the English. He spent some time in England when he was young. Reach him, and we're safe. I've told Lech to tell the Brotherhood.'

'How strange it all is,' said Jenny. 'Friend and foe; foe and friend! I keep thinking about poor Miriam; that attack on Vinsk by the French. It's all horrible.' She managed a small smile. 'I feel like a child in trouble: "I want to go home."'

'So do I.' Glynde had read between the lines of the story Jan and Genet had agreed, but meant to spare Jenny his gloomier assumptions. 'Thank God for your rubies,' he said now. 'Chichagov is bound to come this side of the Pripet Marshes. They'll pay our way across country to meet him. We must start working out our story.'

'And thinking about transport,' said Jenny. 'Do you think von Stenck is going to risk giving us one of the Princess's carriages?'

'You're forgetting; my stables weren't destroyed. Will you and Marylka mind passing as my young brothers? The Brotherhood are forging me papers in the name of Lord Ringmer. We are to be as aristocratic as possible. Jan Warrington and I learned, years ago, that that's the way to travel.'

'Then Marylka had better pass as our servant. She'll be happier that way too. But what in the world are we supposed to be doing in these parts?'

'Looking for the Russian army. I'm accredited to it from the

389

British government; lost my retinue in a skirmish with the French up north somewhere.'

'You're so sure Britain and Russia are allies by now?'

'Bound to be,' he said cheerfully.

He and Jenny had moved into adjacent houses in the guest village after the Cossack raid, and he was surprised, next morning, by an early knock on his door.

'There's someone to see you, lord,' his Jadwiga told him. 'About the journey, he says.'

'Journey?' But Glynde knew perfectly well that his plans were an open secret in the palace. 'Oh well, show him in, Jadwiga.'

'Two of them, lord. Strangers.' She sounded frightened, as well she might. They lived, these days, at Rendomierz, totally isolated, as if they were on the moon. Glynde automatically reached for a pistol as he awaited his unexpected visitors.

They seemed harmless enough – boys rather than men – and for an anguished moment he wondered if they could be brothers of one of his dead pupils. He tried so hard not to think of them, not to remember how he had failed them.

'We've come to offer our services, lord, for your journey.' The leader doffed his furred cap to reveal cropped dark curls.

'Good God! I'd know your voice anywhere, but you had me fooled for a moment.' He turned to Marylka. 'You too! Amazing.' He was more relieved than he cared to admit. Accepting the suggestion that Jenny and Marylka pass as boys, he had wondered what chance the disguise had of succeeding. 'But you're to be Poles?'

'Yes.' Jenny smiled at him. 'The loose tunic makes a much better disguise. Your brother James lost his clothes in the skirmish. But don't worry! I shall understand nothing but English, and behave every inch the spoiled British lordling. A perfect nuisance I shall be to you.'

'Never that.'

He was wakened that night by a scratching below the trapdoor of the secret tunnel and remembered that Jenny had had it fastened from above. He opened it quickly and Lech appeared, breathless. 'Are you ready to go?'

'Now?'

'The Cossacks are on the move again. This way. Leave now

390

and you have a chance of keeping ahead of them. The carriage is ready outside the school. Provisions. Everything you need. Here are your papers, lord, they came today. Fetch the women. You must be well on your way before the moon sets.'

Jenny argued for a moment, reluctant to leave without saying goodbye to Madame Poiret and her other friends at the palace, then: 'You're right of course. If Lech says so. Tell him we'll be there in ten minutes.'

And, to Lech's amazement, they were; two very convincing young men.

The tunnel was even damper and more unpleasant going away from the palace than Glynde remembered it the other way. How strange to think, now, with Jenny's arm light in his, of those passionate nights, when he could not get fast enough to the Princess's bed. And Jan must have done the same. Disgusting. Not to be thought of. But Lech, in front with Marylka, had paused for a moment, now began to move carefully up a flight of slimy steps.

They emerged in the ruins of the school house, and Glynde felt Jenny's arm tense within his, as she remembered, like him, all those cheerful constructive days of looking after the boys. And he had seen them die, and done nothing. Her hand found his in the dark and pressed it. She knew what he was thinking, and it helped.

The carriage stood ready in the drive where the boys had died, four of the Princess's best horses harnessed to it. He decided not to notice. They were committed now. They must go. Lech was kissing Marylka, commending her to their care. Glynde took his hand; shook it firmly. 'We'll take good care of her, Lech, be sure of that.'

'I am.' Lech helped the 'boys' into the carriage. Then, 'Go with God, lord.'

'The coachman?'

'Is a Brother with messages for the Russians. You have nothing to fear from him.'

'I'll never understand the Brotherhood,' said Jenny, as the man whipped up his horses.

'Best not try, I think.' But Glynde thought Talleyrand's hand must be stretched out all across Europe to protect them, and just hoped it was powerful enough. Now they were committed to it, he wondered if they were not entirely mad to embark on this venture across a country in the first throes of war. 'But what else could we do?' He spoke as if he had been sharing his thoughts with Jenny.

'Nothing. Whatever happens to any of us, I am sure we were right to do this. Never forget that. I know anything would be better than to spend the rest of my days starving in a Polish convent like poor Marta.'

He looked at her and actually laughed. 'You don't look much like a nun at the moment.' It was extraordinary how the ruthless cropping of her hair had changed her from neat young woman to brown-skinned boy, and he remembered with a little shock of surprise how he used to compare her tanned weather-beaten skin unfavourably with the Princess's white elegance. Her boy's shirt was fastened high at the neck and he wondered where the rubies were now, remembering that glimpse of white shoulder. He must not let himself think like this.

'I think you should have half the rubies.' Once again, disconcertingly, she seemed to have taken a thought out of his mind. 'Have you somewhere safe to put them? I've given Marylka some too, just in case we get separated.'

Nothing stirred on the country tracks their driver chose. From time to time they crossed a swathe of desolation cut by the Cossacks on their way north, but had seen no sign of them when, having kept safely south of Lublin and north of Chelm, they crossed the swampy River Bug on a makeshift raft at first light one misty September morning. Their driver had picked up a homeless boy somewhere along the way, and now sent him off for information while he rested his horses beside a sluggish tributary of the Bug.

'Russian territory at last,' Glynde told the two women as they returned from washing their faces in the slow-flowing stream.

'So long as it's not held by the French,' said Jenny. 'To be taken by them, with our papers, really would be out of the frying-pan into the fire.'

But the boy came back with comparatively good news. There had indeed been a battle somewhere to the north, but it was the Russian army that was retreating in their direction, and he had heard news too of another army coming up from the south. 'They look to meet somewhere around here.'

'Then let us await them here,' said Glynde, and the driver was glad to let his exhausted horses rest awhile.

'There's a safe house in the forest between here and Lusk,' he told them. 'Not comfortable, but it will do.'

Resting, for the first time, somewhat at ease that night around the fire they had lit, Glynde asked the driver what other news the boy had brought. 'I thought we would have found a great uprising of Polish peasants here against their Russian lords, now the French are come to support them.'

The man spat into the fire. 'So you would have, lord, if the French had sent Poniatowski and his Polish legion to fight the Russians here in Volhynia. But who's going to rise in support of the bloody Austrians? It's better the devil you know, and that's the Russians.'

'Lucky for us,' Glynde turned to Jenny. 'But sad for Poland, I'm afraid.'

'I begin to think everything is sad for Poland.'

There was no mass uprising, though Glynde suspected that the makeshift raft that had served them so well was also being used the other way by young patriots off to join the Polish army. 'But only the upper classes,' he told Jenny. 'No mass revolt of serfs.'

'And no wonder,' she said. 'All very well for the Duchy to give them their "freedom". You know what happens if they demand it. They're free to go – and lose their land to their landlord. Freedom to starve.'

'Still better than serfdom?'

'How hard it is to tell. For us, who have taken freedom for granted, for ourselves and our servants, for so long.' She turned to him eagerly, firelight glinting in her curls. 'Glynde, if I do get back to England, I want to do so much! It's hard to know where to begin. A school perhaps, to teach our young how lucky they are. Boys and girls! Don't think of skimping, Glynde, the journey comes first, but if I have enough rubies left, that's what I'll do.'

No. Marry me. But he did not say it. Paul Genet's mistress. But did he care? Was he mad! 'I'll be as frugal as I safely can,'

393

he promised, vowing to himself that he would repay her, stone by stone, the moment he came into his inheritance.

'Glynde Rendel!' Admiral Chichagov embraced his Petersburg friend warmly. 'Robert Wilson sent you, of course? He promised me an English adviser and I'm delighted it's you. And your young brother? I didn't know you had one.' He enveloped Jenny too in a warm embrace, and then drew away, looking at them both quizzically.

'Not my brother,' said Glynde. 'And Robert Wilson did not send me.' He plunged into the story of their adventures and Chichagov contrived to listen intently while giving a flood of orders as the Russian army of the south pitched camp around them.

'A splendid body of men,' he told Glynde. 'They're glad to be on the way home to defend Mother Russia. And I'm glad to have you, however you got here. Robert Wilson promised to send me an English observer when he left me at Bucharest. He should be at Petersburg by now, fast as he travels. You'll stay, of course, and represent your government until his man arrives.'

'There was no way out of it. No changing Chichagov, once he's set on something,' Glynde told Jenny later. 'And in fact it's just as well we're to stay with the army. The news is unbelievable! We're lucky to have got here. The Russians have given way all along the front up north. Napoleon is clear across Lithuania and has won a battle at Smolensk. Both sides claim victory, Chichagov says, but it is the Russians who have retreated. He says he is afraid for Moscow itself, the holy city.'

'Dear God! Is there to be no end to it?'

'The Russians have a new Commander-in-Chief, Kutusov. He has ordered Chichagov to march north as fast as possible and cut Napoleon's line of communications. We start tomorrow. Chichagov suggests that you and Marylka maintain what he calls your very fetching disguise for the time being.'

'I should just about think we will,' said Jenny. 'But I don't know what we are to do about this habit Russian men have of embracing each other.'

'You'll have to be a shy young Englishman and hold off,' suggested Glynde. 'And I'm going to come the careful brother

394

and forbid your riding out on reconnaissance with me. Protest how you will, nothing is going to shift me.'

'Thanks,' said Jenny.

The amalgamation with Tormassov's army complete, Chichagov marched his united force swiftly northwards. No need to worry unduly about Schwarzenberg's Austrian army, he told Glynde. A secret agreement between Austria and Russia had guaranteed that the Austrian forces would make only a token show of resistance.

'They'll show their teeth at us, but do nothing,' Glynde explained to Jenny.

'Napoleon's own father-in-law? I think it's disgusting.'

'It's politics. And we should be grateful. There's news of another battle, at Borodino. Kutusov claims a victory, but he's retreating again.'

They were well north of the Pripet Marshes when young Lord Tyrconnel arrived with despatches from Sir Robert Wilson at Petersburg. Napoleon was in Moscow, but the Russians had burned it around him. 'He's beaten, and doesn't understand it,' Tyrconnel told Glynde. 'He's actually complained to the Tsar about Russia's barbarous mode of making war. Well, it is horrible! But you can't blame them. And it's going to be worse when winter comes.' Younger than Glynde, he had been delighted to find him at Chichagov's headquarters and was insistent that he stay. 'Aside from anything else, you should not think of risking that young brother of yours in the desolation Russia has become. It's a holy war. They torture and kill their prisoners, burn and destroy everything as they retreat. You won't truly understand the devastation until you leave Polish Russia for the motherland. If Napoleon does retreat, as he must, his army is going to starve.'

Chichagov took Minsk a few days later, surprising the French garrison and capturing a great mass of French supplies. He had heard now that Napoleon was indeed retreating from Moscow, forced back along the blood-soaked way he had come, and his orders were to march east and join the trap that was to close on the Grand Army as the crossing of the Beresina.

'I think you and Marylka should await the result here,' Glynde told Jenny in the comparative comfort of their inn room at Minsk. 'I promise I'll come back for you.'

395

'You can promise to try,' said Jenny. 'And I believe you. But I know Chichagov by now. He won't let you, and I don't blame him. So, we are coming with you, Marylka and I. She is out buying furs for us all. We'll be even less recognisable, she and I, now it's freezing and everyone is bundled up in so many clothes. Anyway, it's hardly the weather for rape.'

She had shocked him, but he knew in his heart that she was right. In the confusion of either victory or defeat, Chichagov would have neither time nor men to spare for two women left behind. They were safer with the army. Besides, the weather was getting worse and worse, all landmarks obliterated by snow. To travel alone across this war-torn, winter landscape would be suicide.

They reached the Beresina in a flurry of November snow and Chichagov launched his army straight across the long bridge that led to the little town of Borisov on its eastern bank. Glynde thought it a mad venture, until it succeeded. Dombrowski and his Poles, who were holding the town for Napoleon, had been concentrating on the east, from which the defeated Grand Army and its pursuers would come; this sudden attack from the west took them by complete surprise, and the Russians found themselves masters of the town and its vital bridge.

'The whole Grand Army is in a trap now. The wrong side of the Beresina. They'll be desperate for this bridge.' Glynde was putting on his furs to go and dine with Chichagov. 'I hope to God I can persuade the Admiral of the danger we are in, here on the eastern side of the river. Madness to bring his headquarters and all his supplies here.'

Jenny smiled. 'You said it was madness to cross the bridge and attack the town at all, remember.'

'True! But for God's sake don't think of leaving the house. And keep an eye on the landlord. I don't think he likes us much.'

'Why should he? We're still in what was once Poland, Marylka tells me. And it was Poles who were holding the place.'

Marylka joined her after Glynde had gone. 'Pani Jenny, I've been talking to the landlord. Told him I'm Polish. And he told me – You won't tell anyone?'

'Marylka, I can't promise. You must see that.'

'I suppose so, and I do trust you, pani. There are Polish wounded in the cellar, dying of hunger and thirst. And a French officer. You can hear them groaning if you listen at the trap door. The landlord has put a cask on top of it. Better dead than caught, he says. The French army is short of everything. No food; hay used for bandages; nothing warm to cover them. It's even colder in the cellar, damp from the river seeps in. If nothing is done for them, he thinks they will die tonight.' She looked at Jenny with a mixture of hope and despair.

'We can't let that happen. Ask the landlord to come and speak to me, Marylka?'

'The lord wished to see me?' The landlord went through the hand-washing motions of Jewish subservience, but Jenny thought his heart was not in them.

'Yes.' Jenny was every inch the aristocratic young English male. 'My servant has come to me with an amazing story. You are really sheltering enemy wounded in your cellar?'

'Not enemies of mine, lord. Nor yours either! We Poles have always loved you British, hoped for help from you.' He smiled at her suddenly, drew himself from his fawning crouch up to his six emaciated feet, and broke into English. '"And freedom screamed when Kosciusko fell."' He smiled at her. 'You'll not betray me, lord, because I care for my friends?'

'No, but my man says they are dying. What kind of caring is that?'

'What can I do, lord? The Russians are out for blood.'

'We have more than we need: food, clothes, everything. And I have a little medical skill. We'll not trouble my brother with this, landlord; he is out for the evening. Let me see these unlucky guests of yours.'

'You promise?'

'I promise.'

The stench, when he moved the cask and lifted the trapdoor, was so horrible that Jenny flinched, but he was already ahead of her on the narrow ladder, candle in hand. Honour made her follow him, but she wished she had brought Marylka, instead of leaving her on guard.

Too late now. She was on the damp earth floor, following

397

the landlord and his flickering candle which revealed one gaunt, emaciated face after another. They lay on wisps of straw on the ice-cold ground, close-packed, like galley slaves, eight of them, but four, she saw at once, dead. 'They'll all die, if they are left down here,' she turned to the landlord.

'They'll be killed, if we take them up. And so will I.'

'Have you no attic?'

'A loft, yes.' Reluctantly.

'Why not up there?'

'There was no time. We could move them now, it's true. You will promise that no one but you goes up?'

'Yes. But – there's another?' She had heard a breath of a groan from a corner even lower, even nearer the river.

'The French officer!' Carelessly. 'The men made me bring him too. They're beyond caring now. Let him rot where he lies.'

'No. If we save any, we save all. Let me see him, my man.' She managed to put years of domination into the order and he obeyed without demur, turning to light their way into the dank corner of the cellar where a long body lay in half an inch of water. It groaned again as candlelight flickered across the grey face. *'Pour l'amour de Dieu!'*

'Paul.' She could not believe ears or eyes. 'Paul Genet?'

'His ghost. Who asks?'

They had to move the Poles before they could get at Paul Genet, but two more of them died in the process and were left in the cellar with their dead comrades. The others were so skeleton thin that the task of getting them up to the attic was unexpectedly easy. They turned out to have only minor wounds with which Jenny was able to deal, and Paul, when they got to him at last, seemed to have only an immense swelling on his head, enough to have knocked him out.

'But he's dying of cold, pani,' Marylka told her. 'I've seen it before. Put him in that icy attic, you might as well have left him in the cellar. He'll be dead in the morning.'

'What should we do?'

'Dry clothes; get him warm; hot soup.'

'Are there hot bricks in my brother's bed, as I told you?' Jenny turned to the landlord.

'Yes, lord.'

'Then we'll put him there. I'll be answerable to my brother. It's an old friend of his. He'd want it. And build up the fire; heat some soup for all of them; it's food they need as much as anything. I'll leave you to deal with the Poles, landlord; my servant and I can manage here.'

Left alone, they stripped Paul's limp body of tattered shirt and breeches and wrapped it in the officer's cloak Marylka had found on one of the dead Poles, first warming it at the stove in the corner. 'I wonder if the landlord stole his clothes, or if that was before,' said Jenny thoughtfully. 'Put that hot brick at his back, Marylka, and then all our furs on top. Where can he have been to have got so thin?'

'At Moscow, I think, pani. One of the Poles talked a little. Delirious; he spoke of horrors. Death of cold; death by fire; fighting each other for food; and, pani, cutting slices off their living horses as they walked along. Drinking their blood. The horses are so cold they don't feel it!'

'Horrible! Marylka, go and see how the landlord is getting on with that soup. Lord, listen to the wind! Put a little more wood on the stove before you go. It's going to be colder than ever tonight.'

'Thank the good God and his Virgin Mother we're warm in a town,' said Marylka. 'I'll take a look at the poor men upstairs, too. It must be cold as Christmas up there.'

'Do.'

Chichagov and his officers dined well, celebrating the comforts of Borisov and the trap that was closing on Napoleon, and the early dark had fallen when Glynde made his way back from headquarters through flurries of snow tossed on the rising wind. Its sound masked the creak of the inn door and he found the landlord deep in talk with a small man so wrapped in greasy fur as to be only a shaggy outline and a whining, eager voice. Both stopped dead at sight of him. 'There's news?' he asked.

'On a night like this? None, lord, except that my poor neighbour here has been turned out of his house by the bloody Russians. His wife's at the convent. I've said he can stay here if your Lordship has no objection.'

'I wouldn't want a dog out of doors on a night like this.'

399

'Brother!' Jenny appeared from the corridor. 'I thought I heard you. Tell the man to heat more soup, would you? And I think a little brandy wouldn't come amiss. Oh!' She had seen the stranger. 'Who's that?'

'All's well,' said the landlord. 'Soup and brandy right away, my lordling.' Something in his tone made Glynde give the man a sharp look, but Jenny was beckoning.

'He's seen through me, I'm afraid,' she said quietly in English as she held the candle down the long corridor. 'My fault; I forgot. We've got a guest.'

'A guest?'

'Paul Genet.' She pushed open the door of Glynde's room and he saw the still figure on his bed. 'He was dying of cold in the cellar. Marylka found out from the landlord; there were some Poles there he was protecting. They'd left Paul to die in a pool of water. They've come from Moscow, Marylka thinks. One of the Poles is babbling of horrors. I'm so glad you're here. I think Paul is coming round. He wasn't badly hurt; just the cold; and starvation. But what's been happening?'

'Napoleon's Grand Army is dying as it marches. The Russians were exulting about it at dinner. There's news from Kutusov, who is following and letting it happen. Up to now. This is the end for them, now we've taken the bridge. Napoleon destroyed his pontoon equipment back at Orcha. If he can't cross on the bridge here he's caught.'

'Destroyed it? But why?'

'Because the conditions are so terrible. It sounds as if they are all a little off their heads. But so is Chichagov. He plans to go out and attack in the morning, while the baggage train is still crossing. Look! He's stirring!' He was gradually taking in the full strangeness of the position. Here was Genet, Jenny's lover, unconscious in his bed, with Jenny in devoted attendance. Had he really been letting himself dream of a homecoming with Jenny at his side? Mistaking her unfailing good comradeship for something more? Idiot. Fool. This was the end for him as well as for Napoleon.

'Jenny?' The cracked, frost-blistered lips struggled open, and Jenny spooned in a little hot soup. 'Jenny? Or are you another dream?'

'No. I'm real enough, and so is Glynde Rendel, here beside

me. Tell us what has happened to you, Paul. You're safe with us.'

'Safe?' The next spoonful of soup dribbled from clumsy lips. 'Glynde Rendel?' Cogs in his brain began slowly, reluctantly to turn. 'Lord Ringmer?' Another pause. 'Didn't marry the Princess then? I'm glad.' A claw-like hand found its shaky way out from under the coverings and searched for hers. 'Jenny, I'm so glad.'

'No more talk now. You must sleep.' But he was already.

'I don't understand anything.' Glynde took a distracted turn around the room.

'No.' Jenny smiled at him. 'I don't suppose you do. Can you manage on the pallet in here, and will you let me know if he needs anything before morning?'

'Don't worry,' he said savagely. 'I'll keep him alive for you.'

The wind dropped in the night and they all slept late in the great silence of thick new snow. When Glynde roused from his hard pallet at last, it was to meet Paul Genet's eyes, lively and intelligent, gazing at him from the bed.

'Thank you,' said Paul.

'It was Jenny.'

'She was really here? I didn't dream her? I've dreamt her so often.'

'Indeed she is here. I'll call her.'

'Not yet. Tell me, first. Did I say anything foolish last night? I can't remember; only that she was here; only that I love her.'

'Still?'

'Always. And you – you didn't marry the Princess?'

'You knew about that?'

'Not one of Talleyrand's best ideas. He's losing his grip, I'm afraid. Some brandy, Glynde, could I? Mind you, we may all be glad of his good word with the Tsar if things turn out as badly as I fear. The Grand Army's a wreck; it fell to bits in Moscow. And something's wrong with Napoleon; he can't make up his mind. In Moscow . . . in Smolensk . . . fatal delays . . . He sent me to tell Dombrowski this town must be held at all costs, and it fell the day I got here. When was that?'

'Just yesterday. You don't remember?'

'A blow on the head . . . Then nothing . . . I was lying here,

Jenny bending over me. That angel Jenny . . . Glynde, I'm so happy . . .'

'I'm sure you are!' Glynde could stand no more. 'I congratulate you; you're a lucky man. But we have to think what to do for the best. The Russians are in a savage mood. I'll do what I can for you, of course, but Chichagov's a firebrand.'

'Lucky? You call me lucky?' But now, both of them were distracted by sounds of tumult outside. 'What is it?' Genet pulled himself up painfully as Glynde crossed the room to throw open a shutter and let in a great draught of cold air and the sound of chaos outside. Shouts, shots, curses, the scream of a wounded horse.

'The Russian army's in flight.' Glynde looked grimly at the man in the bed. 'And I doubt their supply train is clear of the bridge yet. It's not Napoleon who's trapped now.'

'Where are my clothes? Quick! It'll be Oudinot,' he said, as he struggled into them. 'He's a reasonable man; the best of the Marshals. He'll protect you, if I can just get to him. Where's the landlord?'

'Vanished.' Jenny stood in the doorway. 'The Russians are retreating; what are we going to do? Oh – Paul, I'm glad you're better. What is it?' She turned back to the door as Marylka appeared with two gaunt, bearded men behind her.

'It's the Poles; they say they're going out to fight.' But the two men had pushed past her and hurried over to Paul Genet, greeting him with tears of joy as their little father risen from the dead.

'Good.' Paul pulled the cloak around him. 'You'll have to hide,' he told Glynde. 'It will be savage for a while. A sack. I pray God they don't fire the town. I'll get help to you as soon as I can. You two,' he turned to the two Poles, and in Polish, 'you will stay here and protect the lord and ladies.'

They protested at first, but Marylka said something short and sharp to one of them under her breath and they yielded in a babble of talk. 'It makes sense,' Paul said at last. 'Marylka will be the landlady; Pavel here her husband back from the wars to protect her; his friend helping. And you two in the cellar, I'm afraid, until I can send help. It won't be for long. Just the time it takes Napoleon to get the wreck of his army across the bridge. I hope I'll see you again, but in case I do not: goodbye, Jenny.'

'God bless you, Paul.' She stood on tiptoe to kiss him on the cheek.

'I don't understand,' but Glynde's protest was drowned in an outburst of activity as a new volley of shots outside warned them of dangerous time passing.

'I understand nothing.' He said it again as the trapdoor closed with a thud above them and the cask settled heavily on top.

'Well, we're alive for the moment.' Jenny put down the candle on an empty barrel. 'We've food and wine, and furs to keep us warm. And a couple of stools to sit on, bless Paul Genet for a quick thinker. And Marylka is going to put on the performance of a lifetime as the landlady up there.' The six bodies, now frozen solid, had been stacked in a far corner like baulks of timber. Supplies, wine, warm clothes and a charcoal brazier had been hurried down to the cellar while Marylka changed into women's clothes, presumably belonging to the vanished landlady. 'I think we're going to lose Marylka, don't you? If ever I saw a case of love at first sight! Lucky for us. And trust Paul to make his men love him. I wish I knew how long it is going to take Napoleon to get the wreck of his army across the river. I imagine we had better prepare ourselves for quite a siege here, don't you?' She stood up, candle in hand, and moved carefully down the length of the dank main chamber, gradually diminishing into a dark silhouette. 'It's huge.' Her voice came, carefully quiet, from a distance. 'But going down-hill all the time. The furthest had better be our privy apartments. Not an elegant establishment exactly, but I'm sure we can manage here for the few days it takes Napoleon to get his army across.' She was coming back now. 'What's the matter?'

'Matter? You stand there, in a cellar, in deepest Russia, where we may drown, or burn alive, or be raped, and ask me what's the matter?'

'I don't suppose you'll be raped.' She put down the candle and settled on her stool. 'So if I'm not worrying overmuch, why should you?'

'You're so sure he'll come back for you? It didn't sound like that to me!' It came out savagely, because he had been thinking

403

of nothing else but Genet's casual admission that he was glad Jenny still loved him. Taking her for granted. And failing her. His heart bled for her.

'Come back for me? Who?'

'Paul Genet of course. He told me –'

'What did he tell you?'

'How happy he was.'

'Ah, dear Paul, what a good man.' She shrugged her shoulders, a curiously Gallic gesture that infuriated him. 'He had it all wrong, of course, as usual, but what a good, kind man. Maybe he gets it from Talleyrand, his master,' she said thoughtfully, elbows on the cask, gazing at him.

'Gets what?'

'Why, getting things wrong. Talleyrand believed in peace between France and Russia, yes?'

'Yes.' Reluctantly.

'Well, look at us. And in a marriage between you and the Princess?'

'Yes. How did you know?'

'I'm not as stupid as you think. Well, then, look at you. Here. And I must say, it's a relief to me. You'd not have been happy with her, believe me. Something has gone too wrong with her life. I don't think she is able to be happy any more, poor woman. She doesn't know how.'

'Jan Warrington was Casimir's father!' Explosively.

'Well, yes, I did rather think so.' She leaned forward and blew out the candle. 'Did you think you were?' she said in the sudden, thick darkness. 'If you did, I am so very sorry. I loved him too, you know.'

'But you didn't fool yourself you were his mother!'

'Well, no, I hardly would, would I? A desiccated virgin like me.'

'You? What would Paul Genet say to that?'

'Oh,' she said. 'So that's what you think.'

'It's true, isn't it? And he's gone off and left you, with just a careless goodbye. He won't come back.'

'I don't suppose he will. He's got his job to do, after all. But he'll see us safe.'

'If he can. I can't tell you how sorry I am. If there's anything in the world I can do for you, count on me.'

'Thank you. I do. You're a good friend.'

'I think I must be more. I've been thinking so much about you, since the Princess told me –'

'Told you?'

'About you and Genet. I thought, perhaps, you hoped to find a way to him. That he'd marry you. Then it would not have mattered – our travelling together; all of this. As it is . . .' How could he put it?

'I'm hopelessly compromised,' she said cheerfully.

'And now you think Marylka's leaving us. With her, we might just have managed. As it is, you'll just have to marry me. What in the world are you laughing at?' Angrily.

'I was wondering how long it would take you to get around to it. See my desperate plight. Behave like the perfect gentleman you are. But, thank you, and no. With a little judicious lying, I shall do very well in England. Who knows? I might write my memoirs, make some money out of this adventure.'

'You're indomitable.' He should have been relieved to have his offer refused. 'I'll tell whatever lie you think best.'

'As easily as you believe them?'

'What do you mean?'

'I mean the Princess's lies about Paul Genet and me.'

'Lies?'

'Yes. Think for a minute: about her, about me. Decide which to believe.'

He thought. It did not take long. 'Forgive me. But I still don't understand . . .'

'Anything!'

'You don't love him?'

'Paul Genet? No, it's a pity. He'll make a good husband, but not for me. I finally convinced him of that, dear Paul.'

He was looking back, now, all the way along the years. 'Have I been the world's most absolute idiot?'

'Well, I don't know,' she said. 'It depends, rather.'

'I love you!' He reached out a hand in the thick dark, feeling for her. 'How long have I loved you? Where are you?'

'Here.' The firm little hand found his.

'Jenny!' It was an earthquake, a heartquake, an explosion. 'Jenny!' he said again. He burned to pull her close, but must not yet. 'How long? You're not laughing again?'

405

'Well, a little. Happiness, maybe? As to how long. For ever, in my case. Love at first sight like Marylka just now. No wonder you didn't notice, beglamoured by the Princess as you were. No, not yet –' He was trying to pull her to him.

'No.' He slipped off the stool, down on one knee on the ice-hard ground. 'Jenny, I love you dearly. Marry me?'

'Ah,' she said. 'Now that is something like a proposal. Yes, my darling, I'll marry you. Today, if you like; tomorrow if you'd rather; any time you care to choose.'

'Jenny!'

'Glynde!'

It could have been hours or minutes later that they heard the cask rolled away from above the trapdoor. 'Pani!' Marylka's voice.

'Yes?'

'It's bad. The Russians managed to burn the bridge. The French are casting about for other ways to cross. It may take days, Pan Genet says. You must stay there. Don't fear; we are here; we've dealt with the landlord; it's just to stay, to endure and you'll be safe.'

'Don't fret for us, Marylka,' said Glynde. 'We're very happy where we are.'

'Happy?' He had amazed her.

'Rejoice with us,' he said. 'Congratulate me! We're on our honeymoon, Marylka.'

'Honey?' There was a quick giggle as she took in the Polish phrase. 'I'm so happy, pan and pani.' Then, soberly, 'You're better off down there. Things are terrible up here.' She closed the trapdoor.

They heard just how terrible when they emerged three days later, dirty, dishevelled and immensely happy. The French were gone, except for the thousands who lay dead and dying in the snow. Baulked of the crossing at Borisov, Napoleon had fooled the Russians by a feint to the north, and managed to throw two jury-built bridges across the Beresina to the south. The bridge builders had died as they worked in the ice-cold water, but they had done the job and the bulk of the tattered Grand Army had struggled across. Only the rearguard and the stragglers, who had sat, exhausted, by their campfires when they could have got across on the last night, were horribly cut down by Wittgenstein's guns. Now Kutusov was pausing, like the tired old man he was, to regroup his forces and let his Cossacks go ahead to harry the French as they struggled through blinding cold towards Vilno.

Napoleon's headquarters had been briefly in Borisov. Now Kutusov's were. Glynde and Jenny found Sir Robert Wilson there, so gobbling with rage and frustration that he hardly listened to their story. 'Kutusov won't act!' he repeated. 'He could have had them all, just for a little hurrying! And all he does is smile, and talk about "General Winter".' And then, focusing on them for a moment, 'You're from Poland, you say? Amazing! You have to give it them, the Poles fought well. If all Napoleon's allies had served him as they did, he'd not be in this case now. Poor things.' He thought about it. 'It won't help them when the Russians invade. Damned unlucky, those Poles. Yes, I'm sure I can arrange for you to take despatches for me to Petersburg. Anything to oblige an old friend. Lord Ringmer and –' He looked a question at Jenny, now a very shabby Polish boy indeed.

'Lady Ringmer,' said Glynde.

36

The scavengers had finished their work on the bloodsoaked field of Waterloo. The Allied armies were far away now, encamped in Paris, which had welcomed its exiled King back to the Tuileries with relief, if without enthusiasm. And in Talleyrand's house in the Rue St. Florentin two unexpected guests were awaiting his coming.

Paul Genet arrived first, dusty from the road. 'Lord and Lady Ringmer by all that's wonderful!' He shook Glynde's hand warmly. 'You permit?' He kissed Jenny on both cheeks. 'It's good to see you in such looks.'

'Happiness.' She smiled at him. 'And you, dear Paul?'

'I've survived. And mean to. I'll find myself a second best one day, never fret for me. And in the meantime my amazing master keeps me busy. He's Louis XVIII's right-hand man again, you know. And what he did for France at Vienna!'

'Astonishing,' agreed Glynde. 'I longed to be there, to see the Congress dance and scheme, but could not leave Jenny.'

'You have a son, I hear.' Formally. 'My congratulations.'

'Thank you. But Paul, the Congress. I've come to hear everything. How your master contrived to turn enemies into friends, to put France back at the diplomatic table.'

'He'll tell you,' said Paul. 'He'll enjoy that. You've brought the boy, I hope. He'll want to see him.'

'We have indeed.' So Genet knew of the relationship, though Jenny still did not. 'Jenny won't part with him. But you, Paul –' Smiling. 'We cannot be formal after that hell-hole in Borisov. We were so happy to hear that you survived that desperate retreat.'

'Thanks to you and Jenny! We're lucky, we three survivors. Have you heard about the Princess?'

'Isobel?' Jenny asked. 'Nothing for so long . . . Tell us, Paul?'

'A sad story. She seems to have lost everything with her son.

Prince Ovinski's heir claimed the ruins of Vinsk and the Warsaw house. Rendomierz was destroyed by the Russians . . . She came to Vienna, hoping, I think, that the Tsar would do something for her, but he had just forsworn the fair sex, plunged into this religious mania of his. He's hand in glove with that charlatan Madame Krüdener now. No time for old friends. And another old friend, Murat, has troubles of his own . . .'

'And a passion for our deplorable Princess of Wales, I believe,' said Glynde drily.

'Oh, poor Isobel.' Jenny changed the subject. 'Tell me, Paul, what of Marie Walewska?'

'There's a great lady! You didn't know? She went to join Napoleon in his exile on Elba. Took their little Alexander. Napoleon huddled her off into the mountains somewhere; kept her visit secret even from his mother. Worse still, when he heard that the islanders thought it was Marie Louise and the little Prince of Rome who had come to him, he sent Madame Walewska packing. In the teeth of a storm. And Marie Louise snug in the arms of her lover, Neipperg, all the time. Marie Walewska must have known about that. All Europe does. And never said a word to Napoleon. I said: a great lady.' He smiled. 'And I believe with a happy future after all. There's a Count Ornano lovingly waiting. She cried when she said goodbye to Napoleon at Malmaison the other day, but it was goodbye. He wouldn't take her with him, you know. Ah, here's my master.'

Talleyrand had aged, but his manners as he greeted his unexpected guests were elegant as ever. 'Lord and Lady Ringmer, what a delightful surprise.' He held both their hands, looking from one to the other. 'You are happy.' It was not in the least a question. 'And you have a son?'

'He's at our lodgings.' Jenny was looking from Talleyrand to Glynde, recognising at last the likeness that had always eluded her. 'You're very discreet.' She turned to her husband.

'You're very acute, madame.' Talleyrand's charming smile was so like Glynde's that she could not imagine how she had missed it. 'So now you will understand why you must stay with me. Paul, give the orders? I long to see my grandson.'

'Your British grandson,' said Glynde.

'A citizen of the world, if you please. Or of Europe, if maybe we find our American friends too difficult to understand. And they us! Tell me, what do you hear of that engaging young Mr. Warrington?'

'With whom you conspired against me?' But Glynde's tone to his father was entirely friendly.

'On the contrary. For you!' With a smile for Jenny. 'If it had only worked! My grandson. King of Poland. And my son the power behind the throne.'

'Could you have done it?' Glynde decided to leave aside the question of Casimir's parentage.

'With that delightful child as symbol? I really think so. Spilt milk, alas. What a tragedy that was! Even so, I still thought I was on my way to achieving an independent Kingdom of Poland when that disastrous Napoleon escaped from Elba. After that it was all haste, confusion, desperation at Vienna. No hope for Poland. The Tsar got his kingdom there. All very fine for the time being; he's given it a constitution, but what next?'

'He'll swallow it?' asked Glynde.

'I'm afraid so. It will all be to do again. For, believe me, son and daughter, Europe needs Poland. Our young eagle may be dead, but the white eagle will fly again some day.' He smiled his enigmatic smile. 'Forgive me! I sound for all the world like that visionary Baroness Krüdener who has the Tsar in her thrall. And you never did tell me the news of Jan Warrington.'

'Happy,' said Glynde. 'He and Miriam have settled in Savannah; he's a member of their Congress now.'

'And a useful one, I am sure.' He turned to Jenny with that smile again. 'Do you think his wife is homesick for Poland, Lady Ringmer?'

'I am sure she is,' said Jenny. 'I lived there long enough, Prince, to know that Poland lives for ever in the hearts of her children.'

'And grandchildren,' said Talleyrand. 'I drink to them.'